STONE ANGELS

Also by Helena Rho

American Seoul: A Memoir

STONE ANGELS

A NOVEL

HELENA RHO

GRAND CENTRAL

New York Boston

This book is a work of fiction. Names, characters, places, and incidents are the product of the author's imagination or are used fictitiously. Any resemblance to actual events, locales, or persons, living or dead, is coincidental.

Copyright © 2025 by Helena Rho

Cover illustration and design by Kimberly Glyder
Cover copyright © 2025 by Hachette Book Group, Inc.

Hachette Book Group supports the right to free expression and the value of copyright. The purpose of copyright is to encourage writers and artists to produce the creative works that enrich our culture.

The scanning, uploading, and distribution of this book without permission is a theft of the author's intellectual property. If you would like permission to use material from the book (other than for review purposes), please contact permissions@hbgusa.com. Thank you for your support of the author's rights.

Grand Central Publishing
Hachette Book Group
1290 Avenue of the Americas, New York, NY 10104
grandcentralpublishing.com
@grandcentralpub

First edition: March 2025

Grand Central Publishing is a division of Hachette Book Group, Inc. The Grand Central Publishing name and logo is a registered trademark of Hachette Book Group, Inc.

The publisher is not responsible for websites (or their content) that are not owned by the publisher.

Grand Central Publishing books may be purchased in bulk for business, educational, or promotional use. For information, please contact your local bookseller or the Hachette Book Group Special Markets Department at special.markets@hbgusa.com.

Print book interior design by Taylor Navis

Library of Congress Cataloging-in-Publication Data

Names: Rho, Helena, author.
Title: Stone angels : a novel / Helena Rho.
Description: First edition. | New York : Grand Central Publishing, 2024.
Identifiers: LCCN 2024044011 | ISBN 9781538765180 (hardcover) | ISBN 9781538765203 (ebook)
Subjects: LCGFT: Novels.
Classification: LCC PS3618.H59 S76 2024 | DDC 813/.6—dc23/eng/20241007
LC record available at https://lccn.loc.gov/2024044011

ISBNs: 9781538765180 (hardcover), 9781538765203 (ebook)

Printed in the United States of America

LSC-C

Printing 1, 2024

For my aunt, Kang Pung Ja.
Emo, thank you for being a light in my darkness.

She had been forced into prudence in her youth, she learned romance as she grew older—the natural sequel of an unnatural beginning.

—Jane Austen, *Persuasion*

*Love alters not with his brief hours and weeks,
But bears it out even to the edge of doom.*

—William Shakespeare, Sonnet 116

Prelude

If she let herself fall, maybe she'd wake up.

Heavily pregnant with her third child, Gongju clung to the cliff face of Seoraksan, her protruding belly jammed against the mountain's unforgiving surface. Jagged pieces of granite dug into her palms, slicing her skin. Below her, trees blurred into undulating green against stark blue sky.

Gongju was terrified of letting go. Clutching at the knotted roots of a spindly pine that grew through a crack in the mountain, she felt her gut lurch when the tree ripped away. As she plummeted through the air, she flung her arms around her swollen stomach, trying to protect her baby from the inevitable fall.

Instead, she floated, weightless, onto a lush plateau where clear, bright sunlight streamed onto towering stone angels. They were symmetrically arranged, scattered all the way to the horizon.

As Gongju wandered amongst the beautiful statues, she marveled at the precision of the feathers etched into their wings—it looked as though the women could take flight at any moment.

She stopped in front of a marble angel with a familiar face.

Sunyuh.

Coils of rope filled her hands, and she wrapped them around the statue before hoisting it onto her back, surprised by the angel's lightness as she descended the mountain. When she was no longer constrained by twine, at the bottom, she turned around, wanting to look upon her sister, happy to be finally reunited. But the angel quickly fluttered its downy wings and vanished.

Hands grasping at air, Gongju awoke, weeping.

STONE ANGELS

Angelina

SEOUL, KOREA
JUNE 3, 2006

Angelina should have known this journey was inevitable. She should have known she was going to be in this seat, on this bus, from Incheon Airport to Seoul city center, wilted against a glass pane, tired beyond reason. But how else would she get the answers she needed unless she returned to the country of her birth? Korea, the land where her mother's madness began, the home Angelina left when she was six years old. Korea, the country in which Angelina was now a stranger, an outsider from America searching for family, looking for redemption.

What am I doing here? The words rang out in her head like echoes in an empty sea cave.

She looked out into the darkness of Seoul, illuminated by neon signs and glowing office towers. Everything blurred into unrecognizable shapes behind her slowly blinking eyelids. She could barely make out the words fluorescently lit in a mixture of English and Korean. FACESHOP read one sign—a shop for the face? It made no sense.

Just like this trip, she reminded herself. Angelina's life made no sense anymore. All she'd believed about herself and others had vanished in the past two years, seemingly never having existed in the first place. No evidence that once upon a time, she'd led a perfectly normal life with a mother in her right mind, a loving husband, and two happy children.

Now, she felt like a woman at the bottom of a swimming pool, arms and legs leaden from a force she couldn't name.

Is insanity hereditary?

Angelina looked down at her wristwatch, an antique. Tracing the smooth gold around the rectangular face with her forefinger, a habit she'd formed the day she received the family heirloom, she wondered if she was also doomed to cut her wrists and bleed out in a bathtub. Suddenly, her mother's voice echoed like a bell. *Angel-ah, play Mozart for me.* A Little Night Music *always lifts my spirits.*

The jolting of the airport bus only deepened the ache in Angelina's body. The blinding headlights bounced off frighteningly close brick walls as the bus lumbered in and out of neighborhoods with tiny alleyways. It stopped at irregular intervals, offloading men and women with rolling bags into the warm summer night before it arrived at Konkuk University in Gwangjin-gu, north of the Han River.

One of the young Korean university students who had picked her up at the airport turned around in his seat to face her. "We are getting off here. Please get your luggage ready."

Both of Angelina's temples throbbed, and static was building in her ears. The aura of an impending migraine, always triggered by stress—they were now occurring with alarming frequency. Pushing past the pain, she rose to her feet and grabbed the handle of her red suitcase. She couldn't afford to be ill, not until she reached a bed and had covers to pull over her head. As the bus lurched to a stop, she teetered down the narrow aisle. The same Korean student took her bag and carefully lifted it off the bus.

"Thank you," she said, feeling as though her words were swimming lazily from her brain to her mouth.

The lanky young man bowed, his thick black hair falling forward. "I am sorry, but we must walk about two kilometers to the International Guest House. I know you must be tired."

I feel catatonic with exhaustion, actually.

"How long in duration was your flight from Pittsburgh?" the young man asked.

When she responded that her journey had taken over eighteen hours, what she didn't say was that she'd had to change planes in San Francisco from Pittsburgh before landing in Incheon. That she'd lost an entire day crossing the International Date Line. But she'd finally completed the loop that began decades ago at Gimpo International Airport when she was six years old. In 1971, her family had traveled west from Seoul to Hong Kong, then London, where they'd lived for eleven months before settling in New York, and now, over thirty years later, she was back in Seoul. Back in the country where she'd been born, but where she knew no one and barely spoke the language. Her mother was dead. Her father had remarried and taken flight. And Angelina had lost contact with everyone in her extended family.

What am I doing here? she thought again.

"I am sorry," the young man repeated. "Please allow me to take this for you."

He wheeled her suitcase away from her, his long, thin back disappearing into the dark. She followed. The other two exchange students from the University of Pittsburgh were walking ahead, laughing with the other host students from Konkuk, their boyish faces tinted sepia by the yellow lamplight. Edward and Mike were both nineteen years old, just finished with their freshman year of college. Angelina, forty, was in graduate school. The three of them had been chosen by their professor to study Korean at Konkuk University for the summer.

"What is Pittsburgh like?" the young man asked, his face a study in quiet attention as he carefully rolled Angelina's suitcase behind him.

Even though Pittsburgh was in Pennsylvania, Angelina thought of it as a Midwestern city. Small, friendly, provincial. She remembered her first day in Pittsburgh, three years ago, yet another disorienting time. She and her children had arrived at around midnight from New York. In their new house, hours before the movers were due to arrive, they had slept on newly refinished wood floors, wrapped in blankets. In the morning, after a night of sporadic sleep, Angelina had ventured out looking for coffee and breakfast, passing large, single-family homes—Victorians, Dutch Colonials, Queen Annes—with well-manicured front lawns. Suddenly, she found herself on a wide, traffic-laden street. She'd thought it odd that her car was the only one in the lane until a woman coming from the opposite direction stuck her head out her car window and yelled, "Hey, bitch, you ain't in China no more!" Angelina saw the sign for the bus lane almost at the same time. She'd pulled over onto a side street, put her head on the steering wheel, and cried.

"It used to be an industrial powerhouse, now faded in glory," she said finally. "Did you know the mills of US Steel were so large you could see them from space? Now these enormous smokestacks stand in the middle of a mall they built out in Homewood."

Angelina couldn't stop her disjointed thoughts from pouring forth, as if the sharp pulsing at her temples was forcing out absolute nonsense she had no control over. She wondered if this was what going mad meant.

"There aren't many Koreans. But there is a Korean church in Shadyside, and they have Korean classes for kids on Saturdays. Both my son and daughter go there. We're not Presbyterian, but everyone is so very nice to us." Her words sounded falsely bright, even to her own ears. Had she accidentally revealed how much she'd hated moving to Pittsburgh because of Thom's job?

A row of hydrangea bushes lined the sidewalk to Angelina's left, and a familiar sweet scent drifted into her nostrils. The fragrant blue blossoms reminded her of her small garden in Pittsburgh. Out of the dark, an image of her two children flashed in front of her, a picture she loved and had framed on her desk at home. A photograph snapped that first Halloween. Alex, at age eight, and Emma, eleven, crouched next to a neon orange jack-o-lantern in the blue slate entryway of their Victorian, their noses red from cold, arms entwined. She could almost hear the clear peals of their laughter, almost smell the cool autumn air. That was nearly three years ago. Before the divorce. Before their father moved out. Before the ugliness.

The warm night air grazed Angelina's cheeks, comforting her in a strange way. Staring at a green blur in the dark, she watched it unfurl into a large willow tree. Remembering her mother's love of weeping willows, she fought the urge to cry. Angelina had always imagined Korea as a land blanketed by weeping willows because of a song her mother used to sing: *I long for my beloved lost home in the tallest of mountains, amongst the most beautiful of flowers... when a south wind blows, willows dance on the riverbanks...*

Now, at the edge of a loosely oval-shaped body of water, Angelina watched as the willow's draping leaves fluttered like the fingers of a dancer.

Jerking her head side to side, as if that motion could erase the feeling she was about to cry, she squinted up at the young student. "Did you say something?"

His quietly composed face smiled. "Thank you for answering my question about Pittsburgh. I will be an exchange student there in the autumn semester."

The way he said "autumn" was so precise and delicate she could feel herself tearing up again.

"I hope you have a great time. I'm Angelina. What's your name?" She knew she should've asked earlier. As the younger person in Confucian Korean culture, he couldn't solicit her name first. It would have been considered incredibly impudent.

"Keung-nae is my Korean name, but you may call me Kevin, if you wish."

"My Korean is pretty bad, but it isn't so bad that I can't say your name."

"Americans find it easier to use our English names." He shrugged his shoulders in an almost imperceptible way.

"But I'm not American. I'm Korean."

"I apologize. You speak English perfectly, without an accent, and you use your American name."

It was true. She preferred to use her English name. It was so no one could butcher the pronunciation of her Korean one. She remembered the times she'd corrected people when she was younger, to no avail. Eventually, she'd simply given up. She would just smile when they inevitably said her name wrong. Even her sisters called her Angelina—only her mother had used her Korean name. But Sunyuh and Angelina were different people, even if the meaning of both names remained the same: angel.

She'd just turned five when her family converted to Catholicism, and a priest gave them all saints' names. Her mother, Gongju, became Columba. Her father, Minsu, became Paul. Her sisters were renamed Lucia, Catherine, and Lydia—Dia for short. Her mother said when it was Angelina's turn, the priest had looked at her and, knowing what her name meant in Korean, said she looked as beautiful as an angel. Angelina remembered the priest in his long black robes, stooping down, tilting her chin, the scent of tobacco lingering on his long warm fingers.

Her older sisters' names in Korean were *Jewel* and *Pearl*, so Angelina's should have been *Ruby* or *Sapphire* or something, but instead, her younger sister was *Ruby*. Her mother had a dream while pregnant with Angelina, involving marble angels on top of Seoraksan, a mountain range near the East Sea, and it had moved her so deeply she named her third daughter *Angel*. She used to say that the stone angels against the blue sky were so beautiful she had no choice but to take one. The image of her tiny, barely four-foot-nine mother lugging a statue down a mountain always made Angelina suppress a smile.

"Would you like me to call you by your Korean name?" the Korean boy asked, deference inherent in his question.

"Angelina is easier."

The complicated permutations that Korean demanded of its speakers were beyond her capabilities tonight. As the hubae, or *junior person*, in this dynamic, the Korean boy had to speak to Angelina in an elevated form of speech because of the immutable hierarchy of age—she was twenty years his *senior*, a sunbae. To address her otherwise would be inconceivable in Korean culture. Besides, could she really ask him to speak to her in Korean? She could barely string a sentence together in her mother tongue. And the boy would be disturbed to hear her speak to him in honorifics, no matter how much she'd insist she only knew the polite form of speech. He would insist she speak in banmal, the *half talk* Koreans use when speaking with children or friends or younger colleagues, which she, of course, didn't know.

She was *Angelina Lee*, not Yi Sunyuh.

Skirting the man-made lake, they arrived at the tallest building on Konkuk's campus, a glass-enshrouded structure ablaze in light, more modern than the 1970s-era campus buildings surrounding it. Kevin pushed open a large glass door and they entered the building's cavernous lobby. Angelina shivered against the sudden chill of air-conditioning. Another young man sat at a circular laminated wood reception desk. Kevin approached him, and they spoke rapidly in Korean. Angelina understood only *room* and *woman* from what she overheard of their conversation.

"Welcome to the International Guest House," Kevin said, bowing. "This is where our international faculty and students receive accommodations."

"Thank you." Angelina bowed in return. She wouldn't be told until days later that she shouldn't have bowed to a younger person like that, but thankfully, the boy was kind enough to ignore her mistake.

Kevin bowed again. "Your room is on the fifth floor." He pointed to the bank of elevators and handed her a set of keys. "Is there anything else you require before I leave?"

"Thanks again for meeting me at the airport. It would have been a disaster without you," she said, feeling lost and unmoored.

Did I tell this Korean boy I'm looking for my family?

She didn't want him to leave. She wanted to grab his arm and beg him to help her. What would he say if she told him she hadn't seen her grandmother in over thirty years? All she had to go on were faded blue envelopes with black Korean letters, postmarked decades ago, that she'd found mostly unopened and stashed away in the back of a closet when her mother died. Angelina had sent a simple letter to the return address on those envelopes that she was going to be at Konkuk University studying Korean in the summer, and asked her grandmother to please contact her. She hadn't received a reply.

As if he could sense her longing, he said gently, "I will see you again tomorrow for your orientation."

Her upper lip beaded with sweat, but she felt cold. She suppressed the urge to press her palms into her face. Angelina didn't know why she wanted to tell this Korean boy all her secrets—the sudden violence of her mother's suicide, the inexplicable estrangement from her mother's family.

I must be crazy.

With a deep inhale, she walked away, rolling her suitcase to the row of elevators. Edward and Mike were engrossed with the other host students. Alone, she stepped into the first open door, pushed the button for the fifth floor. She noticed an *F* instead of the number 4 in the column of numbers—she would learn later that the number 4 was considered unlucky and sounded similar to the word for *death*, so many elevators and buildings in Korea skipped it; other times it was labeled with an *F* for the word *four* because Koreans were so enamored of English.

Angelina walked down the fifth-floor hallway, her footfalls echoing in the pristine white corridor. She stopped at a large plate glass window and stared out at the man-made lake, at the ring of tall, black, old-fashioned lamps that surrounded it. Lights twinkled as the willows swayed in the breeze. When she crossed the threshold to her room, the door closed behind her with a soft hiss. The compact space was carpeted in gray; the light-colored wood veneer desk, wardrobe, and matching single bed all efficiently arranged. There was no décor—no paintings or prints, no flowers in vases. She was back in a dormitory, feeling like a college student.

Pretending to be young again.

She turns the glass doorknob, cut like a diamond. The white wood door swings open and she sees a woman's arm hanging adrift in a white clawfoot bathtub. She looks down at her bare feet and watches with horror as blood floods the black and white tiles and rises to her ankles. The next instant, she is standing in front of the bathroom of her mother's old house, a forgotten paean to tasteless 1980s modernist imitations—Formica countertops, naked light bulbs over huge swaths of mirror, fake crystal cold- and hot-water tap handles. She hears shouting and looks up to see her friend Liz frantically blocking the doorway. Angelina can't breathe. In the gaudy mirror, she catches a glimpse of her mother's face in repose, as if she is sleeping, her head tilted down, the curve of her neck delicate and—

Angelina woke up weeping. She coughed as mucus slid down her throat and coated her vocal cords. She clutched her arms in front of her belly, slamming her head against her bent knees. The dream had been so real. She could still feel the cool glass doorknob against the palm of her hand.

"It's not true. It's not true."

Her own words startled her. The vehemence, the insistence, the guttural tone sounded like someone else. But it was true—her mother was dead. Her body found by her downstairs neighbor of only four months, whose bathroom ceiling had rained pink, diluted blood. The young woman, still in shock days later, had pointed to the exact spot on the pristine white plaster when Angelina had visited the building to remove her mother's belongings.

The luminescent dial of the bedside clock blinked 4:58 a.m. It was her third day in Seoul. She groped for the box of tissues on the bed stand and hugged it tightly, as though that would ward off her pain. Moonlight filtered in through the slats of the blinds, but shadows were everywhere. The tall, narrow wardrobe loomed large; the black desk chair seemed to have grown wider. The mini fridge wheezed, emitting an occasional gurgle.

She swung her feet off the platform bed onto gray carpet, swiping up used tissues as she walked the few steps to the tiny bathroom. When she pressed the light switch, the square mirror above the porcelain sink reflected her ashen face. In the harsh glare of fluorescent bulbs, the purple shadows under her eyes looked elongated. The wrinkles between her brows furrowed deeper. She pushed away her long hair, only to have it fall back as she slumped forward.

Angelina didn't recognize her reflection. Her facial features were the same, her eyes and nose and mouth all in the same place. But she felt like a stranger to herself, fractured somehow, rearranged in a different order. During the past two years of her divorce, she'd realized that her family—a loving husband and two happy children—was a lie. But she'd fought to keep the illusion of her life as normal, ordinary. Then her mother killed herself. And Angelina could no longer pretend she wasn't submerged in sorrow. Blow after blow of brutal truths she couldn't face. And she was afraid the upheaval she felt inside would look like wildness, unhingedness, and would be reflected in her eyes for all the world to see. She avoided her own gaze.

God, I look old. When did this happen?

The last time she'd looked into the mirror of an unfamiliar dorm room, disoriented, she'd been twenty years old, in London, studying Shakespeare for the summer. The time when she *should* have stood up for herself against her parents and changed her major from pharmacy to English literature. Instead, she was doing it now, as a forty-year-old, getting a PhD. Back then, she'd been surrounded by peeling floral wallpaper in a decrepit Georgian mansion, which University College London had designated as a dormitory.

During those months in London, she'd started speaking with a

British accent, like when she'd lived there as a seven-year-old. She wasn't consciously trying to mimic it, but a return to the place where she'd first learned the language had unlocked a primal part of her brain that she couldn't shut off. Her American classmates used to tease that she was faking it. She didn't tell them she still confused *lift* for *elevator*, and that *lorry* always sounded better than *truck*.

She went searching for her old neighborhood of New Malden after class one day, around the old Korean embassy, where white working-class Brits had once stared and pointed at Angelina, her darker skin and almond-shaped eyes a misfit amongst pale freckled faces. The town had seemed completely new, yet exactly the same. The fish and chip shop was still a hole-in-the-wall, its red and white tiles perpetually coated in grease, its air fragrant with burnt oil. The beauty salon next door still had the same neon pink sign overhead. But there'd been a freshness to the paint on the storefronts, a sharpness to the windows. All signs of gentrification and the old world disappearing.

Angelina turned the lights off in her dorm bathroom and sagged against the doorway, wondering when the jet lag would wear off, when the nightmares would end. She knew she couldn't go back to sleep, couldn't bear staring at the ceiling. In front of the only window in the room, she pulled up the blinds. Her friend Liz had been her usual goofy self when Angelina talked to her a few days ago, and their email exchange last night had glimmered with Liz's peculiar brand of humor: "Are you getting laid soon?" Angelina had laughed before logging off.

Why was Liz in my mother's bathroom in my dream?

She could still feel the texture of the warm night air blowing in through the screen door as she'd held the phone to her ear in August, almost a year ago now. Dia's frantic words echoing, *Mom killed herself.* Angelina had abruptly slid to the floor of her kitchen. The wood had felt cold, the overhead lights too bright, a migraine exploding. She couldn't breathe then, either. She'd called Liz, someone more family than friend since their college days twenty years ago. Her voice must have sounded stilted, because instead of a greeting, Liz had immediately asked, "What's wrong?"

Angelina had felt like the slightest graze against her forearms would shatter her. And it was so trite, but she kept repeating again and again, "Why? Why would she do that? I don't understand." She'd blurted out random things about her mother—the sapphire ring she always wore on her right index finger; the large yellow roses she cultivated in every garden of every house they ever lived in; the celebratory dinner of bulgogi and japchae she cooked when Angelina became valedictorian in high school. But there was one incident Angelina never told Liz about, a day that still lingered, pricking at her years later.

When she'd been in high school, their next-door neighbor had called the police once because they'd heard glass shattering in the house. Her mother had been hospitalized—her father said she'd suffered a mini stroke. He'd driven Angelina to the hospital after school one day, his manner patently jovial, and Angelina hadn't wanted to incur his displeasure by being melancholic. She'd opened the door to her mother's hospital room with a smile painted on her face.

"Mom, I'm here."

Her mother turned her face toward Angelina, eyes blank.

Angelina forced herself to keep smiling. "Did you have a good day?"

Her mother looked away, not moving in her hospital bed.

"Did you hear me, Mom?"

She kept her face turned away.

"Umma, Sunyuh-yah," Angelina said in Korean, hoping that hearing her mother's native language would help her.

Swiveling her head, she squinted at Angelina, her eyebrows furrowing. Then her face cleared, a smile beaming. "Sunyuh-unni? Where were you?"

"Unni?" Angelina said, confused.

Instead of answering, her mother flung out her arms, squeezing Angelina into an embrace. Stunned and stiff, Angelina looked down at the top of her mother's scalp, gray roots defying a forest of brown. The touch of her mother's fingers felt shocking. She couldn't remember the last time she'd been held by her mother, who deliberately avoided physical contact with her husband, with her children. She once told Angelina that people touching her felt suffocating, that their arms and hands felt heavy with need.

Angelina tried to push out of her hold, but her fingers clung tightly. Her mother's face, open and vulnerable, smiled up at her.

"It's okay, Mom." Angelina tried to smile back. Her mother was ill, but her behavior was beyond bizarre. Her mother rarely smiled, but now, she was practically laughing.

"Unni!" she continued in Korean.

"Mom, you don't have a sister. Your two older brothers are in Korea," Angelina said in English, increasingly uncomfortable, increasingly alarmed.

"I was afraid. Scared for you. Where did you go?" Her voice rose an octave, childish in tone.

"I'm right here." Angelina tried to say this patiently, pushing down panic. A tremor took hold of her hands.

Her mother smiled. "I'm so happy you're back. I've missed you." Then she frowned, her lower lip pushed out at a petulant angle, her head shaking like she was a little girl. "But I waited in the plum orchard. For hours. When you left that night, I thought you would be back by morning. You should have returned sooner."

Angelina stared at her mother, speechless.

She stared back at Angelina, tossing her head, crossing her arms. "I hope you are sorry for keeping me waiting. It was not nice. And you are usually so nice to me, not like our mother." Suddenly dropping her posturing, she grinned. "That is why I love you so much."

"Umma, what are you saying?" Angelina said, her voice high and frantic. Her mother was delusional, spinning stories. "Mom, it's me, Sunyuh."

She looked at Angelina, narrowing and then widening her eyes.

"Sunyuh?" Closing her eyes, she collapsed onto the hospital bed. Her keening reverberated in that blank white space. Angelina touched her shoulder, but she shrugged away, squeezing herself into a fetal position, and screamed louder and louder, her body rocking back and forth.

Angelina's father had been dismissive when she told him what happened. "Your mother was talking about an older female cousin. She just had a stroke. She does not know what she is saying." Angelina had accepted his words. But the yearning in her mother's eyes still haunted her.

She stared at the reflection of her own eyes in the dark dorm room window. She thought she could trace the paved path behind the International Guest House that led to the top of a hill and tall trees beyond. The university was constructing new dorms there, and the sound of hammers ringing started as early as seven in the morning. She imagined she could see the outline of a building not yet built, the skeleton formed, the flesh missing. She wondered if it would resemble the International Guest House with glass and steel, or if it would look more like a traditional hanok, which was gaining popularity in Seoul again after almost disappearing in the 1970s because so many Koreans had wanted American-style houses, embracing the Western aesthetic and abandoning their past.

As stars faded in the sky, Angelina stood at the lone window, waiting for light.

Gongju

Gwangju, Korea
April 1944

Gongju ran, almost windmilling her arms, to catch her sister. But her six-year-old legs couldn't keep up. Sunyuh-unni's pale-pink dress was quickly fading from sight, her long dark hair mingling with that of all the other teenage girls running toward the kite fighters. In the blazing blue sky, green, yellow, and red rectangular kites dipped and swayed. Gongju had just barely escaped their family compound, with its elaborate courtyards and lush gardens, peony buds ready to bloom, orchards soon to be heavy with plums and peaches, and, of course, the watchful servants. But she'd already walked over three li, *almost a mile*, to get to town, passing the humble hanoks of tenant farmers, flat green rice fields, wildflower meadows, and the lake with the majestic willow tree. Gongju was tired. She knew that once Unni turned the corner, past the low stone wall capped with dark blue clay tiles, she would be lost. The market square, with its broad lanes and shopkeepers' stalls, was a maze Gongju couldn't navigate by herself.

"Unni! Wait for me!" she cried out, her voice high-pitched and petulant. Gongju was the maeng-nae, the *last child*, and accustomed to having her demands met. She was satisfied and also slightly relieved when her older sister stopped and turned around.

"You should go back to where our mother is," Sunyuh-unni admonished. "You'll get hurt in all this mayhem." She reached out and tucked Gongju's hair gently behind her ears.

Gongju smiled back, panting, happy.

For two sisters, Gongju and Unni could not have been more different. Stocky and short, Gongju resembled her mother's side of the family, whereas Unni was slender and moved with the fluidity of a dancer. Gongju was considered merely pretty, especially when compared to her sister, with her round, placid face instead of her sister's oval one. But her temperament was fiery, ephemeral. She was as stubborn as her sister was docile. Even their names fit: Gongju was a *princess*, and Sunyuh was an *angel*. Gongju, the youngest, the spoiled one. Unni, the oldest at sixteen, the responsible one. She and her brothers knew Sunyuh-unni was their mother and father's favorite, but Gongju and her brothers never minded—she was their favorite, too.

Gongju, unlike her sister, was impatient and willful. She was bursting so much of the time, full of ideas and things she wanted to do, although she was constantly being told she was too young. She didn't agree, of course, and was deeply resentful whenever the boys her age were allowed to do things that were forbidden to her. Such as chase kites without supervision. When they grew older, only the boys would get to compete and see whose kite could fly the longest without the string being cut by their opponents.

Gongju had been determined not to be left behind this time at their ancestral hanok. It was one of the first warm days of the year, sunny and clear, and the annual kite-fighting contest wasn't something she'd ever miss. It was a celebration of spring, unique to their town, and an event their Japanese oppressors monitored but didn't dare to stop. The ritual allowed all the townspeople to mingle—the rich landowners and the workers in the field usually harvesting rice, the shopkeepers and the butchers hawking their wares at the market. Gongju loved Yeonnalligi as much as she adored Chuseok, *the fall harvest celebration*, with its warm persimmon-flavored honey teas and gelatinous sweet rice cakes embedded with pine nuts. She'd eaten so many at last year's festival she'd given herself a tummy ache so bad she'd cried.

"Unni, please, I want to see the kite fighters!" she begged.

Sunyuh-unni knelt so their noses were almost touching, her hands reaching for Gongju's face. "Gongju-yah, I love your spunk," she said, smiling.

Her sister's fingers felt like soft feathers against Gongju's skin. As she looked up, the light in her eyes was less blinding; the smell of fish water in the street was less odious; the squealing of pigs penned nearby wasn't as tiresome. She gazed at Sunyuh-unni's face framed against the brilliant blue sky. Unni's dark eyes glowed in the shadow of the sun, and Gongju wondered if wings would sprout from her sister's back. She wouldn't have been surprised if the sun's rays forged a halo around Unni's head. At that moment, Unni looked exactly like an angel poised to take flight.

Instead, Sunyuh-unni rubbed at a dirt streak on Gongju's cheek and combed her fingers through Gongju's hair, smoothing and untangling the unruly mass. Gongju felt loved, cherished, like she was precious.

"Don't let our mother see you like this. You know she's going to reprimand you, right?" Unni said.

Gongju nodded solemnly, pretending to be chastened. But she didn't care about her mother's disapproval today. She grinned, succumbing to her sister's gentle attempts to impose order. She normally wore her hair in braids, but she'd run out of the house today heedless of her hair, because she'd been dying to see the kite fighters. Gongju knew Joonsuk-oppa, the mayor's son, would be amongst them. Joonsuk-oppa, of the lithe frame, the raven hair, the dreamboat face, with whom she was madly in love.

"I know you're looking for Oppa. Take me with you!" Gongju demanded. "I want to see him win."

"You've already decided the outcome?" Her sister sounded amused.

"Of course, Oppa is going to win! He's the best kite fighter in town." Gongju was indignant, offended by her sister's lack of faith.

Unni laughed. "Oppa is blessed that you have such confidence in him, *Little One*. I can only hope that he wins."

"Unni, what are you saying?"

"I don't know what's going to happen," her sister said. "I never do anymore. I know you're young, but you've seen what this war has done. What we live with every day."

Gongju couldn't quite describe what her sister's face looked like at that moment—Unni seemed like she could spiral into tears or break down laughing. Sometimes, it seemed to Gongju that her sister was already an adult like their parents, not a stupid teenager like her brother Haneul.

But Gongju was accustomed to pushing away discomfort. She lifted her chin at an imperious angle. "I want Joonsuk-oppa to win, so he's going to win," she announced with certainty, dismissive of fate and the vagaries of life.

"Let's find out, shall we?" Unni smiled.

Gongju reached for her sister's outstretched hand, clinging to the solid warmth. Side by side they advanced toward the cheering crowds.

"Joonsuk!" Gongju's father called out. "Well done!" He walked quickly over to Joonsuk-oppa, grasping his arm to congratulate him.

"Thank you, sir," Joonsuk-oppa said, bowing.

Gongju looked up at the two men she adored. Both were long and lean with thick black hair and high cheekbones. Oppa's face had the smoothness of youth; Abeoji's had the creases of experience. Her father's hair was also graying at the temples, which gave him a distinguished air. Gongju thought he looked so dashing, especially in the mornings as he was about to go to work at the bank in his pinstripe suit, his fedora seated low and slightly tilted. Standing next to Joonsuk-oppa, her father looked younger, more excited than she'd seen him in a long time.

"The way you maneuvered your kite at the end was exceptional!" Her father clapped Oppa on the back. The sound of it echoed in Gongju's mind.

"Thank you, sir," Joonsuk-oppa repeated, bowing again.

"It was marvelous! Your opponents cutting each other's kite lines while you waited patiently, keeping the glass on yours sharp for the last fight. A flawless strategy to narrow your field of enemies. Your father must be very proud."

"I hope I am not a disappointment to my father, sir," Joonsuk-oppa replied.

"My dear boy, you're a great source of pride to your father. I'm certain of it," Abeoji assured him.

The look on her father's face made Gongju believe that he loved Oppa as much as she did. That Abeoji wanted Oppa to be his son, not his son-in-law.

"You are too kind, sir." Joonsuk-oppa bowed again.

Gongju's mother interrupted quietly. "It's good to know that despite your many accomplishments, you're still so humble, Joonsuk." She stepped closer to Oppa and patted his arm, her affection palpable in the gesture.

Gongju knew that her mother eagerly anticipated the union of Joonsuk-oppa and Sunyuh-unni and their families. She pictured a beautiful day for their paebaek, *wedding ceremony*, with delicious, sweet and savory tteok, *rice cake*, along with the traditional chestnuts and dates on display. Oppa and Unni in blue and red hanboks bowing to one another, drinking from the same copper cup. A day just like today, sunny and clear. Gongju had overhead her mother talking to Unni about her wedding trousseau, offering to buy the more expensive items over the merely serviceable and cheap. Gongju hoped her mother would be as happy when Gongju married as she was for Sunyuh-unni.

"Oppa, Oppa, you were wonderful! I knew you were going to win!" Gongju knew she should have been quiet as the youngest, and a girl at that, but the words spilled out.

Gongju's mother turned toward her and started to scold, but her father nodded and smiled.

"Thank you, *Little One*," Oppa said. "I hope I earned your faith in me." Grinning, he tousled her hair, his touch surprisingly gentle.

She laughed, joy unadulterated. She wanted Oppa to hug her, as he sometimes did, so she could smell his unique aroma of smoky wood and refreshing tangerine. But Joonsuk-oppa was looking at Sunyuh-unni. Unni had stayed silent during their family's admiration of him. Still, she seemed to be avoiding his eyes.

"What did you think of my kite-fighting skills?" Oppa challenged.

"Quite admirable," Unni said.

Their eyes met as Sunyuh-unni looked up. Gongju could almost hear Joonsuk-oppa's breath stop, and she smothered the urge to laugh. They were so obviously in love, their eyes yearning as they looked at each other. Gongju wished the moment would last forever, this moment when everyone was happy.

"It's getting late. We must get home," her mother finally said.

"Joonsuk, join us for dinner. I insist. Why don't you walk Sunyuh home after you gather your kite pieces?" her father said.

"It would be my honor, sir," Oppa said.

Unni said nothing.

Gongju tried to pull away, but her mother only tightened her grip and tugged. She looked back at the two lovers standing together in silhouette. She walked slowly, letting the tension in her arm go slack until she felt her mother's grasp loosen. Then she broke free. Hearing her mother shout for her to come back, Gongju ran faster. She could still see Unni's pink dress. This time, she knew she could catch up.

Gongju followed her sister and Joonsuk-oppa as they slipped into an empty alley. She hid behind wood crates and peeked through the slats, crouching into a small ball. They were so immersed in one another that they didn't see her. She suppressed a giggle, her hand pressing against her mouth. Gongju felt like she was watching one of those romantic American movies, the ones she snuck into at the town theater.

Unni leaned away from Oppa. Her hands remained behind her back, not quite touching the brick wall, her shoulders pushed up. Oppa looked at Unni with longing, his hand clasping hers before he pressed her fingers against his cheek. He kissed the palm of her hand.

"You have the most beautiful hands I've ever seen," Oppa said, his voice hoarse. "Marry me now. Our parents want this union."

Gongju wanted to swoon, her heart exploding with happiness, like fireworks lighting up the night sky on Buddha's birthday.

"What about me, Oppa? You just want to marry me because I am beautiful. Do you not love me?" Unni teased gently, her voice light and free.

"I've loved you since I was seven years old. I'll never forget the first time I saw you at the playground in school. I even remember what you were wearing. What your hair looked like, parted to the side, tucked behind your adorable ears."

Unni laughed. "You certainly never showed it. I did not think you knew I existed."

"Apparently, I hide things well." Oppa shrugged.

"Maybe, too well," Unni said. "I almost gave up on you. I was going to marry the scholar's son if he asked me first." She smiled and tilted her head to give Oppa a sideways look.

Oppa pretended to be outraged. "*What?* How could you doubt me? No matter what I was doing, if someone told me where you were, I'd always try to find you."

"I did not notice," Unni said, a tiny smile playing on her lips.

"Liar," Oppa said quietly.

"My friends all loved you because you were so polite to them, even though you could have been rude, as an *honorary older brother*. But they always teased me mercilessly after you left, making fun of my flushed cheeks," Unni said, almost petulantly. "But now, you will go into the army and forget all about me."

"I will never forget you. I will love you until the end of time."

Oppa said this with such intensity that Unni flinched, and she clutched his arm.

"What's wrong?" Oppa sounded alarmed.

"I love you," Unni whispered. "I want us to have children, to live for a very long time in the same house, to grow as old as our grandparents. What if that never happens?"

"There's nothing to be afraid of, my love." Joonsuk-oppa smiled and kissed Unni's forehead. "We'll live a good life."

Unni said nothing. She stood so still Gongju was afraid her sister had turned to stone. Gongju suddenly felt panicked, as if something bad was about to happen. A dread rose in her body, a weight brushing against her chest. She felt like running and running, like she needed to get away. Gongju rocked back on her heels and clapped her hands over her ears, squeezing her eyes shut, tamping down her fear.

"When the war is over, we'll get married," Joonsuk-oppa said with absolute certainty.

In the shadows of the narrow alley, Gongju watched Unni lift her head from Oppa's shoulder and look at him, her face so full of love. Gongju wanted to clap at her sister's radiant beauty and Oppa's impossibly handsome face. They looked so good together, so well suited. Gongju pressed her fingers to her lips, her smile widening as Oppa pushed back the ebony curtain of Unni's hair. Gently cupping her face, he leaned down and kissed Unni's parted lips. They both seemed to hold their breath as their mouths opened and melded together, and Unni's arms reached up to encircle Oppa's neck. He slid his hands down her rib cage until they came to rest at the small of her back. They looked as though they were breathing and moving as one being.

Gongju never forgot the beauty of that kiss. It was the moment she knew she wanted to find such a love when she grew up. Joonsuk-oppa's tall, lean frame curving toward Sunyuh-unni's petite slenderness, two bodies arcing toward one another with infinite want.

Angelina

SEOUL, KOREA
JUNE 13, 2006

Angelina fought gravity, each footfall a struggle against the steep ramp of Konkuk's Foreign Languages Center. She felt like her body was continuously pitching forward in a circular motion. She'd been doing this every weekday for more than a week, and each time her lungs burned anew. Out of breath when she reached the third-floor landing, she wondered if she'd yet again made a mistake in not taking the straightforward vertical staircase at the exterior of the building. Her body felt decrepit, geriatric rather than nubile, and she'd barely reached middle age. She braced her hand against the cool glass of one of the coffee vending machines clustered in the entryway, panting. She pretended to peruse her choices, knowing she would get the same thing she did every morning—coffee with sugar, no milk. The machine revved up when she slipped a five-hundred-won coin into the slot, and it spurted out a paper cup with her burnt-smelling beverage. She sipped the sweet, hot liquid as she walked down the austere hallway to her classroom.

It was her mother's death that had spurred Angelina to learn Korean, the language she'd mostly forgotten. She understood most of what her mother used to say to her, but then, her mother had always spoken to her in simple words and simple sentence structure. She'd never forget the day her mother told her she spoke Korean like a toddler. Angelina had felt like a fool. At twenty, she should have been inured to her mother's criticisms, been accustomed to her careless disparagement. Instead, she'd been hurt like a small child.

Angelina was surprised at first by her yearning to learn Korean, to be fluent again in her mother tongue. She'd shunned her culture by marrying Thom, an American who had no interest in Korea or anything even remotely Korean. He told Angelina once that he thought of her as white since she spoke English flawlessly, without an accent, and was beautiful, not like most flat-faced Asian women, who were always bowing and shuffling. At the time, she'd felt grateful instead of being horrified. Angelina had wanted blond hair and blue eyes when she was a seven-year-old in London, wanted to fit in so desperately she'd prayed for those features every night before falling asleep in her family's semi-detached house on Cromwell Avenue.

When Dia had called with news of their mother's death, Angelina had expected an explanation, a note of some kind. But there was nothing, not even a will. She and her sisters took days to clean out their mother's apartment because their father, who'd inherited everything by default, had no interest in their mother's personal things. And they held no wake, no funeral service. At the crematorium, the four sisters had pragmatically divided up their mother's ashes before separating and going back to their own lives. It was in a dust-covered shoebox stowed at the back of her mother's bedroom closet that Angelina had found the letters from her grandmother. A relic from the past. Filled by the desire to read those words, she suddenly became desperate to be literate in a language she hadn't spoken since she was a child, to know her mother in a new way. A burning. Surely the reason why her mother had done something so drastic had its roots in the country she had abandoned.

When Angelina had asked about their relatives in Korea long ago, her mother had said "My family? They disowned me when I moved to America. I do not wish to speak of them ever again." But Angelina didn't so readily believe that anymore. Maybe it was the texture of the almost translucent blue pages or the aching curve of her grandmother's handwriting, but as Angelina squeezed those letters between her hands, she decided then and there to go back to Korea. Her sisters thought she was deluded, especially Lucy, her oldest sister, and Dia, the youngest. They were adamant they wanted nothing to do with the letters. "Mom was always depressed. Why go looking for trouble? Let sleeping dogs lie." But Cathy, Angelina's least combative sister, resigned herself to what she referred to as Angelina's *whims*. It was why she'd agreed to keep Alex and Emma for part of the summer so Angelina could study abroad. "They can swim at the country club and take tennis lessons with Maggie and Conor. It'll be like summer camp."

When Angelina talked to Cathy last night, after she'd spoken to her children, Cathy seemed excited when she asked, "Did you find anything yet? Lucy and Dia asked about you." Her response, "Oh," after Angelina said it was too early, had been subdued. Disappointed. Maybe her sisters wouldn't explicitly say so, but they were curious about their Korean family, too.

Maybe they wanted to know just as badly as she did.

Despite having studied Korean in the US for a year, Mike and Edward had placed in Beginner Korean at Konkuk University, but Angelina was in the intermediate section. At first, she'd felt lonely. But now, she was relieved the other Americans weren't in her class. In Pittsburgh, they had been young, fun-loving college students, but in Seoul, their attitude was careless. They were always too loud, their gestures too big, completely oblivious to the behaved restraint of the Korean, Chinese, and Japanese students surrounding them. And they made fun of the constant bowing in Asian culture, a custom they had not grown up with and thought was ridiculous.

In Angelina's classroom of eighteen, there was only one open seat. Surprisingly, it was next to a very popular student, Keisuke Ono, also an American. Something about the thirty-three-year-old journalist made Angelina uneasy, though. Perhaps it was his juvenile attempts to blend in with the hypermasculine Chinese twentysomething-year-olds, who were learning Korean so they could audition to be K-pop singers and waste their wealthy fathers' money. Perhaps it was his dark good looks. It seemed like he wanted to appear nonchalant, rather than draw attention to the agility of his mind. He never apologized to their teacher for not completing his homework, yet he always answered her questions correctly, clearly showing mastery of the subject matter. Angelina generally tried to avoid Keisuke—nothing beyond polite exchanges of "Hi" and "Goodbye."

She usually sat next to Song-ah, a Korean Chinese woman from Jilin Province, whose Korean parents had found themselves in another country—the far northeastern part of China—after the borders shifted because of the Korean War. Song-ah was also forty with two children, like Angelina, but married to another ethnic Korean. She was in Seoul to learn her mother tongue for a very practical reason: her husband's import-export business had opened a new branch in Incheon. Sadly, neither of them was able to speak or write in Korean enough to conduct business, so she was happy to be in school—not to mention child-free—for a few months.

"Who doesn't want to venture out into Seoul's teeming nightlife and pretend to be single?" Song-ah had laughed, extolling yet another evening spent in a nightclub and then a noraebang, singing until the early hours of the morning. Angelina had laughed, too, but didn't share the fact that talking to Alex and Emma nightly over Skype was her preferred method of diversion. Mostly, she spent her evenings reading or listening to Korean TV and doing her homework, waiting for the phone to ring—any indication that her grandmother had received her awkward letter.

She slipped into the seat of a wooden desk and chair combination, a reminder of grammar school, not college, and placed her Korean textbook and workbook on the narrow, splintered surface.

"Good morning," Keisuke said in English.

"Good morning," Angelina said in Korean, shifting her seat away from him, avoiding his gaze.

"Are you ready for class?" he asked.

"No, I am too tired this morning," she persisted in Korean.

"Why?"

"I was partying last night."

"Where was the party? And why didn't you invite me?"

"I am kidding. I am too old."

"You look younger than I am."

"You are being too kind." Speaking in honorific Korean seemed proper, less intimate.

"It's hardly a secret you're beautiful."

Angelina wanted to roll her eyes at him. His words sounded careless—a throwaway line amongst many such meaningless sentiments she was sure he stored away in his arsenal as a single man. After all, Keisuke was good-looking, and he probably knew it. The young women in their class never tired of gossiping about him: Did he have a girlfriend? Was she in Korea? Why was he learning Korean when he was Japanese and already spoke English perfectly?

Song-ah had proclaimed she'd seen billboards in Seoul with less handsome models than Keisuke. But alas, she was married. The more she prodded Angelina to flirt with him, the more Angelina avoided him. And now, she suspected Song-ah had engineered this uncomfortable seating arrangement. She looked up to see her friend giving her a knowing grin. She glared and mouthed back in return, *Why?!*

Clearly, she'd made a mistake when she told Song-ah about the first time she'd seen Keisuke. Like a scene from a movie, she'd been told by someone in the language department, on the first floor, to go upstairs and take her Korean placement test. She'd put her hand on the painted railing and looked up. Keisuke was standing at the top of the stairs, and their eyes met. A jolt of electricity had rushed through her, but she'd refused to look at him as they passed one another, pretending she didn't feel the intensity of his gaze or the racing of her heart.

Then he turned up in her Korean class.

Song-ah had declared the encounter *love at first sight*, but Angelina didn't believe in such things, had absolutely no faith in serendipity. But Song-ah had insisted. "It's *fate*."

Looking away from Keisuke's bare, tanned arms now, Angelina opened her workbook, tried to focus on the pages.

"Did you do your homework?" he asked.

"Yes, of course. How about you?" She didn't look up, her long hair a dark curtain between them.

"Some of it. I'm not like you—the perfect student," he said.

Her head swiveled, and she glared at him, lapsing into English. "That's not true!"

"You always know all the answers. You're a teacher's pet," he taunted.

All her life, Angelina *had* been the perfect student, obligingly giving the right answer when called upon, staying quiet when the rest of her classmates were unruly. She'd always been proud of her behavior, but the way Keisuke said *perfect student* made her sound like a sanctimonious prig. She felt like someone had played a joke on her and she was just getting it. Years after the fact.

"I like homework. It gives me something to do while I wait," she said, an edge of defensiveness in her tone.

His attention intensified. "Wait for what?"

She instantly regretted her unguarded statement, but then mentally shrugged. "For my grandmother to contact me."

"Why?" Keisuke asked, softly.

"I haven't seen her in decades. I know almost nothing about her." She bit down on her lip but couldn't seem to stop the words that were suddenly rushing out of her mouth. She couldn't believe she'd almost let slip that she was trying to find her family.

"What happened?"

Keisuke's voice contained no judgment, but Angelina felt belligerent, wanted to shout at him to stop asking her questions to which she had no answers. Her face flushed with shame.

"That's all very complicated—I don't feel like talking about it." She turned to stare at him, daring him to say something, furious she'd revealed her innermost thoughts to a man she was sure she disliked.

Keisuke leaned back in his seat, his long limbs stretching over the too-small chair. "Fair enough." He nodded, seeming to acknowledge her anger and not begrudge her contradictory behavior. "What did you do after class yesterday?"

"I spent the afternoon at the National Museum of Korea, near Yongsan."

She didn't say that she loved going to Yongsan—*Dragon Mountain*, because the peaks were shaped like the back of a dragon—in the center of Seoul. That she found the walk from the subway to the museum lovely. Soothing. Whenever she approached the hill leading to the entrance of the building, Angelina felt like she was transported to a small bamboo forest. In the quiet, amongst the tall, thick stalks of bamboo, whose deep green leaves almost obscured the sky above, she felt shielded from the world.

Keisuke quirked a smile at her, crossing his slenderly muscled arms and resting them on his desk. "Is that what you call fun?"

She tried to ignore the unaffected grace of his sloping shoulders, tried to infuse a breeziness into her voice. "The museum has amazing artifacts—crowns, vases, exquisite jewelry from the Shilla, Goryeo, and Joseon dynasties. Did you know your people kidnapped entire villages of Korean ceramicists during the Imjin War? What you think of as Japanese pottery actually originated from the sixteenth century in Korea."

"Thank you for that fascinating fact," Keisuke said.

She couldn't help herself. She glanced back at him, certain he was mocking her, but he seemed genuinely appreciative.

"But a museum is amusing?" he asked.

"Being informed is a form of fun," she declared.

"You're what Bart Simpson calls a nerd."

She laughed. "Really? A *Simpsons* reference?" It seemed so childish for a grown man to say that, yet she found it surprisingly charming. "I hate Bart."

"It's nice to hear you laugh. You're so quiet in class, I was afraid you didn't have a sense of humor." His voice held a tint of satisfaction.

"What? I'm funny. Hilarious, in fact," she said, pretending to be outraged. She wondered why she suddenly cared about his opinion, why she was joking and laughing with him at all.

Keisuke smiled, raising his eyebrows.

She nodded her head emphatically to hide the fact that her face was aflame. "You haven't seen me when I'm drunk—that's when I'm really entertaining."

This is mortifying.

He cocked his head at her. "Let's go drinking then. I love soju."

"Sure, let's go to Cheonggyecheon and find one of those pop-up restaurants by the stream. We can drink until oblivion. Yeah."

Keisuke ignored the sarcasm in her voice. "I love sitting by the water. I grew up in Seattle, surrounded by ocean and gray skies and rain. I can look at water for hours—the more desolate the landscape, the better. That's what I missed the most in Iraq, embedded with the troops, dripping with sand and sun. I was thirsting for the sea."

Angelina was astounded by his revelations. They were so casual, so matter of fact. As if the most dear, secret things in his life could be shared effortlessly without embarrassment or pain. *Where does he get that ease? Is he really Asian?* She was torn between admiration of his shameless openness and deep indignation that an Asian person was behaving so carefree. She'd always believed caution and restraint were typical Asian traits, and while these characteristics were sometimes frustrating, they were also admirable. Now she wasn't so sure.

Is it that simple to break free from what's expected of you?

She just stared at him for a moment, unable to ask the questions swirling in her head. Instead, she said, "You're a crusading war journalist?"

Keisuke hiked one shoulder. "I wouldn't go that far. I wanted to expose the malfeasance of the Bush administration in Iraq. So I patiently followed the money trail until I found the evidence. I have a healthy dose of justice built into me, for whatever reason—probably my parents' fault. They were insistent I grow up to be a responsible citizen," he said wryly. "Plus, I love the chase that comes with a good story."

Again, Angelina had no idea how to respond.

Thankfully, the teacher chose that moment to enter the classroom. "Good morning, students!"

When it was time for the midmorning break, Keisuke stood up, stretched his arms overhead, and let out a yawn. "Let me buy you a cup of coffee."

"Not necessary," she said, trying not to notice the beauty of his long, slender fingers, his short, clean nails.

He raised an eyebrow. "It's only a fifty-cent cup of coffee."

Not wanting to appear petulant, she conceded. "Why not?" she said, trying not to infer anything from a simple gesture. She ignored the heat rushing up her neck.

As she sipped another bitter coffee from a paper cup, she stared out the window of the third-floor landing into the garden below. She didn't know the name of the bright yellow flowers, which were so attention-seeking next to the soft pink roses. When she turned back to Keisuke, she became acutely aware of how close he was standing next to her, and she could feel herself start to perspire. The scent of smoky cedar and bright citrus pervaded her nostrils, and her heart started beating faster. Her skin tingled. She felt fifteen years old again, sitting in the bleachers mesmerized by the captain of the high school basketball team. Angelina would have gulped the scalding liquid if she could, just to hurry back to their classroom.

Please stop talking to me.

"Where is your grandmother?" Keisuke asked.

"In Gwangju, where I was born. And where my mother was born." She couldn't seem to ignore him.

"Where is your mother?" Keisuke asked this question slowly, his voice almost hesitant.

"I'd rather not say." Angelina didn't elaborate on the fact that every day in Seoul, she saw the face of her mother everywhere—a consequence of being in a country where everyone looked like her in some faint, recognizable way. Sometimes, a woman with the same height and build as her mother, the same upright carriage of her head, would startle Angelina so much she could almost convince herself that her mother was still alive and living a secret life in Korea.

"It seems there are many things you'd rather not say. Why?" His voice had a deliberate lightness to it, like he was trying not to upset her.

Angelina ignored the urge to soften her voice. "Keisuke, we're not friends. Please. Let's not pretend otherwise."

"You don't want to be friends with me?"

"No." She shook her head unnecessarily to emphasize her desire. A blatant attempt to convince herself as well as Keisuke.

"Why?"

"Have you heard of the expression 'When hell freezes over'?"

He reached up and clutched his hand comically over his heart. "You're hurting my feelings."

She was about to toss off an apology without contrition, but when she looked at Keisuke again, there was a vulnerability in his expression that she wasn't used to seeing in men. Instead, she said, "I'm sorry," very softly.

Who is this guy?

Keisuke grinned. "Make it up to me by having lunch with me. I'm buying."

Suspicious that she'd been played, she demanded, "Were you just pretending to be hurt?"

"No, you hurt me. But I'm willing to forgive you." He was still smiling.

"I'm not sure I need your forgiveness, and I'd rather not go to lunch with you." Her tone was testy. "Besides, I have a boyfriend."

"No, you don't," Keisuke said without hesitation.

Nonplussed, she stared at him. "How do you know?"

"I can already tell when you're lying."

"I'm not lying." She leveled her gaze, tried not to flinch.

"You don't have a boyfriend." He stated it like a fact, which it was.

This is so embarrassing.

"I think your gang of boys will be waiting for you," she said, lips pursed.

"I don't have to eat with them."

"Really? It seems you like the company of raucous young men," she said, sure that her attitude and complacent judgment would cool off, if not kill, his interest. She wanted nothing to do with a younger man, especially a handsome, immature one.

"Sometimes I do. Do I have to be the same person every day?" Keisuke said casually.

"What does that mean?" Angelina's voice was sharp.

Keisuke rocked back on his heels and crossed his arms. "I'm in a new country, so I'm trying a new persona."

"That's ridiculous. You're the same person regardless of where you are in the world," Angelina insisted, yet a part of her wondered if what he said was possible.

"Being who you are is a choice you make," Keisuke said calmly, his face a picture of beatific serenity.

"Really? I have the option *not* to be a forty-year-old divorced woman in Korea?" Sarcasm dripped from her voice.

"Who you are exists only in your mind."

She rolled her eyes. "This conversation is going nowhere."

"On the contrary—this is fun," Keisuke said, sounding amused. "Let's continue our sparring over lunch."

The flash of heat she felt was annoyance, she told herself. It couldn't be that she was pleased he found her interesting. *Definitely not.* Keisuke had no boundaries and was making her more and more uncomfortable. She was finding it hard to think around him—she was suddenly preoccupied with making sure she didn't touch him, that her hand didn't accidentally brush against his.

A young woman approached them and bowed to Angelina. "Excuse me, Miss Lee?"

"Yes?" Angelina was taken aback by the interruption. Most young Korean women waited patiently to be noticed because that's what was expected of them. They never spoke first.

"There is a telephone call in the office for you." The young woman bowed her head again.

Angelina inhaled sharply and locked her gaze on Keisuke. "It must be my grandmother. She's the only one who has this number."

He nodded, as if he understood her sudden apprehension. "Do you want me to come with you?"

She had no idea why she'd even looked at Keisuke in the first place. Like she needed his comfort, reassurance. He was just another pretty face, and she wasn't in Korea to look for a man. She was here for two reasons only: to relearn Korean and uncover her mother's past.

She turned away from him. "No, I'm fine."

The young woman swept her hand forward and bowed, waiting for Angelina to proceed first.

Heat spread across Angelina's face, sweat accumulating above her lips. She was sure the young woman could hear the rattling of her heart against her rib cage. She slid her wet palms down the skirt of her dress, trying to wipe away her panic.

When she looked at the curved beige receiver of the phone, she froze. She had no idea what to say to a relative she'd never met. Proper Korean telephone etiquette, which had been covered in last week's lesson, totally escaped her. Her mouth tasted like it was coated in sand.

"Hello?" she said in English.

"Hello," a woman with a British accent replied.

Angelina was so disappointed she couldn't say anything in response.

"Are you Angelina? Also known as Sunyuh?" the British-sounding voice continued.

Suppressing the need to clarify that only her mother called her Sunyuh, she said, "Yes. Who are you?"

"My apologies! I am your cousin Una, the daughter of your oldest uncle. My father told me about your family leaving Seoul many years ago."

"I'm sorry," Angelina replied. "I don't remember your father." The sea of faces that day in 1971 was a blur—not a single one distinguishable.

"No need for concern—I can't remember you, since I was not born then!" Una said, laughing. "I am very sorry that it has taken this long to telephone you. When our grandfather died ages ago, Grandmama sold our family home, and your letter was much delayed in reaching us. Before he passed away, my father was a tree farmer, and my mother has carried on the business with my brother in Gwangju. Our grandmother lives with them on the farm. They send their most heartfelt condolences on your mother's death."

Angelina let out a deep breath and quietly confessed her shame. "Thank you, Una. When my mother passed away last year, I couldn't inform our grandmother because I didn't know how to write in Korean then."

"It is so lovely that you are learning Korean! But I did graduate studies at Oxford, and I would be happy to be your interpreter, if you should need one."

Una's offer sounded sincere, but Angelina didn't want her cousin's pity. "I'm getting much better, now that I'm in Seoul."

"Grandmama would like you to visit her in Gwangju. Is weekend next convenient?" Una said this calmly, as though cousins who'd never seen each other before meeting for a weekend in their ancestral hometown was a normal occurrence.

"May I come sooner?" she blurted before she could stop herself.

"I am afraid the business of the farm is quite complicated. I live in Busan, and I do not normally visit at this time of year."

Angelina swallowed her disappointment. "Of course." She didn't want to scare off her cousin with her neediness, her yearning to belong to her Korean family.

Una's voice grew soft through the phone. "I do have to warn you that our grandmother, at ninety-six years of age, is showing signs of progressive dementia. Her lucidity varies day to day. She is a rather cantankerous woman. We can speak more about it when I fetch you at Gwangju Station."

Angelina ended the call with her cousin with a promise to email the details of her journey on the high speed KTX. She thanked the young woman for the telephone call and tried not to fidget as she walked out of the language office. Doubling over as soon as the door closed behind her, she leaned on the nearest wall, the smooth surface cool against her back. She was tempted to turn around and rest her forehead against the whiteness. The buzzing in her ears would soon crescendo, spreading a wall of pain behind her eyes. A full-blown migraine. She could taste gastric acid at the back of her throat.

Without another moment's hesitation, she walked down the circular ramp of the language school to the lobby and pushed open the front door. A small act of defiance. She was no longer the perfect student Keisuke thought she was.

Angelina

Seoul, Korea
June 15, 2006

When the phone in Angelina's dorm room shrilled, she immediately reached for the receiver.

"Hello?" she said, a bubble in the back of her throat.

"Miss Lee, a gentleman is trying to reach you at the front desk. May I transfer the call?"

"Of course." She put the receiver down, deeply disappointed it wasn't her cousin Una inviting her to Gwangju sooner. It had only been two days since their conversation and already the wait felt excruciating.

She should've been relieved it wasn't Emma on the phone again. Not for the first time, Angelina marveled at how different her two children were. Ten-year-old Alex, with his eager-to-please personality, and thirteen-year-old Emma, with her melodrama. Two siblings almost completely opposite in their inherent natures. She thought many times that if she'd borne only Alex, she would think she was the best mother in the world, and if she'd had only Emma, she would think she was the worst.

She knew Alex would be quietly sighing but obediently following his older cousin's demands while relegated to the narrow top bunk of Conor's bed. She knew Emma was ecstatic about sharing a room with her cousin Maggie, probably keeping her up at night chattering nonstop, Maggie too polite to tell her younger cousin to please be quiet. Angelina missed the physical presence of her children—the soft crush of their flesh, the milky scent of their breath after breakfast, the high-pitched delight of their giggling voices. But she didn't miss the constant cycle of laundry and dishes and the rushed routine of getting them to school each morning.

Angelina had been talking to Alex last night, asking how he was doing, how Conor was treating him.

"I'm fine," he said, but his voice sounded uncertain.

She knew he didn't want to talk about it. "You have to tell Aunt Cathy if Conor is bullying you, okay?"

She couldn't hear his answer because, at that moment, Emma had snatched the phone from her brother. "Give me the phone, you loser!"

"Stop being rude, Emma. Don't call your brother that." She didn't know what to do with her daughter, didn't know how to get through to her.

"I need new bras from Aerie," Emma demanded.

"What happened to the half dozen you already have?"

"You never let me buy anything new!"

"That's not true." She felt exhausted, repeating the same things over and over.

"It's been ages since you let me buy new clothes. I shouldn't have to wear bras with holes!"

She knew it was useless to argue with Emma. "Ask Aunt Cathy to take you to the mall next time and charge it to my credit card, okay? Now, please, put your brother back—"

"Thanks, Mom!" Emma had shouted before hanging up, not bothering to listen to the rest of Angelina's instructions.

Two weeks into Korean classes, Angelina had learned that Koreans thought about "homesickness" as an illness. A disease you could catch. An affliction you could recover from. She wasn't homesick for Pittsburgh, the place. But, sometimes, she missed Alex and Emma so badly she couldn't catch her breath, felt like she had a fever coming on. She would experience a squeezing of her heart so intense that when she spoke to her children, she was convinced her chest was mangled, despite its perfectly normal physical appearance. But each passing day without her children was starting to feel almost normal. She could just *be* without the obligation of thinking of anyone else first.

When the phone rang again in her dorm room, she picked up. "Yes?"

She was met by an amused baritone response. "Is that how you answer the phone these days?"

"Lars?"

"Would you believe me if I said no?"

"Lars Nylund, I would recognize your voice anywhere. What the hell are you doing calling me in Korea?"

"I'm in Seoul."

"You're not funny," Angelina said unequivocally.

Lars Nylund was her best friend from medical school. He was also the biggest joker she knew. He was quite capable of prolonging a ruse for as long as he wanted. Angelina hadn't seen him in five years. Not since Paris.

"I'm at the Royale Joseon in Yeouido. Come over for dinner."

"I'm really not in the mood for this, Lars." A mock sternness in her voice.

"Lee." His voice dropped in timbre from baritone to bass. "I'm really in Seoul, speaking at an ophthalmology conference at Asan University."

Lars almost always called Angelina by her last name. It was his thing. When he wanted to irritate her, he called her "Angie," a diminutive she hated.

"Why are you just telling me now?" she said.

"You were gone before I had a chance. I couldn't get ahold of you, so I called your sister. Dia says hi, by the way."

Dia lived on the Upper East Side of Manhattan and occasionally went to see Lars, if she felt the need to visit an actual eye doctor.

Angelina ignored what he said about Dia. Lars knew her relationship with her sister was tempestuous at best, downright dysfunctional at worst. Dia resented Angelina, hated the fact that she'd constantly been compared to Angelina as the younger sister.

"Are you serious about dinner?"

"Lee, don't I always take you to great places? The concierge tells me that the Royale has the best restaurant in Seoul. I have reservations for two at seven thirty."

Angelina looked at the clock. It was almost five o'clock. "Cutting it kind of close, aren't you? What would you have done if I couldn't make it?"

"You know me, Lee. I have no problem eating alone."

It was true. To Lars, the experience of fine dining was a worthy endeavor in and of itself. The company of other humans didn't matter. He ate at restaurants alone; he went to movies alone; he went to art museums alone. Sometimes, he would check into a hotel and stay for days, visiting galleries, watching movies, and reading books, and not speak to another soul.

He told her once during his ophthalmology residency at New York Eye and Ear Infirmary in the 1990s that he would often go to the World Trade Center after brutal thirteen-hour-workdays, head for the observatory in the South Tower, and look down at the sidewalk at all the people milling around in the plaza, going about their ordinary lives. He said it was the only place in New York where he could look down from that many stories, that high up in the sky. He said he'd just stare. He didn't know why it made him feel better. Why it restored his faith in the world. Sometimes he would go to the North Tower and have a drink alone at the bar at Windows of the World.

Angelina never got over that image of Lars. His forehead pressed to a window of a building that no longer existed, staring down at life on earth.

"Please, don't remind me how truly strange you are," she deadpanned.

"Are you coming to dinner or not?"

"I can't resist a good meal."

His baritone deepened to bass. "Maybe you can't resist me."

"Delusions are the first sign of dementia," she retorted. "Or is it schizophrenia?"

He laughed. "Ever the charmer, Lee."

"Happy to oblige," she said wryly. "I'll see you at seven thirty."

It was so typical of Lars to surprise her like this. He prided himself on being unpredictable.

Maybe he doesn't realize that's not a good thing.

Angelina had always thought Lars had too much bravado, too much testosterone—like he could pick a fight with anyone, at any time, driven by an insatiable need to prove himself. He refused to drink coffee but drank at least five cans of Coke a day, insisting it was the sugar that was addictive, not the caffeine. He'd joined the track team in high school for just one year because he was told by the coach that he wasn't built for running, given his too-tall height and too-wide shoulders. Now he bragged about running a mile in under five minutes, even though he didn't enjoy doing it.

Still, Angelina had always thought of him as the boy she should have married.

Whenever she was in New York, she called Lars and he took her to the most expensive restaurants in the city. They had multicourse tasting menus that lasted for hours, dining on luxurious sea urchin with cucumber foam, miniature tureens of foie gras, Kobe beef charred on the outside, rare on the inside, placed on cauliflower purée made to look like mashed potatoes with shaved black truffles.

Five years ago, when Angelina was still working for Astral Pharmaceuticals as a manager in clinical drug trials, Lars had called her unexpectedly at her hotel in Paris, inviting her to the Hôtel de Crillon and its Michelin-starred restaurant. It was February and cold. When she'd arrived at the ornate baroque dining room, Lars was already seated at their table. He rose with a wide grin, and she still remembered the warmth of his lips brushing against her cold cheek. They'd talked about their children, their spouses, their jobs, catching up on the minutiae of their lives. After dinner, instead of heading back to their respective hotels, they'd meandered through the worn-stoned side streets of Paris, ending up at a café near the Jardin des Tuileries for a late-night coffee.

The wine flight at dinner that Angelina had painstakingly sipped had taken effect. But instead of muddling her mind, the alcohol gave her clarity. She'd stared at Lars with his ice-blue eyes, blond hair, and lean muscled frame, and thought, *Why didn't I go out with him?*

She had never wondered that before, never felt the conscious pull of physical attraction toward him until that moment.

It was unsettling.

He'd been her best friend during those difficult years when she'd hated medical school and wanted to quit every day. They would study together in the library until it closed at 1:00 a.m., then go to the East Village and have beers at The Red Lion or cappuccinos at Café Vivaldi and talk passionately and endlessly about movies and books. During one of those visits to the unfashionable part of town back then, they'd run into the late-night film set of a Robert De Niro movie, and she'd insisted they stay to get a glimpse of the actor. Lars had patiently waited with her, hours passing, until the sky lightened.

She had wanted to be a writer, and he had wanted to be a painter. When they ventured to the Frick Collection, Lars waxed poetic about the cloudscapes by Constable and the genius of Vermeer while she rolled her eyes at him. But secretly, she'd wanted to cradle his face between her palms and tell him that he was marvelous. They were both from immigrant families, hers from Korea, his from Finland, and had only gone to medical school to please their parents. When she broke up with her boyfriend Grady, someone she'd pictured marrying, in the spring of their second year, Lars had confessed he'd been in love with her since they'd met in Gross Anatomy Lab, the first day of school. He proposed they date. Instead, she'd run away. Away from him. Away from medicine.

Despite her parents' vehement objections, she took a job at a chain pharmacy store. After all, her father had insisted she get an undergraduate pharmacy degree before going to medical school. She'd even passed the pharmacy boards. Every day, she counted out pills and put them into orange-colored plastic bottles, affixing paper labels on them by rote. Occasionally she spoke to patients about which water pill they were taking for high blood pressure and how it could interfere with the blue arthritis medicine they were taking now. And sometimes, she called doctors' offices to clarify the dosage and frequency of the drug prescribed because the doctor's handwriting was so horrendous she could barely make out the patient's name. She found the routine soothing at first, but quickly became bored.

Six months after quitting medical school, she was living in Zurich. She'd left the pharmacy to work as a research associate at Astral Pharmaceuticals, overseeing clinical trials in Europe. At that point, Angelina hadn't seen Lars for over a year. But one Saturday, a knock came on the front door of her apartment on Fredrik Strasse, a cobblestone street leading to Lake Zurich. Lars stood in her doorway with a bouquet of white calla lilies in his hands. A peace offering, he'd said. They had dinner that night, and he stayed on her couch for the rest of his trip. They talked into the early hours of the morning, watched movies, and read books. Sometimes, she would look up from her novel and catch him watching her from the other end of the couch. She would take her foot, nestled under the cushions, and prod his thigh or hip and swat at him, admonishing him to pay attention. He would laugh, capture her feet, and tickle her. They fell back into the old comfortable rhythm of their friendship.

It made sense to Angelina that Lars, someone who was so intensely visual, would become an ophthalmologist, a surgeon who operates on eyes. It suited his exacting and obsessive personality. He could determine cuts on the visual field to the millimeter. It was easy to picture him incising cataracts that clouded vision, practically counting the rods and cones in the retina.

A decade after Zurich, in that same café in Paris, Angelina picked up her latte cup, inhaled the creamy scent of espresso, and took a sip. She looked at Lars over the rim. The graying hair at his temples gave him a distinguished look, and the laugh lines around his eyes added texture. He was a good-looking man in middle age. Angelina stared out the large picture window of the café, the lights twinkling in the Jardin des Tuileries, and wondered again why she had rejected him. She gripped the seat of her wood and rattan bistro chair to keep her hands from fidgeting with her cup.

"Why didn't we date?"

He didn't seem surprised by her question. "You turned me down."

"Are you saying it's my fault?" She tried to smile.

"You said no."

"Of course. It is my fault," she said, her smile fading.

He shrugged, as though he didn't care. "You were a beautiful girl with lots of boys chasing after you. I don't blame you for not choosing me."

"Am I ugly now?" she joked, not wanting to pursue this line of inquiry. Not wanting to talk about what happened over ten years ago.

"You're a beautiful woman," he said. "Were. Are. Always will be."

She hadn't been prepared for his answer, hadn't known that was how Lars saw her. She responded as honestly as she could. "I don't know about that. And I certainly didn't know it then."

"How could you not know? All those guys asking you out?" He arched his eyebrows at her.

"I'm shy. And I don't know what to do with compliments. I don't believe any of them. Flattery all sounds fake. What I wanted was not to be noticed." She thought she'd changed the subject to something safe, but this felt dangerous, too.

"I used to sit several rows behind you in the med school lecture hall. I could see you, but you couldn't see me. You always had your head bent, never looking up, your hair a curtain around your face. What were you hiding from?" He asked the question like he didn't really need an answer.

"I didn't want to be there." She didn't get into how tired she was of looking different from all the white people she lived her life around. How she always received a second glance because her face had the wrong angles, the wrong color. How she'd felt suffocated by all the expectations surrounding her.

"I thought you'd come to accept it. Instead, you quit med school. I didn't see that coming," he marveled.

"Brave or foolish. I still can't decide which." She forced her face into a semblance of a smile. Pushing the white porcelain cup and saucer away from her, she craned her neck, looking for the waiter. "I want a glass of wine."

He shook his head. "Are you sure that's a good idea? For someone who can't hold her liquor, you drank a lot at dinner."

She stared back at him. "I want another glass of wine."

"Fine." He gestured for the waiter and ordered her a glass of Sancerre.

Angelina swirled the light gold liquid. The base of her glass scraped against the surface of the marble table, the sound reverberating in the chasm between them.

Suddenly, Lars leaned forward. He tapped his long fingers on the table. "I was in love with you. I tried for two years to get you to see that. And when you finally broke up with Grady, I thought, 'This is it.' But you refused to give us a chance." He didn't raise his voice or rush his words, but he spoke with a harshness she'd never heard before—there was an ice-cold fury in his controlled tone. Every word felt like a physical blow.

She fell back in her chair. "I'm sorry. You were my best friend. I couldn't lose that."

"We should have gotten married," he said, his voice sure and confident, allowing no room for ambiguity.

She felt nauseated. "I'm sorry." She could apologize again and again for making a mistake all those years ago, but somehow, she knew it wouldn't matter to him. He'd suffered a broken heart.

His ensuing smile had no warmth. "It's fine. We're friends, remember?"

She wanted to pretend that it was fine, that heartbreak was normal, that loss was inevitable. "It was all for the best. You married Stephanie and had your kids, and I married Thom and had mine."

"Life has turned out the way it was supposed to." His tone was impassive, but the look on his face belied what he just said.

Angelina stared down at the gray and white pattern of the marble café table, chipped in some places, stained yellow in others, wishing she was anywhere but here. She looked up to find Lars with his arms folded across his chest, settled back in his chair, legs crossed. From the look on his face, she knew he was toying with something.

"What is it?" she said slowly, not sure she wanted to know the answer.

"What if we had an affair?"

"That's a terrible idea."

"Indulge me," he said, whirling his hand in the air. "Let's just say you came to my hotel room, and we had sex. Then what would happen?"

"I would probably never speak to you again."

"Probably?"

"Definitely."

They stared at each other across the table.

"Or would you leave Thom?"

"Yes." She said it quickly, the answer surprising even her.

Their eyes remained locked.

"And I would leave Stephanie."

"You would leave your kids?" Nils was seven, Katarina six; Erik was only three.

Lars didn't hesitate. "Yes."

She looked away. For a moment, she had a glimpse of what their life would be like: the two of them laughing while making dinner in an apartment in New York with a view of Central Park. He, at the stove sautéing, and she, leaning into him with a glass of wine dangling from her hand. The possibility of it felt excruciating, and she willed herself not to cry.

Seizing the stem of her wineglass, she said, "This is crazy. Can we please stop?"

"I'm just talking about possible scenarios. Not definite outcomes."

"This is pointless." She stood up and shoved her arms into the sleeves of her long wool coat. "I'm going for a walk in the garden. Goodbye, Lars."

"Hold on, let me pay the bill. We can walk together." He sounded rushed and conciliatory, like he regretted his words.

Angelina waited, slowly winding her pink scarf around her neck. They left the café, not touching, and stepped onto the crosswalk to the Jardin des Tuileries when the pedestrian light flashed green. Angelina trailed behind Lars, feeling awkward, not sure how he was going to behave. Suddenly, Lars reached out his hand. She stared for a moment at his open palm, his extended fingers, before grasping onto the warmth. They ran across the street together and then walked arm in arm, not talking. Sometimes they looked at each other and laughed. Occasionally, she pressed her face into his coat, the camel hair fabric soft against her cheek. They reached his hotel first. Seamlessly, as though he'd done it a thousand times, he turned and took her into his arms. It all felt so effortless. Like it was supposed to happen.

She looked up at him.

"Do you want to come upstairs for a drink?" He said this without urgency, almost a studied casualness. But there was a look in his eyes that she didn't understand. She wanted to say yes. She wanted to find out what it meant to have these feelings for him, but she couldn't bring herself to betray Thom. Standing on tiptoe, she kissed Lars, a brief yet infinite slice of time where their lips touched and pressed together. "I have to go." She turned and walked away.

That had been the last time she'd seen him.

After she hung up the phone with Lars, Angelina stared out her dorm room window, thinking of what it would be like to be in the same room with him again. She could see the construction on the building up the hill progressing. The metal skeleton was complete. It possessed structure. Now it awaited everything else—floors, windows, walls, doors, lights. The guts to fill it.

She thought about that moment again when Lars had asked, "Do you want to come upstairs for a drink?" The look in his eyes. Still not knowing what she saw there, she was certain she'd made the right decision. She and Lars were just friends. Nothing had happened five years ago. Nothing was going to happen now.

Angelina walked into the marble lobby of the Royale Joseon looking for Lars. Lounging in a black leather armchair, his head swiveled at the sound of her high heels echoing in the large, modern space. His face eased into a smile. She watched him unfold his lanky frame in a light charcoal suit, his narrow feet sockless in supple leather shoes. She embraced him in greeting but barely skimmed his back with her fingertips.

In the soothing green of the dining room, Angelina's chopsticks played with the white radish purée accompanying an immaculately cut slice of raw tuna. Surreptitiously, she glanced at Lars. Grayer at the temples, more lines around his lips, but the same brilliant blue hue to his eyes. The same soft lips. It was possible he was getting better-looking with age. Her sleeveless linen black dress suddenly felt too tight. Wishing she'd put her hair up instead of letting it trail down her back, she pushed at the strands clinging to her neck.

"How long are you in Seoul, again?"

"Five days."

"Just enough time for the jet lag to get better before you have to turn around."

He shrugged. "It's the state of my life. I would love to be here for a month, but the kids have too much going on. I came alone."

He poured more soju into her delicate white cup. She drained it, losing count of how many times the vodka-like liquor eased down her throat. The heat of alcohol burned. Soju was insidious. Colorless and practically tasteless unless it was infused with fruits or flowers, it was easy to become inebriated without intention. Especially since Angelina was susceptible. She'd learned in medical school that she was missing the enzyme that broke down alcohol at first pass through her body. She became flushed and giddy after consuming small amounts, and if she kept drinking, the drunkenness could last for hours, as her liver struggled to process what it perceived as poison. Angelina had learned to mask the effects, to slow down her speech and movements so she appeared sober.

"Show me around Seoul," Lars said, tilting his head toward her, smiling.

"I've only been here a couple of weeks. I'm sure the Royale would be happy to set you up with a professional guide."

"Where's the fun in that? Come on, I'll buy you dinner every night."

Lars sounded flirtatious, seductive. But she was tipsy—maybe she was imagining things. Angelina resisted the urge to shake her head, wanting to clear it of these silly, dangerous thoughts. "First, you always buy dinner whenever we go out, so that's not really an incentive. Second, I have class every day. For hours. 'Jang-nan ah-ni-yah,' *it's no joke* when it comes to homework with Koreans."

"This weekend, then?" Lars insisted.

"Maybe. If you're lucky."

"Lee, I'm always lucky." Lars was, if nothing else, persistent. It had served him well in medicine, but Angelina wondered if there was an entitlement to his compulsions that she hadn't seen before.

After he signed the check for their meal, he asked what she wanted to do. She told him it was late, that she needed to get back to Konkuk and her studies. When he pulled her chair back, Angelina's body wobbled. Dizzy, she gripped his arm. Lars held her steady.

"Why don't you come upstairs? I don't think I should put you in a cab right now."

"I'm taking the subway," she said. "The Koreans are so damn efficient. Do you know that every two minutes a train pulls into a station in Seoul? State-of-the-art public transportation, not like New York, where I once waited forty minutes for an F train in the company of rats because the tracks were so filthy. Not to mention the too-many-to-count unidentifiable stains on the subway platform." She rambled, giving herself time to concentrate on standing upright.

Lars pulled her body tightly to his. "You want to take a train, in this state? Now I definitely can't let you leave."

Angelina wanted to contradict him, but there seemed to be a problem with her legs. The only solution was to go to sleep and let the effects of the alcohol wash over her. She trusted Lars, so she leaned into him, let him guide her to the sleek metal elevators and down the carpeted hallway to his room. Angelina was so sleepy she barely noticed the tufted leather headboard and plethora of silk pillows on the bed.

Unzipping her dress, she let it fall unfettered to the floor. She crawled under the sheets and exhaled audibly as her flushed cheek pressed into a cool pillow. Lars asked her a question, but she couldn't make out what it was before consciousness slipped away.

For a moment, after she opened her eyes, she didn't know where she was. Her left eye was enveloped in white, and her right was half-focused on an elegant bedside lamp. Lars sat on top of the covers, reading a book on the other side of the hotel bed.

She squinted at him. "How long was I asleep?"

He glanced at his expensive wristwatch. "Fifty minutes."

"Thank god. I feel so much better."

"I wish I could pass out for a little while and be as good as new, like you."

"Oh, please, you can drink vats of alcohol and be fine."

"Doesn't matter. I still can't sleep."

"I have to pee." She pushed the covers away, then pulled them back when she realized she was only in her bra and lace panties. "Look the other way. I'm getting out of bed."

"It's nothing I haven't seen before."

"You haven't seen me."

Lars snapped his book shut. "On the contrary, you undressed in front of me less than an hour ago."

"I was drunk."

"Do you remember the time when you had too much tequila in med school and threw up on the side of the road? You passed out in the car. I had to carry you to your apartment and get you into bed." He didn't move from his seat on top of the silk bed covers.

Angelina glared at him, pulling the top sheet up to her chin. "That was a long time ago. And I was unconscious, so it doesn't count."

"How about the time we went to West Palm Beach on spring break? All you had on for most of that week was a teeny, tiny bikini."

"That's different. We were at the beach." Angelina had forgotten how irritating Lars was sometimes, insisting that he was right all the time. A disposition he had no interest in controlling. She no longer restrained the edge to her voice. "I haven't seen you in years. Why do you have to make everything so difficult? For the love of god, just look away, okay?"

He turned his head away from her.

She rolled to her side and swung her legs out of bed. As she approached the bathroom, she looked back instinctively and caught Lars appraising her body. Their eyes met, and he gave her a small, unapologetic smile. She pulled her gaze away and continued walking without a word.

Lars was still seated on the bed when she stepped out of the bathroom. He looked up. She ignored him and walked to the floor-to-ceiling windows spanning the length of the room. A small pool of light spilled from his reading lamp. Angelina could see the Han River shimmering below and the Millennium Bridge outlined in white lights.

She stood, unmoving. She heard the shifting of his body, felt the featherlight touch of his fingers on her shoulders. She shivered in pleasure.

It was all the encouragement he needed.

He wrapped his arms around her; the scent of musk and sandalwood was overpowering. She leaned back into his chest, reaching up to stroke his neck. Lars inhaled sharply before sweeping her up into his arms and carrying her to the bed.

The softest lips she had ever kissed loomed large before they engulfed her.

Angelina lay on her side, head nestled on Lars's chest, her hand tracing his collarbone. Her fingertips made narrow oval circles around the protruding bone, dipping into the hollow of his throat before wandering briefly up his neck and down the slope of his shoulder. His chest hair felt soft and springy beneath her palms, the strands more white than blond now. All the years she'd known Lars, Angelina had never touched his bare chest before. The intimacy of that act crossed a barrier she hadn't known existed. Reaching up, she scraped her lips across the stubble of his chin before meeting his mouth. When she pushed herself up onto her elbows, her long hair fell between them.

"I want to keep fucking you. But you're married," she said, her smile as breezy as her words. Wanting him to think she was being playful, wanting not to care that Lars was unavailable. He was supposed to be her friend. Her *platonic* friend.

"Let's just enjoy ourselves. Stop thinking about what's going to happen in the future." He pushed away from her and sat up in bed.

She forced her smile to stay in place. *What just happened? Sex? Love?* Still pretending to be nonchalant, she fell onto her back. "Was it what you expected, after all these years?"

"It was definitely worth the wait."

She laughed, propping herself up onto her elbows again. "Well, I was surprised. I didn't expect the sex to be any good." A fake grimace contorted her face. "Who knew it would be great?"

"Well, thanks very much." His tone was droll, his eyebrows hitched. "So happy to exceed your expectations."

"You aren't surprised we're a good fit sexually?"

"No. Why wouldn't we be? We're compatible in so many other ways."

"Compatibility in conversation doesn't always translate to the sexual arena. I thought we'd be terrible together."

"Why?"

"Because I tend to think of you as my brother."

"Please, don't."

"Clearly, not anymore. As evidenced by what just happened." She smiled up at him.

He smiled back, his fingertips grazing the top of her shoulder and sliding down her back. "Lee, I like having sex with you."

Angelina blushed and looked away, tugging the white sheet higher over her breasts. She and Lars had been friends for a long time—she should be comfortable talking about sex with him. But she wasn't. They'd never spoken about such intimate subjects before.

"Do you feel guilty?"

"No." His voice was emphatic. "Stephanie has no illusions about us. We barely sleep together."

"It's one thing to know that your husband doesn't love you, and that you don't love him. It's another thing entirely to know he's having an affair."

Lars flicked his gaze over to her. "Did you know Thom was having an affair?"

"No." Angelina looked away. "I was the stupid cliché—the wife who was the last to find out. I found it shocking, and yet completely unsurprising. I was never in love with Thom. I thought I was making a safe choice with him, ironically enough—I thought he was nice, that he'd make a good husband and father. I knew he couldn't truly hurt me. I suppose he knew, deep down, I didn't love him, which is why he cheated. But he blames me for it."

Thom had left for work one morning and didn't return. At first, he made the excuse that he was stressed, that their lake house was calming, so he wanted to stay there for the night. At dawn, when Angelina couldn't stand the not-knowing any longer, she called him, asked if there was another woman. Still half asleep, Thom had confessed. Not just to his current affair, but to others. It seemed like he wanted to absolve himself, that by telling her, he could shift the blame onto her, and therefore no longer be at fault. But when Angelina told Thom's mother, he vehemently denied it, accused her of being a liar. Angelina had thought things couldn't get worse. She was wrong.

She'd chosen "irreconcilable differences" as the reason for their divorce when she could have accused him of infidelity in court. She wanted to spare herself and her children from ugly court battles, discussing her case with only one attorney, asking for the quickest and most painless way she and Thom could untangle their lives but still raise their children together amicably. But Thom consulted six different lawyers before retaining the most mercenary one, the one who would accuse Angelina of lounging on the sofa eating bonbons every night. He spun a story in which Thom was a devoted father who was unable to pay child support because of a carefully constructed façade of poverty, after a bogus bankruptcy filing. And Thom claimed he was the primary caregiver for their children, conveniently forgetting he wasn't home for days if not weeks out of every month, traveling for his job as a senior vice president at Astral Pharmaceuticals. Angelina had quit her position as a clinical research trials manager at the same company four years prior. Both couldn't be gone when their children were growing up. Yet Thom claimed he cooked, cleaned, and did the daily chores, including packing lunches for their children, when it was Angelina who did almost everything: the grocery shopping, the dinner making, the bath and bedtime routines for Alex and Emma. She even dropped off and picked up Thom's many suits from the drycleaners, laundered and ironed his shirts, like so many wives and mothers who become unpaid and unacknowledged domestic workers.

But Thom found a coworker and two neighbors in Pittsburgh who signed affidavits swearing he was all he was asserting himself to be.

They claimed Thom cooked breakfast and dinner, although it would have been impossible for them to witness such unlikely events since none of them had ever been inside Angelina's kitchen. She wondered what these three white women—Mary, Sheila, and Patti, whom she'd always thought of as decent people—had against her. One of them even wrote that Angelina was an *unnatural mother*. Angelina always wondered if they had been manipulated by Thom into thinking that she'd accused him of terrible things, when, in fact, Angelina had readily agreed to joint custody of their children at the beginning of their divorce. There'd been no need to besmirch her character when she'd made no accusations against Thom or mentioned his infidelity in court or any court documents. Maybe they'd been tricked into defending his nonexistent honor. Or, more disturbingly, perhaps Mary, Sheila, and Patti had done it of their own accord, avenging themselves for whatever wrong they felt Angelina had done to them.

What Angelina really wanted to know was what those women would say now if they knew Thom had had several affairs. If they knew Thom had cut both Alex and Emma out of his will and named his new wife his sole beneficiary. That the persona Thom showed most of the world was an illusion, a pretense he spent a great deal of time shoring up and shaping. A narrative in which he was always the victim, the one wronged.

Angelina had once met a nurse manager on Thom's team at Astral Pharmaceuticals, who Thom said didn't like him. When Angelina replied that not everyone had to like him, he responded with a strange declaration, an even stranger expression on his face. "Everyone likes me. There's something wrong with *her*." When the woman remained resolute in her dislike, despite Thom's many attempts at being charming—making jokes, bringing her cookies, offering her extra time off—he turned everyone on his team against her. The woman eventually asked for a transfer to Sydney, halfway around the world from Zurich. Angelina never saw her again.

Lying next to Lars in bed, Angelina wondered if she could find that woman again and tell her that she'd been right about Thom before anyone else, even Angelina.

Lars shifted his body. He didn't ask Angelina any more questions about Thom, and instead surprised her by saying, "Stephanie doesn't care that I don't love her."

"Are you sure about that?" she said, doubtful those were actually Stephanie's feelings. It seemed a husband never really knew his wife.

"We're separating once Erik goes off to college."

Angelina wondered if Lars told himself these things to make staying in his marriage more palatable—if such a plan did indeed exist. "Erik is only eight. Ten years is a long time in the same house. You could change your mind."

"Stephanie had an affair last year." Lars leaned back against the leather headboard, saying this like he was informing her of a change in the weather.

"You stayed? You, who values loyalty above all else?" She sat up, astounded by his revelation.

"Strange, isn't it? It's temporary. I know I'll be gone in ten years," he said, his voice suddenly hard and cold.

"So, you're punishing Stephanie." Angelina stared at his rigid, unforgiving face, wondering if she really knew Lars like she thought she did. "You can hold a grudge for that long?"

"Longer."

"You know you can be scary, right?" Angelina tried to say this like it was a joke, but it felt like the truth. The sensation was sharp, like a thorn was being pressed into her side. She pushed the feeling away.

Abruptly he turned and punched the pillows behind him. "Don't betray me, and there'll be nothing to worry about." He couldn't seem to find a comfortable slant against the headboard.

When he caught Angelina staring at him, he looked away while pulling her body closer. She offered no resistance but couldn't help feeling uneasy.

"What are we doing?" she said, surprised at the urgency in her voice. She was confused by whether what had happened was love, or just attraction combined with curiosity. Angelina wondered if she'd had too much to drink on purpose, so she could have an excuse for this to happen after so many years of push and pull. Maybe Keisuke was right. She could become a different person in a different land. Someone without obligations, without tethers.

Lars shrugged. "I don't know."

"I need you to know."

"I don't know." He sounded resigned.

Angelina inched down her shoulders ever so slowly, no longer bracing for impact. She didn't know what they were doing and neither did Lars. To her surprise, her anxiety dissipated. She actually felt relieved. And she was mystified by her reaction, because just a moment before, she thought she had to know what was happening. What the future held for them. Instead, it was comforting not to know. She didn't want to be the woman at the bottom of a swimming pool, being dragged down by obligations. She wanted to be a woman who had no promises to keep, no duty to fulfill.

Nestling into his chest, she wrapped her arms around Lars and settled into uncertainty.

Gongju

GWANGJU, KOREA
FEBRUARY 1945

Gongju crouched outside her parents' bedroom, trying to slow her breath, trying not to get caught. She knew the opaque handmade paper plastered over her home's wood lattice doors wouldn't completely block the transmission of sound. Not their voices, not her excited breaths. She tried not to squirm, but squishing herself into a ball was harder than she'd imagined, and for the first time in her life, she was glad she was short for a six-year-old. Gongju clutched her favorite doll tightly to her chest.

Eavesdropping on her parents was the only way to know for sure what they were planning for Seollal, *Lunar New Year*. She was jubilant that the holiday and her birthday fell within days of each other this year, so she could pretend the ensuing celebration of the New Year was really for her. She hoped her father would sneak in a reference to her birthday, but she was afraid her mother would ruin everything.

"She did not run away," her father said, his voice raised.

Gongju wasn't sure who he was talking about. Much as she wanted to sometimes, Gongju would never run away. First, she would miss their cook's delicious soondubu stew too much. And as annoying as her brother Haneul was because he thought he knew everything, she would miss Byeul, her quiet brother, the poet-scholar of the family. How strange that their practical father, a banker, named his sons after such whimsical things: Haneul had ambition as wide as the *sky*, and Byeul was a mercurial *star*, bright and beautiful.

"She went missing the same day Joonsuk was supposed to go into the army last August," her mother replied.

Are they talking about Sunyuh-unni? Gongju pressed her doll into her chest, squeezing her eyes shut. She missed her sister so much it physically hurt.

"Stop talking nonsense," her father snapped, so uncharacteristic of his usual patient nature.

"It is possible," her mother insisted.

"Joonsuk is with the Japanese battalion at Iwo Jima. He's sent several letters to his parents, asking about us, about Sunyuh. If that wasn't proof enough, Sunyuh would never worry us that way. We must accept that something terrible has happened."

"No," her mother said firmly. "She simply ran away with Joonsuk."

Through a slit in the door, Gongju saw her father's shoulders fall, his body sagging.

"Sunyuh has been taken away to the brothels." Her father's voice was flat, but his face was tortured.

Gongju heard her mother scream. "You said the Japanese wouldn't do that! What were the bribes for, then? Why would they want her? She is a virgin with no knowledge of men."

"They *want* virgins. For the officers, especially the high-ranking ones. They believe it's good fortune to take a virgin before battle," her father said, his voice weary.

"That's insane! This is our daughter we are talking about."

"I'm sorry. I wasn't allowed to say. Joonsuk's father swore me to secrecy. As mayor, he's privy to the plans the Japanese are implementing to subjugate our people. He told me to bribe the Japanese and do whatever was necessary to keep Sunyuh out of the Service Corps. You've seen those banners plastered all over town asking girls to 'volunteer.' It's their cover for recruiting young girls for the soldiers."

"How can they do this and call themselves human? You should have told me. I'm your *wife*. How could you not trust me? We have two daughters, and you did not tell me about this danger?"

Gongju heard her mother start to sob, the sounds jagged and raw. Like something in her had shattered. She'd never heard her mother cry before, never heard such heartbreak. Gongju couldn't move. But even when she crushed her hands against her ears, she could still hear everything.

"There are spies everywhere. If one word got out about the scale of their plans, they would have arrested me for sedition and tortured and killed me," her father said.

"Better you than our daughter," her mother snapped, a coldness to her voice that Gongju had never heard before.

She didn't understand what was going on, but she was terrified. Why would the Japanese kill her father? And where would they have taken her sister? The silence stretched so long she feared she had missed the end of the conversation. Gongju peeked through the sliver where the wood doors didn't quite meet and saw her parents facing off, staring at one another. Not for the first time, she thought their names, Daeshik and Jarang, suited them—her father, solid as a *strong tree*, her mother full of *pride*.

"I told Sunyuh never to walk alone, never to be out by herself. I told her she's only safe at home. Here, she can do as she pleases. But the world outside is a hostile place," her father said. "I bribed the Korean police not to recruit Sunyuh as a 'volunteer' for their quotas. But I have no control over the slave raids the Japanese military conduct under the National Mobilization Law. No one can stop them."

"Why would she go out alone? At night? Without any of us knowing? It makes no sense," her mother said, squeezing her hands so tightly her fingers looked as pale as a ghost's.

"It doesn't matter anymore. We have to hope she's already dead by now."

"Why would you say that?" her mother cried.

"Those young girls don't survive long in those conditions. The soldiers either kill them or they die from infection or forced abortion."

Gongju didn't know what *abortion* was, but she knew it was bad. A flash of heat burned its way from the top of her head to her stomach. She'd seen her sister that night, sneaking out. Gongju had giggled, and her sister had startled at first, then gestured for her to go back to her room. The last time Gongju saw her sister, she'd been smiling, on her way to see Joosuk-oppa. Unni had the most beautiful smile, especially when she smiled at Gongju. It was always filled with love and warmth, unlike their mother's pained facial expressions whenever she looked at Gongju. Like their mother had smelled something unpleasant, or at the very least something to be borne.

Gongju remembered an incident, months ago, when she'd gone into her sister's room, crying yet again because of their mother's scolding. Her mother had not been particularly harsh, just disparaging about the unruliness of Gongju's hair, but it had hurt her deeply. She despaired of ever pleasing her mother. Her sister hadn't said one word. She just opened her arms, and Gongju had run into her sister's embrace.

It was not possible that something bad had happened to her sister. Unni and Joosuk-oppa's story was a beautiful romance, not a tragedy. Gongju was sure of it. Her mother was right—Unni had run away with her fiancée. Unni never disobeyed their parents, not like Gongju. Unless it was about Joosuk-oppa. She imagined Unni living in Seoul, cooking dinner for Joosuk-oppa when he returned from the army base. The two of them kissing like they did on the day of the kite festival.

Nothing bad has happened to Unni. Unni is fine. It's not my fault. She was startled by that last thought. But it kept circling around in her head, as hard as she tried to push it away. And it suddenly occurred to Gongju that there was a reason why her mother had been more irritated with

Gongju lately. If there was a daughter gone, she would have wanted it to be Gongju, the difficult one, not Unni, the obedient one.

And Unni was the only family member who truly loved Gongju as she was. Her father, of course, loved her. But he was so busy, so preoccupied with what was going on with the war and the bank and his employees and her mother. He worried about her brothers' futures because they were boys and more important than girls, which was so unfair and made her so angry. But her father would never let anything bad happen to her sister.

It is my fault. Gongju desperately wanted to go back to that fateful night. If only she'd stopped Unni. Instead, she'd giggled.

"We must make up a story about Sunyuh joining the Women's Voluntary Service Corps, how she went despite our objections. After a suitable period, we'll tell everyone that she died. No details," Gongju's father said, his voice anguished.

"No. We must never speak of her again."

"Never speak of Sunyuh? You are behaving too harshly. There is no need to go that far."

"Do you want to save this family or not?" her mother demanded, her voice rising and breaking.

"Yeobo," her father pleaded. "Sunyuh was our daughter." But he was already talking about Unni in the past tense.

"Our remaining children will not survive the shame of being associated with a prostitute for the Japanese. No one will care that she was kidnapped or forced. She is ruined. We must cut her out of our lives." Her mother sounded almost calm, ominous and cold.

Gongju couldn't believe what was happening. She felt like she couldn't see or hear clearly, because everything was moving too fast, too blurry, too loud. Even the doll in her hand didn't feel like it was actually there. A tidal wave of nausea threatened to expel the contents of her stomach. She swallowed, gagging at the bitterness in the back of her throat. The ondol heating under the pine floor suddenly felt like it was burning Gongju's knees. She unfurled from her crouching position in front of her parents' door. The soles of her feet were damp, but a coldness started to spread through her body. Gongju wanted to scream so badly she clamped her hand over her mouth to stop herself. She jumped up and ran down the breezeway, leaping off the steps and landing on her knees. Throwing her doll away, she sprinted toward the plum orchard, the harsh ground scraping and cutting her bare feet.

Angelina

Gwangju, Korea
June 24, 2006

The white Victorian-style house in the middle of her uncle's tree farm in Gwangju was a startling sight. Angelina couldn't believe she was still in Korea. A wide cedar deck, encircling the house, was the single deviation from late nineteenth century Western architecture. Otherwise, with its white clapboards and steep pitched roofs, Angelina would have believed she was back in her Pittsburgh neighborhood of circa 1800 Victorian homes. When her cousin Una had picked her up at Gwangju Station that afternoon, this was the last thing she had expected in a Korean home. The European-style house seemed incongruous in this bucolic Asian setting. Miniature pine trees, their trunks twisted and gnarled, were at the center of a garden in front of the house. Dotted amongst the balsam were shrubs of light pink mugunghwa, Korean hibiscus, the petals glistening in the sun after a drenching by the start of rainy reason. The *eternal flower* was a national symbol.

Una climbed up the steps to a stained-glass front door. "Our grandmother is waiting for us."

Angelina followed, removing her shoes immediately upon entering. Yet again, she felt disoriented. Pine lined the floors, and the ceiling was low, unlike a typical Victorian home. On the inside, the house was a strange amalgamation of 1980s American glass and mirrors and traditional wood hanok. A tiny elderly Korean woman stood in front of her.

Angelina bowed and recited the traditional greeting in Korean: "Ahnyeong haseyo."

"This is Halmoni, our grandmother," said Una.

"It is very nice to meet you, Halmoni." She was proud that she'd retained enough Korean to say this phrase without hesitation.

The woman's dark eyes remained fixed on her, unblinking. Angelina would later remember the sudden clenching of her stomach, a chill running through her body.

Una put her hands around their grandmother's diminutive shoulders and gently squeezed. "Halmoni, do you remember Sunyuh, the daughter of Aunt Gongju? When you last saw her, she was only six. She has returned as a grown woman."

Angelina's mother closely resembled this resolute person. They had the same petite height, the same broad face, the same coldness in their eyes.

"How is your mother?" Halmoni demanded.

"I thought you knew—" Angelina stopped speaking when Una shook her head, her index finger at her lips.

Her grandmother didn't seem to hear. "She was always so foolish, without caution or sense."

Startled again, Angelina said nothing. Angelina would never have described her mother as impulsive.

"She never knew when to be quiet, was never obedient like a good Korean daughter. She caused catastrophe for our family—what kind of woman fails to have a son? But running away to America? I could never forgive that."

Angelina stayed silent, afraid any interruption would stop her grandmother's revelations. But unasked questions raced through her head: *Why did she stop opening your letters? Why did she leave and never look back?*

Halmoni pushed out of Una's arms and took a step toward Angelina. "I wrote many letters asking how she was, asking if she was still alive. What a tragedy it is, not having a single son. I knew Gongju was suffering. I begged for news. My own child ignored me. What kind of daughter does that? She might as well have plunged a knife into my heart." Finishing her tirade, she fell to the floor in a full wail.

From what Angelina had understood of her grandmother's letters, they had been addressed to *"My Dear Daughter"* and had asked the same things over and over: *Are you passing the time well? Have you been eating?* Expressions of love, of concern. And yet her daughter had cut her off without any explanation. How hurt she must have felt. Angelina wanted to say something to comfort her grandmother. But Una looked at Angelina and shook her head again to indicate that Angelina should not speak.

Bending down to their grandmother, Una stroked her back. "Halmoni, please stop crying. Everything will be fine."

Just as abruptly, their grandmother stopped crying. She sat on the floor, erasing tears from her cheeks. She looked up at Una crouched over her. "I am tired. When is Sunyuh coming home?"

Starting to say she was standing right here, Angelina stopped. She felt the same strange sensation she'd had in her mother's hospital room all those years ago.

Una coaxed their grandmother to stand up. Angelina cradled her grandmother's arm while her cousin guided them down a wood-paneled hallway to a bedroom. Her grandmother's forearm was so frail Angelina was afraid she would break it if she applied too much pressure. As she knelt on the light pine floor, taking off her grandmother's slippers, she felt Halmoni's fingers stroking her hair. Angelina looked up. The tenderness on the older woman's face was riveting.

"Sunyuh-yah, where have you been? Don't you know I worry about you?" she said, her voice breaking.

Angelina stayed still, waiting, listening.

"My precious daughter, I have missed you," she said, before turning away and lying down on the bed, curling her body away from Angelina.

A puzzle piece clicked into place.

Angelina stayed kneeling on the floor until Una pressed on her shoulder. They left their grandmother's sparse bedroom and walked down the hallway to a living room with two oversize leather couches, a huge wall-mounted TV, and several glass curio cabinets. In the adjoining open kitchen with light wood cabinetry and wood countertops, Una took out a celadon-green Korean teapot and put a kettle on the stove. She looked at Angelina but said nothing.

Angelina struggled to keep her voice from wavering. "Please, don't lie to me. Did my mother have a sister?" Suddenly, she was sure. This wasn't the first time she'd been mistaken for someone else. Her mother's ramblings in the hospital, when she'd kept repeating "Sunyuh" over and over again—the memory was starting to take a new shape.

Angelina's family was keeping secrets, and she wanted to know why.

Una reached into a kitchen cabinet and took out more ceramics. "Please have a seat. Allow me to finish making tea, and then I will answer whatever questions you have."

Angelina waited, hands tightly gripped, knuckles protruding. She refused to look at her cousin.

The kettle whistled, and Una poured boiling water into a celadon bowl instead of the teapot. She sat and faced Angelina. Two tiny cups lay empty between them.

"The water has to cool to at least eighty degrees Celsius for this particular tea, otherwise the flavor profile will be ruined," Una said.

Is she really going to pretend nothing just happened?

"I am sorry," Una continued. "This must be frightfully shocking to you."

Letting her shoulders fall, Angelina leaned back in her chair. "I'm tired of people obscuring the truth. My mother was hospitalized when I was a teenager, and even though she'd never spoken of a sister, I think she mistook me for our aunt. Her name was Sunyuh?" Angelina was just starting to comprehend her mother's yearning in that moment.

"I only learned about Aunt Sunyuh five years ago. A conversation with my father as he lay dying from stage-four lung cancer. All the chemicals the Americans dropped on the peninsula during the Korean War, they—" Una stopped, looked down.

"I'm sorry. I didn't know about your father."

"Why should you? Your family in America had no contact with ours in Korea." Una said this without reproach, like she knew how dysfunctional families could be. "I am certain that your mother wanted to leave all this sorrow behind."

"Only to kill herself in America." Angelina shut her eyes, exhausted. All these secrets, all these tragedies. She came to Korea to search for answers, but now she wasn't sure she wanted to know.

Una startled, her shoulders twitching. "Your mother died by suicide?"

"I didn't want to say that explicitly in my letter to our grandmother. Too shocking. So—abrupt. But it's true. And I didn't know she would do that."

Una's gaze was soft, apologetic. "Please, do not blame yourself."

"How can I not? I was her favorite child, even though we weren't close because of so many things—personality differences, cultural gaps, generational drift. But if anyone should have seen it coming, it was me. I failed my mother." Angelina's guilt shadowed her, and she felt like it always would.

"Aren't we all destined to fail our parents?" Una's face was mournful, resigned. "My father hid his cancer from me until the very end. He thought he was a burden, but I felt like something was stolen from me. The time we could have had, the things I wanted to tell him. I think it was the trauma. The wars he barely survived. A dead sister. A dead brother. Your mother, who ran away to America and refused to speak to him. He tried to telephone her many times. She would not even say hello."

Angelina was stunned, tried not to let her jaw go slack. It was as though her world had turned upside down. All her life she'd assumed it was her Korean family who had abandoned her mother because of their sense of shame—her parents had left Seoul after her father had refused to impregnate a surrogate for a son, defying his parents' wishes. Naturally, she'd blamed her Korean relatives for the estrangement. Assumed they'd turned their backs on their single wayward shoot in the States. Her mother had once said that her grandmother was a cruel woman but wouldn't say more. The only thing her mother ever said about her grandfather was that he grew the juiciest, most beautiful strawberries. As for her uncles, Angelina didn't even know their names. Since she was the youngest of her siblings, her mother only used the honorary title "Oppa" for her brothers, and she refused to speak about them at all.

Una pressed on. "My father always thought it was the death of Aunt Sunyuh that pushed your mother away from the rest of the family. Apparently, your mother adored her sister. And Aunt Sunyuh was easy to adore. Easy to get along with. Beautiful. Sweet. Your mother had a reputation for being strong-willed and impetuous. But Aunt Sunyuh understood her, loved her as she was. Our grandmother, on the other hand, was harsh, demanding," Una said. "And of that I have personal experience, not just my father's words."

Angelina could see how her mother's moving to America allowed her to justify not contacting her family in Korea anymore, to distance herself from her pain. Angelina felt empathy for her, for the loss of her beloved sister. "How did she die?" Angelina was surprised at the urgency in her voice, her desperation to know what had happened.

"My father searched the war records at the Ministry of Foreign Affairs and the National Archives for his sister. There was nothing. But he knew she had most likely been kidnapped. Everyone knows now that the Japanese colonial government used the guise of the Women's Voluntary Service Corps to lure girls and young women into sexual slavery. Of course, that's before the Japanese military blatantly resorted to violence, undisguised force and raids, slaughtering family members who tried to stop the abduction of their daughters. In 1991, Chungdaehyup, the Korean Council for the Women Drafted for Military Sexual Slavery by Japan, established hotlines for survivors to report their abuse, and my father hoped Aunt Sunyuh would call. She did not. But he found a testimony from another victim who'd spent most of her imprisonment in Jakarta. When she was briefly in Nagasaki, she had an encounter with a girl from Gwangju whose Japanese name was Sakura—Kang Sunyuh in Korean. Apparently, Aunt Sunyuh shared her food with this girl. She would have starved otherwise." Una paused. "And of course, we know what happened after the Americans dropped the nuclear bomb."

"And you're sure she didn't survive?"

"How could she possibly have survived that?"

"What if she was taken elsewhere before the bomb was dropped? What if she's still alive?"

If there is even the slightest chance. Her mother had lost a sister. A sister she had never spoken about, never mentioned, except for one single, delusional moment in a hospital. The more Angelina thought about it, the more she was convinced that the answers she was seeking about her mother were entwined with what had happened to Aunt Sunyuh. A woman with whom Angelina shared a name. *It must mean something.*

Angelina had to find out.

Una shook her head. "That's highly unlikely. Victims of sexual slavery rarely survived, even before the bomb. There's no trace of Kang Sunyuh after Nagasaki."

"When was the last time your father looked for her?"

Una tilted her head, her brows furrowing. "I presume it was in the 1990s. Before he became ill. He passed away in 2001."

"Do you know how many years it had been since Kim Hak-soon came forward and testified as a victim?"

Angelina had just learned about this courageous woman. Kim Hak-soon was the first "comfort woman" in Korea to go public with her story, in 1991, almost fifty years after the end of World War II. Angelina had been watching the news on TV at the International Guest House when coverage about the weekly protests staged by survivors and their supporters in front of the Japanese embassy in Seoul was featured. The military had systematically trafficked hundreds of thousands of girls and young women from all corners of the Pacific, from China to Guam to Malaysia to Borneo to Papua New Guinea to Korea—but it all started with Japan's quest for empire in the late nineteenth century and its ruthless invasion of its neighbors, years before World War II. After Japan won the First Sino-Japanese War against China in 1874, it was emboldened to dominate the rest of Asia. The Asia-Pacific War officially started with its invasion of Manchuria in 1931; the Imperial Japanese Army established the first "comfort station" in Shanghai in 1932. Then, it was only a matter of time before hundreds of thousands of girls and young women were transported and dragged along with millions of soldiers in battlefields all across the Pacific.

Angelina had had no idea this piece of lost history included a member of her family.

Una shook her head. "My father was absolutely certain Aunt Sunyuh had died."

"But there's more information available now. I heard it on the news. It may be possible to find traces of her. We could find out what really happened."

Una looked at her, a frown on her face. "Halmoni would absolutely forbid it. She was frightfully angry with my father for searching for his sister. It is only with the onset of her dementia that she started talking about Aunt Sunyuh. But when she is lucid, she denies any such daughter existed."

Angelina and her cousin both fell back in their chairs, silent. Maybe Una was right, and Aunt Sunyuh was dead. But she had to be sure.

"We don't have to tell Halmoni." Angelina pushed forward in her seat, wanting to persuade Una. "I have a friend who's a journalist. I'm sure he has contacts all over the world, especially in Japan. He can help us."

Calling Keisuke a friend was bordering on a lie, and Angelina didn't really know how connected he was. But she assumed an investigative journalist embedded with advancing troops in Iraq was savvy and experienced enough to know where to look for a missing person. Hell, she'd *become* friends with Keisuke if that's what she needed to do to find out what happened to her aunt, even if she'd carefully avoided him after their strange and unsettling conversation two weeks prior.

During their drive to the tree farm, Una had suggested that Angelina stay for the weekend, but now, she knew she'd be uncomfortable without Una, who was traveling back to Busan later that night. Angelina had already bought plane tickets to Jeju Island, just in case she needed an excuse not to remain in Gwangju. If she hadn't already agreed to meet Lars in Jeju because he'd insisted on joining her, she would be returning to Seoul now to start searching for her aunt.

"Do you understand the vast expanse of the search you are proposing? The number of archives and international agencies involved?" Una said, her voice weary. "Please, let us not torment our grandmother. Dredging up the past will do no one any good."

"Don't you think she'd want to find her own daughter?" Angelina was shocked by Una's words. Their grandmother had been so tender toward Angelina when she'd mistaken her for Aunt Sunyuh—it was clear their grandmother still loved and missed her oldest daughter. Angelina would be forever haunted by the heartbreak on her grandmother's face.

Una sighed. "You are not Korean. You do not understand. For our grandmother, having a daughter who was a sexual slave for the Imperial Japanese Army is worse than a daughter who died."

Angelina flinched. "That can't be true. That's a terrible thing to say."

"You do not know our grandmother. She is a mother who can discard her own children." Una paused, swallowed. "Uncle Byeul died because of her. He had post-traumatic stress disorder after fighting in Vietnam. Not able to stay employed in Seoul, he returned home, progressively getting more and more depressed until he became a shut-in. He walked into a river nearby with stones in his pockets."

Angelina clapped her hand over her mouth and uttered a gasp so loud and long it sounded like a wheeze.

"Halmoni refused to acknowledge what Uncle Byeul had done. She had stopped him from getting help, insisting he was not *crazy*. He felt so ashamed. He told me that when he drank, he could forget." Tears started running down Una's face.

"I didn't know Koreans fought in Vietnam." Angelina uttered the first thing that came to her. The rest of what Una said seemed beyond belief.

"Ironic, is it not? Koreans felt so burdened by the help supposedly given to them by the Americans during the Korean War that thousands of young Korean men went to fight America's war of hegemony in Vietnam. In reality, of course, we were just pawns for the Americans in the Cold War. As a professor of history, I find that tragic." Una wiped her face with her hands, refusing the tissue Angelina offered her.

"History will repeat itself if we don't change the pattern of secrecy. Don't you think it was the consequences of keeping secrets that killed my mother and Uncle Byeul? I think the truth is sometimes unbearable, but eventually, it releases you. You may not like it, but at least you know. I need to know what happened to Aunt Sunyuh to make sense of my mother's suicide. So I can move on."

Una clasped her hands, as if in prayer, and placed them on the table. "I do not agree with you. I believe Aunt Sunyuh is dead. I think the truth is sometimes so painful one cannot live with it. But I will not stop you from looking for Aunt Sunyuh. And I will not tell our grandmother."

"Thank you." Angelina wished Una was as invested in looking for Aunt Sunyuh as she was, but she knew that not telling their grandmother was all her cousin could do for her. Angelina was disappointed with the seeming chasms between her and Una and between her and her grandmother. It was irrational, unreasonable even, to think she'd find an instant family, but it still hurt when she didn't. Sitting back in the ornate wood dining chair, she picked up her teacup, her hands encircling the warmth. She inhaled the light woodsy yet floral scent of her tea before taking a long, slow sip.

Sunyuh

Nagasaki, Japan
February 1945

Sunyuh walked on the beach, battling bitter cold and raging wind. The sounds swirling around her reached a crescendo so loud and visceral she felt the vibrations in her body. Snowflakes latched themselves onto her eyelashes, a blinding white haze. She took a deep breath and held it.

A storm was coming.

A lone seagull squawked above. The sea crashed next to her. A rushing wetness soaked her tattered, thin-soled shoes. The relentless march of waves diving into sand, spraying white foam, was a ceaseless roar. This deserted strip of sand was her refuge in a world that had become incomprehensible, an escape from the noise and terror of the *comfort station*, her prison. She was called ianfu by the Imperial Japanese Army, a sexual slave, raped every morning, afternoon, and night by a rotating cast of soldiers.

The Japanese manager of the station had initially been unwilling to let her walk next to the sea, but his wife had laughed. "Where is she going to go? Into the waves and drown? Be smashed onto rocks? Leave her alone."

The wind whipped in ever-capricious directions, at times plastering her threadbare shawl to her head, at times pulling the brown, burlap-like material into a canopy above her head. The wind beat at her, molding the dark jacket and skirt of her hanbok to her body. And the water sounded angry, the whitecaps belligerent. It was a desolate, pewter landscape of shifting water and sky, almost indiscernible where one ended and the other began. She was disappearing into gray.

What went wrong?

She kept asking the same question, unable to find an answer. For an instant, she felt a flicker of yearning. She wished the sea would swallow her whole, only her footprints imprinted in sand before disappearing as well. The tears on her face were obliterated by the wind, wiped clean as though she had never shed them. Unable to take another step, she teetered. Falling to her knees, she prayed the water would wash over her, carry her out to sea. She looked for rocks to weigh her down, but only broken shells lay in the sand, pounded by the surf.

She squeezed her eyelids together, willing darkness to come. But the image of Joonsuk's face would not go away. He haunted her. He was everywhere—his lips full, his cheeks smooth, his eyes liquid ebony. The bliss, which had once warmed her body, now felt like a steel blade, slicing open her heart. She screamed into cold, empty air.

Water seeped through the worn fabric of her skirt, the damp numbing her knees. Pulling the forlorn shawl tighter across her shoulders, she stood up. Snowflakes danced around her, pristine crystals melting as soon as they touched her outstretched fingertips. If she closed her eyes and wished as hard as possible, could she compress herself into a tiny white speck, float above it all?

No.

Turning, she faced the onslaught of wind and water. The gunmetal sea drew back in slow motion into a crescent, suspended, before filmy tendrils broke from the peak like wisps of smoke and geysers erupted in the aftermath of the fall. She leaned into the unforgiving wind. And kept walking.

Sunyuh struggled to sit up in the makeshift cot, dizzy and so tired she could have slept for weeks. The rusting metal roof of the shed used as a hospital ward for girls like her blurred and she fell back onto the thin mattress, the cot creaking. When she opened her eyes again, the face of a male Japanese doctor came into focus. This wasn't her first visit to the Imperial Army hospital. Last month, suffering from severe belly pain and foul-smelling discharge, she'd been told she was infected with something called a sexually transmitted disease. She'd wept uncontrollably from the shame. Now the same doctor hovered over her.

"Sakura, are you awake?" His voice sounded uncertain, soft, even in Japanese.

Sunyuh squeezed her eyes closed. She hated her Japanese name, and she hated the doctor for using it.

She heard the scraping of a metal camp chair and then the sound of a body settling into it. "I'm glad you're recovering. I was worried when you failed to wake for two days. You lost a lot of blood."

At the mention of blood, Sunyuh's hand reached down to her pelvis, frantically searching for wetness. The last thing she remembered before passing out in her tiny room was a glint of steel and screaming over and over again from unbearable pain. Her fingers clutched at a dry hanbok skirt. Someone had changed her clothes.

"The soldier cut you with a knife, and there were areas that were already torn. We'll have to see how extensive the damage is. Urination will be painful. Sometimes a hole forms between the parts down there, and you may be dealing with a wound that will never heal." The doctor's words were clinical, but his tone was judgmental. As if it were her fault her womanly parts were destroyed. As if she wasn't used every day by as many as fifty men.

Sunyuh turned her face away, looked at the snow falling outside the only window of the shed.

"You must be careful when moving around. You will bleed for several days, if not a week more. But you must clean yourself meticulously and change the dressing on the wound twice a day without fail. Otherwise, you will develop an infection." The doctor sighed before continuing. "I don't know why you chose this kind of work."

Sunyuh's head whipped to face him. She felt a burst of fury. This doctor, oblivious to what was going on in the army base where his own hospital was situated. Her embarrassment gone, she narrowed her eyes. "I didn't choose this."

The doctor's eyes widened. "I knew you were educated, of a higher class than most of the other girls. Your father named you Sakura, which means 'cherry blossom,' but it can also mean 'virtuous'—a symbol of spring and renewal. I was sure that you weren't of the peasant class." He looked at her with pity and condescension. "Were the conditions in your country so poor your parents allowed you to work here?"

The man was not listening to her. Sunyuh fell back onto the cot. She was starting to panic, hyperventilating, sweating, her heart ready to burst out of her chest. *I was kidnapped* repeated again and again, each word slowing and stretching until it became one giant echo inside her head. Sunyuh debated whether to repeat what she'd told him, then decided it wasn't worth the effort. This Japanese doctor was never going to hear her.

Turning her head away, she waited for him to leave. Several excruciating minutes later, she heard the camp chair being moved, heard the doctor getting up.

"I can give you two weeks to recover. And that's only because the soldier you were servicing also broke your wrist and forearm. I wish I could give you the full four weeks that are necessary, but the cast will come off in another ten days. Then you must go back." He didn't need to say prisoners like her received substandard treatment, were forced to leave before they were healed.

The doctor's voice, patronizing and loud, finally stopped, and she heard his footsteps recede. Sunyuh exhaled. When she opened her eyes, Jina was looking at her with compassion from the cot next to hers.

"Sunyuh-yah, it's going to be fine. I'll help you with your wound," Jina said in Korean. Her saturi, *regional language and accent*, would have once confused Sunyuh. But with each passing month, Sunyuh became more accustomed to the less educated girl's speech patterns. Ha Jina was also sixteen, but from a region near Pyongyang, in northern Korea, and Sunyuh knew scant else about her.

"Don't worry about me. I can do it by myself," Sunyuh said quietly, turning her face away from Jina.

"Yah, don't be so proud. Take the help when you can get it. I'm the one who's been changing your bloodied dressings anyway. Your arm is broken," Jina said, blunt in her kindness. "I'm going to be stuck here because of those bastards' sex infections, anyway. They're injecting me with arsenic. I'm only a country girl, but even I can tell that rat poison is a terrible cure." Jina laid back in her cot. "I understand only a few words in Japanese. Like Kira, the name they assigned me after they said it was law that our Joseon people have Japanese names. What did you say to that doctor?"

Sunyuh didn't cry as she told Jina about the night she snuck out of her house to meet Joonsuk-oppa. The moonlight so bright and beautiful in the plum orchard of her father's estate, her fiancé's strong and sure arms encircling her, their laughter mingling like music. But after Joonsuk-oppa left, she'd felt such a foreboding she'd run after him, getting lost in the dark. Then the glaring headlights of a truck, her body pinned against a stone wall before being thrown into the back. The sobbing of girls snatched by the wind while their bodies were dragged far away from their homes.

"He actually thinks we chose this life."

"What?" Jina scoffed before vomiting suddenly into a bucket by her bed. She wiped her mouth and rested her cheek against the metal of the cot, curling her thin body toward Sunyuh. "Jeollanam-do, huh? So, it wasn't as many hours in a truck to the East Sea. They say the best cooks come from that region, but I'd argue it's really women from Pyongyang who make the best noodles, like my mom." Jina's voice stalled, like she had run out of the desire to speak, before finishing quietly, "I was lied to about a well-paying job in a silk factory in Manchuria."

"Your parents must be worried sick about you. They must be waiting for your letters, hoping to hear from you." Sunyuh wondered if her mother was searching for her, yearning for her as much as Sunyuh did for her. Maybe the years of rumors circling the girls mobilized for the Service Corps had stopped, the truth revealed.

"I miss my mother," Jina said, sniffling, pushing her hand against her nose. "I don't think my father cared about me. I was just another mouth to feed, but I wish I could see my brothers and sisters. It's been more than three years."

Sunyuh didn't say that this month, February, was her little sister's birthday, and how she longed to see Gongju. And Sunyuh missed her father, his gentle hand on her shoulder, patting lightly, making her feel loved. She wondered if he would still plant his strawberry seedlings in the spring, harvest the fruit he'd become famous for in town.

The physical pain she was experiencing didn't compare to her heartbreak.

Rolling onto her back, Sunyuh let the tears fall, soaking the thin pillow beneath her head. She stared at a rusting hole in the metal roof, willing herself to push through that small space into the winter whiteness.

A small speck washing out to sea.

Angelina

Jeju Island, Korea
June 27, 2006

The waves crashed onto shore below her, the sound muffled by the large plate glass windows that spanned the hotel room. Angelina looked out at the vast expanse of seemingly endless water, occasionally dotted by rocky archipelagos. If only she could find the answers out there, in the blue forever. Staring at the watery mass, Angelina couldn't help but think of her aunt, a woman whose existence she'd known nothing about until three days ago.

Did Aunt Sunyuh die in Nagasaki? Or is she still alive?

Angelina's desperation to find out stemmed from an uncanny sense that her mother and Aunt Sunyuh had been more than just siblings. Una had said the two sisters had forged deep and unusual bonds of love, beyond those of duty and responsibility. Not what Angelina assumed was typical for Koreans of that generation and time, struggling through the war and Japanese occupation. Angelina's grandmother had denied for decades that Aunt Sunyuh existed, probably at the cost of her happiness. But her erasure of Aunt Sunyuh hadn't been complete. Angelina's mother had held on to her memories, even as she was forbidden to speak of her sister.

It seemed Angelina's mother couldn't live without Aunt Sunyuh. It had taken decades, but the blinding grief, so deep and wide, had caught up to her, and because of this, Angelina couldn't escape the feeling that if she could find out what happened to her aunt, she'd finally understand why her mother did what she did.

If Aunt Sunyuh had survived Nagasaki, Angelina wondered where she could be. Maybe she was still in Japan. Angelina had read that many victims had become stranded in the countries they were taken to, after surviving both the trafficking and the army's attempts to erase evidence of its war crimes by mass murdering the victims at the end of World War II. Much like what the Nazis had done with the victims of the Holocaust. But if Aunt Sunyuh had been transported before the bombing of Nagasaki to another prison in the Pacific Theater, like Palau or East Timor or Myanmar or Hainan Island, Angelina's search would become more complicated. She'd said it on a lark that Keisuke would know how to find Aunt Sunyuh, but now Angelina was in the difficult position of having to ask for his help. She'd composed and recomposed an email to Keisuke asking if he had friends in Japan, if he knew how to go about finding a missing person from the war. But she found herself unable to send it, feeling unsettled at the thought of Keisuke's involvement. The pull she felt toward him was inexplicable. She told herself it was physical—objectively, Keisuke was a very attractive man. But in that moment, when their eyes had locked on the stairs at Konkuk's Language Center—it had felt like more. It seemed ridiculous, but it'd felt like recognition, like an acknowledgment of a shared connection. A bond.

And she was afraid to lean into it.

Angelina turned away from the blinding blue outside the hotel window. The king-size bed, with its luxurious high-thread-count sheets, was unmade. Clothes, worn to dinner the night before, lay scattered on several surfaces—the chaise, the armchair, the bench at the foot of the bed. Angelina picked up her black lace bra and stuffed it into her carry-on bag. Her flight back to Seoul was departing in a few hours, her sojourn in Jeju-do coming to an end.

A week ago, Lars had suggested she fly to Tokyo for the weekend because he was giving a lecture there, but when she'd told him she had plans to visit Jeju Island, a short flight from Seoul where her parents had honeymooned as newlyweds, he'd insisted on joining her. She didn't tell him she'd gone to Gwangju to see her family the same weekend. She didn't tell him she had an aunt, missing, presumed dead. It was strange that she was keeping secrets from him, supposedly her best friend.

But is he?

She had only spoken to Lars once or twice a year since her marriage. And five years had passed since she'd last seen him in Paris, before their dinner in Seoul almost two weeks ago. Liz was really the only friend she kept in touch with consistently. Liz called her every month, regardless of Angelina's response or lack thereof, leaving funny messages and calling back until Angelina answered. Not Lars. And Lars had invited himself to Jeju Island when she'd been unwilling to go to Tokyo. He'd persuaded her to upgrade her basic hotel accommodations to his luxurious suite at the Donghwa, an upscale eco-resort in Seongsan-ilchulbong. Angelina hated to admit it, but Lars didn't persuade so much as she'd readily agreed.

She was having an affair with a married man. She never lied to herself about that fact. But the thought of being labeled the "other woman" made her squirm. When she found out Thom had been unfaithful, she'd felt only contempt for him. And she wasn't the one cheating on her spouse, her family, so there was no need for her to feel guilty, she rationalized. But what about Lars? Surely what was happening between them was more complicated than an extramarital affair. She couldn't quantify the span of so much time and history between them.

Angelina was surprised at the sex they were having. Uninhibited, inventive. For two precise, compulsive personalities, she'd expected the sex to be awkward. But instead of halting, ungainly motion, they were fluid and unorchestrated with their bodies. Lars moved her from position to position without hesitation, and she was compliant to his demands. She allowed herself to float free from thought, experiencing everything without being mired in anticipating his climax, or wondering if he wanted something from her.

Sex with Thom had been anxiety provoking, hardly enjoyable. It'd been over thirteen years since she'd had an orgasm. Angelina remembered clearly the day she realized she'd never experienced pleasure with Thom, and probably never would. He'd lifted himself off her surrendered body, murmuring his contentment before rolling over and going to asleep. She'd trudged to the bathroom to clean herself, caught her own gaze in the mirror, and the truth had landed in her belly, doubling her over. Coward that she was, she'd shut off the lights, slipped back into bed, and convinced herself that she'd never had the thought in the first place. She'd already agreed to marry him. It had felt impossible to break that promise.

Angelina zipped up her carry-on bag, set it on the floor next to the bed, and walked back to the windows. She wondered if there was a comfort to knowing someone for over a decade before having sex with them that dispelled inhibitions, unlocked unforeseen pleasure. She thought the more sex she had with Lars, the less she would want to prolong their relationship—that they would become bored with each other. Instead, she wanted more. Three days and they'd barely left the hotel room except for meals. They were totally absorbed in each other, talking until all hours of the night like they used to when they were in school, never running out of things to say. And now, making love at dawn, at dusk, in the languid afternoon. They'd returned from lunch at the hotel restaurant and spent most of the afternoon in bed until she'd said she needed a nap. He said he needed more exercise.

Lars was swimming in the hotel pool. She could picture him diving under to make flip turns at the end of each lap, his head in a red swim cap, his goggles tinted blue. He was methodical in the way that he always started with the butterfly. The two-hundred-meter individual medley used to be his race when he was in high school in St. Louis. He was a very good butterflier, a good backstroker, a decent breaststroker, and an excellent freestyler. Which made him perfect for the IM with all four strokes, being freakishly formed with a wingspan wider than his height.

Lars used to say that Katarina, his middle daughter, had the same long arms and legs. She also competed in the individual medley, the only swimmer amongst his children. Lars joked that warm humid air strongly scented with chlorine smelled like home to him. He seemed wistful that neither of his sons had chosen to swim. Nils was a soccer player, and Erik was devoted to basketball.

Despite having known Lars for many years, Angelina had met his children only twice. She'd heard a great deal about them, but she didn't know them. It was oddly a relief that she'd never been a part of their lives, now that she was sleeping with their father. Feeling guilty, knowing what it could do to them, she still wanted Lars to leave his children. They hadn't talked about the future since the night they'd had sex at the Royale Joseon, but they spoke on the phone almost every day and exchanged long emails back and forth. She wondered if she was falling in love with him, and thought he already felt the same way about her. That he'd felt that way for years.

Lars had been incessantly calling her since their night at the Royale, calling until she picked up, always sounding relieved, always happy to hear her voice. At first, she'd been annoyed by his borderline stalker-like behavior, but when he said it was because he was passionate about her, she'd softened. Lars had deliberately sought the lecturing opportunity in Tokyo to see her again. And Angelina had felt wanted. No longer just a middle-aged woman with two children—she was an object of desire. Beautiful. Certain he would be invited back to Asan Hospital next month, Lars had asked whether they should return to the Royale or try the new W Hotel in Gangnam, the most fashionable neighborhood in Seoul.

It was jangma, *rainy season*. Last week, walking in a steady drizzle, she'd fantasized about the two of them arm in arm, crossing San Marco's Square in Venice amidst a spring rain. It made no sense, because she detested getting wet, and Venice wasn't even one of her favorite cities.

Before she even met Lars, the summer of her junior year in college, she'd traveled to Venice by overnight train. She met a student from Cambridge in the same cramped train car, both with a book in hand. She'd exchanged her copy of *Mrs. Dalloway* for *A Room with a View*, and sitting upright through the night, unable to sleep in the crowded, rocking passenger car, she'd skimmed more than read Forster's dreary romance. Angelina didn't fully appreciate Lucy Honeychurch or her predicament in Victorian England, bravely breaking her engagement to a man she'd been bound to by duty in order to marry an entirely different man for love—until she saw the movie by Merchant Ivory.

She'd been in medical school by then, and her boyfriend at the time had been obsessed with Julian Sands, the actor who played Lucy's lover. The plaintive cry of Maggie Smith's character, "We want a room with a view," later echoed in Angelina's head whenever she searched for apartments to rent in every city she ever lived. And Florence became the place she longed to go to one day—she had this romantic, impractical notion that she would fall in love in that city of art and beauty.

Venice's canals had been rank and malodorous. The supposedly quaint cobblestone streets were suffocatingly crowded when Angelina finally stepped off the cursed night train on that long-ago, humid summer morning, and when she left, she had no thoughts of returning. Rome was the Eternal City, not Venice. Paris was a moveable feast, not Venice. And Lars had never been to Venice. But the image of the two of them walking along the canals in the rain, huddled under one umbrella, laughing at themselves, suddenly made Angelina yearn for it.

The lock on the hotel door disengaged. "Hello?"

"In here."

Lars leaned his head into the living area of the suite and smiled. "Good! I thought I might have missed you. I'm jumping in the shower," he said before disappearing.

She turned her head to the window again. The sun, glinting off the water, added a silvery sheen to the waves lapping against the deserted outcroppings of rock. A boat glided across, its white sail curved and full, and she wanted to be on it, cleaving away at the pointed tip of the bow.

"What are you thinking about?" Lars's amused baritone whispered into her ear.

Her cheek nestled naturally into the hollow below his collarbone as Lars pulled her into his embrace. She inhaled sandalwood. The scent was a little too strong, eliciting an involuntary grimace.

"I don't want to leave."

"We're going to see each other in two weeks when I return to Seoul."

"I'll miss you."

"Don't be sad. I'll call you every day."

His attempts to placate her only fueled her desire to cling to him. She caressed his bare shoulders, sliding her hands down his sinewy arms. Her palms grazed the bath towel around his hips before touching his flat, hard stomach. Lars inhaled sharply. Gliding up his torso, her hands wrapped around his neck, pulling his lips toward hers. She wanted to stay at this beautiful hotel by the East Sea and talk and walk and laugh and make love to Lars forever.

"I want us to be together." Her words rushed out as if a dam had burst, her longing flooding the room.

Lars pulled out of her arms. He pushed back wet strands of his hair, crossed his arms, and looked out at the sea.

Angelina clenched her hands, fingernails digging into flesh.

"Lee, we're friends. Remember?"

"What does that mean?" Her voice was shaky and uncertain.

"I care about you. We're good friends. And we have great sex."

"Yes?" She wanted him to give her more.

"That's it." Lars shrugged.

"That's what we're doing?" she whispered.

"For once, I just want to enjoy myself." He was avoiding her gaze.

"That's what you want? Friends with benefits?" Incredulity leeched into her voice.

"It's not like that. Don't make it sound tawdry. You know I came to Seoul and Tokyo solely for you."

"An affair is the very definition of tawdry. I can't believe what I'm doing." Her voice continued to crescendo, as if it didn't know how to stop.

"Calm down, Lee. There's no need for hysterics."

"When I asked you if you'd fallen back in love with me, you said you were confused. Are you still confused?" Angelina had asked this question during a phone conversation last week, and she'd pretended she hadn't been bothered by his tepid answer.

Lars sort of shrugged. "I used to feel a spark. But now? There's no spark."

She stared at his confused face, confused herself. "Do you love me?"

"I don't know."

She couldn't stop herself from asking the same question again. "Do you *love* me?"

"No."

Pain exploded in her chest, like there was no place for the air to go when she inhaled. She abruptly sat down on the blue velvet sofa. Lars sat down next to her, clasping the towel around his waist. He didn't try to touch her.

"At least you're honest." She forced her face into a smile.

"I don't want to lie to you."

She wanted to scream, *Lie to me! Tell me you love me!* Instead, she stared into the blue abyss.

"Lee, I love my kids. Nils will be off to college in a couple of years, then Katarina, then Erik. I have to see this through. I can't ask you to wait for me."

"I would wait for you," she said quietly.

"Please, don't." Lars turned away.

"I'd wait for you. But you don't love me."

"I waited for you for years in medical school." His tone was belligerent.

"Are you ever going to forgive me?"

He backed away from the sofa. "I'm not asking you to apologize. I'm just stating the truth."

"Which truth? Your truth?"

"There is only one truth," he insisted.

"That's your opinion."

Angelina wanted to laugh. The whole situation was so macabre. But what she'd said sounded so trite—a punch line to an elaborate joke. Not an appropriate response in an argument between two people who'd known each other half their lives.

"Are you sure this wasn't about revenge?" She searched his face, looking for evidence that her good friend hadn't been deceiving her, that he hadn't had an ulterior motive for seducing her.

"Lee, I never meant to hurt you." He looked like a schoolboy caught in a lie, unsure if he should admit to the truth or persist in a fabrication.

She felt like a fool. "Right. Sure."

"Lee, I'm sorry."

"I don't need your pity." She got up and started stuffing the last of her belongings into her carry-on. Smiling blithely, she walked to the door.

"Angelina, please don't leave like this. We're still friends, right?" Lars gripped his towel like it was a lifeline.

"I'm fine. We can talk later." A smile still plastered on her face.

Out of the hotel suite, she walked rapidly down the hallway to the elevator. Stopping at the front desk, she asked for her bag to be held until she was ready to take a cab to the airport. A wall of glass separated the lobby from the lawn and its scattering of tables and chairs and four-poster outdoor beds with billowy white curtains. Wide-open views of a suddenly cloudy sea. Passing through the sliding doors, she left behind the wood and metal furniture, the beds a painfully romantic reminder. She walked along the cliff, the surf pounding below her. Angelina could almost hear the sound of her heart breaking.

What happens when you meet the man you're supposed to marry at twenty-three and you don't recognize it? Is redemption still possible?

The famed black soil of Jeju Island splattered on her short boots, a drizzle falling from the sky. She'd bought these boots specifically for the trip to Jeju, indulging her vanity, wanting to appear smart and sophisticated for Lars, who was used to stylish New Yorkers. At Hyundai Department Store in Seoul, she'd turned and twisted in front of a mirror, pleased with the look of her legs. The neutral-colored square heel popped with metal studs, and the black leather body was sleek, the short zipper unobtrusive.

At the top of the headland, Angelina looked back at the hotel. The tears on her face were inseparable from the wetness dripping from the dark clouds above. Numb with cold, she descended the muddy trail back to the hotel.

When she picked up her luggage at the front desk, the receptionist insisted on handing her a towel, distressed by Angelina's dishevelment. "Would you like to have your clothes dried before your travel to Seoul?" the young woman asked.

Angelina wiped her face and rubbed at her hair. "No."

"We would be happy to clean your shoes for you before your journey to the airport," the pretty young woman said, staring at the ruin of what used to be pristine leather, mud obscuring the bling on the heels.

Angelina paused. "Thank you." She handed her shoes to the woman and took out a pair of leopard print flats from her bag, putting them on her feet. "Actually, please don't bother. Just throw them away." She walked away before the young woman could respond.

Angelina got into the waiting cab and drove away from Lars.

Gongju

Seoul, Korea
June 1960

Through the gauzy wedding veil, Gongju stared at her reflection in the mirror. Dispassionately, she took stock of her appearance: a long, white, silk A-line dress with formfitting lace sleeves and a boatneck. A white pearl-encrusted headband pulling back her hair, white pumps peeking from beneath her dress. She gripped a bouquet of white roses in her hands. White was the color of mourning in her world—a white hanbok was what she'd worn to her grandfather's funeral last year. Buddhists believed death was devoid of color, an absence rather than a presence. Yet in the sanctum of her Protestant mother-in-law to be, white was what a bride wore to church.

When she'd fantasized about her wedding as a six-year-old, Gongju had never imagined she'd be wearing white. She'd complained to her fiancé, Minsu, that his mother was like a steamroller without regard for anyone else's opinion, but it was to no avail. They had originally planned to have the wedding in Gwangju, Gongju's hometown, but Minsu's mother had insisted that Seoul was better, more cosmopolitan. His mother was the only Christian on either side of the family, yet everyone was yielding to her wishes for a Western wedding, Western fashions and religions being what Koreans were adopting these days as supposedly modern. And because of this idiotic fact, Gongju was now trapped in this ridiculous getup. It gave her no solace that Minsu would just be as uncomfortable in a tuxedo.

At least, after this farcical ordeal, a proper ceremony in traditional hanbok would take place, as it should, with her dressed like a queen of the Joseon dynasty, elegant in imperial red and green; Minsu wearing flourishes of gold like an emperor. Their hanboks would match, as they also should, to signify their union. On their wedding altar, there would be a pair of wooden ducks painted blue and red, hand carved and bound by silk cloth—mandarin ducks, known to mate for life, symbols of fidelity and love.

Their wedding banquet would be sumptuous, and she was looking forward to all the delicacies prepared for days by her father's cook, especially the wedding tteok. Gongju loved sweet *rice cake*. She'd been told she should refrain from indulging in sesame honey–filled tteok and sweet red bean purée sticky tteok and green tea–flavored tteok. But they were all her favorites. Repeatedly warned by her mother that her short but trim figure would only expand with age, Gongju had responded with rage. She was only twenty-two—she wasn't going to worry about that yet.

Looking down at her bouquet, Gongju thought perhaps white was appropriate today. *If only Sunyuh-unni were here to see me.* Unni had loved roses, especially pink ones. A wetness slid down Gongju's cheeks, her breath burning in her chest. *Don't cry.* No amount of crying was going to bring back her lovely, lost sister. Gongju tried to halt the images of her sister from filling every crevice in her mind: Sunyuh at twenty-two; Sunyuh at thirty-two; Sunyuh at fifty. *Unni should be in her garden.*

Gongju wondered what Unni would have thought of Minsu, wondered if she would have approved or if she would have tried to dissuade Gongju from marrying him. One thing she knew to be true: Unni would have only considered Gongju's happiness. Her sister had known her so well—the only one who saw the deeply passionate, painfully sensitive side of the spoiled child that Gongju had been.

Her parents were relieved she was marrying Minsu. They didn't consider whether he was well suited to be her husband. He was a doctor from an *aristocratic family*, a yangban, and that was all that mattered. As far as her mother was concerned, Gongju was marrying up.

But Unni would have asked if Gongju loved Minsu. And she did. Minsu was the perfect man for her. Smart, loving, passionate. The one who filled the hole in Gongju's heart that Unni had left behind. She imagined Unni smiling and nodding, asking if Gongju was ready to be somebody's wife, no longer a college student. She could almost hear her sister ask, *Is he a good man?* Gongju would have said, *He is a wonderful man. He loves me. He sees me for who I am, just as you did.* She could almost see her sister's beautiful face transform from uncertainty to radiance. Unni would have said, *If you love him, then I will love him too.* And Unni would have held her in her arms, just like when Gongju was six years old.

The sound of a door opening broke Gongju out of her reverie, and she stared again at her reflection in the white dress. She looked like a ghost. The sight was horrifying. And she dreaded the church service—all those people watching her, probably finding her wanting.

Gongju's mother frowned at her. "Why are you wearing shoes in this house?"

Her mother's criticism felt unbearable, especially today. "Uhmonni, please, not now." Gongju spoke as calmly as she could.

"Wearing shoes inside your mother-in-law's home is disrespectful and careless. She already thinks you're a country bumpkin without any refined manners, and now you're going to prove her right."

Her disapproval was crushing. Today, of all days, Gongju thought her mother would not criticize her so incessantly, would try to be kind to her. She was marrying for love, yes, but she was also doing exactly what her mother wanted her to do, abandoning her dreams to become a wife and a mother, a woman who would live only for her husband and children. Gongju had graduated from the Teacher's College for Women in Gwangju because her parents had forbidden her to attend Ewha University in Seoul to study literature, but teaching children wasn't her passion.

She loved literature in translation, especially the works of Hemingway and Tolstoy. But becoming a writer was unrealistic. Gongju was a woman, and the support she'd need to study further or have the time to write wasn't possible after marriage. She would just have to satisfy herself with achieving success through her husband and children, live through them like all good Korean women were expected to do.

Yet even as she fulfilled her duties as a filial daughter, her mother wasn't happy. But Gongju told herself that she wasn't going to let her mother goad her. Not today. "I had to try on the silly shoes to make sure the dress was not too long."

Uhmonni continued to frown. "You should know better. Of course it fits perfectly. It's been measured and done right."

Gongju fought the urge to snap. "I was making certain," she said instead, swallowing an acrid taste in her mouth.

In the mirror, Gongju's lips thinned and tightened. It was only a matter of time before her face would contort into ugliness. The thought of it displeased her. It felt like a bad omen on what was supposed to be a joyous day. She turned away and pushed at her veil, struggling to lift it over her head. When she felt her mother's fingers on her neck, she tensed, but her mother was simply removing the barrier between them. In the mirror, she saw her mother's reflection in a pearl-gray hanbok next to hers. They looked expectantly at one another.

"I suppose you'll have to do," Uhmonni announced, like she was making peace with an unfortunate fact.

Gongju's shoulders fell in the mirror.

Her mother gestured at a bouquet of white lilies she'd placed on the table nearby without Gongju noticing. "Your mother-in-law wants you to change your flowers. She thinks lilies are elegant, not ordinary like roses."

Gongju hated being bullied. "No."

"She isn't asking, and I'm not having a discussion with you. Please, for once, do as you are told."

From the hard edge to her mother's voice, Gongju knew it would be useless to protest. But she still felt compelled to say something. "I do not understand why I must be the one who accommodates, who yields. It is my wedding day."

Uhmonni looked almost pained. "A daughter-in-law must obey her husband's parents, no exceptions. So don't make a fuss. Please." Surprisingly, that last word was said slowly, like she wanted to be conciliatory, not combative.

Gongju chose not to respond.

Uhmonni smoothed the voluminous skirt near her hips, as if she were drying her palms. "I've been meaning to talk to you about something." She fiddled with the long sashes of her hanbok, the perfect bow now askew.

"What is it?" Gongju asked.

"Your wedding night." Uhmonni hesitated before continuing, "You should know what to expect."

Gongju blushed, looking down at her feet. "Mother, please, this is not necessary."

"Your husband will want to do certain things. You must not be afraid or disgusted. They are part of a wife's duty. Just close your eyes and pretend something else is happening," Uhmonni said, her voice subdued.

For a moment, Gongju felt scared. What could be so repugnant about a man and a woman loving each other and expressing that love physically? Her mother was talking nonsense, and she was not going to listen.

"It's important you please your husband. If he's not happy, your mother-in-law will not tolerate you. You must not bring shame or dishonor on our family."

"Why do you always assume I will do something wrong?" Gongju was so fed up with her mother's criticism, her constant haranguing.

"You've always been difficult. A true maeng-nae, *last child*. Willful. Wanting to do whatever you wanted, no matter the consequences." Uhmonni's voice was full of contempt. "Why can't you be more obedient?"

"You mean, like Unni?" she demanded.

Her mother blanched, as though Gongju had physically struck her.

Gongju turned and touched her arm, wanting to apologize.

Uhmonni recoiled and pulled away. "How dare you mention your sister today. Of all days." Her voice was so low it was almost guttural.

"I am sorry." Gongju was ashamed she'd been so vindictive.

"She was my daughter." Uhmonni's voice trembled, but her face was like stone, unmoving. "There is a hole in my soul that will never heal because of her death. Not a single day goes by that I do not think of Sunyuh."

Gongju despaired of ever understanding her own mother. "Then why do you never show it?"

"Would it bring her back? Is that what you think? Foolish girl!"

"It would mean you care. Instead, you have forbidden everyone from ever speaking of Unni. Do you not miss her?" Gongju voice's trailed to a whisper.

"Nothing good will come from talking about Sunyuh. It is pointless," Uhmonni said, impatience in her eyes.

"That is not true!" Gongju cried.

Uhmonni lifted her chin and drew herself taller. "We must get on with our lives. We must behave as if she died an honorable death."

"An honorable death? What does that even mean?" Gongju clenched her hands, wanting to shake sense into her mother.

"You know nothing about honor. By what she did, Sunyuh brought dishonor on our family." Uhmonni's voice was calm and cold.

"What are you talking about? Sunyuh-unni did *nothing* wrong. She was taken from us!" Gongju was horrified by what her mother was equating with honor, horrified by the extent of her denial. *Isn't the truth important?*

Uhmonni visibly startled. "How do you know Sunyuh was abducted?"

"I heard you and Father speak of it when I was a little girl." Gongju looked away. She didn't say that she blamed herself for her sister's disappearance. How she wished she'd stopped Unni from leaving that fateful night. How she wished she was the daughter who had disappeared instead.

A silence.

"Then you know Sunyuh was a prostitute for the Japanese. She died in some brothel." Uhmonni's voice was unyielding.

"We loved her. How can you erase her this way?"

"It has cost your father a great deal of money to keep this from coming to the attention of Minsu's family. The lavish gifts, the exorbitant dowry—it's why his parents aren't asking questions. About anything. Do you think they would let him marry you if they knew the truth?" Her mother seemed to be taunting her.

"Minsu loves me!" Gongju was certain about Minsu's devotion, certain he would never abandon her. "He would marry me no matter what his family said or did."

"Is that what you think happens in real life?" A sneer crossed her mother's face.

"Minsu loves me. We are a couple. A family. I am not listening to this anymore," Gongju said, her lips thin and set.

Mother and daughter confronted each other in the mirror, their eyes locked. Gongju told herself that she wasn't going to budge, even as heat expanded from her cheeks down to her neck, burning and unbearable. She wasn't going to give in. She wasn't going to let her mother frame what happened to Unni as an embarrassment. A shame. But she wondered why she hadn't told Minsu about Unni. What was keeping her silent.

Gongju broke away from her mother's gaze.

"I don't want to fight with you on your wedding day. I care about you." Uhmonni sighed. "And I feel it is my duty to warn you."

"Warn me about what?" Gongju dismissed, unable to keep the irritation from her voice.

"You must be careful." Uhmonni paused, lowered her voice. "Minsu is the jangsohn of his family. And they will not tolerate him being the last one. If you cannot bear a son, his family will punish you."

Her mother looked at her with pity, but Gongju remained defiant. "I do not know what you are talking about. Minsu loves me, and his parents treat me like a daughter. Minsu and I are going to live a good life together."

"Gongju-yah, I hope you live a long and happy life." Uhmonni gave her a long look before leaving the room.

Gongju stared at her reflection in the mirror. Despite her bravado, she was frightened. *Am I going to live happily ever after?* She wondered if Minsu would love her no matter what. If he would value her, above his family honor. She wished Sunyuh-unni were here to reassure her.

Gongju knew her husband-to-be was the jangsohn, *the oldest son of the oldest son*. She knew what that meant, especially for the yangban, the *aristocrats*, sent into hiding by the assassination of the empress and the subjugation of Korea by Japan in 1910. Traditions were inflexible. Sons were valued, and the oldest son was always the most precious. The jangsohn was the de facto leader of the family. She had to give birth to the next jangsohn—the last son of Minsu's family line could not die with her. She would not survive the shame of it.

She remembered that Joonsuk-oppa was the last jangsohn of his family. Gongju knew what losing him had done to Oppa's mother. Almost every night, Gongju had seen his mother at dusk, on the edge of the lake, under a weeping willow, standing like stone. She seemed unable to cry, unable to ever fully grieve her loss. A year after his parents found out about Joonsuk-oppa's death, his mother passed away. No one said of what. But everyone knew it was suicide.

Gongju

Jeju Island, Korea
June 1960

*M*insu wrapped his arm around Gongju's shoulder and pulled her close, taking another drag of his cigarette. Seated side by side on the beach in Jeju Island, "Honeymoon Island," his thigh pressed against hers. Even after four days together, Gongju felt self-conscious about her husband's displays of affection in public. She did not pull away from his touch, but she stiffened. And she could tell that he felt it by the way his shoulders twitched.

"We're married." He sounded hurt. "I'm legally allowed to touch you."

Gongju blushed, her hand fidgeting with the beach towel next to her. "I'm sorry. I don't know how to act." She flattened her suddenly wet palms against the coarse weave of the pale straw mat they were sharing.

As though he understood her discomfort, Minsu released his hold on her shoulder. Crushing out his cigarette, he placed his hand gently on top of hers and gave it a light squeeze. Without thinking, she reached up, cupped his cheek with her hand, and kissed him on the mouth. As if stunned by her sudden impulsive gesture, Minsu's lips were motionless at first, but soon softened, his tongue flicking against hers. She inhaled the fragrance of tobacco and coffee. Everything was as it should be between her and her new husband. There was no doubt in Gongju's mind that their marriage would be a success.

"Let's go back to our room," he murmured.

She gasped. "It's only eleven o'clock in the morning!" But she was giddy with bliss.

"I can't get enough of you," he whispered, his breath like warm wind in her ear.

Heat flashed through Gongju's body. Her fingers and toes tingled as blood rushed to the ends of her body and a warmth collected between her legs. The image of her pulling Minsu down to the straw mat and wrapping her legs around him shocked her. Yet she longed for it. Physical proof that she and her husband belonged together, like Sunyuh-unni and Joonsuk-oppa. The memory of her sister and Gongju's first crush embracing one another had never loosened its hold on Gongju. It was imprinted in her mind like a photograph. And she loved the fact that Minsu was bold. He knew what he wanted, and he went after it—he was passionate just like she was. Not alarmed by her intensity, not always telling her to be sensible. Still, she felt shy around him, wasn't always ready to be herself.

"We have reservations for lunch at the hotel's dining room and then the photoshoot afterward. Don't you remember?"

Minsu fell back onto the mat, groaning. "Whose idea was that?"

"Your mother's, of course. She needs our honeymoon portraits so she can boast to her friends that her son, the handsome doctor, married a respectable and obedient girl." Gongju couldn't keep the resentment she felt toward her mother-in-law out of her tone.

Minsu jumped up. "I'm going for a swim." His feet flicked sand grains onto her arm, sharp and stinging as he ran toward the sea.

Gongju reached out her hand, trying to catch him before he left, regretting her rancor, but Minsu didn't seem to notice. Gongju watched him dive fluidly into the waves, propelling his body toward the horizon. His arms sliced through water, his feet like the tail of a whale, churning a wake behind him. But the calm with which Minsu swam was a revelation. Gongju didn't expect him to flail or gasp for air, but she was still surprised by the leisure in his motions. No frantic activity, no urgency in the turning of his head. Instead, there was grace. His body floated effortlessly in the sea, inexorably moving away from her.

Gongju stepped out of the hotel dressing room, smoothing her Western skirt over her hips. She was pleased with how she looked in her pumps, loved the inches they added to her height. Now she could stand closer to Minsu in the portraits, no longer dwarfed by the distance between them. The photographer, lamenting their vast height difference, had clicked his tongue when they'd first walked in, had looked at her with pity. And Gongju was irritated that, for the first few shots, she'd been obligated to wear a hanbok, like she was a character in some damn historical drama, while Minsu had looked modern in a Western suit. But now, she and Minsu would match.

Gongju heard a mellifluous exchange of words between a male and female voice as she approached a turn in the hallway. *Lovers*, she thought, coming around the corner. But then she stopped short. Her smile wiped away. She couldn't believe what she was seeing—Minsu, with a woman she didn't know. His head was tilted toward the pretty hotel employee, and he was whispering in her ear. The young woman blushed.

"What are you doing?" Maybe she was in a nightmare, and she just had to wake up. What was happening felt completely surreal.

Two heads popped up, eyes startled, mouths open.

"What are you doing?" Gongju repeated, struggling to keep her voice down.

"Nothing." Minsu shook his head decisively.

The young woman clapped her hand over her mouth. "I am sorry. I am so sorry." She turned and swiftly walked away.

Gongju glared at Minsu. "What's going on?"

"You're misunderstanding the whole situation," he said calmly.

Her heart was fracturing into a million pieces. "Don't lie to me."

"I'm not lying." There was not one crease of concern on his face.

"I saw you," she whispered, her gaze steady. But in her head, she was screaming and stuttering. *How could you do this, on our honeymoon, no less?*

"Nothing happened."

"So, something could have happened?" she demanded, wanting to stab him with something, wanting to hurt him as much as he was hurting her.

"That's not what I said."

She squeezed her eyes shut, angry at the desperation in her voice. "You've done this before, haven't you?"

"No! Yeobo, please, listen to me."

Blindly grabbing a vase from a side table, she threw it at Minsu. It shattered on the wall next to him as he covered his face and turned his body to shield himself. Shocked at what she'd done, Gongju stood still for a moment. Minsu remained crouching, cowering, and she seized the opportunity to turn away and run in the opposite direction. The carpet erasing her frantic footfalls.

Gongju gripped the wood handle of the large red umbrella, holding on as if her life depended on it. Water dripped from the metal ends. Rain splashed off the dark wood pier and pelted her stockinged ankles. She was not appropriately dressed for the rain. But then, she'd run out of the hotel, grabbing the proffered umbrella from the bellboy at the last second before venturing heedlessly into the deluge. Walking without thought, she found herself at this fishing pier. She didn't particularly like the sea—the smell of moist seaweed and fish didn't appeal to her, not like the clean scent of pine in the mountains. Verdant landscapes were her preference—fresh air, lush green against brilliant blue sky. No people.

But Minsu loved the ocean, so Jeju Island had been the perfect compromise for their honeymoon. There was hiking in Hallasan, the tallest mountain in southern Korea, and swimming off the many beaches. They chose Jeju City as their base, making day trips to tea plantations and, of course, the easternmost point on the island, Seongsan-ilchulbong, *Sunrise Peak*. Just yesterday, they'd driven in the dark and climbed the steep grade up to the caldera of an extinct volcano to see the sun rise. They had shared a blanket, laughing as light beamed onto their faces.

With the rain and most of the fishing boats out to sea, Gongju was only one of a handful of souls on the dock. There was no thunder, no lightning. But a capricious wind blew, scattering showers onto her face, her arms, her naked knees. She shivered in her sleeveless blouse, black lace over silk, that she'd worn for the photo shoot. Her white skirt drenched dark, a Rorschach of shadow and light. But she refused to go back.

A few hardy women squatting on the pier, hauling crabs out of their traps, looked up at her as if they were shocked by her behavior. The clatter of shells rang out from metal buckets. *Where is her sense of nunchi?* was what she imagined buzzed in their heads. But she was accustomed to people passing judgment on her, expecting her to behave a certain way. It bothered her, even though she had spent years pretending otherwise. Gongju wasn't tough, like her mother assumed. She shouted to drown out pain, and because she refused to cry, she was seen as insensitive. Even her father thought she was selfish but still indulged her, and Gongju perpetuated this myth because she would rather be seen as a bully than a weakling. Only Sunyuh-unni had known how easily Gongju could be hurt.

Under the umbrella, tears ran down Gongju's cheeks, as steady as the rain drumming above her head. *Was I mistaken about Minsu?* She'd been so sure he was The One, believed he was the only man in the world for her—the one person who saw her for who she was and still loved her. She'd fiercely clung to this, yearned for it with all her might. But now, she felt stupid for being so sentimental, so foolish. And she knew she was being nonsensical. There was no other way to explain why she was crying. She detested crying, a habit she so often refused to indulge.

Was she one of those pathetic women who thought that a moment of happiness was worth a lifetime of tears? A person who extrapolates one incident from one day as the harbinger of what will happen the rest of her life?

When Gongju first met Minsu six months ago, in a traditional tea shop in Insadong, she had been there as a favor for her cousin, Yesul, who'd needed a chaperone to meet her fiancé, who happened to be Minsu's best friend. Gongju remembered the moment she'd looked in Minsu's eyes, those beautiful brown eyes in that handsome face. She felt as if time had stood still, the wavy grain of the wood table and the delicate celadon teacups forming a frozen tableau. She fell in love in an instant. She thought Minsu had, too.

But she'd been a fool, blind to this aspect of his personality. How could she not have known? She yearned for him one moment, wanting him to hold her and tell her everything was going to be all right, and in the next, she wanted to inflict harm, wanted to pound her fists into Minsu's chest and ask him why he was such a bastard when she loved him so much.

On the fishing pier, Gongju stared at the sea. A haenyeo, one of the famed *women free divers* of Jeju Island, in a formfitting white cotton outfit, shoulders and legs bare, walked slowly but purposefully to the end of the pier. The diver pulled on her goggles, adjusting them over the white cloth that bound her hair, and hurled her buoy away from her body, the swing of her arms a graceful arc. Dropping her green net into the water, she plunged in. With just a couple of strokes to her buoy, she tucked it under her body and swam away like a large seal. Water rippled behind the diver, her legs propelling her, invisible beneath the surface. If only Gongju could swim away from her life like that, seemingly effortlessly, without regret.

She turned her back on the sea and retreated from the pier. Chilled, her hands trembled from the cold. While searching for a taxi back to the hotel, she saw her husband across the street. Their eyes locked. Minsu's face was expressionless. They stood for a full minute without moving.

Finally, he reached for her, palm open, his long fingers slightly curved. He gave her a slight smile.

She took a deep breath and held it. A puddle filled the palm of his hand, but he kept reaching for her. Exhaling in a rush, she ran to him, flinging her umbrella away. Minsu held her tightly in his arms for a long moment before taking the jacket of his suit off, wrapping it around her shoulders. The warmth of his body lingered in the silk lining enveloping her, his rich aroma comforting. He pulled her body closer, pressed his lips into her dripping wet hair. She told herself that Minsu had made a mistake, that he was just bored; he wouldn't actually cheat on her.

He loves me.

Minsu squeezed her tightly, as if he didn't want anything to tear them apart.

Warmth spread through Gongju's body, all the way down to her frozen feet and toes, thawing her heart.

Angelina

Seoul, Korea
June 27, 2006

Still feeling bedraggled but no longer wet, Angelina stepped through the glass doors of the International Guest House at Konkuk University. She clutched her carry-on bag from Jeju Island and quickened her steps, hoping not to engage in conversation with the polite Korean man who was usually at the reception desk.

She'd already hurried past the little gimbap shop tucked in a side street just outside Konkuk's campus, avoiding the ajumma, the older woman, who toiled there twelve hours a day, six days a week. The gimbap place was tiny, a hole-in-the-wall, which endeared it to Angelina, who loved such things—unassuming stores owned by ordinary men and women, working to improve their children's lives.

The ajumma had two sons, one running a fabric factory in Buenos Aires, the other an office worker in Sydney. She said she was proud of her boys—and of herself. As a single mother, she'd given them their starts in far-flung places with her earnings from the shop. Angelina enjoyed practicing her Korean with the ajumma, coming almost every night to pick up her usual dinner—one roll of vegetable gimbap and one roll of kimchi gimbap. She inexplicably felt a sense of homecoming whenever she stepped into the brightly lit store with the narrow serving counter, the stainless-steel industrial-size rice cooker, the menu handwritten on the back wall.

But after her disastrous weekend in Jeju Island with Lars, Angelina only wanted to get to her dorm room, crawl under the covers, and hide from the world.

She'd just crossed the threshold of the International Guest House when she heard her name.

"Miss Lee!"

She stopped and turned around. Unnerved to see Keisuke standing next to the young man at reception, she practically demanded, "What are you doing here?" Angelina hated the way her heart rate picked up. She was already feeling fragile and didn't need a confusing man anywhere near her.

"I think you'd better sit down." Keisuke gestured at a slat-wood bench next to the circular desk.

"I'm fine. What is it?" she said, her voice high and tight. She couldn't stand the compassion in his voice, in his eyes. *What the hell? Does he know about Lars?*

"You haven't been in class for two days, so I was worried about you. I wondered if something had happened." His words were slow and deliberate, almost too careful.

She couldn't keep the impatience out of her voice. "I told you, I'm fine." She just wanted to get away from everyone.

"When I came here, a package had just been delivered. The staff was distressed because they couldn't find you." He continued to speak, as if he wanted to elongate every word. "I happened to see the return address—a lawyer in New York. I think your ex-husband is serving you with legal papers."

She heard what he was saying to her, but after the words *return address* and *lawyer*, she seemed to have lost her hearing.

She must have looked baffled because Keisuke stopped speaking. Then he repeated what he'd just said, placing the summons in her hands.

"I'm being served? Now? But this was postmarked weeks ago," she sputtered, as if her protest could change what had already happened.

"I think your ex-husband meant for you to get it late."

"Why would he do that?" She was still perplexed, unwilling to believe what was going on. *Why is Thom serving me legal papers in Korea?*

Keisuke didn't answer. He was still looking at her with an irritating amount of compassion. "Please, have a seat. Do you want me to open it?"

Falling onto the bench, she tore open the large manila envelope and read through everything quickly. Thom was going after full custody of their children, claiming Angelina was an "unfit" mother. He'd filed the complaint a month ago, just as she was leaving for Seoul.

"I have to be in court in New York. In two days." She looked up at Keisuke, completely panicked.

"We can find you a flight out tonight. Why don't you go upstairs and pack? I'll call a taxi for you." His voice was low and soothing.

"Why would Thom do this?" Her mind refused to accept what was written in black and white.

She kept her gaze on Keisuke. If she could concentrate on his face—if she only looked into his eyes, and he kept nodding—then everything would be fine. Because if she looked at those papers again, she would throw up. Or pass out.

She had no idea she was shaking until Keisuke wrapped his hands around hers. He sat down next to her, holding on to her. Warmth spread through her body, and she felt like she could finally breathe again.

As Angelina's awareness of her surroundings returned, she became conscious of Keisuke's fingers entwined with hers. Slipping out of his hold, she pressed her suddenly damp palms against her jeans.

"Are you feeling better?" Keisuke asked.

Swallowing audibly, she blurted, "I don't know what to do. I can't leave now, I—so much has happened since I last saw you. I've been in Gwangju, I found my family, I—I have a missing aunt. She was taken to a Japanese Military 'comfort station' during World War II. Can—could you help me find out what happened to her?" Immediately after the words left her mouth, she ducked her head, embarrassed by her request.

"I've heard about these girls." Keisuke seemed unsurprised. "If you give me a little more information, I have contacts in Japan, and I can start the search while you're in New York."

Relief expanded her chest. "Thank you. I've wanted to ask you for days, but I didn't know how. I didn't want to impose." Her voice reflected the uncertainty she felt. "I was just with my grandmother. My cousin Una said my aunt, Kang Sunyuh, went missing in August 1944. One of my uncles looked for her sometime in the 1990s and she was traced to Nagasaki. Everyone in my family thinks she's dead." She hesitated before finishing quietly, "I didn't even know I had an aunt."

Keisuke looked intently at her, nodded, still saying nothing.

His composure was starting to aggravate her, and she raised her voice. "Aren't you shocked? Because I was and still am. I don't understand what's going on or why. But I have to find her." Then Angelina's voice grew softer and quieter. "I have the same name as her—Sunyuh. My mother must have chosen it for a reason."

"I'll help you. Don't worry, you're not alone in this," Keisuke said, confidence and compassion mingling in his voice. "Why don't you go upstairs and pack? I'll wait for you."

Angelina stood up, careful not to touch his long, elegant fingers, and walked to the elevators. She hurried along the corridor to her dorm room, making a list in her head of the things she would need for this unwarranted trip to New York. She tried not to think about Thom, his vengefulness, his malice. Angelina knew Thom had been angry about her trip to Korea. "What am I supposed to do with Emma and Alex while you're gallivanting all over Korea? And why are you going? You were only born there. It's not like you're really Korean, for god's sake!"

When she'd said the trip wasn't a vacation, that it was for her doctoral studies, he'd been unmoved. "If you wanted to be a doctor, you should have finished medical school when you had the chance. Now I'm the one stuck with two kids this summer because of you."

Funny—he never phrased it like that for her, that she was the one *stuck* with two children most of the time. When she pointed out that between her sister, Cathy, and his mother taking their children for six weeks—that he would, in fact, only have them for three weeks—he remained petulant, no longer pretending he was a "nice guy." But Angelina still found it shocking how much his demeanor had changed since they'd announced their divorce. A literal Dr. Jekyll and Mr. Hyde.

What happened to the man who'd shown up at her door on Valentine's Day with a dozen red roses, reciting the Shakespearean sonnets she'd loved so much when they were still dating? The one who'd gone trick-or-treating dressed like a ringmaster, a gaggle of balloon circus animals tied around his waist, Alex and Emma laughing so hard they had cried? The man who'd gone on Easter egg hunts with Emma, seemingly happy to be holding her small hand, whispering excitedly, "Shall we go look around that flowerpot?"

Angelina couldn't understand why Thom was doing this. He'd insisted he get a month every summer with their children in the custody agreement they had worked out eighteen months ago, but he came up with an excuse as to why he could only take them for two weeks. Last summer he dropped Alex and Emma with his mother for the remaining two, claiming he was too busy. But Thom's mother had complained about his negligence, hadn't been home the few times he'd driven over with Alex and Emma. Angelina had told Thom that he didn't have to take their kids for two weeks immediately after Christmas this year—he could drop them off that very night with her if he wanted to, and not have to rely on his mother. He could go to Aspen, ski with his new wife of one year, without any encumbrances. Angelina had thought he'd been mollified for the summer, had enough enticement to satisfy his superficial interest in their children while still maintaining his appearance as a devoted father.

But now Thom had filed for full custody, in tandem with a reduction in his child support. Angelina knew it was a game he was playing: to appear concerned about his children while coercing her into accepting less money for their care. He'd used the same tactic during the divorce, going back to court again and again. But filing papers while she was halfway around the world was a new low, even for Thom. He seemed intent on scraping and sanding her down, not just into exhaustion but into an unrecognizable shape.

This was all about his ego. And now she had to be strong.

Angelina stared out the plane window into inky blankness. In her exhausted state, a blinking light on the wing was hypnotic. She pulled the thin blanket closer to her chin and wished it would block out the chill in her body. Because of the last-minute nature of her trip, the only flight she could find back to the States was from Incheon to Frankfurt, Frankfurt to New York. A part of her appreciated the irony of going west to eventually arrive east of Seoul. Another part was furious she had to do this—be yanked around the globe on the whims of a petulant man. Shivering in the thin air of the plane, she desperately wished she could sleep. She forced her eyes closed but couldn't quiet her mind. Just thinking about being in court again made her want to throw up. She swallowed hard, but her mouth was parched. She wondered if the flight plan would take her over Zurich and its lake. In a feverish state, she remembered a conversation she'd had a long time ago with a complete stranger. If only she'd paid more attention.

Angelina had been living in Switzerland and working for Astral Pharmaceuticals in 1991. She hadn't been able to speak German. Neither the high German of her colleague Nana from Munich, nor the Zurichers' local Swiss dialect. But with her long dark hair and almond-shaped eyes, no one expected her to. She saw the blatant lift of eyebrows and the widening of eyes when she spoke English. Perhaps they expected a Japanese accent. Everyone assumed she was Japanese, the most admired and well-known East Asian culture at the time.

Learning German had been at the top of her list when she first moved to Zurich, and a list had been exactly what she'd needed—anything to distract her from the unspeakable grief of disappointing her parents. To this day, Angelina remained confused about her act of disobedience—finally speaking up and telling her parents she wasn't going to become a doctor like her father. She had dropped out of medical school without their permission, and the anguish in her mother's voice still echoed in her ears: *How could you do this to me?* Her mother's hand over her mouth, tears rolling down her cheeks. Angelina had bowed her head and remained mute through her parents' rebukes, their questions, their denial, her gaze fixed on the gold fleur-de-lis pattern of her mother's French Empire–style reclining chaise as she'd swallowed silent tears.

The gray cobblestones of Fredrik Strasse felt warm beneath Angelina's feet, as though heat from the worn rectangles seeped through the soles of her leather boots. From sheer habit, she found herself at the lake. Zürichsee was flat and expansive, the sky above it a blazing blue. Angelina almost winced from the aching beauty. She could have stared at it for hours, but her stomach was growling. Turning away, Angelina caught the eye of an older gentleman. He smiled at her, tiny lines fanning out from the corners of his dazzling cerulean eyes.

"Excuse me, Fräulein, do you know the way back to your hotel?"

"I live here," she said with a smile.

"I apologize," he said, his English sharp, every syllable pronounced with precision.

"It's unexpected, isn't it? A Korean woman living in Zurich."

He tilted his head to the side. "Why?"

Angelina liked the directness of this tall, middle-aged German. His blond hair and crystal eyes reminded her of Lars. She imagined this was how Lars would look at fifty. Distinguished. "I don't know."

He held her gaze, steady and strong. "There must be a reason."

Angelina became very still. "I was running away."

He tipped his head again. "A broken heart?"

Angelina laughed. "A good guess. But no."

His blond eyebrows remained raised.

"It's a long story. It involves a wayward girl, Shakespeare, Jane Austen, the human skull, and dropping out of medical school," she said with a small smile.

He bowed formally and swept his right hand out, dramatically gesturing to the street. "Please, come this way to my restaurant and tell me your very interesting story."

She laughed. "You own a restaurant?"

"A humble family restaurant. Nothing I can show off about."

"Are you the chef? Or does your wife cook?"

He shook his head, smiling. "My wife never cooked. Liesl was an architect. She designed and undertook the renovation, a labor of love for me. She ate there frequently, saying that she could only see me if she came to the restaurant rather than our home. She passed away last year."

"I'm sorry." Angelina had assumed he was one of those older men who flirted with younger women, looking to have an affair. She'd been approached before.

"Cancer. That is life, no?"

"I suppose."

"Life is joy and heartbreak. Tragedy and beauty. What you wise Asians call yin and yang, yes?"

"I'm afraid I'm not very Asian. I was born in Korea, but I grew up in London and then New York."

"Ah, more of your interesting story." He pointed at one of the narrow cobblestone streets. "Please indulge an old man for a few hours. I can give you a good meal and good wine in return."

"If you have schnitzel and spaetzle, it's a deal. I have a particular weakness for fried pork and fluffy dough."

"It would be my honor." He led the way down yet another cobblestone street.

Angelina learned that his name was Heinrich. A German from Bavaria whose parents came to Zurich when he was a child and started the restaurant to support themselves because his father could not find work as a physicist. Heinrich had gone to university for an engineering degree like his parents had wanted. But upon graduation, he'd enrolled in culinary school. He'd had dreams of becoming a renowned chef, of owning a Michelin-starred restaurant, but didn't want to move to Paris or New York. He loved Zurich and decided to stay and marry his high school sweetheart. Once they had children, he thought his dream had died, and resigned himself to being a chef in a small city not known for its food. But as the years passed, he realized he enjoyed cooking his grandmother's recipes more than he liked classical French cuisine, the supposed haute cuisine. The comfort of making the same dishes his grandmother had when she was a young girl gave him a sense of purpose. He was carrying on generations of his family through food, through the art of cooking. An act of love.

Heinrich told her that the ritual of prepping and cooking something like wiener schnitzel—pounding the veal, dredging it through the egg wash and flour, each step important to the final taste—was meditative to him. But he was older now, and couldn't sustain all those hours on his feet, so he'd hired a chef. None of his children wanted to cook at the restaurant, but he hoped, one day, they would come to know what food really meant to him.

Heinrich's lean frame bent over the rustic wood table as he placed silverware and a perfectly ironed white cloth napkin in front of her. Rich dark walnut and clear-paned windows made Heinrich's restaurant seem cozy but airy. A painted red wall was unexpected, bold and bright. It seemed to Angelina that his place had been curated to induce people to sit and while away the hours.

Sipping a glass of crisp Riesling, inhaling hints of pear and grapefruit, she told Heinrich that her first love was literature—Shakespeare and Austen and the Brontës. But she'd been the good Korean daughter. She told Heinrich she'd been offered the job of a clinical research associate with Astral Pharmaceuticals before she started medical school but had turned them down and deeply regretted it, so she'd decided to course-correct. And now, two years later, she was working for them in Zurich and traveling to research hospitals in London, Paris, and Geneva. She enjoyed overseeing clinical trials. Unlike some of her colleagues in the Zurich office, she looked forward to her regular route. What wasn't to love about being in Paris for several days every couple of months? She even had a favorite Korean restaurant in Saint-Germain-des-Prés in the Sixth Arrondissement. Once the tourists were gone for the day, the charming little restaurant on the charming little street was exactly how Angelina imagined Paris would have been like if she'd lived there in the 1920s like Hemingway.

"What about love, Fräulein?" Heinrich asked.

"What is love, anyway?" She pretended to be carefree, her voice studiously light and unconcerned.

Heinrich arched an eyebrow. "No boyfriend? Not even a lover?"

She shook her head, looked away.

"I do not believe a word you are saying."

For a second, she wondered if Heinrich could read her mind. When he'd asked about a lover, she'd immediately thought of Lars. But that made no sense. She and Lars had never dated, never mind been lovers. Thomas Findlay should have been the man who came to mind.

"There is a doctor I'm seeing. Well, we've been dating for a month. He seems nice." She frowned. "But I'm not sure I like him."

"Why are you seeing him then?"

"He seems safe." She shrugged. She didn't want to say out loud what some of her friends had said about Thom. *It's good that he's nice, because he can't match you in looks, Angelina!* Her friend Liz had been particularly harsh. "He's not even as smart as you. Do you think you'll be happy with just a nice smile in your old age?" She didn't really want to admit it, but it was true that she'd chosen to date Thom because he was a sensible, respectable option. So, what if, in exchange, he was a bit bland? If he was bland, then he couldn't inspire any passion. He wouldn't be able to hurt her.

"He's a doctor. My parents would love it if I married him. Except Thom's not Korean. But strangely, that's why I like him. His Americanness, for me, is a form of rebellion, I suppose. Besides, I avoid Korean men like the plague."

Heinrich laughed. "You are with this uninteresting man because he is a doctor?"

"There are worse reasons for being with someone."

"There are also better ones. I could say many things about Liesl, but I can say for certain that *safe* is not an adjective I ever used. Love is not supposed to be safe, Fraulein."

"I don't know what I want. Why should I not be with a man because it's practical?" There was more than defensiveness in her tone, there was belligerence. She was annoyed with Heinrich and his advice.

"You are settling for this man? Because you think you should be safe in love? Because you think marriage is a check box?"

When phrased like that, Angelina's choice sounded ridiculous, stupid even. As though she'd put her life on autopilot as something to be endured, not something to be enjoyed. This stranger was dissecting her approach to love and pointing out its flaws, as if they should be obvious to her. But he was mistaken, she told herself. He didn't know her. She lifted the wineglass to her lips and took a gulp, not responding to his questions.

"And why not Korean men?" Heinrich asked.

"Because of my father. He's a narcissist. And a cheater."

"Was it a pattern or a onetime incident? Husbands can be led astray once in their lifetime."

"Did you ever betray your wife?"

"I was very tempted once."

"Did you cheat?"

"No. And Liesl knew. She never said one word about it."

"See? You're proving my point. Men and women can wonder if they made the right choice in marrying a particular person. But to carry out an act of betrayal takes more than temptation. It's a character flaw."

"That is harsh, isn't it?" Heinrich said this more like a statement.

"It's what I believe. I divide the world into the faithful and the faithless. Those who betray and those who do not."

"Smugness does not become you, Fräulein. And life is not that easy. People are not that simple. Liesl and I had a complicated marriage. A good one, but complex. From one point of view, you might say that she was burdened with me. From another point of view, you might say that I tolerated much that I should not have. Humans are intricate, labyrinthine, if you will. You are going to regret simplifying or distilling marriage to just one thing."

"I want it to be easy. Life is hard. I don't want love and marriage to be hard." Angelina knew she was whining. She didn't care.

"Fräulein, think more carefully about what you need for a good marriage. Not a perfect marriage. A good one. You should take all the time you need. Marriage is one of the most important decisions you will make. Your partner in life determines where you live, what you do, who your children will be."

Heinrich was right—who you married changed everything. But Angelina didn't know what to look for in a healthy relationship, never mind a marriage. She just knew what she didn't want. From the time she was six years old, she'd heard whispers of disappointment and reproach between her parents. Her father's cheating and excuses. Her mother's anger and pain. She was determined to never make the same mistakes as her parents.

Thom fulfilled her criteria for what she thought a good husband and father should be. Angelina wanted someone predictable. She wanted no surprises, no sticky emotions. Thom evoked none of the anguish that Grady, her first boyfriend, had. When Angelina broke up with Grady for the last time, after she accepted the fact that he'd never fully commit to her, she'd spent hours listening to sad love songs like "It Must Have Been Love" and "Nothing Compares 2 U." She'd promised herself never to be that vulnerable again. The hours she'd wasted, limp in Lars's arms, her shoulders heaving, wetness flooding the hollows of her collarbones. She'd felt like her heart was tired, bloodless from the wringing, twisted from the pain. How silly it all seemed now.

Angelina made a conscious decision after Grady to be pragmatic and sensible about love and marriage. Her parents wanted her to marry, now that she wasn't going to be a doctor, so she had to make a good marriage. An advantageous marriage. Since she had no desire to marry a Korean man, she needed to marry a doctor. At least then her parents could brag to their friends that their daughter had married someone successful.

Thom was a doctor and a researcher who also worked for Astral Pharmaceuticals. He was a director of clinical trials, a vice president—one of many, but still, he was a rising star at a global company. He seemed dependable, bordering on boring, but he had a title and a good salary. He could support a wife and children. They would own a lake house to go to on weekends. And after they moved back to the States, they would travel to Europe every summer on the pretext of broadening their children's minds. Together, they would make a perfect family—one with two children and a large house with a white picket fence. Angelina could almost see it happening, the picture manifesting into reality.

Gongju

Upper Saddle River, New Jersey
October 1992

Gongju sat gingerly on the edge of the pew, staring at Christ on the cross. *How pitiful*, she thought. His ceramic tears, unconvincing, the scarlet of his palms, gaudy. If only the nails were actual nails pounded into the wood. While she didn't want actual blood dripping from his palms, she did enjoy the image of everyone in the church screaming and fleeing from the sight. But it was Christ's gaze, up and away, that troubled Gongju. He made her feel guilty that she had become a nonbeliever, a prodigal daughter of the Catholic Church. After all that trouble to convert when she lived in Seoul, the classes in catechism—time completely wasted. But then, her motives hadn't been honorable. After the birth of her fourth daughter, she'd been inconsolable she couldn't have a son, and her mother-in-law had urged her to convert, convinced that was the problem. Gongju had no interest in being Presbyterian like her mother-in-law, so she became a Catholic because that seemed to require effort and discipline, something worthy of her time. But those masses in Latin had become the scourge of her weekends, never enjoyable, just aching knees from all that kneeling. And it still hadn't worked. When had religion ever solved a problem, anyway?

But here Gongju was, sitting in the front pew of this church because her daughter Angel was getting married. "Mother of the bride!" exclaimed

Pearl's husband, who'd ushered her to this seat, bending over to hug her tightly, even though her limbs were stiff. *Get away, get away!* The mantra shouted so loudly in Gongju's head she was sure she'd said it out loud. *No such luck.* He was so uselessly tall, his blue eyes so irritating. But that was her second son-in-law, a clueless white man who insisted on violating her personal space every time she saw him. *Why did Pearl ever marry him?* Of course, she wasn't Pearl anymore—she was Cathy. All of her daughters insisted on being called by their Catholic names, although they, too, were no longer believers. But she still thought of them by their Korean names: *Jewel, Pearl, Angel,* and *Ruby.*

Shifting in her seat, Gongju tried not to sigh or slump her shoulders. She resisted the urge to look back—that would be undignified.

Behavior more appropriate for a peasant. Gongju could almost hear her mother-in-law's often-said words.

She thought she'd left behind her mother's harshness when she married; instead, she'd gained another voice of disapproval. When Minsu had been offered a job in Hong Kong, she had been the first to say yes, grabbing her chance to be free from her mother-in-law's judgmental utterings and her treatment of Gongju, like she was some indentured servant. Minsu's parents never forgave her for taking their precious son away from them, even though it was Minsu who'd chosen to move the family abroad—to run away from the prospect of a surrogate rather than face his parents head-on. Even years later, after the girls were fully grown, her in-laws had never forgiven her for not giving birth to a jangsohn, the coveted first son.

She wished, perhaps for the hundredth time, that Angel would not marry this man. Gongju despised Thom, knew in the depths of her being that he was not a good man. He reminded her of a snake. No possibility existed in which a man with such a cold gaze could be trusted. She fantasized that her daughter would come to her senses and choose not to walk down the aisle with Minsu. Or Minsu might ask that classic question, *Are you sure?*, and Angel would say, *No.*

Gongju wished she had answered that way when her father had asked her about Minsu, his lips pursed with a slight frown between his brows. But instead, she had said, *I am sure. He is the one.* Her father's face had wreathed into a smile. She'd thought she was going to live happily ever after, like Cinderella, in some damn fairy tale. Instead, she and Minsu were hardly speaking, sleeping in separate bedrooms.

She had tried to tell Angel that marriage was not easy, was not what she thought it was going to be. Commitment to one person had an unyielding practicality that could not be ignored. But her daughter was so determined to ruin her life. When Gongju first met Thom, she'd been struck by his surface charm, his practiced smiles. How he pretentiously insisted on having the extra *h* in his name. Why did he not simply go by Thomas if that *h* was so precious? He bragged about his Irish Catholic ancestors from Belfast going back five generations, running his hand through his blond hair, pretending to be modest. *Try going back five hundred years to the daughter of an emperor.* Westerners and their limited knowledge of Eastern history and culture was beyond frustrating. But it was their arrogance, their presumption that Western civilization was the oldest in the world, that Gongju found suffocating. How shocked and comical their faces would look if they knew Koreans used moveable metal type and printed books more than two hundred years before the Gutenberg press.

Minsu had had the same easy charm. But Angel wouldn't listen, even as Gongju tried to warn her away from making the same mistake she had with Minsu—trusting a man's appearance and words without any evidence of gravity or substance. Threatening to boycott the wedding hadn't worked, either. And she would never forget the look on Angel's face when she'd suggested it, as if Gongju had physically struck her—she'd been plagued by guilt afterward. And now, she was stuck at this stupid wedding. *In New Jersey, no less.*

Before she'd been taken to this seat of torture, she had seen her daughter in the little room behind the altar. Angel looked beautiful in her simple white dress, silk shantung with tiny pearls sewn on the skirt.

"Do I look okay?" Angel had asked.

"Of course. You are the most beautiful bride I have ever seen."

Angel looked vulnerable, unsure of herself. "Thanks, Mom," she said, voice shaking.

Gongju had wanted to hug her daughter, something she rarely did, tell her there was no shame in choosing not to walk down the aisle, no shame in admitting to a mistake. She resisted asking her to reconsider her decision, resisted urging, *Please, don't do this.*

Instead, she'd given her daughter a strand of pearls, the "something new" of the cliché, as well as the antique watch that had belonged to her mother, the same watch her mother had given her on the day of her wedding. Something old. The watch was unusual—it had a rectangular face and was custom made with prized white gold, not yellow gold, in 1920s Korea. A gift from her father to her mother upon their engagement.

Her mother had wanted the watch to be passed to Gongju's daughter, at a time when they both thought there would only be one daughter. It was why she and Minsu had named their first daughter Jewel. Only one gem had been expected—and wanted. Instead, three more girls had come, all in the quest for one son. But Gongju had not given the watch to either Jewel or Pearl on their wedding day—she had been saving it for Angel, her favorite. Her youngest daughter, Ruby, insisted she would never marry.

Four daughters and no son. She loved her girls, but this was an unforgiveable sin for which she was still being punished. She was now an outcast from her family, an exile from her country.

"Please rise, please rise," she heard from the priest in his ridiculous white and gold ceremonial dress. The church organ vibrated, low at first, then rising to resounding decibels. She turned and saw her daughters descending the aisle in order of increasing height and age. Ruby, Pearl, and Jewel were followed by Thom's clumsy sister, Mary, in dusty pink A-line dresses. "Trumpet Volunteer" banged out of tune from the church organ, and she winced, but then she saw Angel standing at the precipice of the long red aisle. *She looks so tall*, Gongju thought, proud of her daughter's height and beauty. Angel's hair was pulled back into a French twist, a tiara-like band perched on top of her glossy hair securing the veil, her long neck exposed. Gongju wondered if she'd looked as lovely on her wedding day, wanting to remember herself as a hopeful young woman.

It had been a disaster. A memory best forgotten. It had rained that June day in 1960. Her mother-in-law had insisted on changing the flowers to white lilies from white roses, despite Gongju's objections. She had felt silly in lace gloves, holding the harbingers of death, the scent of the long stamens too sweet and cloying. Those lilies had been bad omens, she now knew. She would never forget the scent of tiger lilies the first time she'd found Minsu with her only friend when they lived in Virginia.

Just six months in their new home and her husband had been cheating. Minsu had been forced to repeat his medical residency in America, and she had foolishly thought he would be too busy to have an affair, but he had managed to sneak off with her friend, his new colleague's wife. She found them in a guest room of the house where they had gone for a New Year's Eve party, kissing and groping frantically. It would have been hilarious, how quickly they flew apart when she'd banged the door shut, if their betrayal hadn't been such a travesty. Gongju never trusted him again, no matter his pleas, no matter his earnest declarations of love. It had been his fourth time cheating, and in that moment, she knew he would never stop.

She hated to admit it, but she'd done everything she could at the start of their marriage to make sure they were a perfect pair, a matched set like the blue and red ducks that had been displayed on their wedding altar. She'd bought Minsu several Russian novels in translation, particularly Tolstoy, so they could share the same interest. She'd tried to tolerate baseball because he loved it, even tried to drink alcohol, which he liked. It all failed. Minsu couldn't care less about novels, and she could never understand why grown men ran around a baseball diamond—didn't a circle make more sense? Not to mention the fact that she despised Johnnie Walker, the taste thick and bitter.

Angel carried a bouquet of pink roses down the aisle. Gongju hoped they weren't as nauseatingly fragrant as the damn lilies she'd been forced to carry all those years ago. No, the scent of roses was always delicate and refreshing. Never oppressive. She grew bushes and bushes of roses to remind herself of Sunyuh-unni. And like her father, she was good at growing plants. Not humans, as clearly evidenced by her quarrelsome and unhappy daughters. Pink was Unni's favorite color, just like Angel's. The resemblance between her third daughter and her dead sister was unnerving at times. At the right angles, they looked so alike that Gongju sometimes imagined her sister was still alive.

As the priest droned on—it was an hour-long ordeal—she couldn't stop a long sigh from escaping her lips. She resisted squirming on that unforgiving wood bench, her buttocks numb and unfeeling. And she fought the urge to cry as an image of Sunyuh-unni in wedding regalia flashed behind her closed eyelids. Her sister would have looked so lovely in a red silk hanbok, her long hair arranged artfully at the back of her head, her hands folded elegantly as she bowed to Joonsuk-oppa's parents. Her sister's traditional wedding dress had already been tailored and fitted by the town's best seamstress when she disappeared.

If only she had lived.

In the cavernous reception room at the Manor, Gongju sat at table 1, facing the bride and groom. Minsu sat next to her, craning his neck, pretending to look at the other guests. He was needlessly avoiding her gaze. She had no interest in talking to her husband. They no longer had anything in common. They'd never even shared the same sense of humor, Minsu always accusing her of being mean when she thought she was being hilarious. He'd never understood that Gongju had to laugh at the bitterness in life to survive it, to keep going when she thought she couldn't take one more step.

Her eyes flicked Minsu a scornful glance before settling on Angelina's husband and his sly smile, the midnight blue curtains behind him pulled back to reveal a spouting fountain. She saw Angel dipping her head toward Thom, nodding, but her brows were knitted, lips thin. What on earth was that ugly man saying to her daughter that made her look so unhappy on her wedding day? Gongju wanted to walk up to her son-in-law and slap him. Now that would *definitely* be the behavior of a peasant. But it would be the action of a caring mother. Gongju had vowed that she would not be self-involved like her mother, blind to her children's emotions, but she was discovering that she was just as flawed.

Gongju saw the other white boy, the boy Angel claimed was her best friend, sitting at a table near the back of the reception hall, not talking to anyone. She almost felt sorry for him. *He looks like he's lost something.* She knew she'd been right when she warned Angel about that boy.

"He's in love with you."

"Absolutely not," her daughter had replied with vehemence.

That boy was not a good match for her daughter, either. He and Thom were so alike—supposedly in love with Angel, but really in love with the men they thought could be with her. Gongju worried about Angel: she was too much like Sunyuh-unni. Too accommodating, too eager to please, not combative when necessary.

Gongju saw her daughter pull out an empty chair next to the boy and sit, slipping her feet out of her shoes. Angel smiled and leaned back in the upholstered seat, face unguarded for the first time that day. The boy's expression transformed into a fake smile, just like Thom's.

When Ruby slid into Minsu's unoccupied chair, Gongju visibly jumped.

"Are you okay, Mom?" Ruby said, squeezing Gongju's arm.

"Fine. How are you?" She tried to smile at her daughter.

"You don't look so good," Ruby said.

"I just wish your sister hadn't married that man." She switched to Korean because it was easier to express herself in her mother tongue.

Ruby rolled her eyes. "Not this again! Please, it's her wedding day. Be happy for her."

"Fine."

"This is why I'm never getting married," Ruby said, crossing her arms, flattening her already flat chest.

"Do not dare to blame your selfishness on me. You're choosing not to get married because you want to do everything just as you please without considering or consulting anyone else. Just like your father." Gongju said this firmly, trying not to let Ruby provoke her into saying something she would later regret.

"Yeah, of course, it's Dad's fault. I know, I know, he's selfish. A Korean man."

"Not all Korean men are like your father. My father was a gentleman."

"Sure. Whatever you say. Because there are so many Korean men around here. Look at all my options." Ruby gestured at all the white men at the white-cloth tables, her mouth tilted and curled in an ugly way.

Gongju wondered where she had gone wrong with her youngest daughter. Ruby didn't seem to have any common sense. Gongju had had only one viable choice when she was a young woman: become a wife and then a mother. She could have delayed her fate by working as a teacher, but there was no point when she wasn't passionate about it. Wanting more for her daughters, she'd encouraged them to achieve success and status on their own before they married. Ruby had become a lawyer, but surely, she knew it was time to get married and have children, to continue their lineage, to usher in the next generation. Gongju wondered if it was her fault. Maybe if she had been a better mother, Ruby would not be so foolish as to fight biology and societal rules and expect to win. Her spoiled daughter didn't seem to realize that if she didn't find the right man and have children, someday she would be old and alone.

"Ruby-yah, please try to be happy. Life is too short to live miserably." Gongju said this as kindly as she possibly could.

"I'm a partner in a New York law firm, living in a penthouse on Park Avenue. Why would I be miserable?" Ruby twisted her lips. "Isn't that what you wanted? A successful daughter?"

Gongju winced.

"But what good is that to me?" Ruby continued, "You only love Angelina."

"That's not true."

"You gave her Grandma's watch. We all saw it. We know." Ruby crossed her arms again, glowering at Gongju.

"I gave it to her because she'll take care of it. And she will have a daughter to pass it on to. That is what my mother wanted. A matrilineal inheritance."

"Cathy already has a daughter."

"Pearl doesn't appreciate antiques."

"Are you serious? Of the four of us, Cathy is the one who adores jewelry—she has a diamond tennis bracelet, and she doesn't even play tennis! Admit it, Mom. Angelina is your favorite." At this point, Ruby was practically shouting.

Gongju started to deny it, then sat back in her chair and stared at Ruby. Her lips thinned. "Angel tries the hardest. All the time. She's pragmatic, driven by reason, always trying to do what's right. You don't. And neither do Jewel or Pearl. I reward excellence. Not sentimentality. Not complacency. Not weakness."

Ruby recoiled like she'd been slapped. She jumped from her chair, moving swiftly away from Gongju.

She didn't try to go after her daughter. Instead, she closed her eyes and wondered yet again why she had been burdened with four daughters. Girls were so hard to raise. So easy to hurt. For the first time in her life, Gongju felt empathy for her mother. Surely, she must have felt the same way. Maybe her mother had been ruthless with her because she didn't want Gongju to make mistakes she would later regret, because society judged women without mercy. Perhaps she had been trying to protect Gongju, and now, Gongju was doing the same with her girls.

She loved all her daughters. She just didn't like them all the same.

But Gongju had done everything with the best of intentions to ensure their happiness, to smooth their way in the world so they wouldn't feel so alone, like she did after her sister died. If Sunyuh-unni hadn't died, their family would have been different. Their mother would have been different, her edges softened and tempered by her favorite child. And then maybe Gongju wouldn't have had to leave Korea permanently. It was possible she might have been welcomed back by a mother who was less harsh, more forgiving.

She wouldn't have had to raise so many girls by herself.

Gongju watched her new son-in-law preen in front of the standing crowd of wedding attendees. Thom had slipped on his mask and was gesturing magnanimously at the wedding cake and his wife. He shook his head when someone in the crowd shouted, "Smash it on her face!"

He smiled again, flashing his artificially white teeth. "What kind of husband would I be? I may be a cad, and I certainly don't deserve this beautiful woman. But I would never treat my bride so callously."

The audience burst into applause. But Gongju saw that he didn't mean one word of what he said. He was simply performing. Seeming rather than being. Goose bumps flared on her body like chicken pox blisters, itchy and irritating. Gongju didn't want to be right about Thom, but her body knew. She was going to be sick. She ran toward the ladies' room, praying she would get there in time.

In the bathroom, Gongju rinsed the acid taste from her mouth and reached for a paper towel to wipe her lips. Blowing out a breath, she dabbed her forehead to wick off the sweat. The rough weave of the towel felt comforting in her hand, and she clutched it tightly. She leaned against the marble countertop and stared at her reflection.

She had been right in trying to avoid this debacle. No good was going to come of this marriage. But there was no use hiding. She had to find Minsu and convince him to leave. The door swung open before her hand could touch the gold-colored handle. Jewel stood there, blocking her path.

"Please, no more confrontations today. I have a migraine and I need to go home," she said.

"Why do you always think I'm going to make your life difficult?" Jewel crossed her arms.

"Because you're your father's daughter. You've never made life easy for me. And Ruby just yelled at me about having favorites," Gongju continued in Korean.

"I know. She told me what you said."

Gongju wondered again where she had gone wrong with her daughters, especially Jewel. She was the neediest and the most stubborn, always arguing with Gongju, insisting she was right when she was wrong. And, Ruby, petulant and always instigating conflict amongst her sisters, wanting so badly to be like Angel, yet hating her sister for the standards she set. Gongju could no longer see Jewel or Ruby as the sweet little girls they used to be, so blatant was their hostility toward her, and so great was her fatigue at holding their emotions, satisfying their demands.

"Dia has always been spoiled. Indulged too much by both you and Dad." Jewel twisted her face into a grim smile. "Speaking of Dad, you have to drive him home. He's drunk again. After I spoke with Dia, I point-blank asked him who his favorite was. And guess what? He just shared with me that it's Angelina, when all this time, I thought it was *me*."

"That's not true. Your father makes many mistakes, especially when he's had too much to drink." Gongju sighed, wondering if any of her daughters had any sense.

"I always knew I was a disappointment to you. But Dad? I thought he saw me, loved me for who I am."

"You are his favorite. You're just like him." If there was one thing, amongst several things, Gongju could change about her daughter, it was that Jewel be less like her selfish and careless father.

Jewel barked out a laugh. "We're both wrong!"

"Your father says things he doesn't mean. All the damn time. Don't listen to him."

"He said he's been waiting for a doctor in the family for years. Now his 'dream' has come true." Jewel's face looked like a clown's, a forced perpetual smile. "All thanks to Angelina. He's so happy that she married a doctor. He said, 'Finally, one of you girls is useful.' Isn't that great?"

"Why do you waver like a stalk of wheat at anything your father says? You're sabotaging yourself. Stop it." Exhaustion crept into Gongju's limbs. It seemed like Jewel would never be happy, no matter what Gongju did. Jewel was content in her marriage and even had a son, yet it seemed like she was still missing something. Something that would complete her life, make her whole, as if such a thing existed.

"I just want him to be proud of me, too," Jewel whispered, a tear falling down her face.

"You're a grown woman. You shouldn't need anyone's approval."

"What I needed was love, and neither of you ever gave it to me." Jewel looked like a lost child.

"That is not true." Gongju had no more energy to insist or protest or cajole. It was mind numbing how her daughters always wanted something from her when all Gongju wanted was to be left alone. She couldn't bear to explain one more time that she had done her best for all of them—Jewel, Pearl, Angel, Ruby. They would probably be surprised, but she did think of them as precious. As precious as the emeralds surrounding the large diamond center of a ring Minsu had bought for her in Geneva many years ago. The smell of their baby skin was imprinted in her memory, fixed and immoveable. Jewel had a smoky scent; Pearl smelled like crisp apple; Angel like peonies; Ruby like early spring chives.

Gongju always carried her daughters with her, but she couldn't help them anymore; she shouldn't *have* to help them anymore. Gongju wondered if her daughters would be happier if she were dead. Maybe they would let go of their bitterness. Maybe they would lead better lives. How exhausting it was to have daughters.

All Gongju wanted in that moment was to lay down the suffocating burden of motherhood. She wished she had never borne children.

"I am tired. I will no longer listen to any of this." Gongju closed the door and walked away, leaving her eldest daughter crying in the bathroom.

Angelina

NEW YORK, NEW YORK
JUNE 29, 2006

Slumped in front of the glowing screen of her laptop, Angelina checked her email. The hotel room in the Upper West Side of Manhattan was tiny and dark, except for a sliver of light escaping through a thin window above the fire escape. The email from her sister Cathy asking why Angelina wasn't seeing her children during her sudden three-day trip to New York was particularly painful to read. If Cathy had been with her in the courtroom this afternoon while Thom had spewed more lies, she wouldn't be asking. But it seemed near impossible for Angelina to describe the depth of Thom's selfishness, his narcissism, without sounding melodramatic.

Instead, she explained again why seeing her children during these court proceedings would have unraveled her. How the precious energy she'd needed to face Thom would, instead, have been channeled into pretending to be serene in front of her children. They, in turn, would have pretended they were fine, that they could endure their father's cruelty without consequences. Like a twisted version of *The Gift of the Magi*, each side going to extremes to protect the feelings of the other. Just thinking about it exhausted her.

She sighed, a small rush of air filled with guilt, when she opened an email from her Korean instructor at Konkuk University. Her teacher was expressing only concern and best wishes, yet Angelina felt even worse.

She gasped, though, when she read Keisuke's email.

He found something.

Keisuke wrote that he'd gone to the Seoul headquarters of the Korean Council for the Women Drafted for Sexual Slavery by Japan, a nonprofit organization advocating for the victims. In Seodaemun-gu, in a humble, third-floor office of a five-story building without an elevator, he'd located the transcript of a survivor who'd been transported from Nagasaki to Bangkok with a Kang Sunyuh from Gwangju. The victim had recounted an incident on a Japanese naval vessel in which several Korean girls had been murdered.

After Angelina had left Seoul, Keisuke had called his contact at the Ministry of Foreign Affairs in Japan, along with a colleague at a major newspaper in Tokyo, to get background information and access to sealed records regarding the registration and transport of military sexual slaves across national borders starting in 1932 until 1945. He'd been told by his Japanese sources that the Korean government, in 2004, had formed a special committee to investigate wartime atrocities of forced labor, military conscription, and the "comfort women." The Truth Commission on Forced Mobilization under Japanese Imperialism was housed in an imposing building near the Seoul Museum of History and Gwanghwamun Square. The Truth Commission reopened the registration and self-reporting of the victims of sexual slavery, which had been started by the Ministry of Health and Social Affairs in 1993. When Keisuke inquired about Angelina's aunt, he'd been directed to the Korean Council because hundreds of new reports were being verified and sorted there. And he'd found a trace of Aunt Sunyuh.

Keisuke ended his email with "I'm going to Bangkok, regardless, to search for any records remaining from the comfort stations there. Do you want to join me? I'll wait for you at the airport, no matter what time your flight comes in."

Immediately, her fingers flew over the keyboard. But instead of sending her answer, she stood up, feeling strangely restless, even as relief coursed through her body. *Why?* Surely, she was just glad a concrete trace of her aunt existed in official records. Or maybe she was just surprised he'd found something so quickly about her aunt when she'd braced herself for weeks of nothing.

No.

It was Keisuke himself—the idea that he'd be waiting for her. Rubbing her arms as if that would create a barrier between them, she sat down again and changed her answer. "Thank you for finding this information about my aunt. But I can't join you in Thailand. I hope you understand."

Her finger hovered over the Send button, but again, she didn't press it. Angelina knew she could go to Bangkok, but she was resisting. It seemed silly, but she was afraid to be close to Keisuke again. They wouldn't be in a classroom setting. Instead, they would be traveling together to find answers about Aunt Sunyuh.

When she'd blurted to Keisuke on that bench at the International Guest House that her mother had a missing sister, Angelina had said it mostly because she'd felt so battered by Thom's cruelty and so befuddled by her Korean family. Keisuke's kindness had breached her notion of decorum, her reserve. With him, she hadn't felt so lonely. Grasping his hands, she hadn't wanted to let go. He'd been so strong and sure and hadn't pulled away.

Now, she paced back and forth in her hotel room, telling herself she shouldn't have any expectations. Not about the possibility of locating her aunt. And definitely not about Keisuke. She sat back down at her computer, deleted what she'd written, and responded with one word. Then she clicked on another tab and changed her flight reservations, adding a stop in Bangkok before landing in Incheon. She leaned back and expelled hope and fear at the same time. *Now what am I doing?* Sudden exhaustion swept through her body, like a deluge in an unpredictable storm. Only five o'clock in the afternoon and she wanted to go to sleep.

But she still had one more thing left to do before her flight the next morning.

The clatter of Angelina's black peep-toe pumps against the pavement of Central Park Loop Road rang out in the dark. She was on her way to see Lars. They hadn't spoken since she'd walked out of their hotel room in Jeju Island, but he'd been relentless with his phone calls and text messages. It was time she confronted the truth.

She chose to walk, knowing her shoes were totally impractical for traversing any distance. These shoes were meant for a woman to walk down a carpeted hallway, take an elevator, and then have a doorman hail a taxi for her. But she wasn't that kind of woman anymore.

When she'd lived on the Upper East Side with Thom, before their move to Pittsburgh, it was the life she used to have. Angelina and her children took innumerable yellow cabs from Waterside Plaza and their school up the FDR Drive to their condo on the East River with views of the Fifty-Ninth Street Bridge and the Roosevelt Island tram. Even stuck in unspeakable traffic on the highway during those bumpy rides over randomly placed manhole covers and potholes large enough to swallow a small car, she always thought that particular view of the East River was unparalleled.

Most of the time, all the concrete and metal in the buildings and bridges gave the river varying tints of gunmetal, but every so often, the water looked blue. And a current ran through the estuary, creating small waves. At night she could see the Pepsi-Cola sign in Long Island City blazing red from the FDR. She used to put the window of the cab down and let the breeze rifle through her hair. It would make her smile for no reason.

Nighttime in New York was magical. The city's harshness was softened by darkness, illuminated by dazzling lights. Even Times Square didn't seem so bad at night, perhaps even glamorous. And the water surrounding the island of Manhattan was inky and bewitching. Angelina missed that view.

She also had a special fondness for the Jacqueline Kennedy Onassis

Reservoir in Central Park. She used to jog around that body of water when she lived on the Upper East Side. A saving grace of the two years she'd lived in that snobby neighborhood, where people in her building regularly mistook her for a cleaning woman. One-point-six miles in circumference, it had been perfect for Angelina, who wasn't a distance runner.

Running around the reservoir set a pattern that would save her life. When she'd moved to Pittsburgh, she intermittently ran in Schenley Park, another Frederick Law Olmsted–designed oasis in an urban setting. Mellon Park was closer to her house in Shadyside, but she felt compelled to drive to Schenley to run. She found it oddly comforting to run in a park built by the same visionary responsible for Central Park. When Thom moved out of their home, she'd stopped running, unable to summon the energy or desire. But after one too many sleepless nights staring at the ceiling of her bedroom, waiting for dawn to break, she'd gotten into her car, and it seemed to steer itself to Schenley. In the semi-dark, she began to run again, and through the years of her soul-numbing divorce, she'd kept running.

At Fifth Avenue, Angelina exited the park and walked past the Plaza Hotel. She could almost hear Emma's shrieks again, the time they had afternoon tea there. At eight, Emma had been obsessed with Eloise, the little girl from the children's series who lived at the Plaza. And she'd begged to take a pedicab to Dia's co-op in Midtown East, where she was supposed to have a sleepover with her aunt. Angelina had had to squeeze her eyes shut against the terrifying speed of cars roaring past their not-too-sturdy mode of transportation on Fifth Avenue, but she'd smiled at Emma's delight.

Angelina crossed Madison Avenue at East Sixty-Fifth and, before reaching Park Avenue, stood in front of Daniel, one of Lars's haunts in New York. Lars said he liked the old-world French style of the place, the chairs upholstered in rich leather, the banquettes covered with plush mohair velvet, the cream-colored arches supported by ornate columns, the white tablecloths starched and crisp. He was already drinking a martini at the bar, waiting for her, had probably arrived a half hour ago, so compulsive about being on time that he was always early.

She stared at the brushed glass doors marking the entrance and smoothed down the satin skirt that flared just below her hips. Her palms were damp and cold. She combed her fingers through her hair, the silky strands sliding through the web of her hand. Glancing at the black face of her watch, a tiny diamond marking the twelve o'clock position, she saw she was actually on time for a change. Briefly, she toyed with the idea of walking around the block for ten minutes. Instead, she pulled the door to the restaurant open and stepped inside.

"Let me go," Angelina said quietly.

"What?" Perhaps he was too sated from their decadent meal and hadn't expected this turn in conversation, but Angelina suspected Lars was pretending to be confused. He moved away from her, leaning back in his chair, and took off his frameless glasses. He tipped his head to one side, his short hair unmoving. "I have no idea what you're talking about."

"Please let me go," Angelina said again, eyes unwavering.

He shrugged, terse and careless. "I'm not keeping you."

"Please don't pretend."

"Is this why you won't let me come to your hotel?" His smile was practically a smirk.

"You don't love me, but you won't let me go. We had a regrettable moment in Seoul when we weren't in our right minds. Jeju Island was a mistake. I've been trying to put some distance between us, but you won't allow it. Why are you behaving this way?"

There was a blatant curve to his lips now. "Like I said, you have free will. It's your choice to respond to me." His long fingers leisurely tapped the table.

"I can't believe we had an affair." Her voice was barely above a whisper.

"It wasn't an affair." He shook his head, voice insistent.

"What do you call it when a married man has sex with a woman who is not his wife?" Lars was being deliberately obtuse, and she couldn't believe she'd had to say those words out loud. "When I let my voicemail pick up, it's because I don't want to talk to you. Yet you won't stop until I give in and answer."

"I'm obsessive." He shrugged. "I need to know what you're doing. I care about you."

Anger surged through her body, which she supposed was a welcome change from sadness. His earnestness was insulting. "Please. Do you know what I went through today? In court with Thom? I had to capitulate to his demands that I move our kids from Pittsburgh back to New York. He's trying to kill me. And it feels like you're helping him."

"Thom is a narcissist who won't stop until you give him everything he wants. You should never have married him. I did try to tell you." Lars took a leisurely sip from his porcelain coffee cup, "Daniel" in gold script scrawled across its surface.

"Is that really what's important right now?"

Angelina had only had one conversation with Lars during her divorce. He'd called and asked how she was doing, offering to lend her money for attorney's fees and court costs when she hadn't asked. She'd thought he was being kind and supportive. Lars had married after her, the year she'd been pregnant with Emma. It seemed unlikely, but now she wondered if he'd been waiting for her all that time but gave up when Angelina started a family. She wondered how hurt Lars must have been, and for how long he'd nursed his grievance.

Angelina knew Lars could carry a grudge to his grave if he so desired. Perhaps rejecting her now gave him a satisfaction he needed. Perhaps he despised the sentimental, lovesick boy he used to be.

He certainly looked outraged. "You make it sound like I took advantage of you."

"I was under the illusion that we might have had a future together." And it *was* an illusion. A brief dream she'd indulged in because she'd needed to believe in something. *Anything.* She'd wanted to hide from the sorrow flooding her life after her divorce, and Lars had almost miraculously reappeared when she was in a strange place, a strange time. A period of flux when she'd thought she'd never date again, never find true love. A time when she'd been under the spell of a deep yearning to belong somewhere. She'd lost herself and thought he was the conduit back to the person she'd been and still could be: strong, passionate, in control of her own destiny.

"If you had felt that way seventeen years ago, we wouldn't be in the situation we're in now." He settled back in his chair, crossed his arms in front of him. The charcoal gray suit of his jacket rode up from his wrist, and his gold Rolex glinted underneath.

It was becoming clearer to Angelina that she didn't know Lars as well as she thought she did. "And what situation is that?"

Lars looked down for a moment, then met her eyes. "A world in which you are in love with me, and I am not in love with you."

Maybe she'd hoped that Lars was Captain Wentworth, the hero of Jane Austen's novel *Persuasion*. After an absence of eight years, Anne Elliot and Frederick Wentworth rekindle their love, defying their families' and friends' expectations, and in a famously passionate letter, Wentworth writes to Anne, "I have loved none but you."

When Angelina read *Persuasion* for the first time in her early twenties, she hadn't fully appreciated the tenderness of two people tempered by life, reigniting their love. It was only in her thirties that she'd come to understand what two people who gave up on love must feel—a loss of soul. Now, at forty, *Persuasion* was Angelina's favorite novel. A beautiful elegy of regret and redemption. But Lars was not Wentworth. And she was not Anne.

Angelina stared at Lars. He looked back at her, unflinching. His blue eyes were like marbles, opaque and without mercy. She'd never realized how troubled he was. How vengeful.

"I'm not the person I was seventeen years ago. We'd have never worked out," she said, mourning the morbidly shy and unconfident girl she'd been at twenty-three, so eager to please, so burdened by expectations.

"I disagree. I give people space and freedom. You would have become whatever you wanted if you'd been with me. If you had made the right choice."

"Maybe I wouldn't have liked that person. I like who I am now," she said, realizing she actually meant her words. She mostly liked the person she'd become, molded by time, experience, and a little wisdom. At times, she'd been so beaten down, she felt like she couldn't get back up again. But it seemed she had the strength of an Energizer Bunny—going and going and going when it didn't seem possible. She was more resilient than she'd ever given herself credit for, and probably more than what certain people believed of her. But, right now, she was disappointed in herself and in Lars. "I hate that I had an affair." She spit out the words like they were an unpleasant taste in her mouth.

"Don't do that. You know what it's like between me and Stephanie. We stay together for the kids."

"No, you stay for the life you've built for yourself—the apartment on Park Avenue, your thriving practice, your kids in private school. You used to have such a chip on your shoulder about being treated like an outsider. Now you're an insider, and you don't want to give that up. Yet you want me without any complications or commitment."

"Why do you make me sound like such an asshole?"

"Because you are."

Lars laughed, breaking the tension. "But you've had fun, right? It was a great time for both of us." He kept smiling.

"You betrayed my trust and used me when I felt untethered in my life. You hurt me, someone who you claim is your best friend," Angelina said, incredulous at the depth of Lars's denial.

His posturing suddenly disintegrated. "Lee, I'm sorry," he said, gaze softening. "Think of all those wasted years. If only we could go back and change everything." He actually looked shattered.

"You can't let go of the past," Angelina said, finally seeing Lars for who he was. She almost felt sorry for him, knowing the blindness with which he was choosing to live his life. She deeply felt his desperate urge to become the person he was when they'd first met. Because she'd had the same desire. With the irrationality of a grief-stricken mind, of course she'd let herself fall into a fantasy where she could rewrite the past, because if she could go back to a time when Lars was in love with her, then she could slip into a universe in which she never married Thom.

Angelina knew she'd never been in love with Thom. She'd been in love with the idea of who she wanted Thom to be. Honorable, loyal, kind. She'd made herself believe he was what she wanted when it was obvious that he was not. Later on, she told herself it was because of her children that she'd stayed, to preserve their family. But the truth was she'd done it for herself. Like Lars, she'd loved the illusion of her life in New York, and with willful blindness had chosen to believe that Thom was real. That she was right to believe in him, to believe in them as a family. That she hadn't wasted years of her life.

And now she'd done the same thing with Lars, wasted even *more* time. Seen in him what she wanted to see. Hoped that by indulging in the what-if scenario that had plagued her for so many years, she could right a past wrong. But revisiting the past like this—it wasn't what she wanted. That flash she'd seen of her and Lars walking in the rain in Venice was just that—imaginary. It wasn't real. If she'd married Lars, chances were she'd be divorcing him, too. She didn't like who Lars had become, and she didn't respect the choices she'd made lately that had led to this moment. Angelina couldn't help but shake her head. She was done with these false representations—done with Thom, and Lars, and any other man who dared try to weigh her down at this point. "I knew this was going to end badly. I came tonight so there would be no misunderstanding. I won't be taking your calls anymore." She shuddered, thinking how narrowly she'd escaped subjugating herself to the whims of another selfish man.

"We've ruined our friendship, and we're never going to see each other again." She closed her eyes, but couldn't stop seeing imaginary flames getting higher, as if their history was combusting. "I made the right decision all those years ago. We should have left whatever we felt for each other as a tenderness of the past. Instead of being blinded by it."

Lars reached across the perfectly starched and ironed tablecloth. "Don't say that."

The smell of musk and sandalwood was nauseating.

"I can't do this one more single minute." She stood up, let his hand hover in the air between them. "Goodbye, Lars."

As she turned to go, she caught the look of complete astonishment on his face, but she didn't stop. She kept walking. Past the opulent reception into the street, into Central Park, into the comforting dark of New York.

Sunyuh

Jakarta, Indonesia
March 1945

In the dark of the ship's hold, Sunyuh heard the sailors talking excitedly about crossing the equatorial line near Jakarta, their shouts easily transmitting from the deck above her. They had been traveling for days on the sea from Nagasaki, briefly stopping in Manila to take on more supplies and offload more girls. Now, it was morning again. Drenched in sweat, Sunyuh lay sleepless. So many girls were still crammed in the hold. The stench of unwashed bodies made her nauseated, and she swallowed to keep from dry heaving.

At least the ship wasn't violently rocking, like it tended to do on open sea. She felt the thud of a forward moving projectile against an immovable object, the scraping of the metal ship against the wooden dock. She didn't flinch. She had gotten used to unsteady landings. Trapped in the dismal belly of the vessel, she searched for a glimpse of light, but there was only grayness and shadows. She told herself to stay calm, but really, she wanted to scream at the heat and humidity. So many things made her want to scream these days.

Sunyuh tried to remember what spring had been like in Gwangju. *Do I even have a home anymore?* Last spring at Yeonnalligi, when Joonsuk won the kite-fighting competition, seemed like several lifetimes ago. If she squeezed her eyes shut, maybe she could go back in time. If she tried as hard as she could to remember that version of herself, maybe she could return to Joonsuk's arms. She'd been right to be afraid; he had been wrong to think that everything would be all right, that they would marry.

Tears slipped from under her closed eyelids, but she didn't make a sound. Instead, she heard the quiet weeping of a nearby girl. The sight of shaking shoulders was unbearable. She navigated the three bodies between them before kneeling and touching the girl's shoulder.

"What is it?" She wanted to be kind, but she knew the girl's crying would soon attract unwanted attention.

The girl pulled away from Sunyuh's touch. "Leave me alone! I am dying anyway!"

"Why would you be dying?" *We're all going to die at the hands of the Japanese.*

"Blood is coming out of my private area, and my stomach hurts! I know I am dying!"

A half smile escaped from her lips. "How old are you?"

"Thirteen."

Sunyuh's lips remained in place, frozen. *So young.*

"I do not want to die!"

"You're not dying—it's just that time of the month. There's no need to cry," she said gently.

The girl sat up abruptly and looked at Sunyuh. "What?"

Her face transforming with relief was heartbreaking. Sunyuh looked away, tried not to think about how small this girl was.

"I am not dying?"

Sunyuh shook her head, tried to smile again. "Let's do something about that bleeding."

The girl's wide face bloomed into a smile. For a moment, Sunyuh could see what her sister Gongju's face would look like at thirteen.

"What's your name?"

"Jisoo." The young girl grasped both of Sunyuh's hands. "Thank you, Unni."

Sunyuh patted Jisoo's shoulder before reaching for the frayed hem of her hanbok skirt and ripped off strips. "Stuff this in your underwear for now. We'll find a belt and pads for you when we get off the ship."

"Why bother? She's going to be dead in a few days," Suki said, her slightly muffled voice coming from a few girls behind Sunyuh.

"She's not going to die. We're going to help her." Suki was only fifteen, but she bullied the younger girls—even some older girls were afraid of her. But Sunyuh knew she was lashing out, desperate to distract herself from her own suffering. "Suki-yah, try to be nice for a change."

Suki smiled and dipped her head in a show of deference. "Unni, of course. I'm always nice," she said, her voice dripping with insolence. Her use of the honorific term *older sister* was an insult because she continued to talk back in banmal, a sign of disrespect.

Sunyuh smiled back. "I know you're capable of better behavior. As Unni to those younger, you need to show more kindness. You're a good person, Suki."

Suki's smile wiped away. "Why do you pretend to be good all the time? We know you're not. We've seen you and that Japanese doctor. He acts like a lovesick puppy around you, giving you gifts. Did you think we didn't see the clementines he snuck into your hands? You didn't stop him."

Sunyuh stared at Suki. "I'm not good. And I don't pretend." Light was starting to seep through the cracks around the trapdoor and the buckling floorboards above them, enough that she could see the hate glittering in Suki's eyes. She understood Suki's hate. She hated, too. There were days when she hated everyone and everything so much she wanted to die. Days when she hated her mother and father and brothers. Even her little sister.

Suki's voice kept rising. "You're a hypocrite! And no one likes you!"

Miyun-unni came to Sunyuh's defense. "Don't listen to her. Shut up, Suki, you little brat."

"Please do not get angry, Miyun-unni," Ara said, her voice level but loud enough for everyone to hear. Ara was always trying to keep the peace.

Miyun, at age nineteen, was the oldest amongst them. Sunyuh and Ara were both seventeen. They had become friends in the Nagasaki camp through sheer proximity—their closet-like rooms were all next to one another, just like their ages, with Sunyuh in the middle. They would knock on each other's walls, a code developed for communicating without words—one to signal survival, two to ask how the other was doing, three to express despair.

High-ranking officers often visited in the evenings, whereas common soldiers came in the afternoons and mornings. Usually, the girls were forced to eat in their claustrophobic rooms, and the tapping saved them from utter loneliness. At least for Sunyuh. She would eat her small bowl of porridge with her head leaning against the wall between her and Miyun-unni, hoping to hear Unni's bare knuckles rapping against the hollow barrier. Sometimes, if the camp was quiet, they would whisper amongst themselves, their voices distorted but still audible. She and Miyun-unni talked about their families, their hometowns, their parents. They cried but tried to hide it from each other. She knew that without Miyun-unni, she would not have survived those months in Nagasaki.

She and Ara were dongmu, the *same age*, so they used banmal when speaking to one another. It was comforting that she could talk to Ara like a younger sibling, their speech informal and free. She and Ara joked a great deal, both sharing a dark sense of humor. Ironic—Sunyuh had never considered herself to be a funny person. Until now. But laughing at macabre things now kept her going, gave her the will to go on living. She had shed her old persona, but still wasn't sure who she had become. She was doing everything she could to survive, but she wasn't proud of the things she'd done over the last ten months.

Ara spoke again. "Suki, why don't you apologize to Sunyuh-unni?"

"I will not."

Hearing this, Miyun stalked over to where Suki was standing and slapped her. A collective gasp erupted amongst the fifty-odd girls as Suki fell to the floor.

Ara rushed over and wedged her body between Miyun and Suki. "Unni, do not hit Suki again. Please."

"She needs to be put in her place." Miyun glared at Suki.

Suki jumped to standing and glared back.

Ara gently touched Miyun's arm. "Please, calm down, Unni. We do not want the guards to hear."

Miyun's shoulders slumped, and she wheezed out her frustration. "You're right. But this one is going to apologize to Sunyuh."

"I'm never saying sorry to that bitch!" Suki pushed Ara aside, spitting in Miyun's face.

"What did you say?" Miyun grabbed Suki and shoved her down, striking her again and again.

"Stop!" Sunyuh screamed. This couldn't be happening. They shouldn't be fighting amongst themselves. The Japanese were the enemy. Not each other.

Shrill bursts of high-pitched whistles filled the hold and sudden sunlight blinded Sunyuh. Water cannons blasted at her, saturating her clothes in an instant, flooding the floor beneath her. She crouched into a tight ball, crossed her arms above her head, trying to shield herself from the avalanche of water.

A male voice blared in Japanese over a loudspeaker. "Shut up, you whores!"

The girls flinched as a whole, as though they were linked by a rope. Sunyuh peered from under her lowered head, watched fountains of water flail before disappearing, leaving them all soaked.

"Get up here! Right now!" the loudspeaker continued to scream.

The girls stood and shuffled to the metal staircase and ascended one by one, as they had been conditioned to do. Sunyuh could smell the sea, the brine and tang of endless ocean, but she didn't make the mistake of raising her face to the sun, as she had once done, earning a stab to her belly from the butt of a rifle, along with an inability to stand up straight for days. She bowed her head so the guard marching by didn't have an excuse to strike her, as he did so many girls before her, shouting, "Insolent prostitutes! How dare you look at me?" She was too afraid to say that most of the girls didn't understand Japanese. She knew these men didn't care.

A Japanese soldier stood in front them and flung out a baton, pointing it like a gun at their chests. "Which one of you sluts is the leader?"

None of the girls moved.

"Don't make me repeat myself." He slammed his baton into a girl's face. Blood flew into the air, the crunch of bone breaking echoing in the harbor.

Miyun stepped forward. "I am, sir!" she said in Japanese.

He turned toward Miyun-unni and smiled. "What is your name?"

"Miyoko, sir!" Miyun said, staring straight ahead.

"Why are you whores squabbling and disturbing my peace?" His voice was quiet, ominous.

"I am sorry, sir!"

His voice was still quiet. "I asked you a question."

"We are stupid, sir! We deeply and humbly apologize for our dirty Korean behavior, sir!" Miyun answered with the rote answer they had all been painfully taught while being pummeled by batons or stabbed by bayonets.

Sunyuh could see the soldier's teeth were displayed, but the look on his face was not a smile. She shuddered.

"I do not accept your apology. There is always a price to be paid for being willful and ignorant," he said, whipping his gun out of the holster. He pointed it at Miyun's temple and fired.

Brain and bone splattered across the deck. Sunyuh tried to take a step toward Miyun's crumpled body, but Ara kept her arm in a vise grip. Everything blurred through a wall of tears, but she didn't make a sound.

"Throw her body overboard," the little man said, stalking away.

Sunyuh watched as two soldiers lifted Miyun and tossed her from the ship, like she was garbage.

"No!"

For a moment, she thought the utterance came from her mouth. What kind of friend was she if she didn't object to the death of Miyun-unni? What kind of person had she become if she didn't protest, however useless, the disposing of her friend's body? Sunyuh was sure it was her. Instead, it was Jisoo, the thirteen-year-old.

"No! No! No!" Jisoo screamed again, running toward the railing and trying to jump for the sea.

"Shoot her!" the little man ordered.

Bullets riddled her body, twisting it midair, arcing her back, her long dark hair trailing like a banner behind her. Sunyuh heard the splash of Jisoo's corpse hitting water.

She fell to her knees, hands clasped white and bloodless.

A month passed, and Sunyuh still could not forgive Suki for what happened to Miyun-unni. Her lower lip, swollen from last night's beating, throbbed, and her arms ached from being thrown against the wall of her room. There were always new injuries. But at least this week, the sadist who liked to carve the flesh of her arm with his pocketknife hadn't yet made an appearance.

She and Ara were hanging their meager wardrobe of underwear, socks, and extra hanbok jeogori, *top*, and chima, *skirt*, after washing them in the camp's communal metal tub. Ara moved directly in front of Sunyuh, blocking her access to the clothesline. "Suki's pregnant and starting to show. The abortion didn't work. They're going to kill her soon, and you know that."

Sunyuh flicked her gaze beyond Ara, staring at the steep ornate temple roofs at the center of Bangkok. The low concrete structures of the compound afforded her a view of the harbor today. Usually, a fog of heat and humidity obscured the seagulls and the sea. The unrelenting rain of monsoon season also frequently obliterated their sight of anything other than gray. She wondered why she yearned for the sea. Gwangju, where she grew up, was landlocked, but the province still had many small bodies of water, ponds and lakes surrounded by weeping willows. She missed the willows. She missed the view of the lake from her father's estate.

Sunyuh stepped aside to avoid Ara's bruised face. She slung the faded fabric of her hanbok skirt over the clothesline, took a wooden peg, and pinned it to the cloth. She wondered why she bothered. There was no wind today, nothing to blow her away from this place. She was already sweating, and it was only morning, and the smell of open sewers and dirty wash water was nauseating. At least it wasn't bitterly cold, like Nagasaki in winter. She reached down for another piece of clothing and found her basket gone. Ara was clutching it to her chest.

"Give it back."

"No. Not until you forgive Suki."

"That's never going to happen."

"Please, Unni, please. This is not like you." Ara spoke in honorific speech, like she wanted to guilt Sunyuh into good behavior.

"That's what living in savagery will do to you." The harsh sound of her own voice stunned her. Was that what she sounded like these days? Was she one of those souls already extinguished but unaware of her plight, cursed to keep wandering the earth?

Ara switched back to banmal, her speech no longer formal. "Sunyuh-yah, you'll come to regret this."

"I don't care," she said, her voice still hard.

Ara dropped the basket. "I'm pregnant."

"What?"

"I missed my bleed again."

"No."

"I must be two months along."

Sunyuh fell to the ground.

"I won't be able to hide it for much longer. And I'm not getting an abortion. I won't survive their barbaric methods." Ara crouched next to her.

"What are you going to do?" Dread seeped into her voice.

"Escape."

"They're going to catch you." She was so afraid for her friend her stomach burned. "And then they will kill you." Just last week a girl had been caught trying to flee. Her flesh had been torn as she was rolled naked over a board embedded with nails, her pelvis shattered by the butts of rifles as several soldiers viciously struck her.

"What choice do I have?" Ara's voice was hollow.

Sunyuh stood and extended her hand to Ara, pulling her up. "We'll go together." She'd made up her mind.

"No. I won't put you in danger."

"We've lost Miyun-unni. My life isn't worth living if you aren't here, either."

"Sunyuh-yah, you still have a chance of seeing your family. Your parents. Your brothers. The little sister you love so much. If you go with me and we get caught, they will kill you. You'll never see your family again. I can't be responsible for that." Ara took a sharp inhale. "You know you kept me going when I wanted to give up long ago, right? Like your namesake, you are an angel."

"Don't talk like that. You and I are sisters. Always. Like Miyun-unni was."

"No. You're special, Sunyuh-yah. You saved me when I thought no one could. If you keep living, then there is hope. Make it back to your family."

"You're my family now. Besides, I'll never see my parents again. I can't go back after everything that's happened."

"What about Joonsuk? He was in love with you."

"He won't be. Not when he learns the truth."

"Then he wasn't worth loving." Ara's voice hardened, like she could protect Sunyuh from Joonsuk's inevitable betrayal.

Sunyuh wanted to cry for the boy she'd been in love with since she was a child. She wanted to cry for the child she'd been, for the sixteen-year-old who thought she was going to marry the love of her life. But crying was no longer of any use to her. She had to save Ara.

"Find a way to sneak out just before the soldiers leave for the night. Meet me right here, okay?" She grasped Ara's arm and held it.

Ara shook her head. "Not tonight. Too many soldiers are here. I heard they're losing. The bastards were talking while they were lined up outside my door. Another air strike is planned for the next two days. There'll be more chaos to hide behind tomorrow evening."

"Are you sure? I think tonight is our best chance. They'll be drinking and pretending to be brave, one-upping each other. They'll be passed out well before the night is over. They won't find us missing until morning."

"No. We'll go tomorrow night," Ara insisted. "It's better that way."

"All right. I trust you."

Ara ripped apart a seam of her hanbok jeogori and pulled out a jade ring. "Here. Take this and keep it for me with the rest of your jewelry, okay?"

How does she know I have jewelry? Of course, Ara would have guessed that she received trinkets and a few tokens from some of the high-ranking officers. Ara's room had been next to hers in the Nagasaki camp, but not here. Now, there was no more tapping between rooms.

She thrust the ring back at Ara. "Bring it when we meet tomorrow."

"It's my mother's ring. I stole it from my father when he was drunk. Before he sold me. You were abducted. Miyun-unni, a haenyeo, was lied to about diving for sea urchin off the coast of Japan. But not me. My own father did this to me. I was his only daughter, his only child."

Sunyuh pressed her fingers to her forehead and covered her eyes, trying to hide her tears. "Ara-yah, I'm so sorry." What she really wanted to say was, *I'm sorry you didn't have a father like mine. A man should never make his daughter feel fatherless.*

"My mother loved me. I knew that. It's how I was able to survive his drunken beatings my entire childhood. Did you know my mother was from a rich family? She married down for love, and her family disowned her, so she couldn't go back. She got sick and died when I was ten." Ara pushed the ring into Sunyuh's palm. "Keep it safe for me."

"No. It's too precious."

"Sunyuh-yah, nothing is too precious. Not even our lives. That's the one thing I've learned in all these years. When we escape, we're going to use that ring to buy our passages back to Korea." Ara smiled. "We should go to Jeju Island. Pay our respects to Miyun-unni's family. We could make a living digging for clams and sea snails, right?"

"Of course," Sunyuh said, wiping away tears.

"Don't cry. Everything is going to be okay. What could go wrong on a day this beautiful?"

Sunyuh nodded, wishing she could believe what Ara was saying with every fiber of her being. She turned away from Ara and finished hanging her laundry. They didn't talk. Together, they walked back to their prison.

Sunyuh stared at the cracked cement ceiling, desperately trying to think of anything besides what was happening to her body. Sometimes imagining herself running through her father's plum orchard, taking different routes through the trees, helped her make it through. Other nights she pictured herself with Gongju in her room, teaching her math. But tonight, nothing was working. Instead, with this soldier on top of her, pinning her down, she was trapped in the memory of her first night: the tearing of her body like it was a persimmon fruit. The screaming of the Japanese soldier. The spit flying into her eye. The unspeakable pain. The blood.

She twisted her face toward a wall, looking for an imperfection to focus on, anything to stop her from fixating on what was happening. She wanted to float above her body.

A shot rang out in the courtyard.

The soldier above her pushed away.

She could breathe.

Scrambling to put her clothes on, Sunyuh avoided looking at the soldier. He left the room before she did. By the time she got to the courtyard, a crowd had already formed. She heard Ara's voice and pushed her way to the front.

The skinny Japanese commander was pointing his pistol at Ara. "You stupid whore. You've been caught in the seditious act of treason and cowardice against the empire."

Ara glared at him. "I'm not stupid!" she said in Korean.

"So stupid you've been here, submitting to us, the superior race," he continued, his voice dripping with disdain. He only spoke Japanese.

"You son of a bitch," Ara spat back.

"What did you call me, you slut?"

"So you do understand Korean! You heard me, you murderous bastard. You killed Miyun-unni for no reason," Ara shouted, spit flying out of her mouth.

"How dare you? You're nothing but a worthless prostitute." He holstered his gun and turned away from Ara.

Sunyuh finally let her breath out. She took a step toward Ara.

But then he whipped around and stabbed Ara in the stomach. "This is what you deserve."

Ara only grunted in response, clutching her belly and falling to her knees.

The little man stooped and sliced open Ara's throat. Blood spurted like a fountain, and her body toppled into the dirt. "Cut off her head and feed it to the dogs," he said, wiping Ara's blood from his sword.

"No!" Sunyuh screamed. She ran to Ara, covered her friend's body with hers. Even when she felt her shoulders being wrenched from their sockets, she pushed her body toward Ara. Even when she felt the explosion of brutal slaps to her face. Even when she heard the shouting of the little man. "Another dirty Josenbbi! Get away or I'll shoot!"

Sunyuh didn't care anymore. She wanted to die.

Angelina

BANGKOK, THAILAND
JULY 3, 2006

Angelina stared at the bureaucrat sitting across the untidy metal table, leaning back in his office chair, a condescending smile on his face.

"What do you mean there are no records? This is the Hall of Records, correct?"

"Well, miss, those records were burned by the Japanese before they retreated from Bangkok in 1945," he said slowly, like he was speaking to a child.

"But the Korean consulate said you have documents in the archives from the Japanese occupation regarding the victims of sexual slavery," she insisted.

"We cannot show the archives to you without proper procedure. There are rules to be followed and protocols that must be met." The man might as well have wagged his finger at her. Instead, he jabbed at the air between them with a pencil.

He was a low-level bureaucrat whose only power lay in saying no, but she was so angry she had to concentrate on speaking in a level tone. Then she felt Keisuke's hand on her shoulder. At first, her body seized. But feeling only the weight of his hand, no downward pressure, she lowered her shoulders. She exhaled quietly. With her next inhale, she smelled fresh cedar with a hint of clementine. The scent of Keisuke. A sense of calm settled in her body.

"How do we get access to the archives?" Keisuke asked, his voice mild, his posture loose.

The bureaucrat leaned back in his chair again and interlaced his fingers over his portly stomach. "There are forms that must be filled out in the Archives Department first. If permission is granted, then you can come back and fill out a new application."

Wanting to glare at him, Angelina lowered her eyes instead. She needed to be patient.

The weight of Keisuke's hand lingered even after he removed it. From the corner of her eye, she saw his fingers, long and thin, hanging by his side. Why that sight disturbed her she didn't know. Maybe it was the awkwardness between them.

The night before, Keisuke had met her at the Bangkok airport as promised, but the conversation en route to their hotel had been stilted whenever they veered away from the subject of her aunt. When she'd apologized for her overwrought behavior at the International Guest House the week before, he'd seemed embarrassed. Which only made *her* feel embarrassed all over again, cringing at the memory of her clinging to Keisuke's hands. In the cramped back seat of the taxi, she'd tried to shift away from him, but their thighs had remained touching, heat growing between them.

Now she tried to focus on the wide, oily face of the man in front of her, but it was too repulsive to be a meaningful distraction. Staring at the paperwork strewn across his desk, she hoped, grudgingly, that she appeared demure, exactly what such a man would expect from an Asian woman. Then maybe he would help her find Aunt Sunyuh. As Keisuke continued talking, she sat without speaking, nodding when it seemed appropriate, keeping her head bowed. When the administrator finally finished lecturing at them to his egotistical satisfaction, she rose to her feet and followed Keisuke out of the Hall of Records.

She pushed back against a wall, expelling a long angry huff. "That insufferable man!"

"They're called bureaucrats for a reason," Keisuke said. "You handled it well, all things considered."

"Are you kidding? I was seconds away from causing bodily harm."

"It would have been totally justifiable if you'd slugged him. He was a sexist pig, but you managed to get whatever information you could from him instead of losing your temper. That looks like admirable self-control to me," Keisuke said with a wry smile.

She'd thought she'd capitulated to misogyny, yet again, and let that unpleasant man win. But Keisuke made it sound like it was a strategic plan on her part. She wanted to believe that. She wanted to believe she wasn't anyone's doormat anymore.

"We'll go to the Archives Department, then back here, then to whatever other place we need to go. We will find any trace your aunt left behind. I'm sure of it."

When Angelina had read his email in New York that he'd found evidence of a Kang Sunyuh being transported from Nagasaki to Bangkok, asking her if she wanted to join him in Thailand, she'd responded with only one word: *Yes*. As she stared up at Keisuke now, she wondered again why he was going to such lengths to help her. She wondered if Keisuke assumed she was a damsel in distress, and he a knight in shining armor. But she resisted asking these questions, because part of her didn't want to know, didn't want to know what Keisuke held dear in his life.

Angelina smoothed her damp palm down her white linen sundress and sagged against the wall. Her joints ached from the eighteen-hour flight she'd taken from New York. She just wanted to lie down.

"I'm really hungry. Can we grab lunch before hunting down more lazy civil servants?"

"Of course. There's a food stall around the corner—it's street food, but I have it on good authority that it's excellent. Or we can eat at the hotel restaurant, whatever you want."

"Street food it is." She turned to walk out of the building. Her hand brushed past his, almost touching but not quite, and her fingers twitched.

Angelina pulled the brown beer bottle to her lips and took a long gulp. Leaning her forehead against the frosted glass, she released a long exhale. The heat and humidity in Bangkok was *no joke*, as the young Koreans would say. She was wearing only a simple shift, but she was sweating profusely. Maybe they'd made a mistake not going back to the hotel and air-conditioning. The fan spinning next to her was somewhat refreshing, but the pungent odor of gasoline fumes from passing motor scooters made her want to gag. Keisuke was sitting across from her at their round wood table, seemingly unflappable in his white T-shirt and linen pants, a jacket slung over the back of his folding chair.

"Why aren't you drenched?" she asked.

"I credit the many lessons I learned in Iraq. One must be Zen with one's surroundings," he said, placing his palms together in front of his chest in prayer, bowing his head.

She glared at him but was secretly amused by his answer. "Oh, please."

"Seriously? I have no idea. I just try to slow things down. Relax. As much as I can whenever I can." He leaned back in his seat, slid his legs out, crossed his feet at the ankles. Even his battered sandals looked urbane.

Angelina decided that Keisuke had a unique style, what she would call "nomad casual." A simple elegance combined with gritty practicality. She'd seen him in a T-shirt, board shorts, and flip flops for Korean class, but also in that undyed linen jacket, a button-down shirt, and jeans. She had to admit she always liked what she saw.

"What was Iraq like?"

"Hot."

"I mean, what was it really like for you?"

"Perhaps I should use an excuse you once gave me: I don't feel like talking about it," he said, but his face didn't tighten. Instead, he was smiling at her.

"Touché." She smiled back. "Since topics like Iraq and my trip to New York are off limits, what should we talk about?"

He paused, clearly wrestling with something. "My mother died of cancer six months ago, and I didn't know she was Korean until after her death," he said, his voice quiet. "My father told me she was ashamed of being Zainichi, an ethnic Korean in Japan. The stigma of not being granted citizenship in a country she'd spent almost her entire life in never went away—the perception that she wasn't good enough to be considered even a second-class citizen. She didn't want to pass that burden on to her children. That's why we moved to America when she was pregnant with me. I was born and raised in Seattle."

There he goes again. Confiding family secrets without reservation, without shame. Keisuke just recited the facts of his past with no inflection. No land mines. He didn't even glance at her to gauge her reaction. She wondered yet again how Keisuke managed to be so calm, so free.

"Is that why you're learning Korean?"

"Yes. But I have other reasons that I can't talk about right now. Not until I have my sources lined up and my intel confirmed."

"Was she—like my aunt?" Angelina asked, her voice cautious.

Keisuke shook his head. "My mother and her family came to Hokkaido from Busan in 1942. She was three years old. Her parents scraped and saved and opened a sewing shop, but they struggled because they were Korean and subjected to ethnic slurs and prejudicial treatment. My mother and father were high school sweethearts. My father knew she was Zainichi, but he defied his parents and married her anyway. Apparently, they called her 'a dirty Korean' when they found out, and he never spoke to them again."

"What a beautiful and tragic love story," Angelina said, unexpectedly touched by the depth of his parents' love.

Keisuke's eyebrows rose in surprise. "Not tragic at all. My father said they had a fifty-year love affair. Of course, not everything was easy, but they fought and made up, fought again and reconciled again. They committed to each other. My father is only sixty-eight, but he says he'll never remarry. 'Why settle when you've had the best?' he always says. I hope I'll find a semblance of what my parents had one day. A true lasting love."

How romantic.

Being around Keisuke was at once strangely comforting and extremely uncomfortable. She felt at home with him in a way she couldn't explain, but also frequently blushed for no reason, which was decidedly embarrassing, especially at her age.

The pretty Thai waitress arrived, smiling, with their food—a ham and duck pâté Bahn mi for Angelina, chicken satay skewers and fresh shrimp rolls for Keisuke. They ate without speaking, just nodded at each other, making indistinct vocalizations about the rich peanut sauce and tangy basil, unhurriedly sipping their beer.

Angelina awoke drenched in sweat in her pitch-dark hotel room, the constant drone of the air conditioner missing. *What time is it?* She dragged herself upright, jet lag making her limbs feel heavy. She pulled her long hair up, but without a restraint, it fell immediately back down onto her sticky shoulders.

Fumbling on the nightstand for the remote control to the air conditioner, she found only her earrings, watch, and a glass of water. Maybe the remote was under the air conditioner across the room. She felt self-satisfied with her progress, wading through furniture, until her knee slammed into a low table she hadn't accounted for in the dark. Crashing onto the bamboo floor, she rubbed her throbbing knee, rocking back and forth. Why hadn't she turned on the lamp by the bed? *I'm stupid*, she decided. She wanted to embrace her inner toddler and bang her fists on the floor and cry.

"Goddamnit!" She couldn't stop the torrent of tears that followed. Everything felt impossible—the search for her aunt, unraveling the mystery of her mother's suicide, the burden of fighting for her children. She couldn't even manage to walk across a room.

She was startled by the loud rapping of knuckles on the door that separated her room from Keisuke's. With their last-minute booking, the hotel had advised them there was only a "suite" available, which in reality meant they had connecting rooms with no lock between them.

"Are you okay?" Keisuke's voice was muffled.

"Leave me alone!" She felt wrecked and didn't care how unhinged she sounded.

Keisuke opened the door but didn't enter her room. He didn't try to touch her or attempt to comfort her or recite meaningless phrases like *It's going to be okay.* And for that she was grateful. The light from his room diffused the dark in hers, casting shadows onto the low carved table she had smashed into and the wicker rocking chair next to it. She propped herself up and leaned against the legs of the chair. Keisuke walked over and handed her tissues but remained standing. It seemed like he was waiting for an invitation, like he didn't want to impose.

Angelina gestured at an empty upholstered chair. "You can sit down."

"Thank you."

They looked at each other across the small space. Angelina didn't feel the need to fill the silence. She wiped her face and blew her nose, her hiccups gradually slowing, her breaths no longer ragged.

"Thanks for letting me cry." She tried to smile, as if she was making a joke.

He smiled back. "You're welcome to cry in front of me anytime."

Keisuke's kindness seeped through her skin and into her bones. Thom, Lars, her father—no man had ever said anything like that to her before. Her nose itched; the back of her throat tightened. But she kept smiling and swallowing to stop the tears.

"Hey, could you grab me a beer from the mini fridge?"

When he opened the door and retrieved two bottles, the light was blinding.

"Yikes. Stop that!" she said, trying to joke again.

"Of course." He handed her one of the cold beverages, the top popped off.

She stopped trying to smile and took a sip of the beer instead.

"Do you want to talk about it?"

Oddly, she *did* want to talk about it with him. And the semi-dark of the unconventional hotel suite allowed her to feel shielded, somehow, in revealing her true feelings. If only she could keep her voice from trembling.

"This feels hopeless, this quixotic quest to find my aunt. She's probably dead. Like so many bureaucrats in so many departments said to us today. There aren't any records here of a Kang Sunyuh, not even under her Japanese name. Besides, how could anyone endure that kind of brutality and survive? The things we've read, the people we've spoken to—maybe she died from a botched abortion. Maybe she committed suicide. Or maybe she was taken to Sumatra or Singapore or Nauru. And if she did, by some miracle, survive the mass executions by the Japanese at the end of the war to cover up their crimes, how could she possibly have made it back to Korea? And if she did, why wouldn't she have contacted her family?" Angelina felt hollow and sad, exhausted by her diatribe.

"Those victims internalized their shame. Nothing was their fault—there was nothing they could have done. If your aunt returned to Korea, she might not have contacted your family because she didn't want to be a burden to them, bring what was considered a 'dishonor' by a misogynist culture back then."

"But I was told she loved my mother. When they were young, Aunt Sunyuh protected her. My cousin Una said their relationship was unusually strong. I'm sure she would have found a way to contact my mother if she were still alive," Angelina said, her voice insistent.

"Your family left Korea and resettled in America."

"Ah, but for our migration to the Western world, my aunt and my mother would have been reunited. Is that what you're suggesting?" She felt forlorn just hearing her own words.

Keisuke hesitated, then nodded his head. "If your aunt is alive, she wants to be found."

"Yet more reasons why we should've never left our homeland." Regret dripped from Angelina's voice.

"Why did you leave?"

"My parents couldn't have a son. Four girls. No boy. My paternal grandfather insisted that my father impregnate a surrogate." She tried to recite the facts just as Keisuke did, tried to remove any emotion from her tone.

Keisuke nodded.

She was relieved that he didn't exclaim his shock, didn't express his disbelief at that long-ago demand of her grandfather's, a terrible truth she'd overheard as a child during one of her parents' fights. Keisuke simply understood.

"What happened to your mother?" he asked.

Angelina choked back bitterness. "She slit her wrists, bled out in a bathtub."

"I'm sorry."

"Thank you," she said, feeling like this was the first time she could accept condolences from someone without wanting to scream.

He paused before asking her something else. "What happened in New York with your ex-husband?"

"The narcissist I lived with for fifteen years? He wants me and my kids to move back to New York, so he doesn't have to go back and forth to Pittsburgh. He uses the broken justice system to torture me. It's soul destroying, going to court over and over. So, I gave in. It means uprooting my kids again, but I'm actually happy to go back to the city, because at my core, I'm a New Yorker. Of course, he doesn't know that," she said, pretending to smile at Keisuke. "Don't you dare tell him."

She wanted to believe she wasn't capitulating to Thom's demands again, that not fighting was a choice born of practicality. Not cowardice, not fear.

"I would never betray you."

Keisuke looked at her with an expression she couldn't quite name before he took another drag of his beer. A prickling started on top of her scalp, and suddenly she felt her heart thumping against her ribs, goose bumps erupting on her skin. She took a large sip, too, before changing the subject.

"Why are you helping me look for my aunt?" She'd wanted to ask him for days, and now she had the liquid courage to do so.

"I'm a journalist—I go where the story is. We haven't talked about this, but I was already doing research about the Japanese colonial era. I'm writing a long-form piece on the Korean diaspora for an editor at *The Atlantic*. I didn't tell you earlier because I didn't want to jinx my story. I'm weirdly superstitious. But I was looking into why my mother's family had moved to Japan, and it turns out many Koreans were 'forcibly migrated' to disparate parts of the world, like Sakhalin Island, long before the Asia-Pacific War started in 1931 and ended in 1945—when Korea was stripped bare, all its resources used for Japan's war. The population of Korea is currently about forty million, yet it's estimated over ten million Koreans are dispersed in places as far as Cuba, Brazil, Australia, and Uzbekistan, where they formed communities and were able to retain their culture and language. I want to write about why so many Koreans left their homeland, and I want to be able to interview them in their native tongue. Because it should have been mine, too."

Keisuke never stopped surprising her. His compassion and curiosity about the world were such laudable qualities. But the admiration she felt was tinged with something else—she was finding it harder and harder to deny the pull she felt toward him. "Is all this some kind of crusade on your part? Are you atoning for something terrible you've done?" she said, half joking, half serious. Mostly curious.

"I believe injustice must be undone. 'Injustice anywhere is a threat to justice everywhere.' Martin Luther King Jr. said that. In sanctioning government-sponsored sex trafficking, Japan committed crimes against these girls and young women. As someone who identifies as Japanese, I'm ashamed of what my country did, and I want to do my small part in righting that wrong. Because I'm proud to be Japanese. After World War II, Japan denounced violence. In article 9 of our constitution, we renounced war as a sovereign right of our nation, banishing the existence of a military. Forever."

Angelina was amazed by Keisuke's honesty and idealism, even if he did come across as a bit naïve. She found his thirst for justice kind of sexy, but she also regarded it as a potential problem. How far would he extend himself in the service of his ideals before he realized it might not be sustainable? Because the world always demanded compromise, if not outright capitulation.

Keisuke set aside his empty bottle and sat down next to her on the floor. "Let's take a look at your knee."

"It's fine."

He reached out and slid his hand up her leg gently. "It's scraped. I can get betadine from my room."

She suddenly felt hot, as if jolts of electricity had just coursed through her body. Terrified he would notice, she uttered the first thing that popped into her head. "Do you always travel with your own first aid kit?"

"Ever since Iraq."

"Oh." She looked down at the welt on her knee, pretending to assess the damage. "I'll just rinse it before I go back to bed, but thanks." She needed to get herself out of this increasingly dangerous situation.

She tried to stand up, but her legs wouldn't cooperate, and she fell against Keisuke, toppling them both onto the floor. Frozen, she stared into his face. Slowly, he propped himself onto his elbow, then reached out and cupped her face with his hand. His touch was gentle and loose. Exhaling slowly, she closed her eyes. A heaviness lifted. It was strange, but she felt truly safe, cherished even, for the first time in a man's grasp. The warmth of his breath on her lips sparked a fire that raced through her body, every cell flaring to life. Angelina gripped his head with her hands and pulled his mouth to hers.

Their tongues collided, their movements growing increasingly urgent with each parting of their lips. The intoxicating scent of cedar and citron erased all coherent thought from Angelina's head. Pressed against one another, they rolled on the floor, like a scene out of a movie, straining to get closer with every touch, every kiss.

Like lovers who couldn't get enough of each other.

Gongju

Westchester, New York
April 2005

"What?" Gongju said, stunned.

"I want a divorce," Minsu repeated.

"I must be hearing things."

"I can't do this anymore."

"What does that even mean?"

Gongju wanted to shout that she'd felt she couldn't go on with their marriage for years. *Years.* But she had stayed because she'd made a commitment, and surely that had to mean *something*. She'd always told herself that she needed to cham-muh, *forbear*, hold it in whenever she wanted to leave Minsu. Now he had the nerve to say that *he* couldn't bear it?

"I've fallen in love with Tiffany."

"You've fallen in love with the blue box I found in your desk?" Gongju couldn't help but make quips. The situation playing out in front of her was laughable.

Minsu shot her a defiant look. "I won't let you demean Tiffany with your sarcasm. I want to marry her." He said this like he was declaring something he didn't quite believe but didn't care anyway. *Ridiculous.*

Gongju knew her dark sense of humor had never resonated with Minsu. He wasn't witty or clever and never seemed to understand what she found riotously funny. So she resorted to the obvious. "You're leaving me for a younger woman? The nurse manager of your office?"

"I'm miserable."

Gongju was outraged by his selfishness. "I'm unhappy, too!"

Minsu looked at her, eyes wide and brows raised. "Then why have you always insisted we stay married?"

"Because we have children, you fool!"

"Why do you have to shout? And call me names?"

Minsu looked like a lost boy, but for once, Gongju resisted the urge to comfort him. She'd always been the adult in their relationship. Now she realized, in many ways, she'd been mothering Minsu along with her children. She'd never had a partner in the rearing of their daughters—she'd done it all herself. No wonder she was exhausted. And still, Minsu wanted more, wanted Gongju to validate him like she was his parent and not his—apparently—soon-to-be ex-wife.

She lowered her voice. "A fool? That's name-calling?"

"Tiffany understands me. You never have. Why are you so cruel?"

Minsu had also never understood Gongju's survival mechanism: to turn tragedy into comedy so she could cope. So she wouldn't have to cry. Ironic, since it was because of him that she'd become like this. His cheating, his carelessness. When she was younger, she'd allowed her emotions to run rampant, for everyone to see and judge. She'd been so easily hurt, so unable to protect herself. Not anymore.

Gongju felt so weary she'd have collapsed onto the oak floor of their living room if she were alone. "Please, get out." She reached for the arm of the chaise longue and squeezed, propping herself upright.

"We're going to work it out with the lawyers," Minsu said. "I want you to have the house. And everything in it. Just let me keep my pulmonary practice."

Gongju fought the urge to laugh. *Of course I'm getting the house, you idiot!* With his talk of getting lawyers involved, she knew Minsu already had one. He was just too afraid to tell her. But she knew him too well.

Unfortunately. And she knew he'd been cheating on her again. She just hadn't known with whom.

On Valentine's Day, when she didn't get the locket she'd found in his desk drawer while looking for a pen, she knew. She'd ignored his callousness, as she'd learned to do for so many years. And now he wanted to leave. *How rich.*

"Fine then. Go."

"I've packed a bag to last me for two weeks. I'll call you later." Minsu looked at her expectantly, as if he wanted her to reassure him that all would be fine.

Again, she suppressed the urge to laugh.

He cleared his throat. "Well, I'll be going."

She turned her back on him and squelched further retorts. No good would come from prolonging their goodbye. No good would come from another battle. She'd never forgotten a fight she had with Minsu years ago when she'd discovered yet another affair, shouting at him to get out, and his cruel reply, *I should have left when the second girl was born. You were never going to bear me sons. I should have run then.* His words had been suffocating and corrosive, and she'd never forgotten the pain he'd so carelessly inflicted.

Gongju desperately wanted to sit down, but she'd be damned if she showed any weakness in front of him. She pressed harder against the back of the chaise. Only when she heard the front door close did she let herself collapse into it. The drumming of her heart was rapid and loud in her ears, and something was wrong with her vision. The gold and cream fleur-de-lis pattern of the cushion was increasingly losing color, as if it were black and white.

What's happening?

Nothing was making sense. All she wanted to do was laugh and laugh and laugh. She wondered if she was about to have a breakdown. Like years ago, when Angel was in high school and Minsu checked her into an acute psychiatric care center, where she'd had to stay for six long, boring weeks. Gongju still remembered her slip, mistaking her daughter for her sister, Sunyuh. She didn't know why that particular affair of Minsu's had undone her. But the sight of a seemingly happy, bright yellow sunflower from her bedroom window had splintered and exploded a dam inside her that she hadn't known existed.

She'd told the psychiatrist whatever he wanted to hear. She didn't tell the doctor that before she'd been taken to the hospital, she'd been waiting for Minsu to promise yet again that he wouldn't have any more affairs. Minsu always begged her not to leave after cheating, terrified that she'd abandon him.

That hideous day, she'd thought that if she cried until there were no tears left, she could purge the sorrow from her body. But after several hours, she knew she had to stop or else she'd be doomed to cry all the time. She tried screaming and screaming and screaming, hoping it would be cathartic. But the noises spilling from her own body horrified her—she sounded like an animal caught in a trap, chewing its own paw to save itself. She'd started breaking dishes in the kitchen, not knowing the windows were wide open. When the police arrived, she'd been carted off in an ambulance.

Gongju fought the well of rage flooding her body. She tore off the sweater she seemed to be habitually wearing these days because she always felt cold. Now she was burning up. The pounding of her heart in her ears was so loud, she couldn't hear anything else. She wondered if this was what a heart attack felt like. If this was the suffering that needed to be released from her body. All the humiliation she'd kept buried, all the hurt she'd refused to feel from the mockery Minsu had made of their marriage.

Even his unwillingness to impregnate a surrogate, as demanded by his parents to continue the patrilineal family line, couldn't redeem his cheating. Of course, she'd been grateful he'd shown that he could be an honorable man. He left Korea for her sake. But the daily humiliation she'd suffered from living with her poisonous mother-in-law for ten years was not anything a loving husband should have asked of his wife. *Confucian traditions be damned.* Gongju had first thought that the suggestion of a surrogate wouldn't change her love for Minsu. But maybe a layer of trust had sloughed off, and now, all those shavings exposed the truth that their marriage lacked a real foundation.

As she walked toward the kitchen, she picked up a full bottle of Johnnie Walker Black from the living room bar cart. She unscrewed the top and poured the amber liquid down the drain. Gongju hated Minsu's drinking, especially the whiskey.

She stared out her kitchen window into her herb garden. "Rosemary is for remembrance," Angel had said last spring when she'd helped Gongju plant the evergreen-like herb, so uncommon in Korea. In that moment, Gongju had remembered her sister, Sunyuh, who'd never gotten to smell the woody stems or taste the brightness of rosemary. Perhaps Gongju would always carry her sister with her. She'd thought that when she left Korea, she would think of Unni less, that her face would fade with time. Instead, Gongju remembered Sunyuh-unni with a clarity that never changed.

She remembered that day in April, Yeonnalligi, when she'd run after the kite fighters with Unni, laughing. Gongju had no way of knowing then what danger Unni faced, what her parents endured during the brutal decades-long Japanese occupation. As a child, she had accepted as normal that there were prolonged food shortages, that the land was barren of trees, that men and girls often disappeared from their town. It was not until years later, after Gongju abandoned Korea, that she allowed herself to remember the signs plastered everywhere. The posters on the side of trains, at the bus depot, on the walls of her school: BE PATRIOTIC! GIRLS, SIGN UP FOR THE WOMEN'S VOLUNTARY SERVICE CORPS! THE EMPEROR NEEDS YOU!

To think that Gongju would soon have a grandchild the same age her lost sister had been when she disappeared. Maggie was almost fifteen. Gongju had never gotten over the tragedy of Joonsuk-oppa and

Sunyuh-unni. She'd felt like it had been her fault for so many years. She felt sorry for her six-year-old self, and even sorrier now, her life so inseparable from grief.

Gongju put down the novel she was reading and looked at the rosebushes out her bedroom window. The pink and yellow blooms wouldn't appear until June, the anniversary of her marriage. She wondered if she could wait that long to see the flowers. Sunyuh-unni had loved pink; Gongju still loved yellow. All her favorite dresses when she was little had been yellow. Sunshine yellow. She hadn't worn that color since her sister disappeared. Where had the time gone? And yet time seemed to drag on. It had only been a week since Minsu's departure, and he'd left several messages asking to come by the house. By the tone of his voice, she could tell he wanted something.

What if he wants to come back?

She couldn't let meaningless sentimentality sabotage her new resolve to cut off Minsu. She'd had a lot of time to think, these last few days. It was inevitable that Minsu would cheat if he returned. The thought of forgiving him yet again, and of him doing it yet again, exhausted her. She wanted to be free. Living alone was better than this hell she'd made for herself, this never-ending cycle of fake forgiveness and crushing betrayal.

In the last week, she'd cooked a hearty tofu and seafood stew, sautéed chunky tofu with bright spinach in a soy and scallion sauce, fried firm tofu with piquant kimchi and rice, and simmered a tofu doenjang soup for dinner. Minsu had always preferred steak or salmon. She'd spent decades of her life adjusting herself around Minsu, accommodating his needs. But now? She slept whenever she wanted, ate whatever she wanted, and watched Korean dramas on the large TV in the living room instead of being relegated to the den. It felt so liberating—and yet.

She still woke up each morning and reached for him, only to feel a cold, blank space. Even after all these years in separate bedrooms. She still listened for the creak in the stairs when Minsu descended in the morning. She still made two portions of rice at dinner, knowing full well he wasn't in the house. As if her hands were incapable of scooping and washing only one cup. There was more leftover rice in the refrigerator than she could possibly eat in a month. Habits were so hard to break. While washing dishes this morning, she'd suddenly remembered Minsu's face one afternoon in her father's garden in Gwangju, back when they were still courting. She had fallen asleep, her head on his legs. She'd woken up to find Minsu gently cooling her with a paper fan. She'd been so moved she'd squinted to avoid crying at the tenderness on his face.

I'm fine.

Gongju picked the novel back up and inserted it into its rightful place on the bookshelf by her bed. She walked to the vanity in her bathroom and sat down, brushing her hair automatically. In the mirror, her face looked old and drawn and hollow. Was she becoming one of those people—an empty shell? Simply going through the motions of life? How trite. How despicable. She put the brush down and turned toward the tub, thinking about how much she'd wanted to renovate the bathroom for years. The 1980s garish gold and chrome was so dated, so tasteless. But what was the point now? She'd be selling the house and moving into an apartment. Who knew this would be her future, at her age.

But then, there were many instances that Gongju had never imagined. Like leaving the country of her birth to live in America, amongst heathens who didn't know what tofu was. Like moving to Westchester, a dreary suburb of New York City. Like having four daughters and no son. And now, Minsu leaving. That was a scenario she had never anticipated. Gongju wondered why she'd stayed after their honeymoon. She'd been lying to herself all these years, thinking she'd be able to forgive his infidelity, when the truth was she'd felt gored each and every time, unable to heal.

Gongju had believed that Minsu had truly seen her. Like Sunyuh-unni had when Gongju was a little girl. For decades, Gongju had tried to deny the existence of the only person who'd ever truly loved her, and the wrongness of that action had left an indelible mark on her heart. She should have talked about Sunyuh-unni, shouldn't have allowed her mother to erase her. To speak of someone is to remember them so they don't disappear. It would have been better if Gongju had been the one who'd died, because pretending like Unni had never existed had shredded Gongju's soul, until what remained eventually shriveled and disappeared. She missed Unni, wanted so badly to see her face again—her third daughter was named Sunyuh because of her dream about Unni. She'd wanted her sister to be free and take flight, away from what was surely a horrific existence as a prisoner of war.

Now all she wanted was to join her.

Gongju regretted being estranged from her family in Korea. Her path to loneliness wasn't intentional. When she'd first come to America, she'd dutifully responded to her mother's letters. But then a month would pass before she wrote back with excuses like "I was busy this summer with the girls out of school." And eventually it wasn't rare that six months would pass before she thought about replying. It was piecemeal, the erosion of her filial piety. But after a whole year drifted by without the need to give in and lie to her mother about how much she was struggling in a foreign land—how unfulfilled she was as a parent yearning to be a writer—she no longer felt guilty. She still collected the blue letters—enough to fill a shoebox—but she stopped opening them. Why read something that would only make her feel worse? Trigger feelings of homesickness and guilt she wouldn't be able to suppress? It was better to just keep the letters out of sight. Occasionally images of her mother kneeling on an embroidered cushion or bending her head over a book would suddenly appear before Gongju's eyes. But she learned to habitually brush those aside until her musings and memories faded to blankness. She hadn't known that her silence would be so complete, so final.

Abruptly getting up from her vanity in the bathroom, she walked back into her bedroom. She knew she should be sorting through her things and packing. She didn't want to be in the house during the sale, didn't want strangers looking at her life. Inexplicably, she found herself in front of the bookshelf, staring at the spine of the novel she'd just put back.

Gongju didn't know why she was reading *Anna Karenina* again. Maybe she'd finally lost her sense of humor. Because the novel was a tragic story, not a farce or a romance. She'd always thought Anna was too dramatic. Stepping in front of a train? That had to hurt. And the blood and body parts? *No, thank you.* But Gongju understood the futility Anna must have felt. Begging her husband, cajoling her lover. How exhausting. Yes, Anna had cheated. But wouldn't any woman who'd married Karenin? Gongju felt sorry for Anna. The only thing Anna had gotten wrong was persisting in keeping her son. *Why?* She should have run when she had the chance. Men were tiresome. And children could be worse.

At least Anna had a son. Gongju had failed, and she couldn't *forbear* any longer. Her daughters were beyond exhausting, not the confidants or companions she'd once imagined they'd be. Those creatures she'd cared for when they were small and vulnerable, scared and ill. The nights she'd spent at their bedsides worrying when they'd fallen or had a fever or the flu. How viscerally her body reacted to the thought of her daughters— her jaw tensing, her neck stiffening, her belly squeezing. It seemed to Gongju that her daughters were human shapes filled with never-ending want. They had not lived through two wars. Never suffered deprivation, never feared for their lives, never seen their country torn in two. They knew nothing of sacrifice or duty, while she had sacrificed the possibility of a career, of a different, happier life, to raise them out of a misguided sense of duty.

Her daughters had taken so much for granted, like steady electricity and safe running water. They'd watched *The Brady Bunch* and *The Love Boat* on color televisions, had loved microwaved American meatloaf and mashed potatoes. They lived in a land of bounty where riches were never-ending. They had no idea the courage it had taken for her and Minsu to come to America and start over. The fearlessness she and Minsu had had in those days when they'd been young and thought they could take on the world. Back when she had still believed in them. Back when she'd believed she couldn't live without him.

The truth was Gongju had chosen Minsu, and she'd thought he had done the same. Maybe she should have let her parents arrange her marriage. Like her brothers. She'd felt superior because she'd chosen her life partner, not been assigned one. But left to her own devices, she'd chosen wrong. She'd been so infatuated with Minsu—he'd been so handsome, so charming—that she'd ignored his flaws as she fell headlong into love. She believed that jeong, the deep connection that blooms between spouses during the course of a marriage, would sustain them. That this bond, forged daily for forty-five years, could not be severed. That it would transcend any loss of romantic love because they had built a family and a life together. Instead, he'd just walked out after forty-five years, no hesitation in his footsteps, no regard for the sanctity of marriage. No regrets. Now she was completely alone.

It seemed silly that she'd put her faith in the supposed sacred vows they'd taken. In that old cathedral in Myeong-dong, under brilliant stained-glass windows, they'd promised to stay faithful and true. *In the name of the Lord, Jesus Christ.* She knew she'd been doubtful when she'd recited her wedding vows, hadn't thought closely about what she was promising. She'd blithely said all those words, not knowing how they would come back to haunt her. *I, Gongju, take thee, Minsu, to be my wedded husband. To have and to hold, in sickness and in health. Until death do us part.* How ironic—she'd meant those words.

She truly believed she and Minsu would be together until death.

Angelina

Seoul, Korea
July 16, 2006

Angelina awoke with a start. Blinking rapidly at the white ceiling of her dorm room, she waited for her heartbeat to slow. *What a nightmare.* It was the same dream she'd had her first night in Seoul, in her mother's bathroom, blood everywhere. Fighting not to cry, she tried to curl into a fetal position. But another body blocked her motion, a warm, muscled, *male* body.

Keisuke.

She liked many things about him, but she didn't like his hogging of the bed. No matter how many times she pushed him away, trying to give herself some space, he inevitably ended up pasted next to her in his sleep. At one point, he'd actually dumped her right onto the floor. Even when she'd yelled at him, he didn't wake up. He'd told her before that his special gift was the ability to sleep like the dead. She believed him now.

She pushed Keisuke onto his side, away from her, but he still didn't wake, so she lifted herself over him to sit on the edge of her bed. His face looked even more vulnerable in sleep, and she resisted the urge to caress him. Instead, she walked to the single window of her room. The glass and metal building at the top of the hill was almost done. All that shine. All that light. She smiled, a lightness easing through her body.

As if she could stand tall, hold her head up without effort. Was this happiness?

What is happy anyway?

These past thirteen days with Keisuke had been magical. Almost unbelievable. Sometimes she held her breath when he spoke, sure he'd make a gaffe, say something that was beyond offensive, something racist like Thom once said about a Black character in the movie *Crash*, or something conspiracy-fueled like Lars once said about 9/11.

Keisuke, on the other hand, was honorable. *Noble*. He really *was* like a knight on a quest. Day after day, he called his contacts, asking for favors. For her, to help her find out what happened to her aunt. He approached their search with single-minded zeal, refusing to take no for an answer. His tenacity was a marvel, not that she would acknowledge it. She was still probing for imperfections, certain Keisuke was lacking in *something*.

Now that they were back in Seoul, she'd insisted on secrecy, refusing to let him sit next to her in class again. Even Song-ah didn't know about her and Keisuke. And Angelina wanted to keep it that way, uncertain of what was going on between them, shying away from labeling it as anything significant. Yet she'd felt a funny jump in her heartbeat when Keisuke had casually asked if he could keep a toothbrush in her bathroom, some underwear in a drawer.

On weekday mornings before class, Angelina and Keisuke had breakfast together in her dorm room. A simple meal of sweet red bean buns and hot instant coffee. They often laughed as they discussed their plans for the day, or the homework she'd completed but he hadn't. There was an easy intimacy between them, as though they were the only ones who mattered in the world. Angelina always left the dorm room first, and Keisuke would follow five minutes later. She took the elevator; he took the stairs. And they never entered their classroom together. But Keisuke didn't complain about skulking around, didn't push her to acknowledge their relationship. He was careful with Angelina's feelings, always acting like being with her was a privilege he'd never take for granted.

They frequently went to Cheonggyecheon. It was sadly funny, but sitting next to that stream turned tourist attraction, drinking soju, eating at a pop-up restaurant, Angelina felt Korean. Like she'd reclaimed being Korean without shame. Maybe Keisuke felt that way, too. There was an inexplicable softness to his face whenever they sat at Cheonggyecheon. Sometimes their eyes would meet, and they would smile at the same time.

Last week she'd asked him if he wanted to accompany her to the National Palace Museum at Gyeongbokgung, the main palace of the Joseon dynasty, which housed artifacts from past kings and queens. She'd wanted to see how her ancestor, the daughter of an emperor, had whiled away her time in the fifteenth century.

Angelina had been there before. She adored Gyeongbokgung, loved entering the palace through Gwanghwamun, the *Great Gate*, with its massive red wood doors and cathedral-like stone arches. She could pretend she lived in the palace, in one of the elegant rooms, in the maze of structures somewhere at the rear of the huge complex. Perhaps next to the queen's quarters or near the large pavilion jutting out into the lush, man-made lake. Keisuke didn't object to going to Gyeongbokgung. He didn't whine. Not like Thom or Lars would have done.

After asking for her permission, Keisuke had read the novels on her desk: *The Bluest Eye* by Toni Morrison, *Housekeeping* by Marilynne Robinson, *Persuasion* by Jane Austen. When he finished them, he'd turned to her and said, "I see why you love these books." The quiet understanding on his face as he said those words had flooded her with joy. *A man who reads novels—why is that so hot?* Keisuke never made fun of her choices, didn't diminish her love of fictional worlds. Like he knew how life-saving books were to her, how if she could lose herself in *Pride and Prejudice* for a chapter or two, her faith in the world would be restored.

Thom didn't read books—in Angelina's eyes, a single Tom Clancy thriller didn't count. Instead, he skimmed medical journals. And Lars only read nonfiction, disdaining what he referred to as "pretend worlds." And his nonfiction tastes were eclectic and bizarre, *The Evolution of Desire* his favorite. Whenever she thought about her affair with Lars, she fought the urge to cringe, no longer justifying her actions. She'd been cheating. Now she understood why she'd done such a terrible thing—not by society's standards, but by *her* standards of what she expected of herself.

My mother was right.

In 1992, on her wedding day, her mother had found her hiding in the bride's room, just after Angelina had spoken to Lars.

Her mother had said, "What did that boy want from you?"

"He congratulated me."

Her mother stared at her. "Then why are you crying?"

She tried to laugh. "It's ridiculous, isn't it? I should be happy." She paused. "I mean, I am happy."

"That boy is no good. Don't be fooled by him, too."

"Lars is a great friend. If not for him, I might not have married Thom today." She tried to smile again.

"What are you talking about?"

"Dad went off to smoke, and I was pacing outside. It's crazy, but I wanted to run away. I was sweating and almost threw up. But Dad came back, and Cathy rushed us back into the church. I didn't want to go through with it. But then Lars came up the aisle, stood at the last pew. I don't know why, but when he smiled at me, I just knew it was going to be okay. So I walked down the aisle."

Her mother stared at her, eyes wide and unblinking.

"Thom loves me, and I love him," she insisted. "It's a good thing Lars was here, right?"

"Angel-ah, you can make a mistake and not let it ruin your life. A mistake is just that—a mistake. Don't stay with Thom because you made a mistake," her mother said in Korean, slowly and carefully, as though she wanted Angelina to understand every single word.

"I don't know what you're talking about, Mom. I'm fine. Better than fine. Thom and I are going to be great."

Her mother had tried to implore her again, tried to save her from herself, but she'd smiled and hurried them both out of the little room back into the loud and chaotic reception hall.

Did she even know how to be *in* love? It was easier to say that she'd loved and lost—that made sense. After all, Anne Elliot in *Persuasion* had loved and lost Frederick Wentworth by the age of twenty-seven. But Angelina was a forty-year-old woman who truly believed, for the first time, that she'd never been in love, with Grady, or Thom, *or* Lars. What kind of cliché was she that she'd been in love with the idea of love? In her language class, Angelina had learned that Koreans talk about love as something a person "slips" into. Was it really that easy? Could she just *slip* into love?

She was so lost in her thoughts that she visibly jumped when Keisuke wrapped his arms around her, briefly tensing her shoulders before letting them fall. Her back landed on his bare chest. His sinewy muscles felt firm yet yielding—there was no need to brace for impact.

"Did I scare you?" Keisuke whispered in her ear. "I called your name, but you didn't answer. Were you thinking about your aunt? My friends in Japan haven't been given access to the war records in Tokyo yet, but we shouldn't lose faith. We're less than three weeks into our search."

She gently pushed out of Keisuke's arms. "No, for once, I wasn't thinking about my aunt. And I know you're doing all you can." She cupped his cheek. "Thank you."

"You were crying." He wiped away tears she hadn't known she'd shed.

"I'm fine."

"Do you want to talk about it?"

"No. I'm really fine."

Angelina thought she was deflecting at first. But as she heard the words out loud, she realized she meant them. She was at peace with what she now knew about herself, about the men from her past.

Keisuke tilted his head, as though debating whether to pursue his line of questioning.

Before he could say anything more, she grabbed his shoulders and pulled him toward her, planting a firm kiss on his mouth. His hands cradled the back of her head as he deepened their kiss and tugged her closer to him. Desire coursed through her body, and then a lightness, a melting she'd never felt before. Their bodies stumbled and lurched toward the bed, she and Keisuke laughing and kissing and touching.

"Why haven't we gone to your place, again? I have a single bed and you keep dumping me off of it. Think how comfortable we'd be in a double bed." Angelina pushed her cheek deeper onto Keisuke's shoulder, burrowing her hand into the nape of his neck. "You do have a bed in your goshiwon, right? Or have you converted to being fully Korean, with a sleeping mattress that you fold up and put away?" She always imagined Keisuke in a *student's studio*, like the size of her dorm but with a slightly larger bed to accommodate his height.

"It's a queen bed, actually."

"What? How luxurious!" Large apartments were expensive in Seoul. "How big is your place?"

"Not that big." There was a sudden studied casualness to his voice.

Now she was definitely curious. "How big?"

"It's a one-bedroom."

She sat up and stared at him. "We're going to your place. Right now."

"Why? We're comfortable here. And I don't have to take the subway to class anymore." Keisuke pulled his arm across his face, seemingly shielding himself from the light.

Here it was—the problem she'd been searching for. Abruptly leaving the bed, she walked into the bathroom, grabbing some clothes on the way.

"Come on, Angelina, is this really necessary?"

She took one step out of the bathroom. "Get dressed, please. You're hiding something."

"No, I'm not."

"Do you live with a girlfriend? Is that why you don't want to show me your apartment?" she said, deliberately keeping her voice calm.

"I practically live with you. Are you my girlfriend?"

"Don't be ridiculous. I'm too old to be your girlfriend." She fought her rising panic, sure he was keeping a secret.

He sat up in bed. "The age thing. Do you know that's your excuse for everything?"

"Stop changing the subject," she said, voice tight. "And get dressed, please."

They stared at one another. Just when she thought she couldn't hold her breath any longer, he looked away. She exhaled without making a sound.

This is suspicious as hell.

They didn't speak while he pulled on his pants and a black T-shirt. They didn't speak on the subway ride to his apartment. Thirty minutes of screaming in her head that she'd been a fool to trust Keisuke. That she was about to be betrayed. *Again.*

Usually, Angelina marveled at how clean the subway cars were in Seoul. How no trash littered the seats and the floors weren't sticky. How orderly the Koreans were, how quietly they spoke when they actually talked to one another. Mindful. Polite. Even the conductors were respectful in their language and tone when making announcements. Not like the New York City subway workers who shouted the names of upcoming stations and yelled angry instructions to not block the closing doors.

When Keisuke led her to a shiny high-rise tower in Gangnam, the most expensive neighborhood in Seoul, Angelina glared at him, still refusing to speak. She followed him into a gleaming elevator and seethed all the way to the penthouse floor. He didn't try to talk to her. He simply opened the door to his apartment and gestured for her to enter.

Shedding her sandals in the foyer, she walked straight to the floor-to-ceiling windows in the living room. She pivoted to him accusingly. "You have a terrace?"

"It's my father's apartment. I'm using it for the summer."

He sounded embarrassed, and Angelina softened a little, but she wanted answers. "Are you rich?"

"No." His tone was emphatic.

"Well, is your father rich? Because this must have cost at least a million dollars," she said, her gaze fixed on the Han River view out the sliding glass doors. She was having trouble processing this—that Keisuke had access to a lot of money when, for weeks, she'd thought he was a working-class journalist, barely making ends meet.

"He's comfortable."

"That's what rich people say when they don't want to admit they're wealthy." She turned back to Keisuke. "What does your father do for a living again?"

Angelina knew very little about Keisuke's family. He was proud of his sister, an animator in Hollywood. Keisuke visited her often in Los Angeles, but he'd been vague in describing his father as someone "in management."

"He's a businessman."

"What kind?"

"He owns a couple of grocery stores in Seattle."

"A couple? Or a chain?"

She could see Keisuke struggling to answer her question. And she was debating whether she was *actually* outraged or if she felt she *had* to be outraged. She decided it didn't matter—watching him squirm was kind of fun.

"My dad came to America with nothing and built a business without any help from his parents. He had no friends. But he had my mother. So I suppose they really did it together, built something from nothing. The American Dream. Yet that doesn't account for the poverty they endured for years, pouring every cent and every second of their lives into the business. It dismisses the cost of family time lost—all the family dinners we didn't have, all the weekends my mom and dad both had to work. I had to babysit my younger sister from the time I was seven. But I guess it was all worth it. My father is now wealthy, as you say."

Keisuke continued to astound her with his ability to change the emotional tenor of a conversation. Moments before, she'd been angry and wanted contrition from him, wanted him to feel uncomfortable. Now, she felt like she should apologize for being callous, for judging him without knowing all the facts.

"Why didn't you just tell me?"

"Because I wanted to avoid this conversation."

"Like why you have an abundance of fresh flowers in vases everywhere?" The scent of lilac and hibiscus lingered in the air.

"The housekeeper comes twice a week, even though I've told her many times she doesn't need to clean for me."

"You have hired help?" She barely kept her jaw from dropping open. "How many?"

"It's my father's money. Not mine. I feel like a parasite living in my father's place. I'm ashamed that I'd rather live in a fancy apartment than in a gritty one-room goshiwon, like I should as a student. But the truth is I don't want to suffer. Besides, how could I let this view go to waste?"

She shrugged one shoulder, as if she didn't care that he'd kept secrets from her. "It's all going to be yours someday."

"No. My dad's been very clear that he's leaving his fortune to charity when he goes. My sister and I don't expect anything. I agree that I should make my own way in the world. I'm in my thirties—I should have a plan for my life, not just bounce from one thing to another. My father disapproves of what he calls my 'lack of ambition.' I haven't told him about an assistant managing editor job I was offered a few months ago at the *Seattle Times*. He says he wants me to join the family business. Settle down. Start a family." Keisuke seemed at a loss, even as he said the words with certainty. Like he wasn't sure if he should bend to his father's wishes or if he should pursue his dream and possibly break his father's heart.

"Do you have any interest in grocery stores?" she said almost playfully, searching for lightness, trying to return equilibrium to their relationship.

"None," he said quietly, looking away.

Angelina turned back to the view of the Han River, the sun shining so brightly the water glared like a mirror. She could look at that view, with Seoul Tower in the background, all day. Especially since she was reluctant to delve into Keisuke's family dynamics. Angelina told herself she didn't want to know.

"I'm still mad that you didn't tell me. But damn, this view is amazing! I can't believe we didn't use this for the last two weeks—should I be mad about that instead?"

Keisuke laughed. "Sure. As long as you're not angry that I come from money, who cares?"

Angelina didn't want to admit that she'd been hurt, even just a little. And she didn't want to admit that she'd just as quickly forgiven him. Changing the subject, she said, "I'm going to check the bedroom to see if you're hiding a girlfriend." She was only half joking.

Walking quickly out of the living room, with its midcentury modern furnishings, she glanced at the kitchen's white marble countertops, luxurious leather stools, glossy kitchen cabinets, and stainless-steel wine refrigerator. She opened a door in the hallway to see a gleaming white bathroom and closed it, still searching for the bedroom.

"Unless you'd rather see the office, why don't you come this way?" Keisuke stood at the other end of the hallway, pointing to an open doorway.

She raised her eyebrows at him. "You have another bedroom?"

"It's small, so I use it as an office."

"So, it's really a two-bedroom penthouse apartment?"

He shrugged.

She stepped into the uncluttered bedroom. A black-and-white photograph above the bed was mesmerizing—grays and charcoals formed mountains, and a wooden pier jutted toward the distant rim of a lake, the water appearing white. The room was capacious, with floor-to-ceiling windows, but there was only a simple curved, black wood headboard rising from a low platform bed, with black metal bedside tables and a Flos lamp arcing over the bed. An acoustic guitar was propped against a wall, and several jang-gu sat in wood supports.

"You play Korean drums?" She examined the jang-gu up close, the animal hide stretched taut on either end of hourglass-shaped wood. She caught the scent of lavender and searched for the source. A drying bouquet on his bedside table.

"I'm learning. Another reason I'm in Korea, besides the language classes."

"You're a talented guy. A journalist, an editor, a drummer."

"I just don't like being bored."

"Where are your books?"

"In the office. I have shelves upon shelves."

"Are you writing a novel in there?"

Keisuke hesitated before answering, "I don't like to tell anyone, but yes, I'm writing a murder mystery set in the Green Zone, based on my experiences in Iraq."

She wasn't surprised by his revelation. *What man but a writer reads novels?*

"Ah. Something like *Murder in the Emerald City*, instead of *Murder on the Orient Express?*"

He smiled. "More like an international espionage thriller involving illegal arms dealers and collusion on the part of the American government."

She suppressed a smile. "How disappointing."

"Why?"

"Because I wanted a book with a flavor of the ancient. Like the murder of an innocent Iraqi child on the Euphrates over a stolen Mesopotamian antiquity that's traced back to a CIA agent in the Green Zone," she said, trying to keep a stony expression on her face.

"Sorry to disappoint you."

"I'm sure it won't be the last time."

Keisuke half-smiled. "Tough crowd."

She laughed, wrapping her arms around his waist, nestling her cheek into his chest. They stood without speaking. The solid beating of his heart, loud and sure in her ears. She liked Keisuke; she was afraid she was falling in love with him.

Is Song-ah right? Is this fate?

But she'd been wrong about love before. She didn't want to make another excruciating mistake. She was forty years old, not twenty-three. And clearly, a forty-year-old could still be stupid, like she'd been with Lars. But having two children whose lives were entwined with hers—it wouldn't just be her mistake if she was wrong. She searched for a lighthearted comment, anything to deflect her feelings. Instead, tears threatened to spill.

As though he detected her shift in mood, Keisuke disentangled himself from her arms. His hand reached for her face. She closed her eyes. The tips of his fingers brushed against her skin, his palm cupping her cheek. She opened her eyes. The yearning on his face was heartrending. Holding her breath, she dropped her head back onto his chest.

"Are you okay?" he asked.

"I'm fine," she said, keeping her face buried. She swallowed and the motion was painful, like a physical lump was in her throat, stuck and growing larger. Not ready to show him how vulnerable she was feeling, she tamped down her sudden swell of emotions, as though she could fit everything into an imaginary box. She gripped a small piece of his T-shirt, the fabric smooth and cool against her fingertips.

"I'm not going to push you. I want you to know you can take all the time you need."

Instead of reassuring her, what he said unsettled her. She plastered a smile on her face. "You know I'm going to make you honor what you said." She pushed out of his arms.

"I'll wait for you."

Her smile wiped away. "Don't say things you don't mean."

"I mean it."

"Stop."

"Why?"

"Because I have trust issues." She tried to say this with a laugh, but it came out like a harsh rasp.

"I know. I'm trying to understand your feelings."

"Feelings?" She took a step away from Keisuke.

"You know, those pesky things you like to avoid? They itch like you're about to break out into hives, right? I promise you won't be hurt. If you sit with your feelings, you'll find they become less uncomfortable. Someday they'll actually feel normal."

"Do you moonlight as a therapist?"

Keisuke stretched out his arms and touched the tips of his thumbs onto his forefingers. "Om."

She laughed before schooling her face into a neutral expression. "I'm still dealing with a brutal divorce—you'd be the rebound guy. Are you okay with that?" She didn't want Keisuke to be under any illusions, and she certainly wasn't going to tell him about her *other* rebound with Lars.

Keisuke smiled. "I'm not in love with you."

She stared back. "Good." *I think.*

"Yet."

"What?"

"I'm not in love with you *yet*."

"Stop complicating things."

"How am I doing that?"

"Don't elevate what's going on between us into something meaningful."

"Why can't it mean something? Why does it have to be casual?"

"Because we're going nowhere," she said impatiently.

Keisuke shrugged. "Who says? We could fall in love. The only way to find out is to try."

"I can't do that." She turned her body away from him.

"Can't? Or won't? You have choices. You know that, right? We may not like the decisions we make, but we have free will. We can decide to move in together and discover what we feel for each other."

"It's not that simple."

"Sure it is." Keisuke took a step toward her. "I'm starting to suspect you don't want to make choices. Because then you won't be responsible for the consequences. Life doesn't work that way."

"No, thanks. I'm done living with men." She backed away from him.

"Love can sometimes expose you to hurt."

"You think I don't know that? My marriage was a fucking disaster."

"It doesn't always end that way." He gently touched her shoulder.

She slipped out of his hold. "Of course, it does. People who say they love you will always betray you."

He pushed his hands into the front pockets of his pants. "Love doesn't always end with betrayal. Sometimes you just say goodbye and wish the other person well. My last girlfriend and I parted amicably. I went to her wedding last year, and I was happy for her."

"Inconceivable. You must not have loved her." She was looking for any excuse to dismiss his logic, to resist being sucked into this fantasy.

"I did love her. But I wasn't passionately in love, and neither was she. It was sticky, but we managed to be honest with ourselves. Not every farewell is ugly." He kept his hands in his pockets.

"Thanks, but no thanks," she said with a fake smile. A pretense at looking breezy, unaffected.

"Let's talk about how sad you are. How frightening it is for you to admit you could love me." His voice was soft, but he was looking straight at her.

She broke away from his gaze. "This conversation is over."

"Do you know you always shut things down when you don't have an answer?"

He was flaying her open. She didn't care that he was right. She just wanted him to stop. "Why do you like me? There's nothing to like about me—I'm cranky, obstinate, melancholic. What the hell is there to like?"

She hated the pleading in her voice. She didn't say that *he* was easy to love. Easy to get along with, easy to be with. There'd been a moment about a week ago at the National Museum of Korea when she'd looked up from the famous Moon Vase and saw Keisuke across the gallery. His shoulders had been sloped, and he'd been intently examining a bronze sculpture. From that angle, the curve of his cheekbone had been heartbreaking. She'd barely suppressed the urge to run over to him, clasp his head between her hands, and kiss him. A deep, long kiss.

"How can you even say you could love me?"

He took a small step toward her. "Because you're smart as hell. Absolutely adorable when you're shy and uncertain. Witty when least expected. I love the way you close your eyes and smile for no reason when sunlight hits your face. You're a joy to be around."

"When you say things like that, I don't know how to respond. You're constantly catching me off guard."

"Now you sound like *The Sound of Music*—how do you solve a problem like Keisuke?" He took another step toward her.

"I hate musicals."

"Shocking. What do you have against laughing and singing?" He was barely restraining a smile.

"Are you mocking me?"

"Life without humor isn't worth living. One of the many reasons I like you." He was openly smiling now.

She remained petulant. "I don't like you. I'm only using you for your journalistic prowess." *And because you're good in bed.*

He smiled wider. "I like you. Really, *really* like you."

No one had ever described her that way. *A joy.* Without saying a word, she engulfed him in her arms.

Angelina

GANGWON-DO, KOREA
JULY 22, 2006

Siberian pines stretched into sky, but Angelina stood above them all, a vertiginous plateau of granite beneath her feet, endless blue and green before her. She and Keisuke had hiked for hours in Seoraksan to reach this breathtaking vista on their first morning at the East Sea.

When Keisuke first proposed this trip to Sokcho and Seoraksan, Angelina had been resistant. She wanted to spend every minute out of Korean class revisiting the archives at the War Memorial of Korea, poring through the transcripts and testimonies of victims at the Korean Council and at the Truth Commission on Forced Mobilization under Japanese Imperialism, and sifting through the records at the Ministry of Gender Equality and Family, the Ministry of Foreign Affairs, and the National Archives. Four weeks into her search for Aunt Sunyuh, Angelina was starting to feel desperate. But Keisuke said it was healthy to take a break, and besides, the halls of government were closed on weekends. Hence their trip two hours out of Seoul.

Angelina faced the sun and closed her eyes, wondering if her mother had stood in this very spot in Seoraksan. One of the few memories Angelina's mother had shared about Korea was her long hikes on this mountain. Looking almost happy, she'd describe the clean air, the sea of green trees, the stony paths she climbed as a young woman. Then, looking pensive, she'd said, "But that was a long time ago."

Angelina remembered that her mother used to call Korea *the land of ten thousand mountains*. It was an embellished, elegiac phrase borne from her nostalgia, her longing, for the country of her birth, for its many peaks and plateaus. Angelina hadn't known that most natives didn't talk about Korea that way until she started learning Korean. Only her mother had given this land such a poignantly poetic name. She had dreamt of stone angels in Seoraksan—it was why Angelina's name in Korean was *Angel*. But she hadn't known she'd shared the sentiment with her mother's lost sister. The beloved sister. The cherished daughter.

The years her mother must have ached in body and spirit, denying the existence of a sister who'd loved her and whom she had deeply loved in return. Losing someone you love also means losing yourself. Angelina imagined that fact alone could have driven her mother to despair. Compounded by the repeated betrayals of her father, and the loneliness of living in America—how doomed her mother must have felt. Angelina didn't blame her mother for her suicide. She blamed herself for not preventing it.

Keisuke touched her arm. "Do you want a drink?"

She accepted the water bottle and took a long, slow swallow. Wiping droplets from her chin, she said, "My mother loved hiking in Seoraksan."

Keisuke gently contemplated her face. "Then why do you look so sad?"

"At every wooden pavilion I saw along this trail, I wondered if she'd rested there. If she'd sat on the platform and shared a snack with her friends. She became a recluse in America, but my mother had friends in Korea when she was younger. I can't help but think if she hadn't left, she could have been happy." Angelina brushed away tears. "I wish she were here."

"Her death wasn't your fault," Keisuke said, his voice level and calm.

She turned away from the view and pushed her face into a smile. "Let's not talk about that today, okay?" She wasn't ready for absolution.

Keisuke's head tilted ever so slightly. "Let's go have lunch, shall we?" He reached out and took the water bottle from her, his fingers brushing against hers. Her skin seemed to prickle from his touch. She wanted to grasp his hand; instead, she looked down at the granite, the surface smooth and worn by rain and sun and the rubbing of hikers' boots. Her hands remained by her side. When she lifted her head, Keisuke was looking at her. With a laugh, he grabbed her hand. Warmth flooded her body. For a moment, she let herself feel happy, and she held Keisuke's hand as they descended from the peak.

Pouring makgeolli, *opaque sparkling rice wine*, into her squat, mustard-colored metal bowl, Keisuke said, "I want to ask you something, but I also want to respect what you said earlier."

They were sitting at a small white table with red plastic chairs, waiting for their rolls of gimbap and mul naengmyeon, *handmade noodles in icy beef broth*, to be served at an outdoor restaurant halfway down the mountain. Grandparents and little children and hikers of all abilities surrounded them, occasionally giving them curious glances, probably surprised at hearing English coming from their mouths. Chinese or Japanese tourists were more common than Americans.

Although he didn't say it, Angelina knew he was referring to her mother. "I guess you can take the journalist out of Seoul, but you can't take the urge to ask questions out of the journalist." The milky-colored makgeolli eased down her throat, giving her a momentary reprieve. "Go ahead," she said, but she wanted to shift her chair away from him.

"Are you bracing for impact?" Keisuke said.

She laughed at his bluntness. "Always. But I know you by now. The curiosity is killing you, isn't it?" She quirked her lips. "I've had enough makgeolli to fortify myself. Ask away."

Keisuke leaned back slightly in his chair and folded his hands in his lap. It was strange—now that he'd obtained permission, he seemed hesitant. Angelina found it endearing, and wondered if this was what falling in love entailed, the odd warmth yet strange discomfort she felt looking at him, watching the fall of his fingers as he tucked one thumb underneath the other, noting the beauty of that motion.

"From everything you've told me, it seems like you blame yourself for your mother's death. Why?" he asked.

"Wow. Already with a tough one. Shouldn't you start with a softball question before you zero in?" She pretended to be joking, managed to keep the smile on her face.

His eyes were watchful. "You appreciate honesty. You wouldn't like it if you thought I was fooling you."

She nodded. "I do hate subterfuge. One point for Keisuke." This time her smile was genuine. "Still. I'm discovering I'm more sensitive than I thought. Apparently, I'm easily hurt."

Keisuke arched his eyebrows. "You didn't know that about yourself?"

"Are you trying to make me feel dumb?" she demanded.

He shook his head. "Nope. But I am wondering how such a smart woman could be so—unaware?"

Angelina burst into laughter. He really knew her so well—her pretenses, her propensity for avoidance. "Fine. No more delaying tactics. Just give me a second." She looked up, searching the sky above her, the leaves and branches of the Korean maple obscuring most of the blue. She looked back at Keisuke, who was sitting quietly, not saying another word.

"I blame myself because I know I could have stopped her." Angelina forced her voice not to tremble, forced herself to finish the sentence. "If only I'd gone to her apartment that weekend." It was impossible to keep her voice steady. "My mother had asked me to visit her, but I was drowning in my divorce. I thought I would be burdening her if I went to see her. She would always get incensed whenever we talked about Thom. But if I had gone that day, if I had just been there, maybe I could have prevented a tragedy." Angelina's shame whipped at her, and it felt physical, like her skin was being flayed. Her hands started shaking, then her legs, then her whole body. Even her teeth were chattering.

Keisuke leaned over and pulled her body into his arms, repeatedly rubbing her back, her shoulders, as if he could transfer the heat from his body to hers.

She dropped her head and cried silently into his shoulder.

Minutes passed.

"Walking around with all that guilt must be exhausting. Why don't you lay it down?" Keisuke said softly near her ear.

She lifted her head and pushed her body away from his. "I failed my mother."

"And blaming yourself is a form of atonement?" Keisuke sounded surprised, as though that logic escaped him.

"Isn't that what Asians do? We're responsible for our parents, our families." She tried to say this with conviction, but her voice stuttered.

"What about a duty to yourself? It's not inherently selfish to think of yourself first. It can be a good thing. It teaches you self-worth and reminds other people of your value. Sacrifice can be a cowardly act sometimes, and it can breed resentment and bitterness."

Angelina didn't know how to respond to Keisuke's matter-of-fact statements. What a concept: to be beholden to no one.

"I don't know what kind of person your mother was, but I do know she wouldn't want you to blame yourself for her death. I think she'd be happy you're looking for her sister. Because if your mother thought there was any chance her sister was still alive, she'd be looking herself." Keisuke paused, like he wanted to make sure Angelina was listening, paying attention to his words. "This grief is consuming you. But holding on to guilt isn't the same as holding on to your mother."

His insight, his generosity, was astonishing, unspooling her, forcing from her an unprecedented honesty. "I feel like I'm suffocating. Like no matter how hard I try, I can't catch my breath. Like I have to force myself to breathe, just to keep going."

Keisuke gently touched her shoulder. "You'll get there—wherever 'there' is, and whatever it means to you. I struggled after my mother's death. I was angry at her for dying, which was ridiculous, but it was still how I felt. It was my father who helped me realize that I wasn't angry with my mother. I was just sad. Really sad. But I had to acknowledge this in order to accept the fact that my mother was gone."

Angelina felt an easing in her chest, a sensation of stillness. Looking down at the white plastic table dusted with pollen, she tried not to think about why Keisuke inspired such trust. When she looked up, he was watching her, seemed to know she didn't quite believe him.

"You're stronger than you think," he said, the timbre of his voice low and sure.

She blinked hard, like she could erase this onslaught of shame by sheer will. And yet, she felt hope, a sentiment foreign and unfamiliar. Embarrassed that everyone at the tables around them had seen her cry, she pretended not to notice the sidelong glances from the older Korean woman behind the counter.

"Maybe I'm not the person you think I am."

Keisuke quirked an eyebrow. "You're not the embodiment of wit, elegance, and beauty?"

Angelina burst into laughter, pure relief landing on her shoulders and loosening the knots. A lightness filled her voice. "Why not? I'll take beauty."

Keisuke smiled. "Let's go back to our hotel room, shall we?"

Their hotel room in Sokcho had commanding views of the East Sea with sliding doors to a generous balcony. Angelina avoided looking at the queen-size bed dominating the room. Swallowing audibly, she hoped Keisuke couldn't hear the sudden increase in her heart rate. After their conversation at the restaurant, she felt self-conscious. It wasn't like she hadn't seen Keisuke naked every night in her dorm room for the last three weeks. But there was an awkwardness, a vulnerability revealed in a hotel room, even between lovers. She felt like they were putting their desire on display, and it seemed crass. She twisted her hands, kept her back to Keisuke.

"Still uncomfortable about sex?" Keisuke's voice coming toward her.

Angelina dropped her knotted hands. "It's no big deal. It's just sex."

He stood next to her, in front of the sliding glass doors. "That's not the case for you."

She swiveled her head. "How do you know?"

He seemed to be suppressing a smile, a corner of his lip twitching.

"What?" she said, irritated.

"You'd be a terrible poker player," he said, his face giving nothing away.

"That easy to read? Is that how you figured out I didn't have a boyfriend when we first met?" She quirked her lips.

"Yes." He broke into a grin. "You look away when you reveal something important about yourself. You stare without blinking when you're more bravado than truth. And you think your shell hides your reticence, but I find your shyness very charming. Adorable, in fact."

Angelina stared at Keisuke's lips as he spoke. So full and sensuous. Reaching out her finger, she traced the smooth ridge of skin at the edge. She heard harsh rasping and was surprised to discover it was hers. She dipped her head away from his steady gaze, away from the longing in his eyes.

"We don't have to do a single thing." Keisuke lay down on the bed fully clothed, still in his hiking shorts and T-shirt. He turned on his side, curling his arms and legs toward Angelina still standing at the window. "We can just lie here and look at each other."

Angelina wanted to make a flippant comment, resort to humor, but this moment felt important, precious even. She lowered her body to mirror his, their faces only inches apart. Keisuke wasn't physically touching her, but she felt held.

"One look from you and I know exactly what you're thinking sometimes. I can almost hear your words."

"Frightening," she said quietly.

"You never have to be afraid of me," Keisuke said, his voice soft. "You can trust me."

She closed her eyes.

"Angelina, look at me."

The way he said her name slowly and deliberately, the vowels of her name elongated—she'd always resented how long and cumbersome her name was, but in Keisuke's low tenor, it sounded practically musical.

"I love how you say my name."

"It's a beautiful name."

"I feel beautiful with you," she said, in wonder.

"Because you are," he whispered, gently dropping his forehead to meet hers, their noses touching. "You're the most beautiful woman in the world to me."

Angelina had never felt what she felt when she was with Keisuke. Like she could be joyful. Like she could be someone more, not limited by fear or a lack of imagination. She felt seen.

Pulled to Keisuke by a force that was almost magnetic, she pressed her body against his lean form. Clasping his head in her hands, she kissed him. His lips, soft and surprised, were still at first before they moved against her mouth, urgent but languorous. He tasted like sweet rice wine and salt. Heat pervaded her body. Even her earlobes felt like they were on fire, burning with want.

She let herself melt into him.

Angelina

GYEONGGI-DO, KOREA
JULY 27, 2006

Angelina ducked out of the tour bus and stared at the House of Remembrance. A house more than a museum, two hours outside of Seoul, it served as a nursing home to the now elderly surviving victims of sexual slavery by Japan. A nonprofit organization opened the House to provide shelter to the often poor and destitute women whose trauma and lack of social status prevented them from attaining meaningful jobs or living with families who could support them. The building was modest, a squat, two-story brick structure at the top of a series of concrete steps. Bronze busts of the survivors who had lived or were currently living at the House filled a circular courtyard below. Angelina didn't know what she'd expected when Keisuke told her about the House. It was difficult to find through English-language resources, but he'd been told about its existence by the Truth Commission, and he was optimistic about visiting a place where a group of survivors lived. "Maybe we'll meet someone who was taken to the same place. Maybe someone will remember your aunt."

Ironically, Keisuke's enthusiasm dampened her expectations. She felt like this was going to be a wasted trip. What traumatized woman in her seventies or eighties wanted to remember the exact details of her imprisonment? Or who she was imprisoned with? Trauma caused entire periods of one's life to vanish, with only fragments remaining of what happened, of what was endured.

Angelina reluctantly joined the line of foreign journalists and tourists filing into the House of Remembrance. The lobby was full of light, a wall of glass framing the entrance. Display cases with pictures and plaques were filled with information about the history of the nursing home and museum, the history of those who survived, once young girls, now old women. Everyone took photographs, except Angelina. She couldn't bring herself to record this much pain, this much grief. She'd wanted to cry the moment she entered the building. Standing as far away from Keisuke as she could, she watched as he went from display case to display case, jotting down notes in his worn leather notebook, taking pictures. He seemed happy to be back in his natural habitat as a reporter, while Angelina felt like she was about to splinter apart.

A woman in a prim suit walked into the atrium. "Ladies and gentlemen, welcome to the House of Remembrance. Please gather in the community room for the testimonies of the halmoni in this special English-language tour." The director gestured to a large room off the lobby.

Two older women sat in wooden chairs at one end of the room, microphones positioned in front of them. Facing them were rows of metal folding chairs. One halmoni sat with her hands over her eyes, her head bowed. The other smiled at everyone as they found seats or sat on the floor, their backs against the wall. When the director spoke a little too close to the microphone, a screech echoed through the room. Angelina winced, pressed a hand to her ear. She immediately felt the urge to flee.

But Keisuke didn't flinch, continuing to scribble notes. He gave her absentminded smiles as he occasionally looked up. He leaned forward in his folding chair as the first halmoni started speaking in Korean.

"My name is Ha Jina. I was born in 1928 near Pyongyang, now in North Korea. My father was a farmer. He worked hard and was able to feed and clothe all five of his children. But when the Japanese arrived, they took more and more of his harvest, and by 1942, we were near starving. I was the oldest child at home, my brother having been conscripted into the Imperial Army, and I felt I had to do something. Even though I was only thirteen, I took a job in a fabric factory in Manchuria. But I was lied to. I was taken to an army station for sex slaves. They lined us up and treated us like cattle, stripping us, poking at our girl parts, opening our mouths to inspect our teeth. I was raped that first night by three men. There would have been more, but I was bleeding so much the soldiers told me I was disgusting. I was imprisoned there until November 1944. Then I was taken to Nagasaki and the Philippines.

"In 1945, after the Japanese lost the war, I thought I would be free. When the Americans took over Manila, they interviewed us, but they didn't believe our stories. They claimed we were prostitutes, and they used us, too. I escaped with the help of a Korean man who interpreted for the Americans. He married me, even though he knew of my past. But he was abusive, beating me whenever he was drunk. He was angry that I couldn't have children because my female parts were so scarred. There are still days that I cannot stand up properly because of the damage to my body.

"In 1960, my husband moved us to Vancouver, Canada, to join his brother. Of course, he fought with his family, so we moved from British Columbia to Québec to Prince Edward Island. I endured my husband's abuse for years, but when he allowed me to visit Korea, I left him. I could not return to my hometown, with the borders closed to North Korea. In Seoul, I worked whatever job I could beg for—washing dishes, collecting recycling, sweeping streets and parks.

"When I heard about the House of Remembrance in 1995, I came. This is a place where I can live without suffering anymore. I cannot change what happened to me, but I have a room here and three meals a day. It is hard for me to make friends, after all the isolation I have experienced, after being imprisoned in cubicles smaller than one meter by one and a half meters, but now I have the company of women who know what

I went through. Please allow me to continue living here. This is my testimony. Thank you for listening."

As the halmoni's testimony was being translated into English for the foreign listeners, Angelina cried, as quietly as she could. She hadn't earned the right to make a sound. If this halmoni hadn't wept telling her horrific story, then Angelina wouldn't either. When Keisuke placed a tissue on her lap, she grabbed it. The pressure of his palm against the cold flesh of her arm should have felt warm, but she experienced no solace.

One American journalist raised her hand and asked, "How did you feel when Kim Hak-soon came forward in 1991 with her story?"

The frail yet determined halmoni leaned forward. "I am proud of Kim Hak-soon. She broke a fifty-year silence that history and our own misplaced sense of shame imposed on us. She told her story without apology, without fear. 'We must record those things that were forced upon us,' she said. Her courage gave me the fortitude to tell my story, so my life will not be forgotten."

A different journalist asked, "What do you want from the Japanese government, after all these years?"

"It is never too late to acknowledge the wrong a nation has done, especially when it comes to human rights. What I endured was state-sanctioned rape and torture. I lived in filthy conditions, under guard, surrounded by barbed wire. The soldiers of the Imperial Japanese Army transported me from camp to camp, where the military set the rules, like the hours of operation, and when I served the sergeants versus the lieutenants. They claimed I was a prostitute and charged fees from the soldiers, although I never received a single coin. Instead, I was assigned debts for food, clothing, and toiletries, which I was never able to repay. I could have died on a Japanese warship being bombed by the Americans in the Pacific Ocean. Yet the government claims my abuse occurred at the hands of civilians. That is a denial of history. I want the Japanese government to formally apologize for what they did to me. I want them to acknowledge my pain, admit to their war crimes, and teach their citizens correct history. I was born a human, but I did not live a normal human life. I was shunned by society for many years and told I should be ashamed of myself. My youth cannot be restored. But my dignity can be. And then the war can finally end for me."

Another journalist asked, "Why do you want to be called halmoni? Why not 'comfort woman'?"

"We were girls. Some of us as young as ten. Most of us were teenagers. 'Comfort women'? How is that possible? And what comfort did they give us, we who were raped every day?" The thin halmoni stared into the middle distance, ignoring the murmurs from the crowd. "I want to be called '*Grandmother*.' It is what I would be called if I'd had children and grandchildren. I was robbed of both. But at my age, I deserve the title."

The same journalist raised her hand. "How did you survive all the brutality?"

"Every day I thought about killing myself. Every single day. But I wanted to see my mother again. I wanted to be held in her arms. I awoke from dreams crying out for her. I still do." The halmoni pressed her hand over her eyes. It was only now that she started to cry.

The room went still, except for the sound of the halmoni's keening. The other halmoni sat with her head bowed, crying too. Angelina squeezed her nose and absorbed the mucus, swallowed the tears. Feeling Keisuke's hand on her shoulder, the weight warm and steadying, she gulped in breath after breath.

The director stepped forward. "Are there any more questions for this halmoni before we get to the testimony of the second halmoni? Both grandmothers will be available for individual questions at the reception after this. There is no need to rush."

After some murmuring amongst the foreign journalists, an American man raised his hand. "Can your story be verified? By witnesses or official records?"

The hunched-over halmoni, her spine curved from poor nutrition in her past, struggled to sit up straight after hearing the translated question.

"Young man, you have my testimony and the testimonies of other victims. The girls I was in captivity with are almost all dead. Those who are still alive do not wish to be identified as ianfu, 'comfort women,' the term the Japanese saddled us with. As for the official records, the Japanese, like the Nazis, destroyed evidence and killed those who could bear witness. I hear the Japanese kept meticulous records, which may still exist, but that the Japanese government refuses to disclose them to the world." She glared at the journalist. "Germany has been held accountable for its crimes against humanity during World War II, and so should Japan. I am living evidence. But what will happen after I am gone? Why can't you Americans pressure Japan into admitting the truth, into doing the right thing? Is it because you cannot admit your own subjugation of Korean women during your occupation of our country?"

The director stepped toward the halmoni and whispered in her ear, a hand over the microphone to block her words.

The halmoni shook her head and reached for the microphone, pulling it closer. "We, the grandmothers, are dying. We are now old women who don't have many years left, and we are in danger of having our stories be forgotten. That cannot be allowed to happen. It would be deeply unjust. While the Japanese government continues to deny what it did to us, the world stands by. I am a human being. This is a human rights issue. I want justice. I deserve peace."

The director grabbed the microphone back and hastily announced a ten-minute break in the proceedings.

Angelina didn't return to the community room to hear the second halmoni's testimony. The emotional deluge of hearing the first halmoni's story had triggered a throbbing at Angelina's temples. Before a full-blown migraine took hold, she swallowed her medication, urgently seeking reprieve. She wandered around the nursing home but attracted no particular attention from the staff. It was comforting to know the angles of her face and the color of her skin didn't merit a second glance here—the anonymity of being Korean in Korea.

Angelina walked past the rooms of the different grandmothers and observed their lives. Some were sitting on their beds looking out the window, some dozing on chairs, some reading books. It was near lunchtime, and the smell of piquant kimchi, the ubiquitous side dish served with every Korean meal, and fatty fried pork made her stomach growl.

She followed the exit signs and climbed up a flight of stairs to a spare, white space. It looked like an art gallery, but the plaques were placed under amateur-looking sculptures and drawings. A painting caught her eye. A pile of bodies in hanbok, a circle of Japanese soldiers surrounding them, multiple rifles exploding fire. On the verge of hyperventilating, Angelina searched for a way out.

She felt like she staggered outside more than walked. Standing in sunshine, she willed her body to stop its clamoring and pounding. She looked up, focused on the shape of the leaves, thin and wispy, of the willow tree she was standing under. The humidity of July in Korea seeped through her linen dress and sweat rolled down her cheeks. Still, she stared up at the willow. That painting—what she'd seen was a group of girls herded into a forest, forced to dig their own graves by Japanese soldiers yelling in a language most of them wouldn't have understood. Then they were shot down, their bodies collapsing on top of one another. She could almost hear their screams. Maybe, if she kept staring at the willow, the images of those girls would recede. If she traced the lines of the leaf radiating into nothingness, then these images would also dissolve into oblivion. Instead, her knees buckled. She clutched at blades of grass and knotted roots.

Finally standing up, Angelina straightened her dress and combed her hair with her fingers. Ahead, stone steps led up a hill to a traditional hanok-shaped house. The path was shaded by pine trees. When she got closer, she saw she'd been mistaken. It was a temple. Hanji-papered wood lattice doors opened to a single, high-ceilinged space. A seated statue of Buddha smiled down at her, and fragrant incense drifted in the air. She took a cushion from a pile and sat on the cool floor. Light wood was everywhere—the walls, the ceiling, the floors. She wasn't a Buddhist, but she felt the urge to stand tall, fold her hands in prayer, then bow and prostrate herself.

On the floor, with her forehead pressed to the wood, she closed her eyes and exhaled. She remained in that position until it was too uncomfortable to bear. She sat up and searched Buddha's eyes. Surely there was a purpose. Surely these girls didn't suffer for nothing. No answers came. *Are there things in life that are unknowable?* Terrible, painful things outside of reason, outside of human comprehension. The stillness and the sound of birds outside conveyed an illusion of serenity, and Angelina tried to convince herself that she felt better. Until she saw the walls lined with portraits of women.

In English and in Korean, the lives of these women, once girls, were written in black and white. Their stories, all these women now dead.

Moon Myeong-Geum, born 1917, age 17, trafficked to Manchuria, China, for ten years.

Kim Oe-Han, born 1934, age 11, trafficked to Hokkaido, Japan.

Lee Yong-Nyeo, born 1926, age 16, trafficked to Taiwan, Singapore, and Myanmar for four years.

Yoo Hee-Nam, born 1929, age 14, trafficked to Shimonoseki and Osaka.

Park Ok-Ryeon, born 1919, age 21, trafficked to Rabaul, Papua New Guinea, for three years.

Kim Ok-Ju, born 1923, age 16, trafficked to Hainan Island for six years.

The photos and stories went on and on.

After each story Angelina read, she bowed to the picture of the woman, doing this until she could endure it no longer. A numbness overtook her body. Stepping out of the temple, she slid her sandals back on and walked away.

Keisuke looked up with a slight frown when she slipped back into her seat. She smiled, trying to reassure him, but she could see he wasn't convinced. Thankfully, he was distracted by the director announcing the end of the question period and the start of the reception. Keisuke jotted more notes in his book as they joined the long line to speak with the grandmothers.

"Did you hear the first halmoni's testimony about how she was in Nagasaki?"

"Yes. She barely escaped being obliterated by an atomic bomb."

He shook his head. "I mean the part where she overlapped with your aunt Sunyuh."

"What?"

"The halmoni was in Nagasaki at the same time. We know your aunt was there in 1944 before she was transported to Bangkok. We need to ask if she was taken to Bangkok with your aunt before being imprisoned again in the Philippines."

Angelina stared at the halmoni answering questions from the foreign journalists through an interpreter. *Did she know Aunt Sunyuh?*

The line moved slowly, and the wait suddenly felt excruciating. Angelina's hands were twisted and numb by the time they were within speaking distance of the elderly woman.

"Halmoni, my name is Keisuke Ono, and I am a journalist. Did you know a Kang Sunyuh in Nagasaki?" Keisuke asked in Korean.

The halmoni looked up at Keisuke, her eyebrows raised. "Ono? Young man, you're Japanese. How do you speak Korean so well? Why do you care about us grandmothers?"

"On behalf of the Japanese people, I offer my deepest and most sincere apology. My mother was Zainichi. I am learning Korean language at Konkuk University."

"Ah, good for you. Since you are a Japanese journalist, I hope you can illuminate our stories for your fellow countrymen. I hope you will write about the atrocities Japan needs to answer for." The halmoni paused, as though she'd been running and needed to take a breath. "Yes, I knew a Kang Sunyuh."

Angelina's head snapped up.

"Were you transported to Jakarta and then Bangkok with her in 1945?" Keisuke's excitement was palpable in his voice.

The halmoni shook her head. "I was taken to Manila."

"Did your path ever cross with Kang Sunyuh's again?" Keisuke's voice slowed down.

"I'm sorry, young man. I never saw Sunyuh again."

No! This can't be true.

Angelina stepped forward, unclenching her fists. "Halmoni, are you sure you did not see Kang Sunyuh again?"

The halmoni was still looking at Keisuke with curiosity and didn't turn to Angelina.

"Please, I am Kang Sunyuh's niece. If you remember anything about my aunt, please tell me." The desperation Angelina felt was physical, her throat constricted, mouth dry.

The halmoni looked at Angelina. "Who are you?"

"My name is also Sunyuh. My mother was Kang Sunyuh's sister, but I discovered my aunt's existence only a few weeks ago. She never reported herself, nor registered as a victim with the Truth Commission or the Korean Council. I am afraid she did not survive. Please, can you tell me anything about her?"

The halmoni was staring at Angelina, as if she'd seen a ghost.

"Please, Halmoni, please help me find my mother's sister."

The halmoni bowed her head, seeming to fight tears. "I can't," she whispered.

The interpreter, who'd merely been an observer and whose skills hadn't been needed, now regarded both Keisuke and Angelina with reproach. She reached down and squeezed the halmoni's shoulder. "Halmoni, I hope you are not distressed. Please, you should rest now."

Angelina fought the urge to kneel in front of the halmoni, to beg for any sliver of information about Aunt Sunyuh. It felt so unfair. She'd finally found someone who'd been in the same prison camp with her aunt and who remembered her, just to be thwarted again. But it would be unconscionable to press this elderly woman beyond her limits. History had been so unfair to her, and now it was trying to erase her.

Angelina didn't remember the reception or meeting the director or eating gimbap and japchae. She didn't remember what she and Keisuke talked about during that hour. The only thing she remembered was the interpreter calling for her just before the foreign visitors went back on the bus. The young woman said the halmoni had asked for her contact information.

Angelina wrote down not only her address and telephone number at Konkuk University, but her address and telephone number in Pittsburgh. And then she added Keisuke's. She let herself feel a glimmer of hope. Maybe the halmoni had been too shocked after meeting the relative of a long-ago girl she'd been imprisoned with to remember anything today. But maybe some small thing would surface with time.

A detail, a face.

Angelina

Seoul, Korea
July 29, 2006

Angelina and Keisuke sat at a pojangmacha, a *pop-up restaurant*, by the stream, drinking soju. The remnants of dinner—unfinished soondae, *blood sausages stuffed with rice*, along with warm odeng soup and spicy tteokbokki—littered the red plastic table between them. The humid day had turned into humid night. Angelina tilted precariously on her elbows, let her head fall forward.

"Whoa! Are you drunk?"

"No." She flopped back on her metal stool, just barely not tipping over. "But I'm on my way. Why do you care?"

Keisuke's lips slipped into an indulgent smile. "Take it easy on the soju, okay?"

"The man who's mastered the art of consuming half a bottle of bourbon is telling me to slow down?"

"Hypocritical of me, isn't it?" he said with ease. Normally, she admired this self-deprecating quality, but right now, she found it irritating.

"I can respect a man who admits when he's being a jackass," she said, her voice mocking, trying to pick a fight with him. But Keisuke wasn't cooperating. Shifting her gaze, Angelina stared at the water flowing by in Cheonggyecheon.

The gurgling of the cold, clear water mostly drowned out the honking cars above them. If she closed her eyes, she could pretend they were in the countryside having dinner by a river, reeds and rocks forming a picturesque background. But Cheonggyecheon overflowed with lights and the laughter of children, the admonishment of adults, families strolling by on the stone pavement surrounding the stream. Still, the air smelled of greenery. The water went on for miles, meandering through the heart of Seoul before emptying into the Han River.

"I can be an absolute idiot, no question," Keisuke said. "But I worry about you. Your alcohol tolerance is shit." He smiled, touching her hand, his fingertips caressing her palm.

She pulled away. "Please. Don't pretend you're concerned about me."

Keisuke frowned. "You don't believe me?"

"I'm tired of men telling me that they're worried about me when, in fact, they just want to *appear* like they care. Not actually care."

He leaned back slightly. "I'm not men."

"Fine. A man." She braced, as if she were about to crash a car.

"I'm not your ex-husband." Keisuke's voice was mild yet firm.

"Of course, you're not Thom. He's white and you're not. I'm not blind." Her voice was brittle. She loathed this feeling—like she could break apart at any moment and there was nothing she could do to stop it.

"This isn't about race," Keisuke said quietly.

"Sure it is. I married Thom so I wouldn't have to be Korean."

"Is that what really happened? Or were you running away from your family?" Keisuke was actually asking questions, not making assumptions, not accusing.

Angelina's shoulders fell, and it felt like the rest of her body would follow. "Being Asian in America sucks. My parents never adjusted to life as immigrants, always feeling not good enough, always striving but never being accepted, always seen as Other."

Keisuke looked at her with compassion, nodded his head, still saying nothing.

"Stupid of me, right?" Her voice splintered.

She pushed her head back, trying to avoid his gaze, and almost fell off her chair in the process. Keisuke held her steady while she regained her balance.

"Thom's stupid for not knowing what he had. It's not your fault, Angelina. You don't have to run away anymore."

She hated the compassion in his voice, hated how much she needed it. But she didn't want it right now. Shaking her head vigorously, as if that motion alone would push away his compassion, she said, "It's absolutely my fault for marrying a fucking selfish man."

"Thom wasn't a good-faith player, so the playing field wasn't level. Your nature is inherently good. Don't waste your time trying to understand Thom's bad one."

"Marrying him was an unforgivably stupid sin." She insisted on castigating herself, not addressing what he'd said about running away.

"I wish you would be kind to yourself."

Keisuke always seemed to know what to say whenever she was beating herself up for making stupid mistakes. His seeming ability to read her mind was scary. With Keisuke, she wasn't avoiding the emotional land mines she'd had to with Thom. But Keisuke evoked a different fear—that she'd be exposed as a fraud. She'd always had to live her life with such caution; she didn't know how to live with joy. His authenticity was unsettling; his kindness was terrifying.

She squeezed the shot glass of soju in her hand, willing it to shatter. A shard piercing her hand would feel less painful than the turmoil that was ricocheting inside her head. Throwing her head back, she tossed the cold liquid down her throat, most of it bouncing off her lips, sliding down her neck, dampening her crepe dress.

Angelina had chosen her best black dress for tonight's date with Keisuke, curling the ends of her hair into soft waves, actually bothering with makeup. They'd attended the Seoul National Theater's rendition of Thornton Wilder's *Our Town*, set in a small village in Korea and performed in Korean. She and Keisuke had argued good-naturedly about the actors' performances, about how a quintessentially American play had successfully and not successfully been adapted for a Korean audience.

Keisuke looked handsome in a natural-colored linen suit, a white linen shirt underneath his jacket. Angelina wanted to enjoy what she had decided would be their last night as lovers, but she was failing miserably. It felt like she was avoiding the confrontation to come, and yet here she was, trying to provoke him. She was a study in contradictions.

"I appreciate you helping me look for my aunt, but it was hopeless. My grandmother and my cousin were both right. I'm sorry I wasted your time, Keisuke." She kept her voice level, trying to restrain her despair.

"Our trip to the House of Remembrance was only a couple of days ago. We can keep looking for Aunt Sunyuh—she almost feels like my own aunt at this point," Keisuke said, still sounding optimistic.

Angelina shook her head, her movements emphatic. "What would be the point?" She swallowed hard. "After what your friend in Tokyo found out?" She didn't really want to talk about the devastating phone call they'd received yesterday.

Keisuke's journalist friend had cajoled his way into the Ministry of Defense, what had been known as the Defense Agency during World War II, and accessed their archives. But there was nothing. There were no primary documents recorded by the Japanese military about the names of the victims of sexual slavery, nothing that survived the mass burning by the Japanese as they prepared to surrender in August 1945. It was said that the mushroom cloud over Hiroshima was rivaled only by the dark smoke clouds over Tokyo from the reams of paper they set on fire. And any records that would have been kept at the thousands of individual "comfort stations" had been destroyed by the Imperial Japanese Army as they retreated across Asia.

"I don't want to accept it, but the historian we spoke to last week was right. We should have stopped looking then." Angelina's voice hardened with suppressed emotion.

She and Keisuke had met with a female scholar at the Truth Commission on Forced Mobilization under Japanese Imperialism who'd been doing research for years on "comfort women." She'd informed them that the victims, numbering in the hundreds of thousands, weren't considered important. That they weren't even considered human. They were just army supplies, listed amongst inanimate objects like "one hundred bayonets," "three hundred grenades," "fifty bags of salt." No names had been recorded. No markers of who they were, how tall they were or how much they weighed, or even where their families had lived for generations. Angelina had been horrified by this fact but had chosen to ignore it, convinced that there were documents undiscovered or most likely hidden somewhere because of what the special rapporteur for the UN Commission on Human Rights explicitly said in her report: "Not all official documents had been disclosed by the Government of Japan and might still exist in official archives of the Defence Agency and the Ministries of Justice, Labour, Social Welfare and Finance."

Even the Nazis had recorded the names of their victims. But these girls and young women had been erased.

"We haven't exhausted all our leads," Keisuke said, his voice measured.

She was furious with his naïveté. "Really? Unless she self-reported as a victim somewhere, you know it's impossible to find her. We got lucky when you found that clue about her being in Bangkok. She was such a good person that the other victims remembered her."

"Nothing is impossible."

"Well, I can't live in this fantasy world any longer. My aunt likely perished in Bangkok. Her body is in some unmarked grave. I'll never find her." Angelina tried to sound firm and resolute. *Because these are just facts*, she told herself.

Everything she and Keisuke had uncovered about Aunt Sunyuh being transported from Korea to Japan to Indonesia and Thailand now seemed meaningless. All those hours spent beseeching the various ministries of government in Korea and Japan and Southeast Asia, the countless calls

Keisuke had made to every contact who'd ever had anything to do with those ministries, the visits to the archives and museums and organizations that could possibly have any information about a Kang Sunyuh had been rendered inconsequential.

Angelina couldn't talk about how sad and angry she was that Aunt Sunyuh was dead, that there was no way to even find out where she had been buried. "I'm going back to the States next week."

Keisuke reached for her. "The language program doesn't end for another two weeks. Why?"

She dropped her hands onto her lap. "Given what happened at the last court hearing, I now have to find an affordable apartment in New York and register Alex and Emma for school, not to mention the logistical nightmare of packing and unpacking. I can't stay here anymore." She didn't say that in her conversation with her children last night, when she'd told them about their move, Alex had sighed and said "Okay" in a weary way that had nearly undone her. Emma had simply hung up.

"I'll come to New York once my position as assistant managing editor in Seattle is finalized. It shouldn't take more than a couple of weeks."

"Please don't." She felt like she was whimpering those words, like she was wounded by her desire to hold on to Keisuke when she knew she couldn't.

She searched inside her purse, pulling out a bookmark he'd given her. Keisuke had it specially made, using as a template a similar one he'd found at the National Museum of Korea's gift shop. Two butterflies, their wings adjoined, fluttered over plum blossoms and mugunghwa, *Korean hibiscus*. The petals were pink emeralds, the butterflies gold. Keisuke usually didn't spend so extravagantly.

She thrust it at him. "These jewels are too expensive."

"It's rude to return a gift." Keisuke's voice contained a barely restrained impatience now.

"I can't keep it."

"I had it made for you. It doesn't suit anyone else."

"I don't want it," Angelina said, avoiding Keisuke's gaze.

He stared at her. "Are you saying you don't like it?"

She placed the bejeweled bookmark on the table in front of Keisuke. "I can't accept it."

"I've given it to you as a token." He made no move to pick it up.

"You've created a burden for me. Please take it back." Angelina was trying not to plead with him.

The golden wings of the butterflies winked in the dark between them.

"No." Keisuke's eyes were unyielding. "Did I do something wrong?"

"This isn't anyone's fault."

"Then why are you breaking up with me?"

"We had a fling. And now it's time to move on." A false smile plastered on her face, a forced nonchalance in her voice.

He wasn't about to let her get away with it. "I love you," Keisuke said, voice quiet, gaze intense. "I want to marry you."

For a moment, Angelina allowed herself to feel a burst of joy. But it was a flash—there and then gone. Tamping the emotion down, she placed it in a compartment far away from her heart. Keisuke was too young, and she was too damaged. Nothing lasting was possible between them.

"Don't be ridiculous. I'm a divorced woman with two children. Think of the gossip." Her demeanor was calm, but chaos raged within, and she wondered if her voice was shaking.

"It only matters that we love each other," Keisuke said, his voice firm and insistent.

"You're wrong. Marriage is much more than that. And I've already failed at it. Marriage is an obligation. It ensnares you, tighter and tighter until you've given up everything you knew to be true. I thought if a man loved me, I owed it to him not to disappoint. I never thought he shouldn't disappoint *me*. How silly is that?" Harsh laughter erupted from her throat.

"You won't fall into an abyss if you give me a chance, Angelina. There's such beauty in the two of us together," he said, quietly.

"You don't mean that," she said immediately, voice raised.

She couldn't allow Keisuke to persuade her into another impossible dream. She would never survive the shattering. "We were lovers in good times. Fun times." She looked away, tone dismissive.

"I wouldn't call dealing with bureaucrats and hearing horrific stories of survival 'good times,' would you?" Keisuke kept staring at her. "I fell in love with you in difficult times. It was through hardship that I realized you are exactly the kind of person I want to spend my life with. Smart. Funny. Kind." Keisuke paused, then smiled. "Maddening."

"I didn't know you were such a romantic."

"Surprising, isn't it? I didn't know meeting the right person would change me." Keisuke looked happy, not confused.

"What about me is worth loving?" Even after everything he'd just said—after everything he'd shown her over and over again these last few weeks—she couldn't believe he truly loved her as she was, heartbroken and flawed. Because she thought she might love him—and in her eyes, he was perfect. She'd rather end things now than lose him, like she'd lost everyone else.

Keisuke took her hand in his, his grasp firm but gentle. "You make me happier than I deserve," he said. "It's the sudden warmth in my belly whenever I see you. It's the way you turn your head, the beautiful, unbroken line of your neck. It's the way you laugh. Your wicked sense of humor. And how sensitive and empathetic you are, despite how hard you try to hide it. You couldn't stop yourself from crying at the House of Remembrance."

Keisuke was saying exactly what she'd wanted to hear her whole life from someone she loved, but now, after everything, it just felt too late.

"Listen, if you want, you can say that our romance lasted for the duration of jangma, *monsoon season*. We were ensconced in a bubble, as if time had stopped. But now, we have to get back to reality. Use any cliché you like—'It wasn't meant to be'; 'I loved her, but she didn't love me'—any excuse, okay? But I have to go back to my real life." She hated saying these words, didn't want them to be true. What she wanted was for Keisuke to pull her close and tell her everything was going to be okay.

"Please, don't," Keisuke whispered. His resolve was starting to crumble—she could see it in his face, in the slight hunch of his shoulders.

She didn't want to be cruel, but she felt like she had no other option. "Are you ready to be a father? You've never married. My kids are thirteen and ten. We'd be a ready-made family. I'm *forty*. I have no intention of having more children. But you? You're only thirty-three. You still have love and marriage and babies ahead of you. Babies who will become toddlers and then kindergarteners and eventually high schoolers. My daughter starts high school in the fall. Go live your life, okay?"

Keisuke's lips pressed into a thin line, but his grip on her hand tightened. "I don't know if I'm ready to be a father."

She pulled out of his grasp. "You see? Thom wasn't ready either, and look where that landed me."

"What's so wrong about not knowing whether I want to be a father? Can't you give me more time? Do you need an answer right now?"

"Yes! Kids can't wait for you. They're not something you put on a shelf and deal with when you feel like it, when you think you've figured things out. You're so naïve. Please go back to your nice, tidy life, and don't contact me anymore." Abruptly, she stood up.

"Please, don't leave. I'm begging you."

She gazed at Cheonggyecheon. "I've already left."

"How am I supposed to let you go?" Keisuke's voice broke. *"You pierce my soul."*

She looked back at him, shocked at the familiar words. That line from *Persuasion* was Angelina's favorite. She'd told him once, pillow to pillow, that it was the most romantic sentence in all of English literature.

"Please, stop."

She'd never seen him cry before.

"Please, stop," Angelina whispered again, hating herself for hurting him. She sat down, reached for her soju glass, and tossed it back, poured herself another shot, then gulped that down, too.

He looked at her with eyes rimmed red. "I love you. I won't let you push me away."

"Please, let's not argue." She was trying to maintain some dignity. "I don't want things to become ugly."

"What's wrong with arguing? It's how we communicate what upsets us, how angry we are."

"I am angry! Are you satisfied?" Angelina barely restrained herself from shouting.

"When you express your suffering, you're being honest. You're being true to yourself and sharing it with me." He said these things without any irony.

"What? Thom hated it when we argued. He said I was being vulgar."

"There's nothing vulgar about honesty. What's vulgar is pretending. I know you're falling in love with me. I can see it," Keisuke said, his voice urgent.

Angelina had always thought it was the epitome of good manners to hide her feelings. To be stoic. She'd always thought she was sparing other people unnecessary drama by not saying what she truly felt. What she'd always thought of as sacrifice and duty, Keisuke believed was the exact opposite. She hadn't spared anyone, had she, least of all herself. What she'd done was subterfuge, pretense, what she'd always claimed she hated so much. It would have been comical, this realization, had it not been so sad. She'd repressed herself for years, for nothing, just as her mother had subjugated her own feelings, had no patience for what she called "weakness." Angelina had followed her mother's lead without any thought as to whether that behavior would serve her, whether that behavior suited her.

How stupid.

"You don't have to be afraid. I'll take on the world with you." Keisuke leaned across the table toward her, his eyes beseeching. "Love isn't something people can take away from you. Love is something that is given to you. And I choose to love you."

She did what she did best—she deflected. "I've tried and failed at marriage."

"We all fail at something in our lives. Whether it's marriage or love or career. The only real failure is not trying. I think we should measure our success in how we deal with disappointment. How we choose to go on." Keisuke extended his hand to her, his palm pale and open. "Please choose us. I won't hurt you."

"Stop saying that! I can't stand it!" Angelina screamed, not caring that everyone was now looking at her.

Leaping from her seat, she crashed into the table, knocking one of the soju bottles into the air. The small green bottle shattered on the paved walkway of Cheonggyecheon. She stretched out her hand, as if she could still catch it. Instead, the sudden lurch landed her on her knees, a piece of glass slicing her palm. She squeezed her hand shut, but blood dripped onto her dress.

Keisuke reached for her. "You're hurt. Let me help."

She hid her hand behind her back. "I'm fine. I'm going to find a pharmacy. Please clean this up for me—I'm so embarrassed. Can you apologize to the ajumma for me?"

And then she ran. She shut off the ringer of her cell phone and, later, the ringer of the phone in her dorm room. She willfully ignored his attempts at conversation in her last few classes, her behavior so rude he started turning his head away whenever he saw her. But the scent of soju mixed with river and reeds lingered in her nostrils long after that night, as though the perfume of another heartache had been imprinted in her brain.

Angelina

SEOUL, KOREA
AUGUST 3, 2006

Angelina stared at the open pages of her Korean workbook, reading and rereading the same question. Only one more day of class before she got on a plane back to Pittsburgh, back to reality. One more day of pretending she was still a student, not a mother with two children unhappy to be moving away from yet another school, another group of friends. One more day she wasn't a divorced woman with a broken heart. It was all so ironic—she'd run away from her life in America to Korea, only to find herself running away from Korea back to America.

She always thought she was leaving her problems behind when she made drastic life changes, but the truth was that even in a new country, she couldn't leave herself behind. This truth was now smacking Angelina in the face. This would be the last time—if she couldn't escape herself, then she'd better start facing her problems head-on, starting now, and become stronger, more resolute.

"Angel-ah, you must take a step. Begin with one step."

Startled by the sound of her mother's voice, Angelina looked around her dorm room. There was no one else. She was hearing things. *Christ, despair has conjured my dead mother.*

When Thom had filed for divorce, Angelina had absolutely dreaded telling her mother. She didn't think her mother would understand because she was from a generation of women who didn't believe in divorce, even though she herself had filed for divorce just weeks before she died. But her mother had surprised her by saying, "Thom is ssiraegi-nom. *A trash person.* You did well to get away from him."

Angelina had forgotten her harsh yet comforting words. Until now.

She wanted to believe that redemption was possible, even within reach. If she unchained her heart, could she make better choices? Not weighed down by guilt or resentment or expectations? Angelina saw herself as a woman ruled by logic, not passion. She'd taken pride in that assessment, but maybe she was wrong. *Again.* Maybe her mother's suicide had nothing to do with Angelina. Maybe she didn't need to punish herself, as Keisuke had said.

Gripping the pencil in her hand, she bent her head back over her workbook. Homework evoked the comfort of a routine, soothing in its dullness. She could lose herself in the conjugations of verbs—the past tense, the present tense, the future. Today's assignment encompassed several chapters, but it was the conjugation of seemingly opposite verbs that caught her attention: *to laugh*; *to cry*. There was only one consonant difference between these two actions in Korean—woot-dah, wool-dah—and the pronunciations were almost identical.

She wanted to laugh whenever she thought of Keisuke's outrageous answers to their teacher's questions. *What are you doing while crossing the river in a boat?* the teacher would ask in Korean. *I'm holding a loaf of bread*, he'd answer, while their classmates erupted in guffaws. Now she wanted to cry while thinking about the same situation. Maybe they weren't so opposite after all.

The sudden shrill ringing of the phone made Angelina jump. It was the young man at the downstairs reception desk. "Miss Lee, may I transfer a call to your room?"

"Who is it?" She was afraid it was Keisuke, and she didn't want to speak to him.

"The woman omitted her name. But she is Korean."

Then it couldn't be Una, her cousin. And Angelina suspected that her formidable grandmother would have announced their relationship if demanding to speak with her. As she waited for the phone to ring again, her hand on the handset, she couldn't think of a single other person who might be calling her.

"Hello," she said in Korean, her voice tentative.

"Are you Yi Sunyuh?" a gravelly female voice asked.

"That is my Korean name."

"You're the young woman who came to House of Remembrance to listen to us, to hear our testimonies?"

"Mrs. Ha?" Angelina slipped into English for a moment before reverting back to Korean, "Halmoni?"

"Are you the niece of Kang Sunyuh?"

"Yes, Halmoni."

"There is something I need to tell you. My time on this earth is short, and I don't want any regrets on my deathbed."

She dreaded what this halmoni had to say to her. Anything to do with deathbeds she wanted to avoid, but the woman deserved to be heard. "What can I do for you?"

"I know where your aunt is living. Do you have a pen? I will give you her address and telephone number."

Angelina froze. Then she clutched at her neck and swallowed hard, certain she was hearing things. She'd been so sure Aunt Sunyuh was dead. Like her mother. "I'm sorry, what did you say?"

"Your aunt was my friend when we were both held captive in Nagasaki, but we got separated. Ten years ago, when I could still get around by myself, I saw her by chance in Jeju-do. I was so happy. I thought she had died. Ara and Miyun were both murdered in the camps. Suki, for all her bravado, became addicted to opium and never made it. For years, I tried to convince Sunyuh to live at the House of Remembrance with me, with the other grandmothers. But she said she couldn't leave her husband behind. He is buried on Jeju-do."

Angelina swallowed hard again. "Are you sure my aunt is alive? We—I thought she was dead."

She wondered if the woman was confusing her aunt with one of the other girls she had been imprisoned with. The extent of Mrs. Ha's sorrow was unimaginable to Angelina, as much as she tried to empathize with what the halmoni had endured as a girl. A world without parents, without family, without joy. That kind of grief would drive anyone mad.

"Sunyuh changed her name to that of our friend, Noh Ara."

"Excuse me?" Angelina lapsed into English again, feeling so shocked she almost fell out of her chair. *Oh my god.* Aunt Sunyuh had assumed someone else's identity.

"Your aunt is now Noh Ara. The Japanese never gave Ara a burial, and Sunyuh said it was insult after injury, after everything they did to Ara, after everything they did to us. When Bangkok was bombed by the Americans and fire destroyed the camp, your aunt was outside hanging laundry. She said she turned her back on that prison and kept going until she reached Korea. The man who became her husband rescued her in Yeosu and took her to Jeju-do."

"I don't understand." Angelina kept reverting back to English.

"I am sorry I lied to you. But it was not my secret to reveal. Call Sunyuh. I hope she will see you. I think it will be good for her, and for you, too, young woman. We all need our families."

Angelina's hand clutched the handset of the phone long after the halmoni hung up. She was afraid if she let go, then she would wake up, and this would all have been a dream. She couldn't believe Aunt Sunyuh was alive, that she was on Jeju Island, only an hour by plane from Seoul. To think Angelina had been in Jeju-do just a few weeks ago, although that time with Lars now seemed like another lifetime. It was possible Angelina had passed Aunt Sunyuh on a street, had sat at the same restaurant, had walked along the same sea. Angelina stayed still for a long time, her palms glued together, fingers pressed to her lips. She wasn't praying, but the mantra repeating in her head might as well have been one: *Please be alive. Please be alive. Please be alive.*

Angelina drew a long breath, held it, and then exhaled before dialing.

Angelina

Jeju Island, Korea
August 5, 2006

Angelina walked along the designated Olle Trail in Seongsan-ilchulbong, the crisp scent of the sea soothing. This part of the coastal path circumnavigating Jeju Island had striking views of the South Sea, and she tried to appreciate the beauty of what she was seeing, but she was too nervous, too distracted. She was meeting Emo, *mother's sister*. Feeling anxious but hopeful, she turned inland and ventured up a winding, narrow path to a hanok sitting at the top of a hill. The traditional wooden structure was simple yet elegant. The dark clay tiles on the roof transformed to a charcoal-blue hue against the setting sun. There were no shoes at the base of the two steps leading to the wide pine platform upon which the rest of the house sat. Her heart tripped at the thought that Aunt Sunyuh must have changed her mind—she wasn't home.

Angelina's disappointment was crushing. But then she straightened her neck, stood tall.

If she's not ready, then I'll keep trying. Angelina was through with giving up.

Suddenly a voice rang out in Korean. "Sunyuh-yah? Is that you?"

She whipped her head around. For a moment, she thought she was looking into a foggy mirror, her features a little askew. The woman's face was wrinkled and weathered, but it was unmistakably Angelina's face. For a girl of her generation, her aunt was very tall.

"Emo-nim," Angelina said, voice catching. "I am so happy to meet you. Finally." It seemed appropriate that she ended with *Finally*. The word in Korean sounded momentous, as if it was marking an occasion.

Tears filled her eyes, spilling over. She had been afraid her aunt didn't want to be found, would be reticent and guarded, and Angelina had so many questions about her mother. What teacher did she love as a young girl? Was there a boy she'd ever had a crush on? What made her laugh when she was little? Angelina yearned to know who her mother had been, what seed of sorrow had been planted when she was a girl that had manifested into someone who would take her own life as an adult. Angelina's need rose like a tide in her chest, threatening to drown her in its ever-growing pull.

"You don't look like your mother," her aunt said, seemingly mystified, stepping closer to Angelina.

"I see now that I look like you. Thank you for seeing me."

Aunt Sunyuh took Angelina's hand and squeezed. "I am sorry Gongju is no longer with us. I was heartbroken to hear of such news. When I was in Gwangju many years ago, I'd heard she'd married an aristocrat. She used to say she wouldn't marry anyone except her true love. I was certain she'd be happy. I never went back to make sure, though." Emo's slender shoulders sank.

Angelina clasped her own hands, didn't know if she should touch her aunt because Koreans of her aunt's generation didn't readily hug— maintaining personal space was a form of politeness. And Angelina didn't know if she should tell the truth. If she should reveal the details of her mother's melancholy, the secrets she'd kept meticulously hidden. Instead, Angelina chose ambiguity. "I do not think my mother was ever happy."

Emo half-smiled. "Gongju was such a sensitive soul. So easily hurt, but always pretending she was strong."

"Was that really what she was like?" Angelina marveled.

Emo looked at her with a strange expression. Angelina wondered if her words came as a shock to her aunt. Perhaps her aunt assumed she knew her own mother well, knew about her mother's vulnerabilities.

"Come. Let's go inside and talk." Emo deftly removed her shoes and stepped up to the entrance of her home. She slid open the hanji-papered wood-lattice doors and gestured for Angelina to follow. "I'll make tea from Hallasan. Mountain tea is the best. Why don't you wait in the main room?"

Angelina stood in awe of all the light warm wood—the floors, the doors, the frames, the ceiling. Her gaze skimmed her aunt's furnishings—the scrolls with calligraphy, the pictures in frames, a pair of wooden ducks tied together with silk cloth. She knelt on an embroidered yellow silk cushion placed by the side of a low plank table. Running her fingertips over the smooth surface, she wondered how old the tree must have been from the many whorls radiating out from the center.

Emo came back carrying a black lacquered tray with white ceramic tea accoutrements, popularized during the Joseon dynasty. She flipped over an hourglass timer. "The tea must steep for one minute, then be poured through. If it sits in water, it will taste bitter. Good green tea is consumed three times from at least three infusions. The first for the scent of the tea, the second for taste, the third for the depth or feel."

Angelina had never been told or shown the ritual around green tea, but she'd loved Korean green tea the first time she'd had it at a teahouse in Insadong. Sitting in her aunt's traditional hanok, waiting for the tea to steep, she actually felt Korean. She finally felt like she belonged.

"What do you want to know about your mother?"

"Everything."

Emo smiled. "My little sister was funny and bright. So passionate. I'm afraid our mother was not a kind woman, and my little sister suffered. But my father and I tried to keep her spirit pure and free." Emo's voice, which had been filled with lightness, became somber. "I mustered the courage to go back to my hometown only once. I wanted to see my sister, how she had grown into adulthood. But she was gone by then, already married."

"She married my father when she was only twenty-two. She used to say it was the single biggest mistake of her life," Angelina said.

Emo shook her head. "I had no idea your mother had been unhappy. She had a crush on my fiancé when she was a little girl. Gongju was so feisty and smart, even at six. So full of vitality. I thought she would have married someone like Joonsuk, someone handsome and kind."

"My father was handsome." Angelina hesitated before finishing what she started. "Too handsome. He cheated on her early in their marriage, and with countless others. He broke her heart."

Understanding slowly filtered across Emo's face. "Poor Gongju. His betrayal must have shattered her, and she would have kept it all inside. She probably seemed angry—she hated looking weak, hated anyone's pity. Gongju could be so self-destructive, so stubborn."

Angelina wanted to cry. *Oh, dear god.*

Her aunt was right. Her mother had seemed enraged most of Angelina's life. She'd thought her mother had felt cheated by her father, cheated by a life gone awry with only daughters and no sons, cheated by an America unwilling to accept a woman from a non-Western country. The truth was her mother had been absorbing her sorrow so endlessly, so habitually, that Angelina hadn't known that was what she was doing.

Emo handed her a delicate white cup filled with green tea.

Angelina inhaled the clean, grassy scent before taking a sip. "I heard from Uncle Haneul's daughter, Una, that you and my mother were close. Is that true?"

"Our mother was autocratic. She was like an empress, always issuing commands, and Gongju railed against the confines of her rule. I like to think I was a loving older sister, someone Gongju could be herself with. There was no need for competition between us. I wanted only to bring her comfort."

"The two of you were unusual siblings. It sounds like you were her surrogate mother, someone who gave her unconditional love. Her parents failed her; my father failed her; I failed her." Shards of sorrow rattled in Angelina's chest.

"In what way?" Emo asked.

Angelina's grief felt physical, like a rope tightening around her chest. "I couldn't see my own mother folding into herself. She lost her grip on reality and cut off contact with the outside world."

"What Gongju did had nothing to do with you. Her actions are not a reflection of you or your duty as a daughter. Gongju was in pain and must have felt that she couldn't endure any more. I understand that. I've been desperate and lonely many times. I only wish I could have been there for her," Emo said, her voice quiet and calm.

Angelina flinched. To think of the bleakness her mother must have felt—the guilt was all-consuming. "Maybe I don't deserve happiness."

Emo grasped Angelina's hand, pressing it between hers. "Do you think if you promise to be unhappy the rest of your life, that serves as atonement? Do you think your mother is somewhere in the afterlife resenting you? A parent always wants their child to be happy. Your mother doesn't want you to live in guilt. She wants you to have love and joy in your life."

Angelina's heart wrenched. "Do you really think so?"

Emo looked at Angelina, as though she was behaving like a child without sense. "Gongju had a generous heart. Perhaps she was unable to show it in the years after I knew her. Child, your mother didn't hate you. She loved you. Forgive yourself for whatever sin you think you committed. That's what Gongju would have wanted, even as she left this world behind."

The truth of her aunt's words landed in her chest and exploded. She suddenly felt absolved, and by a woman she'd never met until today. But she felt like this woman knew her, felt a kinship with her that she had never felt with her own mother.

Emo continued to hold Angelina's hand. "Angel-ah, would it help if

I forgave you? Because I do. Please, free yourself from this burden. You owe it to your mother to live well. The ones remaining owe the ones who are gone to live happily, to at least exert the effort to do so."

Guilt was pernicious and corrosive and so hard to let go of. But in this moment, on this island, staring into the eyes of a woman who looked so much like her, Angelina knew it was time. Her shoulders sagged from the release. She was ready to say goodbye, to wish her mother well in her next life.

I can forgive myself.

Angelina finally allowed the tears to fall. She smiled tentatively at her aunt.

Emo smiled back. "Forgiveness is imperative to move on with one's life. I should know."

"How can you forgive? After everything the Japanese did to you?" Angelina couldn't stop herself from asking, still unable to comprehend the horror of what had happened.

"In life, you must put one foot in front of the other and keep walking. Many times, I thought it might be better to die than to live, but the instinct to keep living is strong. Stronger than I ever imagined possible." Emo took long, thoughtful sips of her tea.

"How did you do it? How did you go on living?" Angelina asked. Disbelief and wonder chased each other around and around in her head. She'd faced so much heartache and pain in her own life, yet her aunt had survived atrocities no human being should ever have to bear. If it had taken Angelina this long to let go of her suffering, how could Aunt Sunyuh?

Emo put down her teacup and folded her hands. "You do one thing at a time. You get up in the morning and have breakfast even if you're not hungry. You go to work. You eat lunch. You come home. You have dinner. Sometimes, a whole day goes by when you don't think about all the girls who were killed in front of you. Sometimes, you don't wake up in the middle of the night from a nightmare that you're still trapped in a tiny room, being beaten and violated. Sometimes, you forget the smell and taste of your own blood. Each day you summon the will to keep living. Until it becomes a habit. Then you realize that you laughed at someone's joke or smiled when you saw a peony. You know your friends are dead, but you don't feel so guilty that you're alive. It happens slowly until smiling doesn't make you want to cry. Until you allow yourself to experience joy. Just a little."

"I cannot imagine how hard it must have been for you. Thank you for surviving."

Angelina hadn't necessarily expected a broken woman, but if she was being honest, she thought Emo would be tortured by the past, unable to move on. Like so many of the survivors she'd read about and seen and met. Angelina had thought she would be the one consoling her aunt, but instead, the opposite was true. She marveled at how resilient Emo was, how practical, how compassionate, and she was ashamed of herself. Nothing in her life had come close to the terrible and brutal things Emo had survived, and yet her aunt had stayed kind. Aunt Sunyuh had endured, refused to stay broken, refused to give up her humanity, while Angelina had let herself fall into destructive patterns, continued to run away when things became too difficult, and resigned herself to a future without nearly as much hope. She felt the warmth of the tea seep through the cup she was holding in her hands. She focused on the sensation briefly, centering herself, and then settled in to hear Aunt Sunyuh's story.

Sunyuh

Jeju Island, Korea
August 6, 2006

A light wind ruffled her pale pink blouse, the cool nylon fabric fluttering against Sunyuh's arms. After a leisurely lunch of hwe, almost paper-thin slices of assorted *raw fish*, and succulent grilled abalone, she and Angelina were walking on a stretch of beach in Seopjikoji. Surrounded by sand and water, Sunyuh couldn't help but remember a fateful time on a beach in Nagasaki, Japan. How young she was. How determined to see her family, her fiancé.

She gazed at Seongsan-ilchulbong in the distance, rising above the sea, a hulking cone of volcanic rock and lush green. A piece of peninsula jutting out like a thumb. Her home for over fifty years without Yoon. The image of his face, impassive yet gentle, flooded her with longing. How she wished she could have done everything differently. If only Yoon were still alive.

After all her niece had confided about her ex-husband and the intriguing new man in her life, Sunyuh felt compelled to ask her more.

Angelina stopped walking, turned to stare at the sea. "His name is Keisuke. And as much as I care for him, I do not know if it is love."

Sunyuh could tell from the look on her niece's face this man was important in a way she didn't want to admit. "Why don't you tell him how you feel? A woman should be able to express her love and desire, as much as a man." Sunyuh had spent most of her life listening to nonsense about how a woman should behave—silent, obedient, forbearing. It hadn't served her well. Those rules had lost her Yoon. She was determined not to have history repeat itself with her niece.

"You do not think a woman should wait quietly and let a man decide her fate?" Angelina raised her eyebrows, as if she were surprised.

"Life is long. But it's still too short to live with regret. Find the right man for you and hold on to him."

Angelina laughed, seemingly delighted. "Emo, I did not know you were such a modern woman."

Sunyuh twined her arm through Angelina's, pulling her closer. "Why bother living if you're never going to grow and change? I'm not going to judge you. I want to help." As they resumed walking, she waited for Angelina to say whatever she wanted to say.

"I am older than Keisuke, with two children. And I have a horrible history of picking the wrong men."

Sunyuh had seen a change in Angelina since she'd first walked through her door—a lightness she hadn't expected. But now her voice seemed weighted with doubt.

"Why can't this young man be the right man for you? Stop torturing yourself with the mistakes you've made. You were living with the wrong person, living the wrong kind of life. Let that go. Surround yourself with the people who love you and let those who don't matter fall away."

"I am afraid to trust Keisuke. That if I allow myself to love him, I will lose him. It has been the story of my life." Angelina's voice was thin, reedy, as though she were trying to convince herself of what she was saying, yet afraid she might be right.

"Keisuke is not your ex-husband."

Angelina rubbed her fingers against her forehead, frowning. "That is exactly what he said."

Hating how tortured her niece looked, Sunyuh clasped Angelina's hand. "You can choose to believe him. You're not the same person who made the decision to marry the wrong man once. You're a different person now and you can make better choices. Don't be foolish. Don't tell yourself a story that is no longer true. I lost Yoon that way. I don't want that for you." Sunyuh didn't confide in her niece that sometimes, when the sorrow of Yoon's loss was too much to bear, she imagined a parallel universe, one where Yoon was still on his boat, his hands large and graceful steering the wheel, his feet planted wide, his face content.

Angelina leaned in, pressing Sunyuh's hands between hers. "Can you tell me more about your husband?"

Warmth radiated from her niece's palms. Sunyuh felt less alone than she had in years. She was grateful that Gongju's daughter had found her. A light breeze played with her niece's long hair, so similar in texture to Sunyuh's when she was young. But gazing at her niece, the curve of her cheek, Sunyuh was also reminded of her little sister. Gongju would've wanted Sunyuh to help Angelina. To live fully, to let go of the past, to experience love in all its joy.

Interlocking their fingers, Sunyuh resumed walking into the wind. "It is the lies we tell ourselves that are the most dangerous. This story we have in our heads about who we think we are sometimes tricks us into living miserably, since we can never measure up to that ideal." Sunyuh gazed at the shoreline, the waves gently lapping onto fine sand. "When I was sixteen, I believed certain things about myself—that I was a good daughter, a good sister, a good girl. I thought Joonsuk-oppa, my fiancé, and I were perfect together when there's no such thing as perfect. I thought our love would weather us through any obstacle. But after I was ruined by the Japanese, I wanted to die. I continued to breathe and eat and sleep, but I abandoned the world of the living. Even after I met Yoon. But do you know what I've learned, after all these years? It's when you think your life is over that it can truly begin again."

"Miss, I can help you. I will take you to Jeju-do."

On a frantic and cacophonous pier in Yeosu in September 1945, amidst the wake of the Japanese defeat and the chaos of the Americans taking over Korea, imposing their rule under the guise of democracy, Sunyuh turned to face a young man. Clenching her fists, she tried to erase the disgust from her expression. Countless times she'd heard this offer from men on her journey from Bangkok, but help wasn't generally what they were offering. She'd navigated the long and treacherous path back to the country of her birth, her home, paying with money bartered from Ara's jade ring and her own jewels, but that hadn't always been enough. After everything that had happened, all that she had endured—she couldn't go back to Gwangju, so she decided to go to Jeju-do, as she and Ara had originally planned.

She took a deep inhale of the briny scent of the sea. "And what do you want in exchange for my passage?"

Nothing was what Yoon had said. His broad shoulders had been steady, his tanned face wide and open as he told her that he'd overheard her plea to the other boat captains, and that he wanted to help her.

She'd been suspicious the entire voyage from Yeosu to Dodu-dong, a harbor on the north side of Jeju-do, even as she witnessed him offer space on his boat to a haggard family of five, an elderly man searching for his daughter, and two orphans who had just reached puberty. Over fifteen hours at sea, and he'd only ever treated her with kindness, sharing his food. Seasoned rice balls with flecks of smoked pork had never tasted so good. When Yoon had asked for her name, Sunyuh instinctively told him her real one, hastily modifying that *Angel* was a nickname given to her by her father. She didn't really know him, but it felt wrong to deceive Yoon, like something in her knew she could trust him. She went on to say that her legal name was Noh Ara, and Yoon had just nodded, didn't seem to notice her voice wavering. Once they arrived in Jeju-do, he found her shelter at his female cousin's house. Still, he asked for nothing.

When she asked him once why he made those long, dangerous trips, battling capricious currents and the ever-changing weather back and forth to Yeosu—not to mention evading Japanese and then American patrols, which, fearing the transport of enemy combatants, aggressively restricted the movement of Korean fishing vessels—he said he felt he had to contribute. He was a cripple, he said, with a useless leg. The resistance fighters had never recruited him for that reason. But he was a fisherman with a boat who could ferry refugees where they wanted to go. He could help. He did it again when the Korean War broke out on the peninsula in 1950. In the three years before the armistice was reached between the North and South, she often waited for him in the harbor, almost hoping to see her family fleeing to the very place she was, knowing they'd probably not recognize the woman she'd become. She'd even invented a whole story to tell her mother and father about how she ended up on Jeju-do. They never came.

Sunyuh should have known Yoon was a man worth loving. But her seventeen-year-old self was so full of sadness, and she couldn't recognize him for what he was, for *who* he was.

For weeks into their acquaintance, she'd either shake her head or nod it once to answer most questions, limiting her words to only those that were absolutely necessary. But Yoon had coaxed her out, engineering their conversations little by little until, before she realized it, she was speaking in full sentences. When he proposed marriage the day after her eighteenth birthday, she'd refused. Yoon asked if it was because he was ten years older, if she was in love with another man. She told him she was no longer capable of love. Not like that. Patiently, he'd waited. It made her breath catch now, how long Yoon had waited. And still, she couldn't give him what he needed: a loving wife. He'd married her to stop the whispers about her past. She'd objected, of course, wanted to believe she could fend for herself. But he'd insisted, worn her down. He'd been stubborn like that.

He never touched her. All those years they slept in the same room, on separate sleeping mattresses. He'd wanted to protect her, in case his mother dropped by unexpectedly, so they shared a room. Yoon didn't want his mother berating Sunyuh, blaming her for the absence of children. More than his mother already did, anyway. Yoon's mother was a haenyeo, a free diver who could hold her breath underwater for five minutes, swim down a hundred feet in the sea to harvest sea urchin and abalone. She was a force to be reckoned with, a woman who spoke her mind.

When Yoon first announced he was going to marry Sunyuh, his mother had tried to get her thrown off the island because she was an outsider, a Jeju nonnative who inspired only rumors from their neighbors. She went so far as to painstakingly alienate her from everyone in the village of Seongsan-ilchulbong, made sure everyone shunned her sea snails and clams at the market. A bounty she'd spent an entire day harvesting. But Yoon wouldn't let his mother bully her. He'd take her harvest and sell it with his catch for the day. She suspected he gave her more money than her work was worth.

Yoon's mother was a community elder, a leader of the village haenyeo, and she wasn't accustomed to opposition from her usually gentle son. Yoon's mother confronted him in public about Sunyuh, commanded him to stop protecting a *parasite*. She said she forbade him from marrying her. But Yoon didn't flinch, didn't shout. He simply said he would marry Sunyuh with or without his mother's permission, then walked away. She remembered the clenching of her heart as she watched his broad back, his head held high, his limping body receding from his mother.

They married on May 20, 1947, only days after her nineteenth birthday. For a spring day on Jeju-do, the wind wasn't fierce, and a riot of flowers were in bloom. A beautiful sunny day. Like that day, years before, when kites of red, green, and yellow flew across the sky in Gwangju, and she'd been young and in love. Yoon's mother came to the wedding grudgingly, but she'd kept quiet, thankfully, and didn't try to ruin anything. She knew Yoon must have said something to his mother, but she never asked him what.

As prickly as Yoon's mother had been, after the wedding, she seemed to accept Sunyuh into her family. She foisted Sunyuh's daily harvest upon the villagers, insisting they buy her daughter-in-law's wares above the other women's. She even prodded her to become haenyeo, harassing, cajoling. "Why do you want to waste your life digging in the mud for food when you can easily pluck it out of the ocean?"

Despite Sunyuh's insistence that she was afraid of the sea, of the dark, Yoon's mother was relentless: "You need to overcome such fear." And when harassment didn't work, she resorted to making Sunyuh an offer. An offer Sunyuh could not afford to turn down: "I will forgive your lack of love for my son. I will never again ask Yoon to leave you."

Sunyuh didn't care if Yoon's mother forgave her, really—forgiveness was beyond what she deserved, but she didn't want Yoon to suffer any longer. As stoic as he appeared, he cared deeply about what his mother said, and her insistence that he leave Sunyuh was surely wearing on him. He rarely defied his mother, and Sunyuh knew the cost it was extracting, how hurt he was by his mother's disapproval, her stubborn belief that he should find someone who could give him children. But abandoning Sunyuh was something Yoon would never do, even though he performed his filial duty and listened to his mother's rants without saying a word. Yoon possessed unwavering loyalty.

She sometimes thought Yoon loved her more than he loved himself.

Six months after she married Yoon, Sunyuh went into the sea for the first time. She'd been so afraid her body had started violently shaking before she'd even entered water. The haenyeo had gathered around an open fire behind a stone wall, protecting themselves from the famous wind of Jeju-do. There was a hierarchy in which the older women were, of course, shown the respect they deserved, but there was an ease in that circle Sunyuh hadn't experienced before on the island. The women laughed and joked and cried and teased. They talked about the wind and the tides and the dangerous places to avoid when diving and where the biggest red sea cucumber could be found. But they also talked about a wayward son, a cheating husband, a difficult sister-in-law, the chore of cooking dinner every night. They helped each other change into diving costumes, cotton covering their chest, abdomen, and hips, a single strap looped over the shoulder holding everything in place, their arms and legs bare. Yoon's mother gifted her a pink one, knowing it was her favorite color.

She met Binna that first day in the circle. They sat next to each other serendipitously, not knowing they would become lifelong friends. Binna, a bubbly, irrepressible spirit who couldn't seem to stop talking, and Sunyuh, wary and practically mute. But Binna wouldn't give up on her. Never let Sunyuh's unblinking stare stop her constant chatter. They were the same age, so they spoke in banmal, informally, freely. She always thought Binna was what Ara would have been like if she'd had the opportunity to grow up naturally, hadn't been exploited and killed.

She and Binna became diving partners under the mentorship of a more experienced haenyeo. As excitable and happy as Binna was on land, she was diligent and careful in the sea. But also daring. She ventured into the caverns without trepidation, unlike Sunyuh, who always felt like she was suffocating the moment she entered those dark spaces. The water temperature in the caves seemed to drop precipitously, and the chill penetrated wantonly through her pores. She would frantically gesture to Binna that they go back up, and sometimes, she didn't check to see if Binna was following her. As soon as she broke through the surface barrier, she would whip off her mask and gasp for air. Huge wheezing gulps that sounded desperate even to her own ears.

Binna would inevitably surface after her and say, "It's going to be okay. You're not going to die." Binna knew about Sunyuh's terror, and she helped Sunyuh hide it from their diving master. Always brightly answering their instructor's questions about where they'd been. "Sunbae-nim, you were so busy with the other students, you did not see us! We were in the sea caves along with Haeri and Hyeyoung. Do not worry about us next time. We will be fine."

Binna's smile could fool anyone into reassurance, a laxness the more senior haenyeo would later regret when confronted by Yoon's mother about Sunyuh's lack of skills.

Sunyuh knew she couldn't hide her terror forever from Yoon's mother. She tried to prepare herself, practiced the things she'd say. When their inevitable clash occurred, she'd still felt blindsided—she never forgot that conversation.

Yoon's mother had stood at the shoreline, watching Sunyuh haul her buoy, her net, her metal tools to chisel oysters from sea rock. "You'll never progress beyond the lowest class of diver if you don't overcome your fear of the sea."

Sunyuh pretended not to hear and kept moving, the rocks under her feet digging into her tender insteps.

"When will you learn not to be afraid?"

She stopped wading through water. "What do you want from me?" She was angry and didn't care that she'd violated the tenets of Confucianism by showing her mother-in-law blatant disrespect. "I did what you asked."

"I didn't ask that you remain frightened of the sea. I asked you to become haenyeo."

"What did you expect?" she said, as calmly as she could. "I grew up landlocked in Gwangju. Not by the sea."

"But you love water. I've seen you stare at the sea, like you're mesmerized. As if you could be absorbed by that fluidity, that movement. I thought you'd be a natural," Yoon's mother countered.

"I look at the sea so I do not have to remember. I want to be carried away by water, not be *in* the water." She turned away to stare at the waves.

"What's done is done. You must make peace with the ocean."

Sunyuh shuddered. "I do not want to be haenyeo. I did not know how dangerous it would be. I am terrified that I will not come back, lost in one of the caverns forever. The water feels cold, even in summer."

"You must be brave. I know you've endured worse. Surely this is nothing compared to what happened during the war."

She swiveled her head toward Yoon's mother. "How did you know?"

"You're someone who is haunted. Someone running away. We've all heard the rumors. We just pretend not to know. I think it's shameful. Not for you girls, but for our country. We, women, are so little valued."

Sunyuh tried but couldn't stop her voice from wavering. "If you know, why are you pushing me?"

"It's because I know you've survived unimaginable things that I'm confident you have the strength to be haenyeo."

"I do not have it in me," Sunyuh said, her legs abruptly collapsing, salty water splashing and stinging her eyes.

"Sunyuh-yah, the ocean will kill you if you don't respect it. But if you're too afraid, it will devour you. Dive with assurance, with the confidence that you will persevere and resurface with food to feed your family."

Sunyuh remained kneeling. "I cannot do it." The clear water before her seemed like an endless abyss.

"You're strong. Not outwardly like me, but you have so much strength, Sunyuh-yah. You must summon the courage to live fearlessly. You owe it to yourself to thrive. Stop living in the past."

The sudden gush of tears and howling that came from her body surprised Sunyuh. But Yoon's mother wasn't startled, didn't jump away.

"Let yourself cry. You've held it in for too long."

Her compassion almost made Sunyuh *stop* crying. Yoon's mother had never sounded like this—her voice had always been commanding, practical. This unexpected gentleness made Sunyuh almost love her.

When Yoon's mother died from a bleed in her lungs six years later, Sunyuh genuinely mourned her passing. Not for Yoon's sake, but for hers. She knew Yoon's mother had cared for her, even as she'd resented Sunyuh for not bearing Yoon any children. And that confrontation with her didn't change Sunyuh, but it did shift something inside her.

Little by little, she began to regard the sea with less fear. She began to anticipate the cold hard shock of water, the immersion into a silence that felt neutral instead of foreboding. She formed a communion with the sea. And she began expressing gratitude to the creatures who would nourish her and Yoon, along with the many people who bought from the haenyeo collective. She began to accept that lives ebb and flow, and that she couldn't control the actions of other people.

Sunyuh became a Buddhist after Yoon's death. The pungency of incense and the clattering of a stick against a hollow gourd, the sound of wind chimes in the breeze gave her an inexplicable solace. She was a lazy practitioner who hardly ever went to temple, but still followed Buddha's philosophy: one is responsible for everything in one's life, and one is responsible for nothing in one's life. It was simple, clear. It helped her accept what had happened to her, her suffering. That she had no control over the vagaries of history, the cruelty of men. But she did have a choice in how she would live her life now.

She sat facing the small courtyard of her hanok after her niece's back melted into the night, happy she was seeing Angelina again tomorrow. Her small plum tree was so fragrant in summer she felt bathed in its intoxicating, sweet scent. She watched as stars flickered above her. She remembered the last night she saw Joonsuk-oppa at their secret meeting place in her father's plum orchard, a star-filled night in late August. He'd held her in his arms and assured her that they were meant to be, that they would live long, happy lives. The teenager she had been believed him.

She was almost eighty years old now, but the aging and decay of her body still surprised her. Only in her mind was she still young, still able to move without worrying the creak of her joints could be heard by a stranger and not just herself. Only in her mind was she still sixteen and running through the plum orchard on her father's estate, the gnarled branches and bloomed flowers a blur as she laughed with her little sister. Only in her mind was she forty and able to squat in the sand flats for hours without feeling like she was cemented in place when she tried to get up again.

Sunyuh had possessed the love of two men in her lifetime. Two possibilities for a life. Joonsuk, with his impossibly beautiful face, forever frozen at seventeen. The boy who'd pulled her pigtails when she was a girl, who'd teased and chased her through her father's estate, who'd become such a serious and responsible young man only to die for the Japanese at Iwo Jima. Something that had happened in 1945 but she couldn't mourn until fifteen years after the fact. And Yoon, with his limp and stout but strong body, the stillness on his face as he maneuvered out of the harbor and into open sea. So loyal and fiercely protective. So generous and kind. There was a curve to Yoon's back when he would bend down to lift a large bucket of fish he'd caught for the day. She'd always found that curve, that arc of his body, so beautiful. She missed him desperately.

Yes, two good men had loved her. For that, she was grateful. She had been cursed and blessed, like every human being on this planet.

Sunyuh

Jeju Island, Korea
August 7, 2006

Sunyuh took a sip of the hot liquid and grimaced. Coffee still tasted strange to her, a lifelong drinker of green tea. There was an unmitigated bitterness to coffee that no amount of sugar or milk could cure. But she was accommodating her niece, trying to like this dark-as-night drink, so excited was Angelina at discovering this artisanal coffee house at the foot of Hallasan. The iconic snowy peak was not visible from here, but a wall of windows showcased the balsam and snowbell trees ascending the mountain. They had hiked to Baengnokdam, the lake at the peak of Hallasan, and Sunyuh was tired. The good kind of exhaustion.

She smiled at her niece seated across the table. Three days into their acquaintance, she was still so happy that Angelina had searched for her. Sunyuh had thought the past should stay in the past, had been reproachful with Jina at first when she'd told Angelina where to find her. But Jina had been right about finding family. And Sunyuh's connection to her niece had been almost instantaneous, perhaps because Gongju had loved them both, had almost cosmically linked them with the same name.

Angelina slid more sugar packets across the wood table to Sunyuh. "I am sorry we will not make it to the green tea plantation today. I promise we will go there and the Haenyeo Museum tomorrow. I had no idea it would take so long to reach the lake. I cannot believe you hike there in the ice and snow. How do you manage such treacherous trails?"

Sunyuh loved the landscape of Hallasan in winter, barren and expansive, stark and graceful. The green stripped away except for the pine and the startling beauty of bare birch. She didn't mind how cold it became because of the clarity, the lack of people on the trails. The moisture of her breath appearing like clouds in crisp air.

"The trail that starts at the Buddhist temple Gwaneumsa is steep, but the views are unparalleled. It feels like a pilgrimage. A meditation. I am fond of talking very long walks around Jeju-do. I believe walking may have saved my life after Yoon died. That and, of course, Binna."

"Your friend, the haenyeo?"

"Binna is still diving at almost eighty years of age, a remarkable feat. She's been my friend for decades."

Sunyuh couldn't quite convey the entirety of her relationship to Binna—friend, sister, mother, confidant. A precious person who'd kept Sunyuh alive after Yoon.

"I thought I'd lost everything—my family, my fiancé, Miyun, Ara. Everyone. What I didn't realize was that I had found a new community with Binna and with Yoon. I felt loved and valued, yet I didn't return Yoon's kindness. I was so immersed in my sorrow that I was trapped, not quite dead but not quite living. A purgatory. After Yoon's death, I had to work to choose life over death again, but I also chose hope." Sunyuh took a calming breath. "I still have nightmares. It's astonishing how fresh the wounds I suffered sometimes feel. How claustrophobic the room I was kept in still gives me attacks of panic and anxiety. The days I go without speaking because my sorrow feels like a thick blanket I can't push away. This is the cost of living."

Sunyuh's hand trembled. She pushed her fingers against her temple as a sudden dampness coated her skin, her heart beating ever faster. Talking about her trauma still induced a physical reaction in her body, especially when those memories were sometimes triggered by ordinary things, like the sound of a child's whistle.

Angelina looked horrified. "Please don't force yourself to talk about this. I can't even imagine the depths of your pain."

Sunyuh wiped away the sweat accumulating under her nose and lips with the tissue Angelina offered her. She took a sip of the astringent coffee. "I suppose that's why I became a Buddhist. I never wanted to live in regret again. To wonder what I could have done differently, what might have come to pass if I'd been brave. That's why I went to my hometown to see Gongju."

She'd gone back to Gwangju in 1960, only to learn that Gongju had married and moved to Seoul and Joonsuk had perished in the Pacific Theater fifteen years prior. Sunyuh had hidden from her mother but had watched her shop at the tailor's for a suit, probably for her father, and then be driven home by their chauffeur. She'd been surprised her parents could still afford to employ servants after both wars. But then, after the uneasy truce at the thirty-eighth parallel and the devastation wrought by America's war on communism, everyone was looking for jobs, willing to take very little for room and board.

She didn't go to the bank to spy on her father, but she did sneak into their estate to stand in the sprawling plum orchard. Gongju's favorite place. All the games of hide-and-seek and tag they'd played there. She could almost hear her sister's shrieking, the laughter they'd shared in that now forlorn piece of land. The moon had peeked from behind a dark cloud, pink plum blossoms fluttering above her, and she knew she could never return home.

"I can't ever go back to Gwangju."

"Why on earth not?"

"Because my mother is a woman who lives by the rules of society, who believes in those unspoken, inflexible rules. She would not survive the shame," Sunyuh said, knowing she'd been kind to her mother by not reentering her life.

"Do you regret not seeing Halmoni? You lived for decades knowing she was alive, but you did not tell her that you were. Is it because—you are ashamed?" Angelina's voice was hesitant and reflected her disbelief.

"I don't feel shame any longer about what happened to me. But I don't want my mother to feel shame because of me. Some people can't change. My mother would not thank me for surviving. She would always see me as a ruined girl. In not seeking her out, I was being compassionate to her and to myself." Sunyuh's voice was calm, like the state of her heart now.

"You sacrificed reuniting with your family for your mother's sake. Was that the right thing to do? Is there not a chance that Halmoni might come to terms with what happened to you?" Angelina implored, seemingly stuck in her resistance to understanding and acceptance.

Sunyuh smiled at her niece. "Every decision you make has a price, but also a reward. I had so much regret after Yoon died because of the pain I had caused him. But you can't go back in time. You must live like you have nothing to lose, so you have nothing to regret."

Five years into her marriage with Yoon, Sunyuh was pacing the courtyard of their hanok when she heard his voice, long before she caught sight of him. She'd never heard him sing before, and the sound was discordant, disconcerting. She pulled the coarse shawl she was wearing tighter across her shoulders and hurried to the wood gate, swinging it open. Yoon lurched into view. His arms were around the necks of two men struggling to hold him upright, fishermen with whom Yoon was on nodding basis with, but not friends. She held the gate open, then hurried to the house, and patted the wooden floor where she wanted Yoon to be placed. The men silently obeyed.

Yoon continued to sing off-key but decreased in volume, less vigor in his voice. He slumped against the frame of the wood door, his hands limp in his lap. The two men bobbed their heads up and down, apologizing repeatedly before running away.

Sunyuh faced Yoon.

His face in repose was beautiful. Relaxed. A sight she was not used to seeing. No furrow between his eyebrows, no downturn of his mouth. His thick black hair fell forward and covered his high forehead, like he was a schoolboy. Even with his skin aged by the sun, aged before its time, there was a carefree quality to Yoon's face in stillness that was never present when he was awake. Sometimes she wondered who she'd married.

Sunyuh knelt on the low pine step and pried off Yoon's boots. She shed her own shoes before stepping up to the main floor. She gently pushed him until he was wedged against a solid wood beam and she could slide open the door. He sat like a large doll, his legs sticking out, his head hanging down. She was kneeling in front of him when he snapped his eyes wide.

"Yeobo, what are you doing awake?" He ran his hand through his hair haphazardly, making the strands stick up instead of slicking them down.

"You drank too much soju and just got home."

"What? I wasn't drinking." He vigorously shook his head, then stopped abruptly, holding his temples between his hands. "That hurts."

"Can you get up and walk to our sleeping room?"

"Of course! Why would you think otherwise?" He smiled, but he couldn't lift his body even as he pressed his back against the wood beam. He held a forefinger up, nodded, then reached across his legs and removed his socks. Satisfied, he pulled his knees up, planted his feet, and pushed. His bottom lifted for a second before landing with a thud. He huffed, long and loud, but didn't try to get up again.

She crossed her arms and waited.

"Why don't we sit for a while?" Yoon proposed.

She smiled, remained standing.

"Yeobo, let's talk."

She raised her eyebrows. Yoon was not prone to chitchat. He was stoic, a man who communicated more with gestures than words.

"Come, come. Sit with me." He slapped at the spot on the wood floor next to him and smiled up at her, his face unguarded.

She hesitated, but Yoon was looking up at her, and the vulnerability in his face was endearing. His face open, his lips soft. She wondered why she'd never noticed the angularity of his cheekbones, the symmetry in the shape of his eyes, how curved and long his lashes were. Her heart tightened like a fist in her chest.

Yoon clapped his hands when she sat down, startling her. He was not normally given to exuberance or displays of emotion. Now he was grinning at her, his hair falling into his eyes again.

"What do you want to talk about?" She fidgeted with her hanbok skirt.

"Anything. Everything. You."

"There's nothing to know about me."

"Oh, yes, there is. Most definitely. You are a woman of mystery." He flung out his hands dramatically. "I hardly know anything about you."

"You know all the important things. Besides, I don't know that much about you."

"What do you want to know? I'll tell you anything," he said loudly, smiling. "Did you know that when I was a boy, my mother said I was a dolphin reincarnated as a human? She used to tease me: 'Yoon-ah, you must be good to your mother in this life. Or you'll come back as a girl next time.' And then she'd burst into laughter," he said, bursting into laughter himself.

Sunyuh just kept quiet, hoping he would continue.

Yoon sighed. "She's right. I should be good to her. She's suffered so much in her life. Did you know that my mother was the oldest girl from a long line of haenyeo? She towered over most men, but not my father. He matched her in height and temper. Theirs was a true love story. My father—a stalwart fisherman—was supposed to marry a meek woman, someone who stayed at home and raised the children and struggled to grow vegetables in the rocky, barren soil of Jeju-do. And my mother was expected to continue the tradition of making a living from the sea, marry a man who would stay home with their children. Both families opposed the marriage. But they defiantly did as they pleased, despite the threats of being disowned. A fate worse than death. My grandparents capitulated with the birth of the first child—me. Then my brother came. He didn't like the sea. He died when he was five from polio."

Yoon turned to Sunyuh. "Do you know I never forgot the sight of my brother laid out in funeral clothes? His small body was so still, which never happened while he was living. My mother stopped laughing after his death. She even stopped diving for a while."

"Did you have any other siblings?"

"My sister was haenyeo and followed my mother out to sea. She died years before I met you."

"Diving?"

"A car accident. She was hit by a drunk driver while walking back from the fish market. She was only fifteen. I couldn't do anything to save her."

He fell back against the wood beam and became so still Sunyuh thought maybe he'd fallen asleep. "Yeobo?"

His head popped up. He tried to sit up straight. "I love the sea. I can open the engine of my boat to full throttle and leave land behind. Leave my awkwardness behind. On water, I'm not a cripple." He looked up at the stars. "I can breathe." He swung his jaw side to side, opened his mouth wide, stretched his neck up, pulled his shoulders back out from their perpetual hunch, as though he were replicating his ease on water.

"I know. You practically smell like the coast." She suppressed the urge to cradle his face. An odd sensation, since she'd never registered wanting to touch Yoon in all their years of marriage, had shrunken from any physical contact, the slightest brush of skin.

"I don't belong on land. I'm like my father, a fisherman. I went to sea as soon as I could walk. I remember having to pull myself up on the side of the boat, on my tiptoes, my eyes just above the painted wood, peeking at the gray-blue sea. I was so happy." Yoon threw back his head and laughed, a clear resonant joy.

"I've never heard that story before," she said. "How adorable you must have been as a child." She pictured Yoon with cherubic cheeks, face wide with mirth, and that image splintered her heart.

"Until I got polio myself. For months I couldn't walk, but I needed to get back to the sea. I didn't give up. I made it back onto a boat. Only to see my father drown."

She clapped her hand to her mouth, but it didn't stop her gasp. She'd known his father had passed, but didn't know the cause, and she couldn't mask her shock.

Yoon tugged at her hand. "Don't be upset. It's what happens when a fisherman goes to sea as many times as my father did. But my mother never recovered. Everyone thinks she's so tough, being haenyeo, being so tall. Do you know she used to giggle? Like a little girl. Now she won't let her mask slip, hardly ever smiles."

"I know your mother has a tender heart."

"Good. I want the two women I love most in the world to get along." Yoon cupped Sunyuh's face with his hands. "Why can't you love me?"

Not plaintive. Not demanding. Not angry. In his touch she felt a sadness so profound she had to squeeze her eyes shut.

"I do care for you," she whispered, but she slipped her face out of his calloused palms.

"But you're not in love with me." He almost smiled. "Whereas for me, it was love at first sight."

"There's no such thing." Her denial was less a protest and more a plea.

"Yes, there is!" Yoon nodded vigorously. "When I saw you on that pier in Yeosu, I knew it was fate."

"I don't believe in things like that. It wasn't fate that I had nowhere to go but Jeju Island." This reminder of her past and the sorrow she battled every day pushed her shoulders away from Yoon, made her pull back into herself.

"It was fate that your energy attracted my energy. I will never forget the sun setting behind you, the blue of the water. Your face in silhouette—the ridge of your eyebrows, the slant of your nose, the gracefulness of your jaw. I loved you instantly," Yoon said softly.

"What a poet you are." It was her only defense against his confession. "But you were infatuated with my face. Not with me. You didn't even know me."

"I recognized your soul," he declared, flinging his arms out wide. "No matter what happens, I will love you the longest. Even when all hope is lost."

Suddenly, he dug his hand into a pants pocket. "Ta-da!" he sang as he held up a jeweled gold butterfly suspended from a gold necklace. "I've been carrying it around for months, waiting for the perfect moment to give you this anniversary present. It's been five years. Thank you for staying by my side."

She stared at Yoon, his face heartbreakingly open, his voice earnest. Instinctively, she drew her face close to his. The puff of his exhale was soft against her lips. "How did I not know you were such a romantic?" She'd known he was kind, patient, unwavering. But she'd never plumbed the deep contours of his devotion.

"I have loved none but you. I know it was calamity that brought you here. But it was, nevertheless, good fortune for me. I'm very grateful that you are my family." Yoon blinked at her before slumping to his side, his head falling onto her shoulder. The golden wings of the swallowtail glimmered in the dark, nesting in the palm of his hand.

In the bright Hallasan coffee house, Angelina asked, "How did you survive Yoon's passing? What could possibly have persuaded you to continue after such remorse? To live with so much regret?"

"It was Binna." Sunyuh's voice was firm and sure. "Every woman must have a person like that in their life. A person who is more than a friend. Someone who will always take your side and yet tell you the hard truths. I hope this kind of priceless person is there for you."

"I have Liz—I am lucky."

"That is good, Angel-ah. We all need a Binna or a Liz. Binna, like Miyun-unni and Ara before her, saved my life when I needed it most."

Sunyuh didn't mean to sound melodramatic. She believed in every word she said, maintained an unshakeable faith in the bonds of female friendship. Because the truth was, if not for Binna, Sunyuh wouldn't be here on this earth. She would have done something dangerous, something irreversible.

A few weeks after Yoon's death, Binna had banged on the hanok's gate, metal clanging against metal.

Sunyuh remained on her sleeping mattress and didn't answer. She kept her eyes closed but Binna wouldn't leave. Instead, she hammered louder. "Sunyuh-yah, get out here right now!" The gruffness and loudness of Binna's voice was startling. Binna, of the mild and sweet disposition—to hear her shouting was so incongruous that Sunyuh abruptly sat up and, almost against her will, trudged from her room, past the sitting room and kitchen of the hanok to open the locked gate.

Binna charged in. "We're going for a walk. Right now. Don't try to argue with me."

Binna eyed Sunyuh's disheveled hair and wrinkled hanbok. She pulled Sunyuh through the small courtyard and into the house, marching her back into the sleeping room. "I can listen to you crying—wailing, if necessary—about Yoon. I can walk by your side for three thousand li without complaining. But I can't let you wither away. So, what will it be?"

Sunyuh shook her head, still not speaking. She'd never again hear Yoon's breathing in that room, never feel him shifting in his sleeping mat across the room before bending at the waist, propelling himself up in the smooth way only Yoon could do. And then there was always the pause—that pause when he stared at the wallpaper of their sleeping room, the Joseon dynasty lettering faded into amber. Yoon would turn on his knees and face his bedding, methodically folding the blanket and thick sleeping mat, quietly putting them in a corner of the room.

Only after he'd slid the wood lattice and paper covered doors closed would Sunyuh open her eyes and stare at the wood ceiling. She would give him time to wash his face and brush his teeth, even though the washroom was in a separate part of the hanok. She'd wanted to keep up the illusion that she was still slumbering because she knew it gave Yoon comfort. Early in their days together, she'd risen with him, only to find that it flustered him. He never said anything, but his movements, usually so smooth and elegant, became hesitant, almost jerky. So she'd feigned oblivion until Yoon was ready to face the world.

Sunyuh didn't know she would miss Yoon's rising in the mornings until he was gone. She stared at the door, couldn't utter one word.

Binna sat abruptly on the floor, not bothering to take one of the silk cushions from a pile to soften the hardness of the wood. "Please, Sunyuh-yah, come back to me."

Sunyuh let her body slither onto the floor.

Binna wrapped her arms around her. "Please, don't do this. Yoon loved you so much. He would never want you to give up."

Sunyuh curled her body away from Binna. "Did you know we always ate breakfast together?" she whispered. "Yoon loved abalone porridge with kimchi. He could make a rolled egg omelet so beautifully, cut the slices so thin and precise—it was art."

Binna's hands moved from smoothing Sunyuh's back to pulling her shoulders up. She took Sunyuh's face between her palms, looked directly into her eyes. "I know you're grieving. But you must rejoin the world of the living. It's what Yoon would have wanted."

Sunyuh stared at Binna, tears still running down her face. "It's my fault he's dead," she said quietly.

Binna wrinkled her forehead. "What are you talking about? You're being irrational."

"He loved me," Sunyuh persisted, her voice dull. "But I couldn't give him children."

"Sunyuh-yah, you're making no sense. It's because he loved you that Yoon would have done everything humanly possible to return to you. And you did love him. You kept diving for years because of the promise you made to his mother. It wasn't your fault he hit an unpredictable storm."

Sunyuh felt like hitting her head against the floor—she thought they'd have more time. "I miss him. I should have told him how deeply I grew to love him."

Binna's hands soothed Sunyuh's back again. "Yoon accepted you as you were. If you want to honor Yoon, live a good life. More than anything in this world, he wanted you to be happy, to be free."

Regret lay like a stone in her belly. Sunyuh hadn't known that she wanted to wake up each morning to Yoon, that she looked forward to their day together. How much she'd loved their quiet routines, the simple harmony of their lives. The loss of their imagined future pounded into Sunyuh so hard she couldn't hold up her head.

Binna was right. Yoon had loved her. Truly. Unconditionally. Sunyuh wished she could go back to that moment when Yoon had confessed his love, back to that night when stars had flickered in the night sky. She wished she hadn't resisted his attempts to hand over his heart. She didn't know that he would be taken away from her four years later. If she had the chance again, she would clasp his face in her hands, gently kiss his eyelids and then press her lips to his. Sunyuh would promise to love Yoon, not for brief hours or weeks but until the end of time.

And Sunyuh had to change if she was to go on living—like a human being, not some wounded animal. Watchful. Skittish. Constantly braced for something terrible to happen. Her blindness to Yoon's generosity, her inability to seize the love that Yoon had offered her—she would regret it for the rest of her life. Never again would she hesitate.

Sunyuh would learn to trust the world again.

Her niece's eyes remained riveted on Sunyuh's, like Angelina was searching for something. "I feel like I am doomed to repeat my mistakes, caught in a loop without end. I would rather not make any choice than make a bad one. I have to protect myself and my children."

Her niece looked so torn, so lost. Sunyuh knew what it was like to wrestle with love and faith and possibility. What the consequences of a single inaction could be and knowing she could've had a joyous life. She wanted to urge Angelina to seize any opportunity that appeared because that chance only burns once, fleetingly, and may never come again. Sunyuh reached up and caught the gold butterfly dangling on a delicate chain around her neck—a Korean swallowtail with its wings stretched back in flight. The gift from Yoon.

Sunyuh pushed away her coffee cup and touched her niece's hand. "No one is going to protect you from joy or pain. No one is going to live your life for you. You must have the courage to live it. If it helps, always know that I'll be rooting for you, Angel-ah."

Angelina

NEWARK INTERNATIONAL AIRPORT
AUGUST 13, 2006

As she dragged her red suitcase through the halls of Newark International Airport, Angelina dreaded seeing her children. Well, maybe not dread, exactly. More nervous that she wouldn't know what to do or say, after not seeing them for the last two months. Emma probably wouldn't even give her a hug. Alex would dutifully kiss her cheek, but she knew he'd be grieving the upcoming separation from his father while pretending he was happy to see her. As for Thom, he would most likely be tapping his fingers impatiently on his crossed arms, ready to berate Angelina for taking too much time to get through customs. Thom had insisted on dropping the kids off with her at the airport, and she hadn't had the will to fight him.

After waving goodbye to Aunt Sunyuh, who'd insisted on seeing her off in the early hours of the morning on Jeju Island, Angelina had transferred from Gimpo Airport to Incheon in Seoul, then connected through San Francisco to Newark. The journey had taken more than twenty-four hours, and it was all she could do to keep moving through the arrivals terminal.

A steady stream of people headed toward customs, and Angelina joined them. With her American passport ready for inspection, she noticed she was one of the few Asian people in line for "US Citizens and

Permanent Residents." Not that she could remember, but she'd stood in another line for nonnationals when she'd entered the US for the first time at the age of seven. She imagined she'd clung to her mother's hand as a child, probably too shy and terrified to speak to the immigration official. She was sad she could no longer ask her mother about that experience at JFK, what she had felt in that moment. Angelina had been drowning in questions she'd wanted to ask her mother when she first landed in the airport in Seoul. She was grateful that longing had been tempered, at least in part, by her newfound kinship with Aunt Sunyuh, of the renewed connection she felt to her homeland, her language, her culture. Emo felt like a bridge to her mother.

In line at Newark, instead of feeling like she'd returned home, Angelina was ambivalent. She couldn't escape the persistent worry that one of these days, she would be denied entry, even though she was a citizen, even though she'd sworn allegiance to this country above the one of her birth. Not once, in all the years she'd returned to America, had a customs agent ever welcomed her home.

She wished she could move to Korea, settle on Jeju Island—she'd found a peace there she'd never felt anywhere else. Angelina had finally accessed that part of herself she thought had been lost after she left Seoul as a child. Maybe it wasn't a preposterous idea that she could reside in Korea. She could get a job at the shipping container bookstore and coffee café in Aewol while she finished writing her dissertation. And there would be the added bonus of living near Aunt Sunyuh. Alex and Emma spoke very little Korean, but they could learn. Angelina had agreed to credit Thom fifty thousand dollars in unpaid child support for dropping his suit against her for sole custody, after he'd served her those papers in June. Even though she was still going through with the relocation back to New York, she could now move with Alex and Emma to Jeju Island without Thom's permission. But uprooting them again seemed cruel, selfish even. But she did wonder if she was using her children as an excuse not to go after what she wanted and make things work with Keisuke, surrendering to her fear of commitment, as Aunt Sunyuh had said.

Angelina shifted her carry-on bag from one shoulder to the other, stretched her neck, and barely stopped herself from huffing out loud. The exhaustion in her body felt like it sank all the way to her bones. Even the fluorescent bulbs overhead looked tired. And everything that had happened in Korea seemed surreal. Did she really meet her long-lost grandmother? A dragon of a woman, but still, she was a mother who had lost almost all her children. Angelina thought back on everything she had talked about with Aunt Sunyuh.

Her mother's suicide hadn't been inevitable—it *could* have been prevented. If only her mother had let herself feel cared for, loved, valued. If only she'd read and responded to those letters from her mother. Angelina had opened them and deciphered some of the idiosyncrasies of her grandmother's handwriting in Seoul. She'd been moved by the sentiments on the page: *My beloved daughter, Gongju, please send news of your health... What is the weather like in the place you live? Rain falls relentlessly here because of jangma. The humidity is unbearable... I remember you as a child. How tightly you clutched a peach as you bit into it, the juice running down your chin and neck...*

Those letters were expressions of love, of the longing of a mother for her daughter. A mother who didn't want to be estranged from her child. Perhaps her grandmother still possessed a fragment of kindness that could supersede her sense of shame and embrace Aunt Sunyuh. Angelina wondered what would happen if Aunt Sunyuh's story was laid bare and there was nothing to hide, no secrets to keep. It was possible that Aunt Sunyuh's story could reunite their fractured family. Maybe secrets didn't have to shatter a family. Maybe revelations could weave together torn fragments, knit them into a stronger unit.

Maybe history didn't have to repeat itself.

The woman ahead of Angelina in the Immigrations and Customs line was speaking into a cell phone. Her Barbie-pink handbag listed like a small boat as the woman said, "Honey, I don't know how long it's going to take. Can you wait for me in the parking lot?"

Will Keisuke wait for me? Angelina wondered briefly, before immediately quashing the idea. She didn't want Keisuke to wait for her. Ruminating on everything she and Keisuke had shared and done together these past two months with Aunt Sunyuh—it was amazing the clarity she felt, after so much doubt, as she'd packed her bags for home. She'd been in love with him but was too cowardly to admit it. And now, whatever they had shared, it was over—she'd hurt him too much to reach back out. Maybe she would, one day, have a healthy partnership with a man. Aunt Sunyuh, after all, had encouraged her to seize happiness for herself whenever possible moving forward. But the more pressing issue now was how to navigate her relationship with her children. How to act with them in ways she wouldn't regret when Alex and Emma were grown.

Truthfully, Angelina had been afraid to have children, afraid she wouldn't be a good mother. There was so much pressure—societal and cultural—but it was the personal pressure that was the worst. *Her* expectation to be a good mother, whatever that meant. Angelina had worried she wouldn't feel love for her children, but the cliché was true—she'd felt bathed in warmth and wonder the moment she'd held Emma in her arms. Despite the pain and the brain fog she'd experienced after giving birth, the instant Angelina's hands had touched Emma's skin, a stillness had permeated her body. She'd wanted that moment to last a lifetime.

Voices suddenly shouted behind Angelina in line, and she visibly jumped. A short woman in a sweatshirt and sweatpants threatened a taller woman, "If you hit me with that bag one more time, so help me god, I'm going to rip it off your shoulder." The tall woman in business attire seemed to shrink. Her skin mottled into red blotches even as she smoothed her neck and apologized. "I didn't know my bag was in the way. I'll put it down. It won't bother you again." Gray sweatpants turned her back on the business suit. Angelina's shoulders inched down. Her body had braced itself, like it was going to be assaulted in some physical way.

It felt like Emma had shouted at her.

If Angelina was being honest, Emma wore at her like surf pounding on rock. The rock seemed immoveable, constant, but the truth was the rock was molded by water, the very nature of it eroded by the never-ending push of tides. Emma's passionate and vocal personality was so unlike Angelina's, so confusing to manage. She thought she was being a good mother, trying to temper Emma's outbursts, but after hearing from Aunt Sunyuh how similar Emma seemed to be to her mother, Gongju, Angelina wondered if she was behaving like her grandmother, erasing the very essence of Emma with her misguided actions.

She wondered if her mother had felt this way about her, if her grandmother had felt the same way about her daughters. She hoped she could change—she wanted to do things differently. There was no need to repeat the same mistakes in raising her children that her grandmother and mother had made. They had done their best, probably convinced they were doing the right thing. But mothers were fallible, just human beings in the end.

When Angelina was a child, she used to catch her mother looking at her and her sisters with a strange expression. Now, Angelina understood the look was one of dissatisfaction. *Disappointment.* But Angelina did feel empathy toward her mother, at what she must have desperately wished for—a son. A son who conformed to what her mother had expected for her life, a validation of her time and effort. No wonder her mother had tried so hard to mold Angelina and her sisters into perfect daughters. But in her quest for perfection, she'd squeezed all the joy out of life, and left her daughters desperately competing for any scrap of her love.

The truth was Angelina had had to learn how to be comfortable touching Alex and Emma, because her mother had rarely held her as a child. She could count on the fingers of one hand the number of times her mother had hugged her. Angelina had thought this might be cultural, but after seeing the actions of her grandmother, she suspected it was familial. A pattern learned in a specific family, compounded by a migration to a foreign land and her mother's unwillingness to bend to American culture. Angelina had found her children's bodies as infants easy to hold, easy to engulf. Their growing bodies sometimes felt bulky in her arms now.

It was one of the reasons Angelina was so grateful for Liz's physicality and affection toward her children. Liz always called to check on her kids, sent gifts on birthdays and Christmas, flew in from the West Coast to spend time with them, together and separately. Liz would take Emma shopping at vintage stores and costume shops in the Strip District, and Alex to the Children's Museum and Fiddlesticks concerts at the Pittsburgh Symphony Orchestra. But their favorite outing with their honorary aunt was a trip to Squirrel Hill for mint chocolate chip ice cream. Both Alex and Emma always cried at the airport whenever they said goodbye to Liz. Angelina was grateful her children felt loved by someone other than herself, that they had someone to go to for advice, for sympathy, without the burden of a parent-child relationship.

As she exited customs bogged down by baggage, Angelina heard a familiar high-pitched voice coming from her left. "Mommy, Mommy!" When she turned her head, she saw Emma hurtling toward her. Astonished, Angelina dropped the handle of her suitcase. Emma hadn't called her Mommy for two years, not since the divorce.

Angelina opened her arms wide, almost falling over from the force of Emma's body crashing into hers. Alex followed shortly thereafter. Their hands clutched at her arms, her shoulders, her back. Tears welled in Angelina's eyes, but she squeezed them away. Wild joy—this was love. The softness of her children's hair, the weight of them in her arms felt like a spot of sunlight on her face expanding until the light was blinding. She reveled in the warmth.

"I'm so happy to see you," Angelina said, again and again. And she meant it. Every word.

"I missed you," Alex whispered in her ear.

She smiled, giving him a loud kiss on his cheek.

"I'm happy you're back, Mom," Emma said, her face open and beguiling, her fingers wrapped around Angelina's neck. Emma's hands overlapped with Alex's, and Angelina could feel their fingers knitting together, their motions instinctive, unforced.

Angelina could have stayed in this moment forever, both of her children in her arms. When they had lived in New York, the three of them would go to the room at MoMA that housed Monet's *Water Lilies*. The paintings of the flowers in his pond and garden in Giverny were resplendent, large-scale panels that dwarfed human form. Angelina loved the triptych, because whenever they stepped into that room, Alex and Emma would immediately run to their favorite image and stand there, mesmerized. Then, after a few minutes had passed, they would join Angelina on a bench. Facing all three canvasses, they'd debate which water lily was the most beautiful. Emma always championed a lavender one, while Alex preferred a bluish one. Angelina would only speak when they asked which one was her favorite. Sitting with her children on either side of her, her hands stroking their small shoulders, she always answered the same way. "I love them both."

Angelina

Harlem, New York
January 1, 2007

*A*ngelina awoke to silence. Last night had been mayhem—firecrackers going off at midnight, car horns blaring all down Frederick Douglass Boulevard, all the neighbors clapping, shouting, ringing in the new year. She'd stood in the cold air, one arm around Alex and one arm around Emma, as the night sky above Manhattan had burst into showers of red, white, and blue. Alex throwing back his head and laughing, Emma shouting and running to the edge of the roof deck while Angelina called out, "Be careful!," her admonition carried away by the wind. Burrowing into her down coat hadn't dispelled the chill, but she'd been smiling.

This could be a good year.

She swung her feet out of bed, pulled on her pink bathrobe, and padded down the spiral stairs in thick raglan socks. She walked softly past her children's bedroom and down the short hallway to the open living room, dining room, and kitchen. A single floor-to-ceiling half-moon-shaped window filled the north-facing wall, and exposed brick lined the other two. She flicked on the bulb above the kitchen island, and white marble countertops reflected the light onto dark kitchen cabinets. While she waited for water to boil in her red kettle, she scooped coffee into the French press and warmed the milk.

Their apartment in Harlem, on the third and fourth floor of a brownstone, was a walk-up, which made it more affordable. They couldn't go back to the spacious three-bedroom apartment at The Gravitas, with its views of the East River and Roosevelt Island. But the apartment in Harlem had two bathrooms, and she loved her bedroom's slanted ceilings. Most of the fourth floor was taken up by a flat roof of stained, cracking concrete, but windows with northern and southern exposures meant the small room up there was always flooded with light. And it fit a single bed, a dresser, her narrow wooden desk, and a bookshelf overflowing with books.

Yes, Emma was complaining ever more steadily—and loudly—that she shouldn't have to share a bedroom with her younger brother, that she was too embarrassed to bring her friends over. "Why do we have to live like this!" she would scream, hurling it like an accusation at Angelina. And more often, especially after returning from her father and stepmother's house, Emma would shut out her little brother from their room. Alex sometimes slept on the couch, forbidden to enter Emma's declared sanctum.

Once Emma came back with a Prada backpack, claiming her stepmother had let her borrow it for as long as she wanted. When Angelina had made it clear to Emma that she had to return it, she'd screamed, "You never want me to have anything nice! Just because you're poor doesn't mean I have to be!" Emma's words had cut Angelina deeply, but she'd kept a stone face, appearing on the outside to be unmoved. She kept hoping that Emma—named for the eponymous heroine of the novel by Jane Austen—would retain her strong opinions, but also become softer and wiser as she grew older. For now, Angelina would continue to brace herself—her daughter seemed determined to hate her. Emma still hadn't forgiven Angelina for changing her plans to come home early from Korea last summer, forcing Emma and Alex to stay with Thom's mother in Newport, Rhode Island. Emma despised going there because, despite her very waspy name, everyone saw her Asian-like features and assumed she was part of the janitorial staff at her grandmother's tennis club. Emma had been furious that she'd spent the week explaining to old white people asking for new towels that she wasn't the help. She'd told Angelina that if she ever had to suffer through that kind of humiliation again, she would run away from home. Angelina knew she wasn't bluffing.

Emma had always looked more Asian than her brother and now hated that fact, frequently lamenting to no one in particular that she was cursed with her mother's genes. Emma seemed to have forgotten that just last year, there'd been a boy in her history class who'd told her she looked like Mulan from the animated movie, a boy who'd been so in love with her he offered her his lunch every day. Emma had been pleased by his attention, pleased with her friends' teasing, even as she pretended otherwise. Emma had loudly proclaimed to the boy that she was Korean, not Chinese, and descended from an emperor of the Joseon dynasty on her mother's side. And in typical Emma fashion, when Angelina had corrected her, telling her they were descended from the *daughter* of an emperor, and that daughters weren't considered an important line, Emma had dismissed it with an imperious wave of her hand. "A princess is still royalty."

But now Emma insisted on dying her hair blond, on wearing blue-colored contacts despite having perfect vision, as though she wanted to shed being Asian. Angelina hoped taking Emma to Korea this summer would change something in her daughter, would shift something ever so slightly in Angelina's favor. She hoped Emma would attach to her Korean roots, would discover the wonder of being part of a rich cultural history she hadn't experienced before, just as Angelina had last summer in Seoul.

Angelina wondered once again if Emma *was* like her grandmother, impetuous and sensitive, as Aunt Sunyuh had claimed. Emma definitely expressed herself without restraint, without filters. Her feelings were overtaking her at all times, it seemed. And Angelina worried for her. If Emma didn't learn to harness all that passion, all those feelings, she might be vulnerable to crushing disappointment, as her grandmother had been. She hoped Emma would bond with Aunt Sunyuh, so wise and grounded and nurturing, like her grandmother had as a girl.

Angelina had told Alex and Emma about Emo, but not the details. They only knew that when she was in Korea, she'd found her long-lost aunt, a woman who had survived sex trafficking during World War II. Emma had been particularly outraged by what had happened to her great-aunt, vehemently declaring she'd join the ongoing protest for recognition and reparations in front of the Japanese embassy in Seoul when they got there.

This morning, Angelina was grateful Emma was still sleeping. She picked up her coffee and walked over to the living room window. The street below, normally humming with steady traffic, was quiet. She could hear the opening and closing of the common front door, two floors down, and even thought about going up to the roof deck but was dissuaded by the cold.

She didn't enjoy winter and the quickly dark days. She always wished for spring to come early, the slight chill in the mornings replaced by warm afternoons and crisp evenings. The kind of nights she relished, walking in Central Park under amber lamplights when there were very few people around. On summer nights, the park overflowed with cyclists, joggers, skateboarders, dog-walkers, lovers. Too crowded for her taste.

But she wouldn't have to worry about that this summer because she was returning to Korea and to Aunt Sunyuh. When she'd spoken to Aunt Sunyuh last night to wish her good fortune in the New Year, Emo had complimented her on her Korean. How it continued to improve, even since last summer. Emo had joked that Angelina was very American because she celebrated New Year on the first day of the solar calendar rather than the lunar one.

More and more, Alex sighed frequently when Angelina asked about the weekends with his father. On Sunday evenings, as Angelina would watch her son get his school bag ready for Monday, meticulously arranging his case of pencils and colored pens, his geometry homework, his social studies textbook, she would ask how he was doing. Alex would shake his head and say, "I think Dad's crazy. He told me to prepare for more siblings. When I asked him why he's having more kids when he can't take care of the family he already has, he wouldn't answer me. He had on his wrinkly, angry face."

Angelina would remind her son that none of it was his fault, and Alex would nod, but his face would remain unpersuaded. She worried about him, too—he was so much like her, holding on to life's many burdens, whether it was the right thing to do or not. And he loved the arts, just as she did. Alex drew skyscrapers of the strangest kind, ones that defied gravity. They were Gaudí-esque in their convoluted, sinuous shapes, brightly colored, gaudy in nonmatching colors. Neon green and orange, purple and lime yellow, Gothic black and flame red fanning out of windows. Alex numbered his creations but never named them. He was up to number 101.

The boy who'd been so deft with a PlayStation controller, bouncing in a virtual dune buggy as Baby Mario during Mario Kart races, laughing as he lobbed bombs behind him, seemed to have all but disappeared. She missed Alex's laughter, a kind of chuckling that increased in volume and magnitude until his peals of joy were so irresistible, she had to join in. She and Alex had watched *Where the Wild Things Are* on the big screen in a long-forgotten movie theater when he was nine years old, the same age as Max, the main character. She never forgot the moment Alex's laughter rang out in the sparsely populated theater, turning heads in their direction. She hadn't admonished him, even as people glared. Now her son barely smiled at all.

Angelina took a sip of her milky coffee and stared at the roof of a red car below, the rectangle of color seeming to shrink and expand as if she were zooming in and out with a camera lens. She was supposed to be spending every free minute writing her dissertation, getting ready for a teaching job at a university, but she found herself distracted.

As it often did over these last few months, her mind wandered to

Keisuke, wondering what he was doing. Emo always asked Angelina about Keisuke during their calls, repeating over and over that she shouldn't use her children as an excuse to protect herself from love. When they'd been drinking coffee at the café in Hallasan, Aunt Sunyuh had told her a heartbreaking story about Yoon, about a moment in their marriage when love glittered like a star in the sky. But Emo had been too afraid to embrace Yoon and their life together. Angelina knew she'd been too afraid with Keisuke, so cautious that she'd let her chance at true love slip by.

Her mind was so preoccupied with tormenting images and questions that she'd barely registered opening the door of her stainless-steel refrigerator. She was standing before the gentle frost without any awareness, letting all the cold air out. A piece of aluminum foil had been crinkled and squeezed to fit the opening of a sparkling apple cider bottle. A silver thumb. She smiled. Her children could be quite resourceful when they wanted to be. The beeping of the fridge startled her, and she abruptly closed it. She opened the door again and scanned the contents for tteok guk ingredients—sliced rice cakes, scallions, beef, egg. But she didn't feel like cooking. Maybe it would be easier to go to Koreatown near Herald Square and get the light, savory rice cake soup that Korean restaurants always served for free on New Year's Day.

She refilled her mug with coffee and milk and was preparing to go back upstairs when the intercom buzzed. Not wanting the noise to wake her kids, she immediately pressed the answer button and hissed, "Yes? Who is it?"

"It's Keisuke. Can you please open the door?"

Her finger jumped off the white button, as if she'd touched burning metal. She stood still, convinced she was hearing things. She wondered if her earlier longing had been so deep it had conjured the real person.

Angelina stared at the answer button for a long while before touching it again. "Is this a joke?" she asked, her voice hesitant.

"No. It's really me. I'm standing at your door."

It was definitely his voice. "Why?"

"Can we talk? Please open the door." His voice wasn't pleading, but it wasn't indifferent, either.

Her finger hovered over the Door button, but she decided against pressing it. "Give me five minutes. I'll be right down."

Angelina didn't wait for his response, rushing up the stairs to her bedroom. The jeans and light pink wool sweater she had worn last night were still flung over her desk chair, so she grabbed them and her winter coat before stepping into the bathroom to quickly run a brush through her hair. There was no time for a dash of eyeliner or lipstick, but she did put on her silver droplet earrings, wondering as she did so why she was being so ridiculous.

She and Keisuke had broken up months ago. Still, she thought about him several times a day. Wondered if he enjoyed walking in the rain of Seattle, if he was eating gimbap, his favorite Korean food for lunch, if he was reading Kafka or Camus before bed. Sometimes she had imaginary conversations with Keisuke, asking him if he'd really been in love with her or just infatuated, but most often, she replayed their last conversation on a loop, punishing herself for everything she had said. Sometimes it felt unbearable, but she'd tell herself that the tightness in her chest would loosen with the passing of each day.

I can't believe he's here. Am I'm hallucinating?

But Angelina could see Keisuke through the glass front door before she reached it. Her heart seemed to stop at the sight of his long, lean body in profile. She paused midstride, wanting to remember the slope of his shoulders, the arch of his neck when he was gone. He turned toward her when she opened the door, the expression on his face inscrutable.

"Thanks for seeing me," he said, voice neutral. Not confrontational, not welcoming.

He looked *good*. His graceful hands were loose at his sides, his thick hair trimmed short and neat. These things were so ordinary, so pedestrian, yet the effect they had on her was annoyingly disproportionate. She shoved aside her sentimentality. "I don't mean to be rude, but what do you want?" Her heart was thumping against her rib cage, and she was afraid she'd stumbled over her words.

He finally smiled, eyes gentle but unblinking. "You."

"What are you talking about?" Angelina remained brusque, afraid to let her guard down, even now.

"I want *you*," Keisuke said, his face completely serene.

"We've gone over this before. You're too young, and I have two kids. Have you changed your mind? Are you ready to be an instant father?" Angelina tried to say these things with a conviction she didn't feel. She tried to school her face into a façade of detachment.

"I still don't know. But I'm willing to try. I promise I'll try harder at being with you than anything I've ever done in my life. I just need you to have faith in me." He said this like it was the most natural thing in the world.

Angelina wanted to joke about her trust issues. She wanted to laugh at the absurdity of the scene before her. And she wanted to cry at the futility of their increasingly problematic union. "What if you disappear from our lives? I can't trust you not to hurt my kids. And I can't trust *me* not to hurt you. We're at an impasse. An impossibility," she whispered, her bravado rapidly dissolving.

Keisuke didn't try to hold her as she crossed her arms and hunched her shoulders. She wondered if he didn't care or if he was just trying to give her space. Not trying to unduly influence her. But the two feet between them felt like a chasm.

"How about you suspend your distrust for a short while?" he asked. "Like when you suspend disbelief and allow magic to enter your brain when you read a book or watch a movie? Just give me one month. Your kids could grow to like me. You did."

"I didn't like you when we first met. My kids are even more finicky. Emma is in the throes of teenage mood swings, and she's impossible to deal with, and Alex is so wounded by the divorce that he won't talk about it." Angelina felt gutted by these truths, yet she recited them calmly.

"I'm willing to wait. Making a family takes time. I'm a patient man."

She took a sharp inhale and held it, her pupils boring into his. That simple phrase, *I'm a patient man*, with all the shades of meaning she wanted it to contain, what she *hoped* it would contain, implied there might be a future for them. That the possibility still existed. Angelina pulled the open edges of her black down coat together, like it was armor. "I can't think here. Let's walk in the park."

He nodded, buttoning his long wool coat.

They walked in silence the four blocks to Park Look Road, their steps falling into a familiar rhythm. Angelina was glad she'd worn her black leather boots with the slight heel, so he didn't tower over her. She was careful not to brush against him, careful to maintain distance. They walked for several minutes up the Great Hill, not speaking a single word. She found herself arguing for and against herself, waxing and waning between absolute conviction that she and Keisuke and her kids could form a family, and absolute certainty that Keisuke would never fit in with her and Alex and Emma. He was too young, had never married, had never been around children. She had failed at marriage. And yet. She was still in love with him. She'd realized it a while ago, but in classic Angelina fashion had resigned herself to the impossibility of their being together. But now? Sheer terror and absolute joy cycled through her body.

What should I do?

As if he could hear her question, Keisuke stopped walking and faced her. "I love you. It was all my fault. Forgive me just this once," he said in Korean, his face tender, his voice earnest. He stretched out his hand toward her, still not touching.

Holy shit. "Are you quoting my favorite Korean drama?" Angelina asked, almost stuttering from disbelief.

"Yes."

The absurdity of what he'd said was making her angry. "Are you playing with me?"

Keisuke's hand remained outstretched. "No. You love your dramas.

I thought it would make you laugh if I said it. And it's true. It's how I feel—please, just this once. Give me one more chance."

This man—this man who'd quoted *both* her favorite lines about love, had flown here from god-knows-where to find her. She didn't know whether to laugh or cry. So she did both.

Keisuke took her into his arms, squeezing her body tightly. Then he pulled back and looked into her eyes. "I love you. I love you because you're flawed, just like me. I don't expect you to be perfect. I only expect you to be you. I will wait; I will not complain; I will win over Alex and Emma. I will remain committed to you. To us, as a family. I know you'd be okay without me. I know, eventually, I could go on without you. But our lives would be *less*. Less full, smaller and fainter. I want so much more for us. I will choose to love you every day. Every single day."

Angelina couldn't speak, didn't even know what to say. She'd already experienced how her life had diminished and lost color without Keisuke. She hadn't known her world could expand, that beauty and joy could multiply when she and Keisuke were together. She'd only seen them being together as a problem to be solved. The most practical and logical solution had been to give up on the possibility of love, so she could protect her children from another man who could walk out of their lives, and that was true. But it also wasn't. Angelina had been afraid to love Keisuke, and she'd used any excuse, including her children, to avoid her own cowardice. Alex and Emma didn't need protection from Keisuke—they could benefit from his kindness, his humor, his steady presence in their lives. Keisuke could be a part of their community, another person like Liz who could help Alex and Emma feel loved.

Keisuke reached into his coat pocket and took out a shimmering gold butterfly dangling from a delicate gold chain. "Emo asked me to give this to you. She said you'd know what it means."

"You went to Jeju Island?"

"Emo called me, got my number from the halmoni at the House of Remembrance. She said you refused to talk about me once you left Korea.

She said she had no choice but to contact me and tell me where you were. I assured her I knew how stubborn you are, but that I wasn't going to give up. Not ever."

Angelina stared at the necklace, wondering if she was hallucinating. It was the necklace Aunt Sunyuh had received from Yoon on their fifth wedding anniversary. A prized possession she kept in a red lacquered box, inlaid with iridescent mother of pearl, by her bed. Yoon hadn't been wealthy, but he'd managed to save and give this jewel to his wife. Yoon had told Aunt Sunyuh that she was like a beautiful butterfly in flight and he was like mugunghwa, the *eternal flower* of Korea—if she needed to rest, he would always be there. Despite the years Yoon spent waiting for Aunt Sunyuh, and the anguish he suffered, he never once took back this precious token of his love. While she and Aunt Sunyuh were drinking tea together, in the house that Yoon had built for her, Aunt Sunyuh had said, "When a man's devotion exceeds your expectations, you must endeavor to deserve him. I hope you find such a man. You can choose to be happy, Angel-ah—you just have to jump."

Keisuke placed the jeweled butterfly in Angelina's cupped palms and wrapped his fingers around hers, his face a study in love. "Families are entities we're born into. But sometimes, families are filled with people we choose. I want to make a family with you."

Angelina stepped into Keisuke's arms. She felt free, like she was unshackled from the past. No longer constrained by her previous poor choices, nor beholden to guilt.

Finally, she could take flight, like the angel in her mother's dream.

Acknowledgments

I want to thank my editor at Grand Central Publishing, Rachael Kelly, for her vision, her humor, and her generosity. Thank you, Rachael, for having unwavering faith in me and my ugly duckling of a novel. Writing a novel often feels like an exercise in failure, but I failed better because of you. I also want to thank my agent, Amy Bishop-Wycisk, for her passion and hard work, for believing I could write a novel, and for listening to me whine like a five-year-old and curse like a sailor—Amy, you are a saint.

Much gratitude goes to my writing mentors and amazing novelists Julia Glass, William Giraldi, Andre Dubus III, and John Dufresne—a truly generous spirit who read the first ungainly words I ever wrote as a novelist and still encouraged me. I don't know what you were thinking, John, but thank you for being so kind. To Steph Liberatore, Karen Kravit, and Teddy Jones, my early readers—thank you for going beyond the bounds of friendship to help a fellow writer. To the Dufresne Collective for slogging through a shitty first draft—thank you. A shout-out to Kim Bradley and to the Seaside and the Crescent Beach workshoppers.

I'm grateful for the support I've received from my generous friends during the writing of this novel: Lorena Savignac, Deb Gieringer, Rose L. Cirigliano, Wendy Berkowitz, and Allison Morris. To my favorite pair of nouns, Elise Viola and Ron Groomes, thank you for the bourbon and the delicious dinners and the warmth of your wood fires.

I want to thank the people who helped me in the research of this novel who aren't historians or scholars: Kang Daeshik, Kim Ja Young, Yang

JunSeok, and Yim Seulki—your knowledge was invaluable, and your patience was remarkable. I'd like to thank Alexis Dudden for being my "annoying" history professor and reading portions of my manuscript, and my eternal gratitude goes to Phyllis Kim for taking my calls and answering my frantic emails, along with her patient translation skills when I needed them the most.

I owe a special debt of gratitude to the halmoni, the victims of military sexual slavery by Japan, whose courage in telling their stories and giving testimony decade after decade has brought to light unspeakable war crimes, which still need to be answered for. The halmoni are indomitable survivors and human rights activists, who I admire beyond measure.

Finally, I want to thank my children, Erin and Liam, for enduring life with a mother who is also a writer. You guys were right—I could become a novelist. Thank you for your love and faith.

Author's Note

I first heard about the "victims of military sexual slavery by Japan" when I was in Seoul in 2006. I was shocked that systematic human sex trafficking had been perpetrated upon hundreds of thousands of girls and young women from thirty-five sovereign countries, city-states, and autonomous territories, and that history had mostly ignored them. But I didn't do more research. As an MFA candidate in nonfiction at the time, I thought I'd eventually do a long-form narrative piece about these women, who had their youth, their dignity, their lives stolen from them. Some of the Korean victims were as young as ten at the time they were trafficked; some were institutionally raped and tortured for more than a decade throughout the Pacific, where the Imperial Japanese Army had garrisons or tents during the Asia-Pacific War (1931–1945). According to a Japanese Ministry of War document, "the setting up of comfort facilities" should be considered "the most critical" action item on its list because these girls were supposedly necessary for the morale of its soldiers, reduced the rates of sexually transmitted infections in the battlefields (proven completely false by data on STIs kept by the army), and minimized the raping of local women—never mind the fact that many victims of sexual slavery came from local villages near any Imperial Army station, which, in fact, did little to reduce incidences of rape. The first official record of a "comfort station" where these girls—euphemistically referred to as *comfort women*—were imprisoned, was in Shanghai, China, in 1932. Because these girls were forced to accompany the soldiers onto battlefields, the imperial military called them *the girl army* as early as 1933 because they really were considered "a part of the army, transported along with provisions through a hail of missiles" before they were later referred to as *comfort women*. These camps proliferated to more than a thousand, by the lowest estimate, at the end of World War II in 1945.

In 2015, I was given an English translation of some of the Korean victims' oral histories, *Can You Hear Us?*, which was published by the Commission on Verification and Support for the Victims of Forced Mobilization under Japanese Colonialism in Korea in 2014. The book changed my life. It took me over a year to read the twelve harrowing narratives—many times, I had to put it down because I was so overcome by emotion, so haunted by the brutality these women experienced. But I couldn't stop thinking about them, about their testimonies, about the fact that so few Westerners are aware that this happened in the Pacific Theater. Unfortunately, I can't read Korean to any meaningful degree, so my search in English about the Korean victims was difficult, and therefore sporadic and haphazard at first. But at a certain point, I knew I would never be able to let go of the story, and I started doing something I'd never done before—incorporating everything I'd learned into fiction.

During a research trip to Korea in 2019, I visited the House of Sharing, a nursing home where some victims still live, and the Museum of Sexual Slavery by Japanese Military, which chronicles the "comfort women system," as well as individual narratives of the survivors who live or have lived in the House. In Gyeonggi-do, about an hour and a half outside of Seoul, I had the honor of interviewing some of the survivors. These now elderly women wish to be called Halmoni, or *grandmother*, an honorary title they more than deserve, for if they'd lived ordinary lives, they would have married and had children and grandchildren. The House of Sharing was the inspiration for a similar facility in my novel, the House of Remembrance. I also visited Seodaemun Prison History

Hall and the Museum of Japanese Colonial History in Korea, where I gained invaluable knowledge about Korea under colonial rule. Trips to the National Museum of Korea, the Gwangju National Museum, and several Buddhist temples also provided important cultural context for my novel because of the role that ordinary and extraordinary objects played in daily Korean life throughout the time period I was writing about. Then, in 2021, I returned to do more research. On this trip, I was fortunate enough to interview several haenyeo, the famous female free divers of Korea who appear in the second half of the novel, and visit the Haenyeo Museum on Jeju Island. And throughout those two years, I continued to scour the internet for English-language resources on the victims of sexual slavery and the history of the Asia-Pacific War, which officially ended with the unconditional surrender of the Empire of Japan in August 1945. Luckily for me, several organizations associated with the victims eventually translated some of their archives into English.

In 2023, I returned to Korea to complete my research for this novel. I visited the Korean Council for Justice and Remembrance for the Issues of Military Sexual Slavery by Japan and the War and Women's Human Rights Museum, the Research Institute on Japanese Military Sexual Slavery at the Ministry of Gender Equality and Family, and the Asia Peace & History Institute, along with the War Memorial of Korea and the National Museum of Korean Contemporary History. I also went back to the House of Sharing.

In addition to my research in Korea, I spoke to many historians, scholars, journalists, and activists in the US and abroad. I'm indebted to them for their knowledge and scholarship, and although it is impossible to include everyone, here is a list of some of those who helped me: Phyllis Kim, executive director of CARE (Comfort Women Action for Redress & Education); Dr. Alexis Dudden at the University of Connecticut; Dr. Peipei Qui at Vassar College; Griselda Molemans, investigative reporter and author of *A Lifetime of War*; Dr. Shu-Hua Kang at

National Taipei University; Kim Jimin at the International Solidarity Department of the Korean Council; Dr. So Hyunsoog at the Research Institute on Japanese Military Sexual Slavery; and, finally, Dr. Han HyeIn at the Asia Peace & History Institute. I'm very grateful for their attempts to guide me, especially Dr. Han.

I encourage everyone to do their own research about the victims of military sexual slavery by Japan. In South Korea, 240 victims used to be registered with the government; at the time I finished writing this novel, only nine were still alive, and most are over ninety years of age. It would be a tragedy if their stories are forgotten. Some resources I recommend, along with a content warning for abuse, violence, dehumanization, rape, and sexual assault:

WEBSITES:

Comfortwomenarchive.carrd.co
Womenandwar.net
Archives814.or.kr

ANIMATED SHORTS AND WEBTOONS:

"Herstory" by Kim Jun Ki
"Tattoo" by Park Seon-woong
"Thread" by Yuri Jang

DOCUMENTARIES:

The Apology (2016)
Shusenjo (2019)
Song of the Reed (2015)
Silence Broken (1999)

MOVIES:

Spirits Homecoming (2016)
Snowy Road (2015)
Wianbu (2008)

BOOKS:

Comfort Women by Yoshimi Yoshiaki, translated by Suzanne O'Brien
Chinese Comfort Women by Peipei Qui with Su Zhiliang and Chen Lifei
Comfort Women Speak edited by Sangmie Choi Schellstede
A Cruelty Special to Our Species by Emily Jungmin Yoon

PUBLICATIONS:

Report of the Special Rapporteur to the UN Commission on Human Rights (1996)
Hearing before the Subcommittee on Asia, the Pacific, and the Global Environment of the Committee on Foreign Affairs, House of Representatives, One Hundred Tenth Congress, February 15, 2007

ARTICLES:

"In Japan, a Historian Stands by Proof of Wartime Sex Slavery" (*New York Times*, March 31, 2007)
"New Era for Japan-Korea History Issues" (*Asia-Pacific Journal*, March 3, 2008)
"The Comfort Women and Japan's War on Truth" (*New York Times*, November 14, 2014)

"Supreme Court Declines Case over Lawsuit to Remove 'Comfort Women' Memorial" (NBCnews.com, March 31, 2017)

"The Money Trail of the Japanese Imperial Brothel System" (JournalismFund.eu, October 31, 2019)

"Japanese Textbooks Don't Acknowledge 'Comfort Women' System's Coercive Nature" (*Hankyoreh*, March 31, 2021)

"How Shinzo Abe Sought to Rewrite Japanese History" (*New Yorker*, July 9, 2022)

"Overlooked No More: Kim Hak-soon, Who Broke the Silence for 'Comfort Women'" (*New York Times*, October 21, 2021)

About the Author

Helena Rho is a four-time Pushcart Prize nominated writer and the author of *American Seoul: A Memoir.* A former assistant professor of pediatrics, she has practiced and taught at top ten children's hospitals: Children's Hospital of Philadelphia, Johns Hopkins Hospital, and Children's Hospital of Pittsburgh. She earned her MFA in creative nonfiction from the University of Pittsburgh. She is a devoted fan of K-dramas, Korean green tea, and the haenyeo of Jeju Island.